The Woman Who Walked into the Sea

Mark Douglas-Home is a journalist turned author. Before writing books, Mark was the editor of a daily newspaper in Scotland. As Scottish correspondent for the *Independent*, he reported on both the Lockerbie and Piper Alpha disasters. His career in journalism began as a student in South Africa, where he edited the newspaper at the University of the Witwatersrand, Johannesburg. After the apartheid government banned a number of editions, he was deported from the country. He is married with two children and lives in Edinburgh.

You can connect with Mark on Twitter @MarkDouglasHome and on Facebook.com/markdouglashome.books

By the same author

The Sea Detective

The Woman Who Walked into the Sea

MARK DOUGLAS-HOME

PENGUIN BOOKS

PENGUIN BOOKS

UK | USA | Canada | Ireland | Australia
India | New Zealand | South Africa

Penguin Books is part of the Penguin Random House group of companies
whose addresses can be found at global.penguinrandomhouse.com.

Penguin
Random House
UK

First published 2016
001

Copyright © Mark Douglas-Home, 2016

The moral right of the author has been asserted

Set in 12.5/14.75 pt Garamond MT Std
Typeset by Jouve (UK), Milton Keynes
Printed in Great Britain by Clays Ltd, St Ives plc

A CIP catalogue record for this book is available from the British Library

ISBN: 978–1–405–92358–3

www.greenpenguin.co.uk

For Colette, Rebecca and Rory

For this book, as with its predecessor, *The Sea Detective*, I have invented a coastal settlement in the north of Scotland. My reason for doing so is the same: to avoid imposing a fictional story on an existing Highland community that has a rich and interesting history of its own.

I am very grateful to Toby Sherwin, Emeritus Professor of Oceanography at the Scottish Association for Marine Science, for his guidance. Others who gave me time and knowledge include Ronnie MacKillop and Patrick Maclean, former coxswains of the Oban Lifeboat; David Dick, former rescue coordination manager at Forth Coastguard (sadly, the Fife station closed after we met); and Brona Shaw, who assisted with her midwifery expertise. I am indebted to them all.

My thanks also go to Maggie Hattersley of Maggie Pearlstine Associates, my agent, for all her support; to Colette, my wife, and Rebecca and Rory, my children, for being encouraging as well as good critics; and to Emad Akhtar, my editor at Penguin.

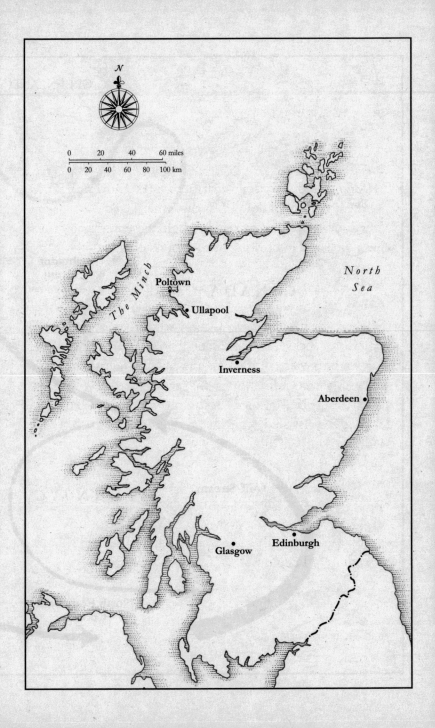

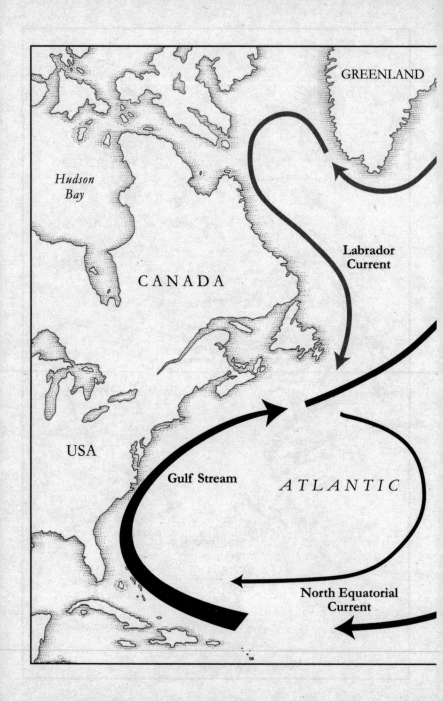

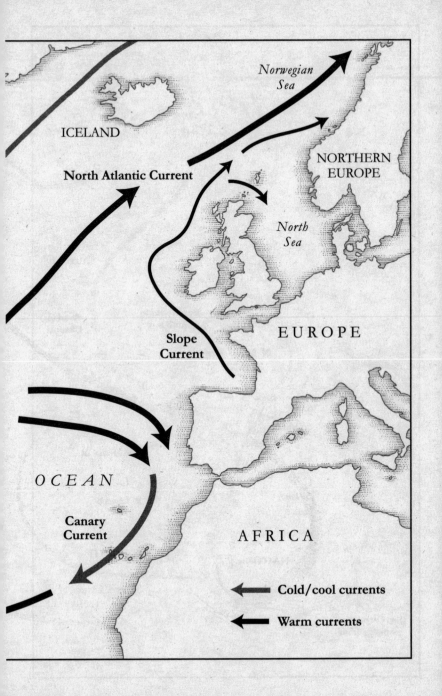

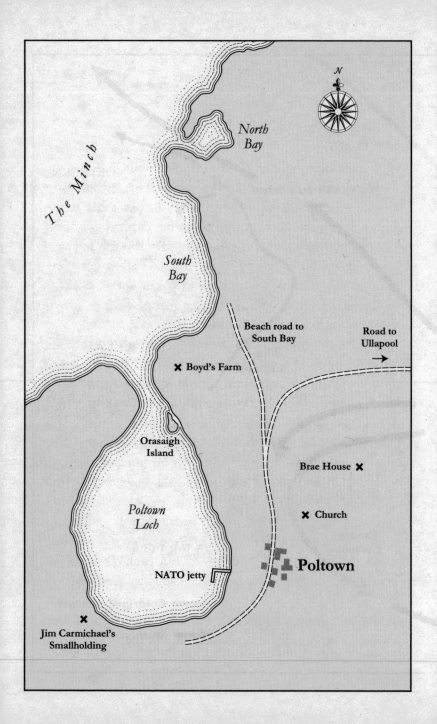

I

A vase of blue African lilies, Diana's favourite, filled the church alcove. Mary Anderson stopped in appreciation before selecting a prayer book from an oak table at the back of the nave. She glanced about her expecting to find other early arrivals already seated, but the church was empty. How fitting, she thought. It would allow her a few moments of reflection to remember Diana and to take her place without having to encounter anyone from Poltown and the unpleasantness that always brought.

As she progressed along the aisle she admired the other displays of flowers: a cascade of reds and burnt orange beside the pulpit and another arrangement of similarly rich colours to the left of the altar. Late summer blooms were Diana's favourites. If Diana had to pass away, Mrs Anderson reflected with a tremble at her own encroaching mortality, then wasn't this the best season for the church to be dressed as she would have liked? She consoled herself with this thought before turning her attention to her choice of pew. The third, or even second, row would be appropriate, considering how close she had been to Diana and to the family. But each of the front four rows, on both sides of the aisle, was cordoned off by blue silk rope. An attached 'Reserved' notice disconcerted her, causing a gloved hand to lift uncertainly to her mouth. Mrs Anderson turned to see whether anyone had followed her in – an usher, perhaps, someone of whom she could ask guidance – but she was still alone.

Inspecting each of the pews in turn, she chose the aisle end of the fourth row on the left. She lifted the rope off its brass hooks and, once seated, felt satisfaction at her decision. From this position, the family would be able to move her forward, as she was sure they would. And if that were to happen when the church was full, everyone would witness her elevation. Mrs Anderson experienced a brief but enjoyable frisson of pleasure at the prospect of such a public display of favouritism. She settled herself, placed the prayer book with its stiff maroon cover on the wooden ledge by her knees and bowed her head.

After reciting the Lord's Prayer in a whisper, she stared sightlessly at the stained-glass window above the altar and remembered Diana; how she was that first weekend at Brae House; already Mr William Ritchie's fiancée, the romance (if that was the word for it) having taken place the preceding months in Edinburgh. How Diana had sought out Mrs Anderson in the kitchen on the pretext of helping with lunch but really to inquire about her husband-to-be. 'He'll bully you,' Mrs Anderson had said in her forthright manner, 'because you're a pleaser.' That much had been obvious after five minutes in her company. Diana was one of those women who, having been abandoned by one husband (Mr William had forewarned Mrs Anderson of that fact), settled on smiling compliance to prevent another occurrence. 'Stand up for yourself, or he'll walk all over you,' Mrs Anderson encouraged her. Not that she'd said so at the time, but hadn't it also been obvious that it wasn't a love match? Oh, Diana liked him well enough, but in Mrs Anderson's opinion the partnership had been a trade-off: financial security for Diana and Alexandra, her six-year-old daughter, and in return Mr William acquired a social secretary, someone presentable who would organize his life in Edinburgh and accompany him to Faculty of Advocates gatherings while making few, if any, emotional demands. There were worse foundations for a marriage, as Mrs Anderson used to tell Diana when she rang tearfully from Edinburgh after more of Mr William's fault-finding with her appearance, her weight or her incomplete education (she hadn't attended university).

Under the circumstances, Mrs Anderson liked to think of herself as the glue that held the marriage together. She'd done for Mr William at Brae, his weekend and holiday house, north-west of Ullapool, for so many of his bachelor years that she had learned to rub along with him despite his distance and moods. Hadn't she deserved the rewards of making Diana her project? The cottage beside Brae's walled garden, her home now for more than thirty years, was the most obvious, but there had been others, presents from Diana as well as innumerable kindnesses in recognition of Mrs Anderson's loyalty. There had also been the privilege (as she considered it) of belonging to a family like the Ritchies. Sometimes, she liked to think, Mr William and she shared a trait. Each recognized weakness and took advantage of it. A rich man like Mr William could do so by bullying and ill temper, a housekeeper by making herself indispensable, and that was what she had become to Diana.

Mrs Anderson closed her eyes and her head shook a little, a tremor from the past.

3

How long into the marriage had Diana broken the routine of accompanying Mr William for every weekend at Brae? Eight or nine years, Mrs Anderson thought. By then Alexandra was fifteen and out of control. She was seeing an older boy from Poltown and Diana had been determined to discourage the relationship by remaining with her daughter in Edinburgh most weekends. Mr William would love having Brae more to himself, Mrs Anderson looking after him, just as it used to be, Diana insisted. The truth, as Mrs Anderson knew, was that by this time Diana needed separation from her husband's unpleasantness just as much as she desired to prise apart Alexandra and her unsuitable boyfriend. If she had an opinion on Diana's strategy, Mrs Anderson thought Mr William would grow to enjoy his weekend solitude and would resent its temporariness as well as Diana when the family was reunited in Edinburgh on Sunday nights. As it happened, both were wrong.

What hadn't entered either woman's thoughts was Mr William's susceptibility to a seductress. Mrs Anderson's neglect of the possibility was mostly practical – that type of woman being as rarely seen in coastal north-west Scotland as pure-blood wildcats – and conditioned by observation. William Ritchie QC had never been romantic or a womanizer. By disposition he preferred the company of men, ideally other lawyers, and was awkward around women, avoiding even a social kiss on the cheek if possible. Then there was his age, late fifties, surely too old for a mid-life crisis, especially for a man who found pleasure in respectability and routine as well as in disapproving the incontinence and mistakes of others.

Mrs Anderson still referred to the affair and its aftermath as his 'madness'. They were desperate times with difficult decisions to be made, an agony for them all: the bloody mess that had to be cleared up. What was done was done, she said to herself with a wondering shake of her head. Not only Mr William's madness; hadn't insanity infected everyone to a greater or lesser degree? Afterwards, Diana had been so frightened he would kill himself she sat at night outside his locked bedroom door. Mrs Anderson remembered his crying. Such emotion: it made her wonder where he'd kept it all this time. Diana forgave him, of course, blaming herself for leaving him alone, as a pleaser would. For his part, Mr William appeared as regretful for the distress he had caused as for his moral lapse. From Mrs Anderson's observations, the shell of the man made a better husband; a better man even, certainly a nicer one. Hadn't he and Diana another twenty years together before his death, good years which Mrs Anderson remembered with affection, with each change of the calendar moving her closer to the centre of the family.

Suddenly she was overcome by a sense of loss: Mr William gone; now Diana too. She found a handkerchief in her bag and dabbed her eyes.

Of course, she'd offered to go to Edinburgh to nurse Diana but Alexandra had turned her down, saying her mother was too proud to let anyone but a stranger do *those* sorts of tasks for her, and anyway wasn't Mrs Anderson too old and decrepit herself now? Mrs Anderson's reply had been sharp – justifiably so. There had also been the hurt over the cremation which had been arranged so quickly, and in Edinburgh too. The lack of notice made attendance by Mrs Anderson impractical. Alexandra apologized in her insincere way and said neither she nor Matt, that weak creature she had for a husband, thought it mattered. Couldn't people like Mrs Anderson attend the memorial at the church by Brae? Mrs Anderson snapped back. *She* wasn't *people*. Sometimes she wondered how Diana had managed to have such an inconsiderate child. *Miss* Alexandra, Mrs Anderson referred to her through gritted teeth.

By now the church was filling up and one or two mourners, presumably members of Diana's extended family, were taking seats in the reserved pews. Mrs Anderson recognized a man with white hair, from Diana's photograph albums. She nodded in polite recognition and he returned the gesture.

How gratifying, Mrs Anderson thought.

Soon the seats behind her were almost full. Some faces she knew from the general store in Poltown returned her stare but she didn't acknowledge them, nor they her. It was propriety in her case (weren't they there to remember Diana?) but jealousy and resentment, she liked to think, in theirs. Again she felt a frisson at the certain prospect of being promoted to a more desirable seat as she saw the family progressing down the aisle: Matt, Alexandra in rustling dark blue silk and the children, Richard and Sophia. Weren't they growing so quickly? Matt's sister was also there, and Diana's nephews and nieces, the children of her brother Malcolm, who was accompanied by his wife. Her name escaped Mrs Anderson, who was trying to catch the eyes of some of the family party as they drew close, any of them really. She'd picked up her prayer book and was sitting on the edge of her seat, primed to move as soon as she was noticed.

A family she didn't recognize filed into the pew in front: a mother and father accompanied by two large teenage boys. They blocked her view, rendering it difficult for her to make herself seen or, more to the point, for anyone to see her.

Then a little man busied at her elbow, asking to be allowed into her pew. She didn't know him, nor, it appeared, did he know her, or else he wouldn't have used that condescending tone of voice. He lifted the rope and she stood to let him pass, but instead of coming in himself he ushered forward four others, two middle-aged women dressed (inappropriately in Mrs Anderson's opinion) in bright colours, green and pink, and two teenage girls, one so overweight that mottled flesh bulged between her trousers and shirt. Once they were seated there was no room for the man, who said in Mrs Anderson's ear, 'Are you sure you're in the right place?'

How was she supposed to answer? Of course, she wasn't in the right place. She should be further forward. She simpered, trying not to take offence, when, thank heaven, she saw Matt noticing her predicament and coming along the aisle towards her. 'It's all right, Henry,' he said to the man, who was still standing beside Mrs Anderson as if he planned to stay for the duration of the service. Mrs Anderson gave a slight shake of her head, letting Matt know that none of this was her fault. He leaned down and she could hardly believe what he said, or the abrupt way he said it. 'Would you move further back?'

What could she do? The congregation behind had gone quiet. She felt faces turning towards her, as if she were the cause of this problem. 'Please, Mrs Anderson,' Matt continued. 'We don't want a scene.' He put his hand under her right elbow and suddenly she was being propelled from the pew. She whispered a sharp protest but Matt either didn't hear or ignored her. He said to Henry, 'Sorry about that, old man,' and Henry promptly took her place. Before she could explain the misunderstanding to Matt, he tightened his grip on her arm and said angrily in her ear, 'Diana felt obliged to put up with you for all these years – God knows why – but we're not going to tolerate it any more.' And then he left her, standing alone in the aisle while he returned to the front pew. She looked around. People were nudging each other, pointing and exchanging whispers. She did the only thing she could. She walked. With every step she was sure her legs would let her down. Instead, her face betrayed her, flushing so red and hot it seemed ready to burst. At the back of the church a young man with short dark hair stood and offered his chair. 'Are you all right?' he asked, but all she could do was sit. Then, mercifully, the priest called the first hymn and the congregation rose. Mrs Anderson was too flustered to stand. Everything was a whirl of humiliation. The door, where the young man had gone to stand, was only a few steps away. It was still open for latecomers.

The next thing she knew, she was outside, on the gravel path, her heart racing faster than was advisable for a woman of seventy-seven. In her hurry to distance herself, she stumbled and fell. The prayer book, which she had omitted to return to the oak table, pitched into the grass at the verge. The pebbles of the path dug into her knees. She cried out just as the congregation started singing 'Land of Hope and Glory', Mr William and Diana's favourite. Mrs Anderson looked in bemusement at pin-pricks of blood oozing through the shreds of her tights and at the fluttering pages of the prayer book. Then she felt herself being picked up by the same young man who'd offered her his chair. She stared at him blankly when he asked if he could help. But all Mrs Anderson could hear was Matt's venomous whisper, 'Diana felt obliged to put up with you for all these years . . .'

Felt obliged . . .

She let out another little cry of pain and shook off the young man. 'Are you sure you're all right?' he called after her as she made her way unsteadily past Mr William's grave, averting her face to conceal her tears. She went through the wooden gate to the path across the moor; the quickest route to her cottage. It took her twenty minutes, longer than usual because of frequent pauses to wipe her eyes. She was still sobbing when she entered her porch and fell back against her door.

She had never been treated so shamefully, she thought as she removed her gloves and placed them on the hall shelf.

To put up with you for all these years . . .

She had always disliked Matt, disrespected him too, as in general she did all men who described themselves as 'dealers' or 'agents' – in Matt's case, property dealer. Now her feelings for him turned to loathing. And for *Miss* Alexandra.

Still distracted, she picked up a letter which had been

pushed through the flap while she'd been out. She recognized the style of envelope, the sort Brae used for estate business. Going into the kitchen where the light was brighter, she opened it, her hands still shaking.

Dear Mrs Anderson

After reviewing the farm accounts following Mrs Ritchie's death, it has come to our notice that you have been occupying Gardener's Cottage on terms enjoyed by no other tenant on the Brae Estate. I have to inform you that it will no longer be possible for your utility bills or council tax to be met by the estate as was the case when Mrs Ritchie was alive. Also, the existing ex gratia rent-free arrangement is terminated; you will henceforth be charged rental at the market rate of £575 a month, all with immediate effect.

Yours sincerely
Matthew Hamilton

Mrs Ritchie. Not Diana. Matthew Hamilton. Not Matt. Not even a handwritten signature.

The letter fluttered to the kitchen floor. Her hands reached for the back of a chair. Her mouth hung open as her breathing became faster, each exhalation accompanied by mewling. Slowly, she looked around and wondered whether she could afford to go on living there.

Hurt heaped upon hurt.

Her pension was small, the house larger than she could afford on her own. A stab of anxiety went through her, a spasm of pain. Her garden, her hydrangeas – she realized they too might be lost. She swayed but managed to stop herself from falling by pressing hard against the chair.

Hurt upon hurt.

She shook her head. Why had this happened to her? Hadn't she been the most loyal of friends to Diana? What would have become of her without Mrs Anderson?

Put up with you . . .

So Diana only put up with Mrs Anderson because she had to. Because of what Mrs Anderson knew. Because of what Mrs Anderson had done when Diana needed her most.

Diana had always been a pleaser, even with Mrs Anderson, it seemed.

Mrs Anderson sat at the square kitchen table. In the middle was an earthenware jar with pens, pencils and scissors. Around about were tidy piles of everyday and useful objects – shopping catalogues, her diary, a pad of paper, envelopes, stamps and the phone book. She reached for a pen and the writing paper. She wrote quickly, two sentences in printed capitals so her handwriting wouldn't later be recognized. She folded the sheet and tucked it into an envelope, the flap of which she had to lick a few times with her dry tongue before it was wet enough to seal. She slid the phone book towards her and copied down the address of the social work department in Inverness. After putting a first-class stamp on the envelope, she went to the front door. As soon as she was outside, she set her face in an expression of indifference, the one she always wore when she took her car to the postbox by the shop in Poltown.

Going down the drive to the road, she talked to herself about her loyalty to the Ritchies: how she had kept Diana's secret, how *Miss* Alexandra owed her as a consequence.

Hadn't Mrs Anderson rescued Diana, getting blood on her hands? How the family shouldn't have let her come so close if they planned to abandon her. How they'd pay for what they'd now done. Oh, how they'd pay.

2

From his position at the back of the church, Cal McGill was beginning to feel conspicuous. As the queue of those paying their respects to Diana Ritchie's family moved slowly towards the exit, sullen faces glanced up at him before turning away. He wasn't sure why he was attracting so much attention. Perhaps it was the odd assortment of clothes he was wearing – a white shirt buttoned up to the collar, a faded black canvas jacket (both in concession to the occasion); black jeans and brown walking boots, wiped clean that morning. Or it could have been because he was a stranger in a place where outsiders were routinely studied for dissection. Whatever the reason, being an object of curiosity was making him ill at ease. Instead of waiting for the end of the queue to reach him, he decided he would go to meet it. Proceeding down the aisle towards the altar, edging past groups of neighbours from Poltown, he picked up remarks about the old woman who'd run from the church as the service started. Cal learned her name was Mrs Anderson and that she wasn't liked. 'Mrs High-and-Mighty,' he heard twice, as if the comments were intended for his hearing, either in explanation of why nobody else had gone to her assistance or, Cal wondered, as a way of telling him he was wrong, as an outsider, to have interfered. 'Who does she think she is? Serves her right,' was typical of the pointedly loud comments he heard on his way along the queue. When Cal was almost at the pews closest to the front of the church – the scene of Mrs Anderson's eviction – a small, round, balding man with a red face held out an arm to usher him into line.

'Thank you,' Cal smiled as the man backed away to open up a space.

'That was kind of you,' the man said.

'What was?'

'Looking after Mrs Anderson.'

Cal shrugged. Anyone would have done the same, the gesture meant.

The man moved closer to Cal and dropped his voice. 'She's not everyone's favourite . . .'

'So I gather.'

'I rub along with her all right, but she can be her own worst enemy.' Then, after checking he couldn't be overheard, he said, 'What happened outside the church? Was she all right?'

'No, not really,' Cal replied. 'She tripped on the path and grazed her knees, but she didn't want my help.'

The man shook his head. 'That sounds like Mrs Anderson, more pride than sense. Did she leave by the side gate?'

Cal nodded.

'That's the way to her house. I'll look in on her later, though I won't tell her why. She'd bite my head off if she thought I was checking on her. I'll say I'm dropping by in case there's anything she needs from the shop.'

Now the man stuck out his hand. 'I'm Jim Carmichael. I drive the shop delivery van. Everyone just calls me Jim.'

'Cal . . .' Cal let go of Jim's hand, feeling stiff and stand-offish. 'Cal McGill.' Not knowing quite what else to say, he added, 'My mother knew Diana Ritchie. They were neighbours in Edinburgh, a long time ago. Mrs Ritchie wrote to my father after my mother's death. She'd have wanted me to be here.'

'You've travelled from Edinburgh?' Jim looked impressed.

'I was coming this way anyway, taking a few days off, going to the far north-west.'

'What takes you up there?'

'My work, I study the sea.' Cal pulled an apologetic face. 'Not what most people call work, I imagine.'

'Is that right?' Jim said. 'Tell you what. Are you interested in odd things that people find washed up on the beach?'

'Sometimes, yes, it depends.'

'Well, there's a farmer here who's always looking and he came across something unusual a couple of weeks ago. A Guinness bottle that had been at sea for . . .' Jim's brow furrowed trying to remember. '. . . Since 1959, I think it was . . . Not a scratch, looks brand new, a collector's item, apparently. Duncan Boyd's his name. As you go north, his farm's first left and left again at the two stone pillars. It looks more like a rubbish dump than a farm. But don't worry about that. Say Jim sent you.' His face clouded a little as though he was having second thoughts. 'Duncan's a bit on the odd side, mind . . . But you'll be OK if it's the Guinness bottle you want to talk about. Not that other stuff, about the wind farm.'

Some days there was nothing, others it was like this, the beach at South Bay littered with detritus. Duncan Boyd gazed at the scene with the excitement of a collector at a junk-shop door. Who knew what he might discover in the next few minutes? Recently he'd found an old brown bottle buried in seaweed. He'd realized its significance straight away. The lead seal was intact and the documents inside appeared to be in the same pristine condition as when Guinness dropped 149,999 other identical bottles into the Atlantic for a bicentennial marketing exercise. Thousands floated on to the east coasts of America and Canada, as Guinness intended; others eventually found land in South America, the Arctic, even Europe; and some continued to come ashore, more than half a century later after countless thousands of miles at sea. One of the documents Duncan teased from the bottle, the King Neptune Scroll, was now framed and hanging from a beam in the barn where he did his sorting. He'd read the colourful document so often during the past few days he could recite the first long sentence and did so then in a voice he considered appropriate for the occasion: deep bass as if emerging from ocean depths.

'To the finder of this document greetings and let it be known to all men (and women) that I, Neptune, Monarch of the Sea . . .' Duncan paused, stuck out his chin and surveyed his imaginary realm. Then he began again. '. . . that I, Neptune, Monarch of the Sea, have permitted the House of Guinness to cast in, and/or, upon my Domain the bottle carrying this document – but in precise particular, the Atlantic Ocean – and allow same free passage, without let or hindrance, to convey to you the story of Guinness Stout.'

Immediately a grin spread across his face, making his weather-beaten skin a relief of crevasses. He rubbed his hand across the grizzle of his unshaven chin and took the rocky path from the headland to the beach below. Half-way down, where the trail descended steeply between perpendicular slabs of rock, he stopped and shouted out, 'I, Neptune, Monarch of the Sea,' and cocked his head to one side. When he heard the reverberation, he smiled. 'This,' he said as he negotiated the loose stones, 'is going to be a good day, Duncan.' He smacked his lips in anticipation.

Almost as soon as he stepped on the sand, his optimism seemed vindicated. A blue mooring buoy was stranded there, a type he hadn't seen before. He turned it over, looking for a manufacturer's name, but couldn't find one. Before lifting it across the beach, he checked whether anyone was approaching. All he could see were the cars at the church for Diana Ritchie's memorial service.

He frowned and pushed out his bottom lip to mark her passing before grinning again at finding he was still alone. 'My kingdom,' he announced, trying for a monarch's resonance. The result amused him: more Darth Vader than Roman god of the sea. He gathered up the buoy before going to the turning circle at the road end where he'd parked his empty trailer the night before. For a moment he wondered whether his find should go with the other blue buoys in his collection – his loose practice was to grade buoys by size and colour – or should it be separate since he had no others the same? As soon as the question formulated in his head he became impatient and gave the buoy a shove, rolling it to the rear of the trailer. His eyes swivelled back to the beach. What other finds awaited him?

Usually he took a few days to fill the trailer, but this morning would be different. The winds and high tides of the last few days had produced a bounty on the beach. He liked that word. *Bounty.* A swirl of greens and blues discolouring the sand suddenly distracted him. He pounced and exclaimed at discovering a rubber ball. He'd keep it for Pepe, the little dog belonging to the new GP, Doctor Bell, who sometimes walked at South Bay after her surgery at Poltown.

For the next hour and more he went backwards and forwards across the sand, dragging a net, two lobster pots, four lengths of black plastic piping, an assortment of softwood planks and other driftwood, a blue fish box, two more buoys (white and orange), broken pieces of polystyrene, an empty oil drum and what appeared to be the blade of an oar. After piling them on the trailer, he stopped to roll a cigarette with the last of his tobacco while trying to remember the day of the week. If Thursday, his delivery box from the general store would be at the farm gate with another packet of rolling tobacco. But he thought it was Wednesday, so he limited himself to two puffs before pressing the smouldering cigarette end between his thumb and forefinger. He stored the butt in the breast pocket of his denim shirt and was about to go back to work when it occurred to him he hadn't checked the road for a while. After all, he didn't want anyone surprising him.

He climbed on to the trailer and slowly straightened his

legs. The high ridge of hills behind Poltown came into view. Then, as he extended his back and finally his neck, the woods around Brae House appeared, followed by the church on its emerald knoll midway between the house and the village. He registered that the cars had gone: the memorial service for Diana Ritchie was over. 'God bless her soul,' he said with a sombre expression, before smirking at realizing he was a god of sorts so had no need to invoke another deity. By now he was almost upright and most of the beach road was visible. He saw his farm gates, the twin stone pillars, the field dotted with old machinery and piles of flotsam and, further to the right, his house and steading. Just as he stretched to his full height, all six feet, he saw the bonnet of a vehicle. It was parked just inside his steading yard. Complaining at another intrusion, he ducked down. Whoever it was hadn't seen him. But who was it? His earlier exuberance at having the beach to himself dissipated. Crouching on the trailer, he began muttering about his land, how he'd never sell, no matter what inducement he was offered or whatever promises they made. In the few seconds after seeing the vehicle, Duncan's features put on a fast-evolving display of emotions – panic, worry, finally defiance. No, he'd never leave his farm.

A plan suddenly popped into his head. He'd paint 'This land is NOT for sale. Turn round here' on the old Ferguson tractor and leave it by the entrance to stop anyone else upsetting him.

Emboldened by this notion, Duncan dared to raise himself up again. He elongated his neck until his big barn came into view. A red pick-up was moving along the rutted track which went from the steading across the field to the stone pillars. His visitor was going away. Duncan's expression changed again; defiance made way for puzzlement. The vehicle looked old and battered and a dent was even visible in the passenger door. The others who had come to talk to him about selling to the wind farm consortium had driven sleek black sports utility vehicles, BMWs and the like. The pick-up headed away along the beach turn-off towards the Poltown road and Duncan waited for it to disappear before loping towards the farmhouse, taking a shortcut through the dunes and climbing the broken-down fence into the field. He paused for breath beside the wreckage of an old horse-drawn cart. His exertion brought back some of his previous high spirits.

'I, Neptune,' he proclaimed in a suitably triumphal voice, as if a great and bloody battle had taken place, a battle of the gods, from which he'd emerged victorious, his enemies in headlong flight. Fired by his conquest, Duncan strode towards home. Only when he was standing between the open doors of his barn did he hesitate. On the packed mud floor was a sheet of paper weighted down by a stone. Its edges fluttered in the draught. Duncan regarded it with alarm before bending uncertainly to read.

Dear Mr Boyd

I was at Diana Ritchie's memorial service and someone called Jim told me about your discovery of a 1959 Guinness bottle. Like you, I'm a beachcomber and have a large collection of artefacts (though having seen your farm I don't think I'm quite in your league). In my case, beachcombing assists my research into how and where currents and winds carry objects across the oceans. My areas of interest are the eastern and northern Atlantic, including the Scottish coast. Because of the length of time you've been beachcombing I'd like to pick your brains (and see your Guinness bottle). Could I drop by again in a few days on my way south? My email address is theseadetective@gmail.com. Look forward to meeting you soon, Cal McGill.

A phone number was added as a postscript.

Duncan guffawed at how a piece of flapping paper had made him scared, one moment a fearless sea god, the next a tremulous mouse.

3

He'd seen something similar before on Texel. Positioned where the North Sea and the Wadden Sea meet, the Dutch island's beaches had a long history of being journey's end for cargoes lost overboard. Cal visited the previous summer because he'd been told of beachcombers there who kept dated records of their finds. He'd matched their logs of high-value flotsam – Burberry bags from Britain, the wooden components of kit houses from Germany, cases of wine from Italy – with the ship-owners' reports of losses. Comparing where they'd gone overboard with where they'd beached, he was able to calculate actual speeds of travel for different weights, shapes and sizes against his computer predictions and to make adjustments. The beachcomber who provided the most useful data went by the name of Olaf, a merchant seaman from Norway who had also washed up on Texel after a shipwreck. His bungalow had been constructed from the spoils of beachcombing – when Cal paid him a visit he found it hard to be certain what was dwelling and what his collection of flotsam.

Duncan Boyd's farm had the same feel, Cal thought, as he drove north. The steading and fields were littered with derelict farm machinery and flotsam. Despite the appearance of chaos, Cal had detected a semblance of order, as there had been at the Texel farmstead. In Olaf's case, his finds were stacked by date, a new pile for a new year. In

Duncan Boyd's, the piles were colour coordinated as well as sorted by type. Cal detected method where others might have seen nothing but mess, a judgement that was reinforced by the sight of footwear nailed to a barn wall. There were fishermen's boots, brogues, sandals as well as trainers, dozens of them. Scrawled at the top of the barn in white paint was 'The Wall of Lost Soles'. Cal found it funny: Duncan Boyd appeared to have wit as well as method.

Then, he thought of the similarities between him and Olaf or Duncan Boyd. Cal lived alone, as they appeared to. At first sight, Cal's rented office-cum-bedsit in a light industrial estate in Leith, the old port of Edinburgh, was chaos. Although his long work table was cluttered with the paraphernalia of oceanography – dozens of maps, files and books all piled on top of each other and in imminent danger of collapse – he knew exactly where everything was. Olaf had a table like that. So, Cal noticed, did Duncan in his barn. Also, they had pinned up newspaper cuttings: reports of notable beachcombing discoveries over the years – a century-old message in a bottle, abandoned boats that beached after crossing oceans, a lock of hair and a love letter in a sealed wooden box, the discovery of sea-beans or even rare ambergris.

Cal's walls were similarly covered, although the subject matter tended towards the macabre. He collected reports about unidentified bodies washing up on Britain's beaches or stories about people who had disappeared after falling overboard in a storm. There were mugshots of couples who had decided to drown together and gruesome pictures of decomposed bodies, hands and legs missing, the stumps of bones protruding. In a few cases, the pictures were printed in newspaper or magazine features about Cal. The headlines had a similar, grim theme: 'Sea detective finds vital clue in severed head murder hunt'; 'Trawler families beg sea sleuth, "Bring home the bodies of our missing men"'; 'Oil tanker collision suspected in missing yachtsman mystery'; 'Ocean detective becomes doctor at sea' and so on. The last of these – the odd one out – was about his PhD, which he had completed three months earlier.

His own Wall of Lost Souls, Cal thought with a wry smile.

Later, he stopped at a roadside cafe which advertised free Wi-Fi. Cal drank black coffee and checked his emails. He had seventeen new messages. Most were inquiries from potential clients, more fathers and mothers, husbands or wives wanting him to guide them towards the bodies of their drowned and missing loved ones. He read the first six. Their tone of desperation was as moving as it was familiar, the burden of expectation too much. He replied with sympathy as well as regret. He cited pressure of work – 'the disadvantage of being a one-man operation'. He hoped to be 'in a position to take on new cases in a month or two'. He'd be in contact if he was.

Cal checked the weather map. The storm would reach land that night. According to the forecast, it would last seventy-two hours, long enough for him to escape. He shut down his computer, slid his laptop into his backpack and finished his coffee. He would drive until he found a deserted stretch of coast where he would walk all day and into the night, where the roaring of the wind and the sea would obliterate everything else.

4

Anna sat cross-legged under the table applying red and glitter pink varnish to her toenails while her mother tried to make the bedsit 'halfway presentable'. But the more Violet brushed, wiped and dusted, the more hopeless the prospect seemed to be. Everything she touched had this wrong with it, or that needing mending or replacing. Her worries about the impression their impending visitor, a social worker from Inverness, would take away extended to her daughter.

'And try not to call me Violet,' she said. Anna had a habit of calling her Violet unless she was cross or upset. Then she became Mummy.

'And *try* to call me Violet,' Anna repeated in the opposite.

'And remember to smile.'

'And remember *not* to smile.'

Anna peered out from below the fringe of tablecloth as Violet removed jumpers and yesterday's underwear from the chair and shoved them under the bed.

'And if he speaks to you, make sure you answer him politely.'

'And if he speaks to you, make sure you *don't* answer him politely.'

Violet gave her daughter an anguished look. 'Anna, love, it's serious. Mr Anwar will be here soon.'

'Mr Anwar will . . . *not* . . . be here soon.' Anna began laughing and kicked out her legs, knocking over one of the bottles of varnish. It made a little puddle of pink on the bare wood floor.

'Oh Anna, look what you've done.' Violet snatched a dirty cloth and ran to her daughter, grabbing at the leaking bottle. 'Why are you so naughty?'

As Violet knelt and wiped the floor, she noticed a pink stain on her jeans. Anna saw too and emitted little sobs of misery in the expectation of another scolding. Violet regarded the wreck of her daughter and blamed herself for being so tense all morning: someone was bound to end up in tears. She wrapped the varnish bottle in the cloth to prevent another spill. Then, crouching beside Anna, she said, 'Come here,' and tugged at the girl's arm. Mother and daughter leaned into each other. Violet kissed Anna's forehead, stroked away the wetness from her eyes and brushed back her dark curly hair. She held Anna's hands and blew on her nails to dry them. 'Friends?' Violet offered.

'I suppose,' Anna replied, retreating to her lair under the table just as the doorbell sounded. Violet wanted to hug her daughter again, to be certain she'd been forgiven, but she couldn't let Mr Anwar see the room like this. What would he think? That she was an inadequate mother too?

She gathered up the other bottles of varnish and hid them in a drawer along with a dirty pan from the sink. On her way to the door she passed by the bed and turned over the duvet to conceal the rip in the cover. She paused to wonder whether the balloon tied to the bedhead should be removed. The legend 'Happy Birthday' had been deflated to a meaningless jumble of letters, 'Hppitda'. The bell sounded again, this time two rings, and Violet left the balloon. She checked herself in the small mirror to the right of the door before glancing back at Anna, whose cheeks were smudged from crying. Violet found a tissue in her pocket and ran back. 'Quickly, your face.'

Anna passed the tissue carelessly across her mouth before throwing it behind her. 'And remember to smile,' Violet said, returning to the door.

Violet made a last despairing inspection of the barely furnished room with its high ceiling and plaster cracks. Nothing was as she wanted.

She pressed the entry buzzer, straightened her jersey and combed her fingers through her hair, a habit from when she'd worn it long. By the time she heard her visitor's footfall on the last flight of stairs she was shaking with nerves. Taking a deep breath, she opened the door.

Mr Anwar, it turned out, was a small man, with tidy black hair and a long face on which perched wire-rimmed glasses. He wore a navy-blue jacket, white shirt and charcoal trousers which were too long. 'Miss Wells?' He offered a hand. Violet took it briefly, detaching as soon as was polite in case he felt her agitation.

'Come in, please,' she said.

After closing the door, she introduced Mr Anwar to Anna, and Anna (*bless her*) did exactly as Violet had asked. She smiled and said, 'Hello, how are you?'

'Your daughter?' Mr Anwar turned to Violet.

Violet nodded. She'd grown accustomed to the

question. 'Anna's father is from North Africa,' she said, explaining the different and honey-brown colour of Anna's skin. That was all she said: nothing about him deserting her in pregnancy to go back to Morocco; nothing about the guilt, bringing a child into the world without a father, repeating the cycle.

'Anna is a pretty name for a pretty girl.' Mr Anwar addressed the compliment to Violet. Anna pulled a vomit face, but Violet didn't mind. In fact she wanted to kiss her daughter. In that short exchange Anna had won over Mr Anwar. Violet could tell by his expression of amused indulgence.

'And how old is she?'

'I'm four and a quarter,' Anna replied with an indignant note of protest that the question was not directed at her.

'Lovely age, when they're like that,' Mr Anwar said. 'A handful, I'm sure, but delightful.'

'Most of the time.'

Violet offered Mr Anwar a cup of tea, remembering too late the milk in the fridge was past its sell-by. 'Do you mind black?'

'No, not at all; in fact, I prefer black, thank you.'

She was beginning to like Mr Anwar and his courteous ways. As she put the teabags into the mugs, she indicated the armchair. 'Please sit down, Mr Anwar.' He hesitated, since that was the only chair in the room, but Violet forestalled any objection by saying she would sit on the end of the bed.

Mr Anwar bowed, a gesture simultaneously of obedience and thanks, and perched on the edge of the chair.

After Violet brought over the mugs of tea, handing one to him, handle first, she said, 'You have something to tell me about my mother.'

'I have, Miss Wells.'

He placed his mug on the floor between his shoes – slip-ons; grey, unassuming and unfashionable like their owner – and brought a white envelope from an inside pocket. 'I hope you didn't mind me contacting Mr Wells . . . I gathered from him that you're not in regular touch . . . that all he has is your email address.'

'It's all right.'

Mr Anwar appeared anxious to reassure Violet there had been no breach of confidentiality. 'I asked him to pass on my details to you: name, phone number and email address. He didn't ask why. Nothing else passed between us.' He paused. 'Your address . . .' He looked around the room, '. . . will remain confidential, of course.' While Mr Anwar was talking, Violet watched his forefinger stroking the edge of the envelope.

'We don't have much to do with each other . . .' Violet glanced up, wondering if she should explain why she'd drifted apart from her adoptive parents, how they'd never really got on. Mr Anwar bowed again, letting her know there was no need for her to say more, and Violet took a sip of tea. Mr Anwar did likewise before holding up the envelope. 'This,' he said, 'arrived at our office in Inverness.'

Violet stared but said nothing.

'You know what happened after you were born?'

'My parents . . .' Violet said, 'my adoptive parents told me.'

'Well, that makes it easier.' His expression was kindly and understanding. 'For both of us.'

He waited again, glancing at Violet. 'Usually we wouldn't pass on anonymous correspondence, but considering your circumstances, your special circumstances . . .' With that he offered Violet the envelope, stretching his left hand across the gap between the chair and the bed.

'My suggestion,' he said when he saw that Violet appeared immobilized, 'would be for you to open it and then we can talk.' His speech was slow and considered, as if he understood the importance of the next few minutes and the speed at which they should be taken. Such things were best not rushed, his tone seemed to suggest.

'Does it say my mother's name?'

He nodded and pushed the envelope at Violet. After taking it, she rubbed the corners between her fingers and thumbs. 'Do you have children, Mr Anwar?'

The question caught him off guard. 'A son . . . yes, a son . . .'

'Could you have done that to him?' Her face showed the hurt.

'No. No, I couldn't.' He shook his head to reinforce the point. Violet was struck by the emphatic nature of his response. Mr Anwar added, 'But not everyone's circumstances are the same. Who knows what was going through your mother's head, what trouble she was in? Perhaps she thought she couldn't look after you.'

A pulse pushed at Violet's neck. 'I've wanted this so much . . . and now I don't know.' She closed and opened her eyes. 'What would you do, Mr Anwar?'

He sighed, considering his reply. 'I'd take my time.'

'But would you read it?'

'I think I would, yes.'

'Even though it changes everything.'

Mr Anwar nodded a number of times. Neither spoke for a minute. Then Violet put the envelope on the arm of Mr Anwar's chair and crossed to the other side of the room. 'What will happen if I don't?'

'It'll be kept for you. If you change your mind, you'll be able to read it.'

Violet put her hands in front of her face, as if in prayer. Why was she being like this? Didn't she spend part of every day or night thinking about her mother? Round and round in her head went the theories about why she had been abandoned.

Had her mother been underage, too young to fend for herself let alone a baby?

Had she been frightened of the consequences of keeping Violet?

Had her mother been deserted by her father?

Mr Anwar let his attention stray momentarily to Anna, who was hugging one of the table legs while staring at the envelope, as if her grandmother might suddenly emerge, genie-like. He smiled at her and Violet asked, 'If I open it, will I have to do anything . . . afterwards?'

'Go to see her, you mean?'

'Yes . . .'

Mr Anwar hesitated before replying, forming the answer silently to be sure of his delivery. 'I don't know if this makes things easier for you . . . or more difficult.' He let Violet prepare herself, delaying a beat before continuing. 'I made a preliminary check to ascertain whether this letter had come from the woman named . . . to be sure it wasn't your birth mother's way of trying to initiate contact with you. Sometimes that happens.'

'Was it?'

'No. No, it wasn't.' Mr Anwar shook his head. 'I'm sorry, Miss Wells. The woman who is named in this letter isn't alive. She died the day after you were abandoned at the hospital.'

Violet didn't move. What transfixed her was not only the news of her mother's death, but also that she hadn't sensed it, not once, not in all the years of searching, of imagining their reunion with such daily regularity that any doubt about it ever happening had gone from her. Not *if*, but *when*: a longed-for moment.

'Oh, she's dead,' was all she managed to say after the first shock. Then, a few seconds later, 'I didn't know.' As if she should have done. As if it was a daughter's duty.

'Gosh.' It was not a word she often used – it seemed to come from childhood. Ever since she could remember, she had felt a visceral connection to her absent mother. It had driven Violet to hunt every street, every crowd, certain that she would have been doing the same. Violet had always been on the lookout, wondering, 'Is this one her?' Sometimes it was simply the way a woman walked, the style or colour of her hair – the same shade of brown as Violet. At others it wouldn't be anything specific, just an inexplicable sensation of affinity. Or, a certain age: someone who would have been a teenager when Violet was born, someone too young to understand what she had done by deserting her baby, someone who hadn't known better. The constancy of her searching hadn't been affected by her living in Glasgow, a bus journey of more than 160 miles from the hospital where she'd been left. As often as once a week she'd see someone who had something familiar about her. Usually it happened when Violet hadn't even been conscious of looking. She'd lost count of the number of women she'd followed. Some she'd even engaged in conversation, asking directions, anything to detain them long enough for her to obtain a sense of them. After each disappointment Violet had lain awake as Anna slept. One day. One day it would happen.

How could she have been so wrong?

In the middle of this rush of memories, regrets and recriminations, Mr Anwar dropped another bombshell. He apologized for doing so but in his judgement it was better she was told now than find out later. 'According to the record, she took her own life . . .'

Violet gasped and crouched, her back to the wall, rocking backwards and forwards.

'I'm sorry, Miss Wells.' Mr Anwar moved further to the edge of the chair, as if preparing to spring to Violet's side should she require support.

'She killed herself . . . after she had held me?' Violet asked.

'I can't say for sure. There's no official record of your birth. We have to assume she delivered you herself or someone unqualified assisted her.' Mr Anwar added, '*If* she was your mother . . .' He paused again. 'Maybe she has brothers or sisters who are still living . . . there are tests you can have done.'

Violet wasn't really listening. 'How could she do that,

33

hold me and then leave me, kill herself?' She was still rocking.

'I don't know, Miss Wells.'

Violet let out a shout of anger and Anna clung tighter to the table leg. She had never seen her mother like this. 'You know,' Violet said to Mr Anwar, 'I'm so angry with her. I'm glad she's dead . . .' Her voice sounded cold. The rocking suddenly stopped. 'Did she kill herself because of me?'

'I don't know. If only there was more information . . .'

Violet noticed Anna's frightened face and beckoned her over. The child walked stiffly across the room and crouched against the wall, copying her mother. Mr Anwar apologized for upsetting Violet, 'for managing a difficult situation inadequately, for making bad worse'.

'It's not you. Really, it's not,' she replied, putting an arm round Anna and pulling her close. Then she said, 'Will you read out the letter, Mr Anwar?'

'Are you sure?'

'Yes. It doesn't matter any more, does it?'

Mr Anwar picked up the envelope, opened the unsealed flap and removed a single folded sheet of paper. He looked at Violet, offering her an opportunity to change her mind. 'As you'll see,' he said, allowing more time to pass, 'it's handwritten, but there's no signature, sender's address or date.' He coughed, adjusted his glasses and began to read. 'A newborn baby girl was abandoned at Raigmore Hospital, Inverness, before midnight on 9 September 1983. Her mother was called Megan Bates and at the time she lived at Orasaigh Cottage, by Poltown.'

He re-read it to himself before folding the page.

'Perhaps the anniversary has prompted this – the ninth was two days ago.' He looked at Violet's birthday cards on the mantelpiece. 'Though it's impossible to say for sure . . .'

'Where's Poltown?' Violet asked.

'It's about eighty miles from Inverness, but on the west coast.'

Violet considered the implication. 'My mother wanted to distance herself by leaving me on the other side of the country from where she lived.'

'You could draw that conclusion, but I'm sure there are others, if only we had all the facts.'

'How old was she?'

'She was thirty-three.'

Violet shook her head again: another of her presumptions confounded. 'So she was old enough to know better.'

'I can't say.'

'Did she have other children?'

'There are no records of any, but there is no record of your birth either.'

Violet pushed back against the wall. Anna copied her. Mr Anwar clasped and unclasped his hands.

'Where is she buried?' Violet asked.

Mr Anwar appeared startled by the question, as if Violet had read his mind. He stammered and coughed. 'I'm sorry, Miss Wells. I didn't want to distress you any more than was necessary.' His mouth flinched. 'She wasn't buried.'

'Why not?'

'Her body was never recovered. She killed herself by

swimming out to sea, according to the police inquiry at the time.'

Violet closed her eyes at her mother's final betrayal. Even in death she hadn't wanted to be found by her daughter. Anna pressed closer.

'I'm sorry to be the bearer of such difficult news,' Mr Anwar said. He placed the letter on the arm of the chair and removed a small brown envelope from inside his jacket. 'I thought you might like to have these. They're newspaper cuttings about Megan Bates and the search for her body . . . and there's a photograph.'

'Of her?'

'Yes.'

Another shock.

The emotion of the moment affected Mr Anwar too. 'It's not a very good picture, I'm afraid, and it's black and white. Would you like to see?' He fumbled among the clippings until he found the one he wanted and carried it over to Violet. 'According to the caption it was taken at the Poltown fair the year before you were born.'

All Violet saw was a grainy blur. A woman half-turned to the camera, the wind blowing her long, dark hair which formed a veil across her eyes. Her mouth was half open in laughter. A woman captured in a moment of happiness. Her mother. A moment Violet would never share.

'Of course,' Mr Anwar said, 'it's possible you're not her daughter. Whoever wrote the letter might be mistaken . . .'

'They're not mistaken,' Violet replied. 'She is my mother.'

She put her hand into the pocket of her jeans and withdrew a small box. 'This is the brooch she's wearing in the photograph.' She handed the box to Mr Anwar. 'The nurses found it when they found me. It was attached to a piece of knitting, something cut from a jersey or a cardigan.' She watched as Mr Anwar opened the box and studied its contents. 'The flowers on the brooch are violets . . . that's why I'm called Violet . . . it was the name the nurses gave me.' She let out a brittle laugh. 'I took it to an expert once but he wasn't able to tell me much except it's made of porcelain and might be worth sixty or seventy pounds.'

'Yes, I see.' Mr Anwar closed the box and returned it. He went back to the chair, where he sat head bowed, as usual allowing an interval for Violet to assimilate each new revelation.

Eventually, Violet asked, 'Was my mother married?'

Mr Anwar shook his head. 'No, no she wasn't. The newspaper reports of the time refer to her as Miss Bates and my information is that the police report also described her as single.'

Violet said nothing and Mr Anwar waited. 'You have many things to think about,' he said at length. 'And thinking is best done alone.' He stood up. 'So I should leave you now.'

Violet made to move but Mr Anwar insisted she stay where she was. He would see himself out. At the door, he turned back.

Anyway a small man, he seemed smaller now, as if shrinking from more revelations.

'I've been dishonest with you. You asked me if I had children.'

'I did,' Violet replied, 'and you said you had a son.'

The repetition appeared to cause Mr Anwar anguish. He made an expression of contrition. 'I have a daughter too.'

'Oh,' Violet said.

'Shereen – she was very pretty, and clever.' There was pride in his voice, that a daughter of his could be such things; but regret too. Violet registered the past tense he'd used.

'Was?'

'I don't see her any more . . . Shereen married too quickly, a rich man. She became ashamed of me.'

He faltered and Violet stood and touched his arm lightly. 'There's no need to tell me, Mr Anwar.'

'Please . . .' He sounded cross for not saying what he meant. Violet took her hand back and waited for him to speak.

His head dropped, pulled down by the weight of regret. 'Every night for the last four years,' he glanced up at Violet, 'every night before I go to bed, I sit in her room and talk to her. Can I give you this piece of advice, Miss Wells? Go to where your mother used to live, talk to her, as I talk to Shereen. It helps.' He retreated along the landing. Violet watched as he turned at the top of the stair. From his expression, Violet could tell he had forgotten to tell her something else and was torn about doing so now. 'What is it?' Violet asked.

Mr Anwar drew in a deep breath.

'When you read the newspaper cuttings, you'll see that there's nothing about the pregnancy, although the police report into her death refers to her being close to full term.'

Violet sounded bewildered, another mystery to add to all the others. 'Why was it not mentioned?'

'I don't know.' Mr Anwar shook his head. 'Although in a small community such as that there will be ... sensitivities.' Now he looked at Violet with concern. 'A word of caution, Miss Wells: if you're planning to visit Poltown, you might be wise to say nothing about Megan Bates being your mother. It's quite possible, even likely, that your father is alive or has family in the area. In my experience of this kind of case, it's better to move slowly and to gather as many of the facts as possible before revealing anything about yourself.'

***

That evening, after settling an overexcited Anna with her friend Izzy in the bedsit downstairs, Violet packed. She checked the times of early-morning buses from Glasgow and, before going to sleep, found a reference to Poltown in an online travel guide.

Question: when is a town not a town? Answer: when it's Poltown. This example of misplaced suburban planning was dropped on the unsuspecting West Highlands for the workforce of the NATO refuelling depot which opened here in 1962. The military fondness for acronyms (POL = Petroleum, Oil and Lubricants depot) gave the new settlement its name. Unwisely, those responsible for designing Poltown allowed themselves an evocative flourish, imagining their creation one day becoming as notable as the famous Scots after whom they designated this ugly collection of cul-de-sacs. To save you the bother of visiting, there is Thomas Telford Court, Sir Harry Lauder Gardens, William Wallace Drive, Sir Alexander Fleming Rise, David Livingstone Neuk and Jenny Geddes Walk. The last of these was named after the spirited woman who threw her stool at the head of the Dean of St Giles Cathedral in Edinburgh for having the effrontery to use an Anglican prayer book. Wouldn't she have aimed another missile at the perpetrators of this more modern heresy had she been alive? Further attractions include a refuelling jetty in the adjacent sea loch, buried fuel tanks in the hillside behind and a collection of disused military sheds, where visiting forces were trained in the theories and practice of covert mountain warfare. Since NATO's retreat and the departure of the military trainers and depot staff, the cul-de-sacs have been used as overspill social housing from the surrounding towns and villages, the Highland equivalent of a refugee encampment, the residents huddled and forlorn, waiting to return to their lost homelands, all hope gone.

5

The gale barged ashore as if dislodging Cal's pick-up was its only purpose for travelling over hundreds of miles of ocean. Like a thug who wasn't getting his own way, the wind shoved, pushed, threatened and howled. A gust thumped against the front passenger door; another bounced off the cab. The vehicle rocked and shuddered from the ferocity of the assault. Cal opened his window wide enough to slide a hand out into the night. When it was dripping with salt spray, he rubbed his fingers against his face. Zipping his jacket and pulling tight the draw-string on his hood, he wondered if this was how his life was going to be. Would he always be alone and in a storm, walking some remote coast?

A few moments earlier he'd been half-asleep, the sound of the radio drifting in and out with his consciousness. Then, suddenly, he was wide awake as if the storm had delivered an unexpected and shocking blow. Cal's reaction, however, was not to the wind, rather to a short news item about a five-year-old boy who had been swept off a pier in the south of England by a freak wave two days ago. The newsreader announced that the sea search was being abandoned. Cal listened to the pained dignity of the parents as they thanked the emergency services for trying to find their child. He heard their agony as well as their tenacity – they said they would keep looking for their darling son's remains for as long as it took. Cal could picture their faces: their hollowed cheeks, dulled eyes and grey skin, the silent tumble of tears and their bewilderment as if they didn't really know where they were. He'd seen too many faces like that recently.

Trying to get them out of his head had been the reason he'd taken off to the coast.

The news bulletin brought them back with a vengeance and also the questions that had been nagging him these last few days.

Did his skill in tracking and finding bodies lost at sea offer people at their wits' end, like the mother and father of that dead boy, false hope? Did he make their agony worse?

He couldn't recall a case when he hadn't. That was never his intention, of course; it was just the nature of his work. Either he'd draw a blank – a matter of regret even though Cal warned in advance about his area of expertise being an 'imprecise science' and the sea having its own unfathomable rules for delivering up bodies – or the corpse he led them to would be bloated, disfigured or half-devoured by scavengers. The media usually described these as 'astonishing discoveries' which provided 'closure for the parents'. It was a phrase, a concept, Cal had come to loathe.

The previous week, for example, he had found the body of a child, an eight-year-old girl. She was from Northern Ireland and had fallen from a yacht off the Antrim coast. The police described her as pretty, blue-eyed and blonde, though none of that was apparent from her remains. By the time Cal found her, she was three months dead. The sea had carried her across the North Channel to Scotland. After walking the west coast of the Mull of

Kintyre, Cal discovered her among rocks. Should he have watched over her until the tide returned, said a prayer as he pushed her back out to sea and saved her parents an unending torment?

Instead, he called the police.

Later, at the mortuary, he met the parents. They insisted on seeing their daughter's body, 'to tell her we love her and to say goodbye'. Afterwards, he looked into their life-less faces and wondered whether he should take on any more cases like theirs.

How was leading parents to putrefying flesh helping them at all? Better, he thought, that their memories sur-vived intact – their dead child smiling, happy and living as in a holiday snapshot – than having them replaced by a horror story, the stuff of continuing nightmares.

After finding the eight-year-old's remains, his name was in the media again. The result was that more desper-ate people asked him for help to find their lost loved ones. More emails arrived every day.

Would the mother and father of that missing five-year-old boy from the south of England be contacting him too?

Cal rubbed his face.

The storm would soon blow itself out. He opened the pick-up's door and headed out into the dark, giving the wind one more chance to fill his head with noise.

∼

Dawn, and the wind died away. Cal sat on the bonnet of his pick-up. He looked at his phone and read a message that had been sent two days before.

43

> Neptune Boyd here – visit
> anytime you want.

Cal understood Duncan Boyd's reference. He had seen a Neptune Scroll before. The bottle drop by Guinness in 1959 was well known among beachcombers, a topic of discussion. Not long ago, Cal had read about a cinematographer who found a number of intact Guinness bottles in the Canadian Arctic more than four decades after they had been put overboard from thirty freighters in the Atlantic.

Cal messaged back.

> I'll be passing Poltown today.
> Look forward to meeting you.

6

On the bus north-west from Ullapool, Violet studied an Ordnance Survey map of Poltown and the surrounding district. She read the newspaper cuttings Mr Anwar had given her, though she knew them so well she could recite paragraphs from memory. How Megan Bates had left her cottage on the tidal island of Orasaigh. How she walked the coastal path to the headland by South Bay, where she descended to the beach. How it had been a still, sunny day – one newspaper made reference to an 'Indian summer' that year. How 'Miss Bates' had been wearing a loose white dress and a raffia sun hat decorated with broad red ribbon. How she also had a leather bag on a shoulder strap. A witness, an elderly woman named Armitage who was exercising her dog on the beach road 300 yards away, had told the police it was 'unmistakeably Miss Bates because no one else wears summer dresses and hats like that in Poltown'. How she hadn't thought anything was untoward because the two women were used to seeing each other at a distance. How Miss Bates had stood at the water's edge before wading into the sea, deeper and deeper. 'She just kept going,' Mrs Armitage told the police, 'she didn't hesitate or stop.' The woman had flagged down a passing motorist to raise the alarm, but not before Miss Bates had vanished. The hat and bag had been recovered later from North Bay, more than half a mile up the coast. A local farmer by the name of Duncan Boyd had found them. The police had searched for seven more days, waiting for the sea to give up her body.

But it never did.

Violet read how that was unusual in waters like those, with a prevailing south-westerly which brought all kinds of flotsam ashore. How the unseasonal and light southerly wind that September might have influenced the natural order of things. How, according to Inspector Robert Yellowlees of Highland Constabulary, the officer in charge of the investigation, there had been 'no suspicious circumstances'.

On a ridge not far from Poltown, the bus driver, an obliging middle-aged man called Stuart, pulled into a passing place. He was five minutes ahead of schedule and 'might as well have a ciggie break here' and let Violet 'enjoy the view', considering she was his only passenger and she'd been asking so many questions about the area. As soon as Violet stepped from the bus she realized why he'd chosen to stop there. The passing place had a 180-degree view of the coastline, 'A veritable panorama,' Stuart said mockingly, taking on the role of personal tour guide. He lit a cigarette and clamped it in the right-hand corner of his mouth. 'Didn't I tell you it'd be worth it?' he said out of the left. Despite his sardonic manner, there was satisfaction that someone as ordinary as him could live among magnificence like that.

Violet managed to nod in reply, but her mind was on the map and the cuttings and translating them to this incredible vista of land and sea across which her mother had made her final journey. She identified the features whose names had become familiar since Mr Anwar's visit the previous day. There was Orasaigh, the tidal island, at the inner mouth of the sea loch. A narrow band of sparkling blue showed between it and the mainland: the tide was in. From there Violet's eye was drawn to the north by a scored line a little inland from the coast. This was the trace of the path which Megan Bates had taken that day. At the headland, a walk of five minutes, she'd descended to South Bay, a long, inviting curve of dunes, sand and sea. Somewhere along its lazy sweep of beach Megan Bates had gone into the water and disappeared. Violet lingered on the view, the scene of her mother's death, before seeking out the final landmark, North Bay, where the hat and bag came ashore. Violet recognized it from the outline on the map, like a mouth that was half-open.

'In case you're interested . . .' Stuart said, his tone suggesting she shouldn't be, 'Poltown is over to the left. It's hidden by the hill. See that grand house?' Violet looked to where he was pointing. 'That's Brae House. And see the church?'

Violet could: a building of grey stone squatting on a hummock of bright green encircled by a boulder wall.

'Well, Poltown's round the shoulder of the hill, out of sight and out of mind . . . best way with Poltown. Bit of a dump, to be honest, run by a family of small-time crooks called Turnbull.' He dropped his smouldering cigarette into the swept-up gravel at the side of the lay-by while Violet's attention was drawn back to South Bay.

'Enjoy the view while you can,' Stuart said.

'Yes, it's the perfect day, isn't it?' Violet replied,

thinking there might have been similar weather twenty-six years before.

'I wasn't meaning that.' Stuart nodded towards the horizon. 'There's going to be a forest of windmills out to sea, hundreds of them . . . and down there. See that little turn-off to the beach?'

Violet looked at where Stuart was pointing. She guessed it must be the road from which Mrs Armitage had seen her mother. 'Yes.'

'Well, see the field the other side?'

Violet nodded.

'And the farmhouse and steading . . . across the field, do you see, this side of the headland? They're planning to put up a building the size of a football pitch . . . for converting the electricity for the grid, or something like that. I don't know the technical detail. It's all progress, I suppose.' Stuart sounded unsure and kicked at the gravel to emphasize the point. 'But it's causing a rare old stushie between the people who rent out their cottages and make money from the tourist industry and the rest who don't give a tinker's fart about tourism or the environment and just want a house and a job.'

Violet didn't reply in case Stuart heard her distress. For the first time in her life she had an address for her mother, a context. She was able to see what *she* had seen; in fact, the last thing she had seen before she died. Now, it was to be spoiled by a 'forest of windmills'.

'Well, that's us,' Stuart said, unaware of Violet's mood swing. 'Last stop before sunny Poltown,' he snorted. 'Bet there'll be a cloud hanging over it by the time we get there, always is.'

Violet said, 'I think I'll walk.'

'Oh, OK, suit yourself.' Stuart sounded disappointed. 'Maybe pick you up again some other time.'

'Yes, maybe . . .' she replied.

He loitered, as if hoping she would change her mind. 'I'll be off, then.'

She nodded without turning, remembering to thank him only after he'd shut his door.

Once the bus had gone, Violet remained where she was, the prisoner of conflicting emotions. She yearned to walk in her mother's footsteps, but also had a gnawing fear of the consequences, of the turmoil that threatened to be unleashed. She found her mobile phone in her backpack and took the opportunity to text Izzy's mother Hilary in case there was no signal later at the coast.

Arrived safely. Love to Anna.
Hugs for you and Izzy.

Hilary lived in the bedsit below Violet's. Anna and Izzy were best friends; so were Violet and Hilary, who had met as students at Glasgow's School of Art. After graduating they shared the same bed to save money on rent. Hilary worked days as a part-time clerical assistant in an insurance office; Violet, nights, waitressing in a pizza restaurant. After their daughters were born four months apart, they moved into their own bedsits, sharing a door on to the street and childcare instead of a bed.

'Leave Anna with me,' Hilary had said when Violet told her about Mr Anwar's visit and her spur-of-the-moment decision to go to Poltown. She had 'due days' to take and

Izzy always loved having Anna to stay. Last night, when Violet returned from work, Hilary had hugged her unexpectedly. 'What's that for?' Violet asked.

'Look after yourself, won't you?'

'I'll be fine,' Violet said. Now she wasn't so sure.

Mrs Anderson sat at her kitchen table. She had done little else since posting the letter. Every so often she would get up to make herself toast and tea or to go to the toilet or to bed, but mostly the days passed in a blur and she watched the kitchen clock and wondered what was happening. Had the letter arrived yet? Had the girl been told? Would she come to Poltown? When would she arrive?

Tick-tock: it was like waiting for a bomb to go off.

The tension was becoming unbearable. Rather than sitting and waiting, she resolved to keep herself busy around the house by doing some of the things she'd been putting off. She drank the last of her soup and mentally prepared herself. Then she got up, crossed the hall and opened the sitting-room door, the first time she'd been in there since her disgraceful treatment at Diana's memorial.

Mrs Anderson looked around the room, at all the photographs, as though she didn't know these people who were staring back, as if she was in the company of strangers. Nine matching wooden frames, scenes of her with the family: *her* family she liked to think of them, or had *before*. These photographs which had sustained her for years – the proof of her indispensability – now seemed to mock her.

Over there, on the chest of drawers, Christmas 2002, the year before Mr William's death: the family and Mrs Anderson assembled for tea in the drawing room. That was the Christmas Diana had given Mrs Anderson a silk scarf, a pretty butterfly pattern of pale yellows and greys. And there, on a Pembroke table behind the door, three more photographs: her 'Easter parade' she liked to call them whenever she showed them to visitors. She remembered the years, 1998, 1999 and 2001; the family and Mrs Anderson by the front door before the start of the Easter-egg hunt, Alexandra's children holding empty paper bags in which to put their finds. Wasn't 1999 the year Sophia ate so many she had to go to bed? The missing year, 2000, she recalled, was the Easter Alexandra and her family went skiing and Mr William and Diana escaped to Paris for the weekend.

On the mantelpiece, in pride of place, were two other photographs: one taken at Alexandra's wedding; the other at Mr William's seventieth birthday party: happy occasions, she'd thought at the time. Next Mrs Anderson examined the group of three photographs on the bookshelves to the right of the fireplace and noticed something of which she had been utterly oblivious until that moment.

For many years now she had regarded her position in every group as unspoken acknowledgement of her importance to the family. Hadn't she been placed on the outside because Mr William stood or sat opposite to her, the two of them like strong supporting columns? Take one or other away and the edifice would collapse. Now her eyes darted from photograph to photograph and she considered the manner in which Alexandra, Matt and the children held themselves; even Mr William. It was in every one, the turn of a shoulder, the swing of a hip, the slant of a head; away, away, always away from her. She hadn't realized it before and now she couldn't bear to look. There was a sign, even then, of what would happen, of what had happened. Why had she been so blind?

Diana felt obliged to put up with you for all these years . . .

Was the conspiracy against her silent or spoken? She imagined the family's private condescension before her arrival for lunch, tea or whatever gathering; their disdain for a servant, allowing her to think she was one of them when she was nothing of the kind. What a fool she had been. Had there ever been an occasion when she had been invited into the middle of the group? If there had, she couldn't remember it. Her temper rising, she went quickly round the room collecting up the frames, stacking them face down so she didn't have to see them again. She hurried across the hall to the kitchen and dropped the photographs into the rubbish bin. One slid away and crashed to the floor, splintering the glass.

She glanced at the clock. Tick-tock.

On the road down to the coast, Violet came upon a poster tied to a telegraph pole. It was announcing a public meeting about the wind farm at Poltown community hall due to take place in two days. 'Fuck the environment, give us jobs' had been daubed across it in red paint. Despite the bus driver's forewarning, Violet was unsettled by the angry note it struck in an otherwise harmonious landscape.

Then she had another shock.

She was following the path her mother had taken to the beach. At the headland, it tipped into a gorge between sheer plates of rock. At first the going was firm – compacted peat – but the path steepened into a flight of stone steps. Some were crumbling under the persistent drips of water trickling from an overhang. Others were strewn with loose stones. A secure footing was hard to find. Violet leaned forward to pick out the safest descent and her backpack and tent pressed against her shoulders. She feared she was about to topple and let out a cry of surprise. Her voice reverberated in the confines of the gorge, changing into a sound she was sure she had heard before, an age ago. It was the strangest experience, not the sort of fey imagining to which Violet was usually inclined. Yet it had the force of absolute conviction: she *had* been here before. Hadn't she felt that same claustrophobia, heard that same echo?

An idea came to her. Had she been here when she was in her mother's womb? Had her mother also walked here once and feared losing her balance, in her case the bulge of pregnancy making the negotiation of the stone steps precarious? Had she also cried out in frustration and worry? Had Violet heard it then? Feeling rather spooked, she carried on down the remaining steps. As soon as she was safe and on the beach, she reflected on the childhood she'd had, instead of that which should have been hers. Her adoptive parents, Tom and Bridget Wells, were kindly and generous though each had an enthusiasm which (in Violet's slowly developing consciousness) provided adult satisfactions against which a child could not compete.

Away from work, as a manager in the council's property maintenance department, Tom's hobby was reassembling old car engines in the garage, whereas Bridget's interest was domestic – keeping their 1970s bungalow spotless.

Violet went between the two, never feeling she belonged with either. She kept that knowledge to herself, aware of its potential for hurt. Perhaps her reticence also owed something to her dim understanding that the disconnection between her and her parents was part of a bigger mystery which one day would be revealed. That day came when Violet was twelve and Bridget sat her down to explain why a woman might desert a newborn baby. 'She'll have been abandoned too, by the father, poor girl. It must have broken her heart.'

Violet recalled every detail of the conversation, not only because of the revelation of her adoption but also because Bridget seemed so troubled. 'Things are better said, don't you think, so we all know where we are? Even if I'd given birth to you, I couldn't love you more.'

Until then Violet thought Bridget was talking about one of their neighbours, or another girl at school.

The thing she remembered most clearly about the disclosure, once she had understood its significance, was her relief. Afterwards she called Tom and Bridget Wells by their first names, not Mummy and Daddy. Every day she expected her real mother to rescue her, and imagined how extraordinary that would be.

Always her mother, never her father, since she accepted without question Bridget's explanation that her mother's action was dictated by desperation, by circumstances beyond her control, by her father's fecklessness.

Later that day she remembered overhearing Bridget's concern about Violet's unfazed reaction. Bridget told Tom she was sure Violet would have a delayed and disturbed emotional response; that they should be vigilant. Bridget needn't have worried. Violet had never felt more reconciled or more curious about mysteries still to be uncovered.

Now, standing at the high-tide mark, Violet felt she was on the point of another revelation. She dropped her backpack on the wet sand, slipped off her trainers and padded towards the water's edge. She stood in accusing silence as she examined the blue sea. How could the water be so calm when she was anything but? When she did speak, all she could say was, 'How could you leave me?' Her words were snatched by a sudden gust of wind, unheard by the man who was observing her from a battered red pick-up at the end of the beach road.

7

Cal McGill peered through his dirty windscreen. There was something compelling about the young woman's stillness, about the length of time she'd been standing there, square-shouldered, erect, staring out to sea, like an Antony Gormley figure waiting for another of its cast-iron tribe to emerge from the waves. By his calculation, she hadn't moved for ten minutes, not a stretch of an arm, a turn of the head – nothing that he had seen. What had brought her here, he wondered. Just as he began to guess at some of the possibilities, she turned round, collected her backpack and continued further along the beach, towards North Bay.

Her impending departure caused him an unexpected pang of regret, followed by the whimsical notion that this woman, whom he had never met, whose face he had never seen, of whom he had been aware for no more than a dozen minutes, might be a companion spirit, someone who found refuge by the sea, as he did. For as long as she remained in view, he let himself be distracted by the possibility of an unexplored affinity between them. The thought was accompanied by a wistful smile. A beach was where he met his wife, Rachel. Their divorce wasn't quite two months old. If he had learned anything by the experience surely it was to be wary of a combination of wide skies, an empty beach and the chance appearance of an unaccompanied young woman?

Still, it was a bitter-sweet sensation as this newest encounter climbed the headland and began to descend towards the next bay. He followed her progress until all that was visible of her above the horizon was her bobbing head and then he closed his eyes. The cab of the pick-up was warm, the afternoon sun making it soporific. He dozed for ten, perhaps fifteen minutes. When he woke, the statue from the beach was coming towards him through the dunes and the path she was following led her to the turning circle where Cal had parked. He reached for a file and pretended to read, while tracking her approach out of the corner of his eye. She was taller than he'd imagined: five foot eight or so, almost his height, and slender too. He feigned surprise when she tapped on his door, taking in her boy's-cut short brown hair, the two silver rings in her left ear and her dark eyes that looked deliberately past him. Her closed expression and the paleness of her small face together gave him an impression of self-containment.

'Do you live here?' she asked before he'd lowered his window, repeating the question after. He shook his head and she seemed disappointed, pulling her mouth to one side and looking around as if hoping to see someone else. 'Try me,' he said.

'The island in the sea loch . . . I'm trying to find out who owns it.' She turned in that direction.

'Orasaigh?'

'You know it?' Her voice lifted and, for the first time, she returned Cal's gaze.

'No, not really.' He'd walked there earlier in the day, killing time, waiting for Duncan Boyd to put in an appearance either at his farm or at the beach.

She sighed and apologized for bothering him. She made to leave but changed her mind. 'You don't know when low tide is, do you?' He took his mobile phone off the pick-up's dashboard and checked the time. 'In exactly one hour and forty-two minutes, at 17.54, and the next one is at 06.36 tomorrow morning.'

'How do you know that?' For the briefest of moments she appeared interested.

'It's a hobby of mine.' He thought he sounded like a nerd and perhaps she did too.

Her interest didn't last. She raised a hand in farewell without looking at him again and went along the beach road.

'Hi, my name is Cal McGill,' he said quietly when she was out of earshot.

8

A knee-deep stream of retreating seawater covered the causeway. After removing her trainers, socks and jeans and putting them into her backpack, Violet waded across the eighty metres to Orasaigh Island. She went ashore at a gravel ramp, beside which was a wooden notice. 'Beware of the changing tides,' it warned. 'If you find yourself trapped, please have consideration for the inconvenience of others before attempting to summon help. A few hours pass surprisingly quickly and enjoyably on Orasaigh.'

Brushing sand and grit from her feet, Violet dressed again. From the ramp she climbed uphill on a grassy track which wound through spindly alder, ash and birch. Wherever she looked she asked herself the same question: how had the island changed since her mother lived there?

Where the trees gave way to bracken, a pitched roof appeared above the skyline. In her impatience to see her mother's home, Violet broke into a run. Soon she found herself standing before a two-up two-down cottage. It was surrounded by a mossy stone wall which enclosed twin patches of lawn and between them a path edged with narrow borders of lavender. Violet lifted the latch of the gate and went uncertainly down the path. Knocking at the outer door of the porch, she noticed a card in one of the side windows. 'For letting inquiries, ring Brae

Estate Office.' The phone number was printed in fading letters. She shouted out, 'Hi, hello.' After waiting for a response, she crossed one of the lawns to what turned out to be the sitting-room window. She peered through the glass on to another life. Had it been like that when her mother lived there, she wondered.

The room was dark and neat with two armchairs either side of an open fireplace framed by matching bookshelves. Violet saw there was none of the clutter that went with occupation. It seemed no one was in residence. She made her way back to the letting notice and tapped the number into her phone. Her call went straight to message. Violet left her name and number. Then she looked in the window on the other side of the porch, at a small dining room with a circular table and four chairs. That, too, was neat, if gloomy. Going back to the porch, she rattled at the locked door in frustration. Having waited so long to discover her birthplace, she found her patience wearing out. With a regretful backward glance, she left the garden and carried on along the track towards the middle of the island until she found a sheltered area of grass below some rowan trees. She took off her backpack and put up her small tent.

Afterwards, she rang Hilary, who was full of the exploits of the two girls. Typically, she ended one story with a burst of laughter before launching into another, until Violet's silence prompted her to ask, 'Are you all right?'

'I've found my mother's house.'

Hilary relayed the message to Anna. Violet heard her daughter shout with excitement. 'Would you like to speak to her?' Hilary asked.

'I can't,' Violet replied.

'Why? What's wrong?'

'Nothing, it's just that I'll cry if I talk about it and I don't want Anna to think I'm upset.'

Hilary seemed put out.

Violet could still hear her daughter's excited squeaks. 'Ask Anna if she'll paint me a cottage with two windows upstairs and two downstairs with a door in the middle. Ask her,' she added, 'to paint her granny's house.'

As he returned along the rough track to Boyd's Farm, Cal noticed a new addition. An old tractor was now parked by the two stone pillars. 'This Land is NOT for sale. Turn round here', was painted across the bodywork. Cal kept on driving past the other abandoned machinery until he was almost at the steading. He parked by the entrance close to the Wall of Lost Soles and smiled again when he saw all the footwear nailed to the barn. The extent of dilapidation struck him more forcibly on this visit. The roofs were sagging and bowing as if close to collapse. There were forlorn heaps of broken slates and fallen masonry in the courtyard below. Rounding the corner of a barn, Cal came upon three men in ill-fitting suits. Two leaned against a car, their arms folded; the other – a big, bald man – stood separately, smoking a cigarette. 'You don't know where he is by any chance?' He sounded weary with waiting.

Cal shook his head.

'Mr Boyd isn't expecting you?'

'Not really. I said I'd look in sometime today but we didn't agree when.'

The smoker's brow creased in mild irritation. 'Well?' He directed the question at his two colleagues. 'What'll we do?'

'It's up to you,' one with a sharp face said. The other, a younger man, nodded in bored agreement.

'Another five, then,' the smoker said before introducing himself to Cal. 'Alastair Henderson. I'm the local councillor.'

Cal nodded. 'Hi.'

'We were hoping to speak to Mr Boyd about the wind farm.' He studied Cal on the off chance he could be of assistance. 'See if he's open to persuasion at all about selling to the consortium. It'd be best for everyone, Mr Boyd included.' He glanced around the steading, a frown forming at the state of the buildings. 'He can't go on living like this. He won't get a better offer, if that's why he's holding out.'

Again it was as if Councillor Henderson thought Cal might be able to exert some influence on the stubborn farmer.

Cal shook his head. 'I can't help you, I'm afraid. I know nothing about what's going on apart from the posters on the telegraph poles I passed on the road to Poltown.' Out of the corner of his eye, Cal noticed a movement at a skylight in one of the barns. Illuminated by a shaft of evening sun, he had the impression of a disembodied head, grey hair and a broken-toothed grin.

Cal assumed he had found Duncan Boyd.

'I don't know where you'll find him,' Cal said. 'But since there's a queue I think I'll try my luck again in the morning.'

9

Mary Anderson's hands clasped a cup. The tea had become lukewarm since her last sip. Her eyes were staring vacantly at the wall opposite, at the space between the cooker and the kitchen clock. On the table in front of her was a collection of seven letters, which she had discovered in Mr William's dressing room at Brae House after his funeral six years ago. They had been in his chest of drawers, concealed under his jerseys and wrapped around with two rubber bands. At Diana's request, Mrs Anderson had been sorting through his clothes, separating what could be given to charity and what should be burned. Diana said she would find the task too distressing but it had to be done, or else the room would become 'William's mausoleum'. Would Mrs Anderson be 'an absolute dear', while Diana removed herself to Edinburgh?

Mrs Anderson hadn't told Diana about the letters, a correspondence from Mr William to Megan Bates that must have been returned to him following her death, nor had she burned any of them. After digesting their contents, she had locked them away in her bureau. She considered them to be a form of insurance. In Mr William's crabbed handwriting was the proof, if she ever needed it, of Diana's motive for wanting rid of the child, of Diana being the instigator of the terrible events of that night – a night Mrs Anderson would never forget.

She glanced again at the clock. It was 2.23 in the morning. The kitchen was in shadow. The only light was from a lamp on the table, which cast a pale glow on Mrs Anderson's face, as if she had seen a ghost. And, in a manner of speaking, she had. On re-reading the letters, she had not only disinterred the remains of Mr William's affair with Megan Bates, but also inadvertently those of Mrs Anderson's marriage, which had ended when Robert, an instructor at the Poltown base, left her for another woman. What made the memory bitter, and the letters poignant, was that Mrs Anderson was pregnant when Robert departed, as was Megan Bates by the end of the correspondence. Mr William's transformation from surprised lover to negotiator when the affair cooled still had the capacity to create a whirlwind of emotions in Mrs Anderson. As with her husband, Mr William appeared to consider a promise of continuing financial support sufficient to resolve 'an impossible conflict' in his responsibilities to two women. The significant difference in the behaviour of the men was which of the women they attempted to placate with money. In Mr William's case, it was his estranged mistress Megan Bates. In Robert's, it was Mrs Anderson, the soon-to-be-abandoned wife. As was usually the case with Robert, it was an offer made in drink, late at night, circumscribed and grudging. It was limited to maintenance for the child and to 'keeping a roof over its head'. A final similarity: in neither case did the man honour his commitment, though in Mr William's case, because Megan Bates died.

As her emotion subsided, Mrs Anderson was left with a bitter aftertaste at the casual trail of destruction left by men and at the women who conspire with them, women like Megan Bates and Alice Forsyth, her husband's lover who became his wife and the mother of his three children. Most of all, Mrs Anderson reserved her bitterness for the loss of her baby daughter, stillborn after twenty-nine weeks, her death the consequence, she would always believe, of the stress she suffered when Robert finally deserted her.

Hadn't that been the story of Mrs Anderson's life: her loyalty always rewarded by betrayal of one kind or another?

The thought was quickly followed by self-pity and by tears which welled at the corners of her eyes. Her hands began to shake and she placed the teacup back in its saucer. She continued to hold on and every time her hands trembled the cup rattled against china, a noise like a distant chiming marking the passage of time. She appeared deaf to it: at any rate she didn't change or release her grip. And so the chiming continued as she rehearsed for the umpteenth time since Diana's memorial service the injustices she had suffered. Having run through those, she fretted about the precariousness of her position, at the household bills which would eat into her savings and pension, at the first rental demand for £575 which was due in a few days, and at the lawyer's reprimanding tone in response to her written protests. Finally, there was the worry that her anonymous letter concerning Megan Bates's daughter was lying crumpled and discarded in some official's waste bin in the social work office in Inverness.

These ghosts and fears assailed her throughout the night, until at 4.20 a.m., exhausted, she went to bed, resolving to leave a message for Jim Carmichael, who would deliver her order from the shop in Poltown the next day. She would ask him to drop in early, for cake and tea, and encourage him to divulge all the local news, the comings and goings, in the hope he would tell her whether any young woman had been in the shop asking questions about Poltown.

She'd let him talk for as long as he wanted and she'd listen to his ramblings for any mention of a last-minute B&B booking, for a stranger walking the beaches, a young woman in her mid-twenties. If Mrs Anderson were the daughter of Megan Bates, she would start the search in the shop, either there or at Boyd's Farm, since Duncan had found the washed-up hat and bag. Just before she fell asleep, Mrs Anderson wondered how Duncan would react to hearing the name Megan Bates again.

Cal woke before seven, his shoulders and neck stiff after sleeping uncomfortably in the pick-up's cab. He'd dozed off four hours earlier to a radio discussion about globalization and had come round feeling weighed down, as though the worries of the world had settled on him. He knew why he was out of sorts. Another day, another coast: wasn't he just looking for excuses not to go back to his office and putting off having to decide how to answer all those waiting emails?

He swore, pushed open the driver's door and jogged across the beach. At the high-tide mark, he stripped off his shirt and, hopping on one leg then the other, his jeans.

He dropped them on the sand as he walked to the sea. When the water was up to his armpits, he let the waves wash past him until his mood improved. Then, after ducking his head, he splashed back through the shallows. Picking up his clothes, he remembered Rachel, his ex-wife, complaining about his habit of removing himself to a distant coast instead of discussing what was wrong with their marriage. He couldn't keep on running away, she'd said. In that, as well as other things, she had been wrong.

Back at the pick-up, he put on a blue shirt, cotton trousers, thick socks and walking boots. Breakfast was half a cheese sandwich left over from the day before and a swig from a carton of milk. Afterwards, he drove to Boyd's Farm. Like the previous evening, he parked by the entrance to the steading. Unlike then, there was no one to be seen in the yard. His progress was witnessed by two feral-looking cats which sat on the slate roof of the back porch and, as it turned out, by Duncan Boyd. He was watching from an upstairs window in the farmhouse – spying a habit, it seemed. Only when Cal shouted his name and why he was there did Duncan emerge into the sunlight, grinning shyly. He wore baggy black trousers and a creased off-white shirt with frayed collar and cuffs which was tucked into his waistband at the front but not at the back.

'Good morning, lovely day,' Cal said.

His greeting caused Duncan to indulge in a succession of facial expressions, from amusement and panic to vulnerability, as if he was trying out each one in an attempt to discover which felt appropriate to the day. He settled on amusement.

'Wall of Lost Soles . . .' He nodded in the direction of the shoes nailed to the barn.

'Yes, I saw it,' Cal said. 'It's funny.'

Duncan grinned at Cal's reaction. 'I stole it,' he said, 'from a woman who lives on the Pacific coast of America. She has a Wall of Lost Soles too.'

'I wouldn't call that stealing,' Cal replied, 'and anyway, the world's big enough for two, don't you think?'

Cal's answer again seemed to please Duncan, who beckoned to his visitor and led him from one ramshackle building to the next. Duncan pointed out some of his beachcombing finds, selecting examples for inspection as if testing Cal's knowledge and interest. Then Cal was taken into the big barn and Duncan ushered him into the presence of the Neptune Scroll with all the comic formality of a fawning courtier. Though the document was squint and in a damaged frame, Cal made admiring comments about it and the Guinness bottle, which was on Duncan's big table where he displayed his most recent discoveries. These included a collection of rusty nails, odd shapes of driftwood, sea-glass, broken pottery and children's plastic toys.

'I collect too,' Cal said. 'Rather like you . . . My favourite is a green turtle shell I found washed up on a beach in South Uist. It's this big . . .' He spread his arms wide. 'Well, not quite that big.'

Duncan frowned as if put out. He glanced at his Guinness bottle and Neptune Scroll before casting around the barn, as though trying to find something which could compete with a turtle shell.

Cal hadn't meant to appear competitive. Trying to

make amends, he said quickly, 'But if I had a Neptune Scroll, that would be the best. Nothing beats that.' Cal went closer to examine the scroll and Duncan leaned in too, his eyes darting from the scroll to Cal. The half-mad grin Cal had seen at the skylight the previous evening spread slowly across Duncan's face. He crooked the index finger of his right hand, again beckoning.

Duncan strode across the yard to the back porch of the house, Cal following and wishing he'd said nothing. The two cats jumped from the roof and rubbed against Duncan's legs. Cal was careful to step around their encrusted food bowls on the porch floor as Duncan carried on inside. Now Cal was walking along a dark corridor, the atmosphere thick with dust and smelling of damp and cats. He emerged into a rectangular, gloomy hall and found Duncan standing at an open door opposite. Cal joined him and looked in.

By the dimensions and size of the fireplace, if not the furnishings, it might originally have been a sitting room, though there was now no room to sit. Tables, old mattresses and chairs were all piled higgledy-piggledy on top of each other. Duncan indicated an open space behind the door and Cal saw a doll's house. Despite being damaged – its walls were rotting and the windows broken or missing – it had a certain style. Close up, it resembled a grand plantation house from the southern states of America. Cal knelt and looked inside. Apart from some pieces of miniature furniture which looked appropriate to the house, each room contained a cheap modern doll, all worse for wear with ragged clothes or missing limbs.

Cal wasn't sure which had been washed up. 'Did you find the doll's house in South Bay or the dolls?' he asked.

Duncan said nothing. He stood in the doorway with his peculiar grin. The scene struck Cal as weird, this man-boy showing off the wreck of a doll's house containing its gruesome collection of residents. 'By the way,' he said, trying to find another subject, 'Did you talk to those men? The ones who were here yesterday evening? One of them said he was a councillor. He wanted to discuss the wind farm.'

The grin faded. Duncan plucked at the sleeve of his shirt. He muttered about his land not being for sale, about the public meeting tomorrow evening stirring up feeling, about people taking sides against him. He wouldn't look at Cal. His eyes darted about.

'I'm sorry,' Cal said, seeing his distress. 'It's none of my business. I shouldn't have said anything.' Then, turning again to the doll's house, he said, 'This is interesting. And so is your collection. Would it be all right if I looked around outside? I'm sure there'll be something there which will be useful for my work.'

When he looked back, Duncan was gone.

By the time Cal was in the hall, all he could hear was a door closing. It came from the next floor. 'Duncan,' Cal called out before going to the stairs at the end of the hall. 'Duncan,' he tried again, ascending slowly. 'I didn't mean to upset you. I'd really like you to show me round outside.'

No reply. No sound at all.

As Cal reached the first floor a rattling began. The

noise seemed to be coming from the door across the landing. Could Duncan be on the other side?

Cal saw that a name was stencilled on it. 'Megan.'

Cal knocked. 'Duncan? Are you in there?'

No reply.

Cal tried the handle and the door sprang open. He looked inside. There was no sign of Duncan but there was a surprise. He looked from the double bedstead with its patterned cover, a teddy bear against the pillows, to the dressing table on which there was a mirror, scent bottles and an open box of tissues. He watched the curtains flutter in the draught from the open window, the reason the door had been rattling, and he thought how odd this room was. In any other house, it would have been unremarkable, but in this one, with so much in disrepair, its simplicity and tidiness were peculiar.

Cal closed the door and went downstairs. He felt uneasy wandering around this strange, dilapidated house and, worried about being caught prying, decided to go outside and look at some more of Duncan's collection in the steading. He might find the man-boy there.

Back in the yard, breathing in fresh air, he wondered about Megan, who she was, when she would be returning and why any woman would choose to live in such a place with someone like Duncan?

A movement in the dunes at the back of the beach caught Violet's eye. She thought it might be the breeze ruffling the grass, or a rabbit until she saw a man's head bob up.

Walking in his direction, she noticed the man seemed to have turned his back and was raking his fingers through his unruly and brittle hair and brushing down his clothes. When, eventually, she was close enough to say 'Hello', he pretended not to hear her. 'Hello,' she tried again, louder, walking round him until she was looking up into his face. 'Hi.'

He indicated with a nod of his head some flotsam which was lying beside him on an old farm trailer. He picked up a lobster pot, followed by a buoy. 'I'll be busy sorting out this lot for a while, I imagine.' The remark was boastful in a juvenile way and his demeanour also that of a self-satisfied child expecting a compliment for his hard work.

'I'm sure you will.' Violet tried to summon up sufficient enthusiasm. 'Haven't you done well?'

After Duncan showed her a length of blue rope, Violet asked, 'I was wondering whether you might know who lives at the farmhouse?'

'Depends.' He squinted.

'On what?'

'Why you might want him?'

'Just to ask him about someone who used to live near here.'

'Not about the wind farm?'

'*Definitely* not about the wind farm . . .'

'Mmh.'

'You don't like the wind farm?'

He shook his head. 'I won't sell, you know.'

'You own the farmhouse?'

He nodded.

'I saw the notice on the old tractor as I walked past this morning. "Land NOT for sale",' she repeated with the correct emphasis. 'Good for you.' She laughed at another strange turn in the conversation. 'So you must be Duncan Boyd. I'm Violet . . . Violet Wells.' She extended her right hand. 'I'm visiting for a day or two, passing through.'

Duncan eyed her outstretched hand with suspicion until Violet withdrew it.

'I was wondering,' she carried on, 'if you ever came across someone who used to live here, a friend of my mother's . . . Her name was Megan Bates.'

Duncan pressed his hands to his ears. His head was shaking.

'Mr Boyd, are you all right?'

'I want you to go now.' He sounded petulant, as though Violet had spoiled a game and her punishment was to be banished.

She said his name again and touched him on the arm to let him know she hadn't intended to provoke him.

'I want you to go now . . . I want you to go now.' With every repetition his voice became louder. Violet thought her departure was the only thing that would calm him. She retreated through the dunes to the beach road, where she stopped and looked back. Duncan was half-running, half-walking towards North Bay, where her mother's hat and bag had drifted ashore.

A little unnerved, she wondered if he was having a fit of some kind and whether she should tell anyone. Back on the road, by the stone pillars leading to Boyd's Farm, she was relieved to come across a blue van. A man in work overalls was getting out of the driver's door with a cardboard box of groceries. A dog barked from the passenger seat.

'Hello,' Violet said. 'Can you help me?'

The man was balding, red-faced and with a friendly expression. He pretended to be surprised by her sudden appearance. 'Oh, you gave me a fright.' He clutched his spare hand to his heart, coughing and spluttering before giving up the pretence. 'What can I do for you, miss?'

'You know Mr Boyd?'

'Indeed I do. I've been delivering this same order of groceries to his farm for more years than I can remember.' He noticed Violet's worried expression and the way she kept looking towards the beach. His tone changed, becoming confiding. 'Duncan's not quite like everyone else, if you know what I mean . . . But there's no harm in him, no harm at all.'

Violet said, 'I think I've upset him. He's run off towards North Bay.'

'Has he now? He must be out of sorts, then.' He put down the grocery box by a pillar. 'Always leave it here, I do. Duncan collects it later.'

'We were just talking,' Violet said. 'I didn't mean to upset him.'

'I'm Jim, by the way.' He held out his hand after wiping it on his overalls. 'Jim Carmichael.'

'Violet Wells.'

'Nice to meet you, Violet.' Jim glanced in the direction of North Bay. 'Now don't you worry yourself about Duncan. We're used to his ways. He'll be up there, standing on the beach like he does and in an hour or two he'll come back, right as rain.' He looked at Violet. The same confiding voice. 'He's been a bit overwrought recently about this wind farm business.'

Jim drew Violet's attention to the 'NOT for sale' sign on the tractor beside the track. 'People trying to get him to sell . . . The electricity's coming ashore over there.' He looked towards the sea. 'And see this field . . .' Jim nodded past the tractor. 'They're going to cover it with a shed; massive, so they say.' He glanced up the coast, frowning as though Violet might have reason to worry. 'Still, he hasn't gone up there for a while. Not a good sign. Usually sticks around South Bay, does Duncan.'

They were where Duncan was standing now: the raffia sun hat with its band of red ribbon and her leather shoulder bag. Duncan had gone from one to the other, not wanting to pick them up, fearful of what they signified. He'd looked behind him, hoping it was a practical joke of some kind, willing her to be hiding among the boulders which tumbled down to the little beach. Hoping it was a game and she would suddenly jump from behind a rock, laughing. Knowing it had been a portent of something else.

The tide was ebbing. The hat and the bag beside each other, both wet. He'd looked up, hoping against hope to see her swimming in the bay, knowing she wouldn't be there. She didn't like North Bay because of all the rocks and because the beach shelved away too quickly. She preferred the wide and flat expanses of South Bay. He touched the hat and the bag, feeling them with his outstretched fingers, as nervously as if he was touching her flesh. He hadn't picked them up or taken them away. Later the police asked him why not. He could tell from their faces he hadn't provided a satisfactory answer.

Instead he'd backed away. Scrambling across rocks, he fell and cut his hands and knees and then he ran to Megan's. Her cottage on Orasaigh, the tidal island inside the mouth of Poltown Loch, was the other side of Duncan's farm. He waited at the causeway calling for her, cursing his inability to swim, waiting for the ebb to quicken, for the narrow channel separating Orasaigh from the mainland to be shallow enough for him to cross. He went up to his waist wading, shouting her name, so by the time he arrived at the cottage he knew she wouldn't be there. He banged on the door before going inside. The cottage was still, still and empty, her spirit gone. He'd pressed his hands to his ears and closed his eyes tight. After calming down, he went round the sitting room touching the places he remembered she'd been, the armchair, the rug at the corner of the coffee table where she'd poured the tea, feeling again the brush of her fingers when she'd told him he was 'a sweet man' for offering to look after her and her baby if the father didn't. If she felt she had to leave Orasaigh so that she wasn't living under a roof owned by him. She had kissed him too, on the cheek. He told the police he'd been there half an hour or so. He judged it by the causeway when he left. By then the water was at his knees.

Later the police asked him why smears of his blood had been found on her desk, the armchair and the rug. He said he'd cut himself on the rocks at North Bay. They asked whether he loved her and he said he did; whether he was jealous of the other man and he said he was, a little; whether he'd killed Megan, whether he'd been destroying evidence when he'd been in her cottage, whether he'd taken her things to North Bay to make it look like she'd drowned. Hadn't there been two sets of footprints in the sand, both his, from when he carried her things there and when he departed? Didn't he have a reputation for being, no offence intended, unlike other people? In his case, they

77

weren't dealing with a criminal mastermind but someone who'd been caught up in the emotion of the moment, who wouldn't have the guile to cover his tracks, who would make elementary mistakes because he wasn't 'overly blessed in the intellect department'?

A crime of passion, said one of the policemen. Yes, the other had agreed. A crime of passion.

Duncan had gone to a corner of the interview room, facing the wall. 'I love her,' he said.

'Did she love you?'

'I love her,' he repeated.

They registered the tense. One wrote down 'Love' and added a big question mark. His colleague raised an eyebrow and tapped an index finger against his temple. *Screw loose.*

The interrogation continued. 'Did you have sex with her?'

'No.'

'Did you hate her for carrying another man's baby, because she'd let another, older man thumb his prick into her, like you wanted to?'

'No.' He wailed at the crudeness. 'No.'

'You knew you'd lose her as soon as the baby was born, so you killed her, didn't you? You took her somewhere and killed her. Did you put her into the sea, Duncan? Did you bury her? What did you do with her, Duncan?'

By then his hands were over his ears and he was stamping his feet. He told them to stop talking like that, about the woman he loved. Later, when they persuaded him to sit at the table for tea and a cigarette, they said they believed him, but they had to be sure. It wasn't personal,

78

it was routine. They were sorry if he felt they'd been rough with him. They didn't like coming on strong. But the job was the job. Was there anything he could tell them about Megan that would help them with their inquiries?

'When did you last see her?'

'Two days before she disappeared.'

'Where?'

'In her cottage.'

'Did she invite you over?'

'No.'

'What time of day was it?'

'The middle of the afternoon,' Duncan replied. 'I'd gone then because it was low tide.'

'Did you wash beforehand? Did you put on clean clothes? Did you want to look your best for her?'

He looked embarrassed. 'Yes.'

They smiled. They would have done so too, their expressions seemed to suggest. Pretty woman like that.

'What was the purpose of your visit?'

'I'd wanted to tell her something.'

'What?'

'I said I would look after her, her and the baby, if the father didn't. I wanted to tell her she could live with me at the farm.'

'A happy family,' one of the policemen said.

He smiled and repeated it. 'Yes, a happy family.'

'And what happened?'

'When?' he asked, suddenly confused.

'When you said that to her, about her living with you, being a happy family?'

'She said I was sweet.'

The policemen looked at each other and smirked. 'Sweet,' they said together.

'Yes, sweet,' he replied.

'Bit of a kick in the teeth,' one said. 'For a man who'd gone to all that trouble, smelling nice and getting all dressed up, laying it on the line like you'd done.'

'Sweet? I'd have slapped her,' said the other.

'Me too,' his partner agreed.

'Sweet,' they said in unison. 'For fuck's sake.' As if they had a script.

'I'd have smacked her, no question.'

'Wouldn't blame anyone . . .'

'Not after that . . .'

'Sweet . . .'

'What an insult . . .'

'What kind of woman would treat you like that?'

They were talking so quickly, one then the other, that Duncan was unable to get a word in. He was confused and worried by these two policemen taking his complicity for granted.

'No question, Duncan; I'd have done the same.'

'She had it coming,' the other said.

By then Duncan's hands were shaking so much he spilled his tea. They let him fuss over it, covering the puddle with a newspaper, but when he looked at them again their faces were hard.

'Afterwards, when you left the cottage, you met Jim Carmichael, didn't you?'

'I think so. I'm not sure.'

'What did you say to him?'

'I don't remember. I was upset.'

'Do you remember if you were crying?'

He thought he had been.

'Do you remember what you said?'

He shook his head.

One of them consulted a notebook. 'Duncan said, "Megan's gone" and when I asked him where she'd gone he said he didn't know.'

'Why didn't you call the police, Duncan?'

'I don't know,' he said.

'Where did she go, Duncan?' one of the policemen asked.

'After you'd killed her?' the other added.

'Where did you put her, Duncan?'

Tweedledum and Tweedledee again.

'I loved her.'

Each looked at the other, significance in their expressions. They'd noticed the change of tense.

'Loved her, Duncan?'

'That's better, Duncan. Now we seem to be getting somewhere.' Then they started up another conversation, how people like Duncan didn't have the control panel 'up top or down below', how the police and the courts knew that, how he'd get psychiatric help and maybe that would be a relief to him, because 'old Mother Nature' hadn't played fair with him, giving him sexual urges and no mechanism for keeping them under control.

Duncan slammed his hands on the table. 'I won't talk any more. You're confusing me, making my head muddled and twisting my words.'

He'd looked from one to the other. 'I love her,' he said and turned his back.

They left him alone. He spent the night in a cell. In the dead of night, when no one was at his door listening, he talked to Megan. Hadn't he shown her the strength of his love? Hadn't he kept their secret? Hadn't she said she would go away one day? Hadn't she promised to leave something behind, something to let him know she would return? One day. Hadn't that been the hat and the bag? 'You're a sweet man, Duncan.' He heard her voice and felt her soft lips on his skin.

He was released the next morning by the custody sergeant, who said more evidence had come to light. A witness had come forward. The police were following a new and positive line of inquiry. Foul play was no longer suspected.

When he returned to the farm in a police car, 'for his own protection', he discovered they'd searched everywhere, all through the house and the farm buildings. As he walked around, unable to settle to anything, his two interrogators dropped by to see how he was, to let him know they'd be watching, every minute of every day, until they got him for what he'd done to Megan Bates.

'Sticks in here,' one said, pointing at his throat. 'That we've been ordered to close the case.'

'And mine,' added the other.

'Out there,' the first one said with a sweep of his hand which encompassed the landscape beyond his few fields, 'is hostile territory for a wee shite like you.'

11

Cal found a pile of bones in a disused stable while looking for Duncan in the steading. He thought a horse must have died and its broken skeleton was all that remained. Then he noticed three skulls. Two were familiar in size and shape. They belonged to porpoises – he'd found a number of similar ones while beachcombing – but the other, larger one was very unusual. He'd heard about a creature whose description matched the skull structure, not only the distinctive hollow at the top of the head but also the large size and the two cylindrical teeth which were still embedded in the bottom of the elongated jaw, near the tip. He was more or less certain the skull was a Cuvier's, an elusive type of beaked whale which inhabited deep water and fed on squid. These details had lodged in his memory after watching a YouTube clip of American scientists examining a beached and dead Cuvier's whale and removing from its stomach twenty-two carrier bags. Apparently the bags – how they hung in the water, how light played on them – confused the whales and they mistook them for prey.

Cal held the skull in both hands and wondered if that was how this one had met its fate. In case Duncan would be interested, he carried it to where he'd left a section of wood, more than a metre long, part of a mast, which had been colonized by goose barnacles. There were so many that none of the wood was visible, except at one end. He would tell Duncan about the considerable distance it had travelled before ending its journey at South Bay. Given the profusion of barnacles it had certainly been at sea for some time. He put the skull down beside the pole as a post van appeared in the yard driven by a middle-aged woman. She had curly red hair turning grey at the temples. 'Is he about?' she asked after driving up to Cal and opening her window.

'Duncan?' Cal asked, shaking his head. 'He was here but I don't know where he's got to.'

'Gone to the beach, I dare say.' The postwoman rolled her eyes. 'Would you sign for these, then?' She retrieved four letters from the passenger seat and followed them with a pad and pen. 'One signature for each letter; if you don't mind,' she added.

Cal examined the envelopes: each had a red stamp, 'Final Warning'. He screwed up his face in apology and handed them back. 'Don't know what I'd be signing for. Not my business.'

She sighed. 'I'll just have to bring them back tomorrow. As likely as not there'll be a couple more by then.'

'Sorry I can't help.'

'Well, someone's got to.' A frown of concern wrinkled her brow. 'Have a look in there.' She nodded towards a lean-to shed, its door closed. 'This can't go on, all these letters and Duncan ignoring them. You don't mess about with an outfit like BRC,' she said.

'That's the consortium that's going to build the wind farm?'

The postwoman nodded. 'What beats me . . .' she

looked around the steading, 'is why Duncan wants to stay. There again, where else could he go? Who would want him as a neighbour?'

Cal watched the van go, glanced at the lean-to and decided to look inside. The door opened halfway before sticking. Cal pushed with his shoulder and it gave some more, revealing a mound of paper, letters and packages of different shapes and sizes. There were so many that Cal assumed this was where Duncan routinely dumped his post. The notion took further hold when Cal noticed some envelopes like the ones he'd returned to the postwoman. They bore the same red warnings.

Cal picked up a handful. Some hadn't been opened but others had – they were about the wind farm, or about Duncan being in breach of environmental or building safety regulations. The common denominator, as far as Cal could tell from his fleeting examination, was the threat of legal or other enforcement action. One letter which impressed itself particularly on Cal was from lawyers acting for BRC. It warned of compulsory purchase and, in that event, 'minimal' compensation for Duncan considering the 'farm's state of dereliction'. 'To prevent imminent court proceedings you must communicate in writing your immediate and unconditional acceptance of our clients' existing and generous offer to purchase Boyd's Farm in its entirety.'

Three weeks had passed since the letter had been written and, presumably, ignored by Duncan.

Feeling sympathy for the man, Cal went out into the yard. He carried the whale skull and the barnacle-encrusted pole to the barn where the Neptune Scroll was hanging and put them by the table. After tearing a page from his pocket notebook, he wrote about the Cuvier's, telling Duncan how rarely beaked whales were seen, and also about the barnacles, speculating how they might have travelled from the tropics on the North Atlantic Current. He thought about adding something about the wind farm, an indication of his support for Duncan's stand against big business ruining the environment, or words to that effect, but instead asked Duncan to ring him.

I'm leaving my phone number in case you've mislaid it.

While he was writing, he prepared a little speech to deliver when Duncan contacted him, how he was right to stand firm against BRC, against business extending its realm over a vast swathe of sea – in one of the protest posters he'd seen, 362 square kilometres was mentioned. When Cal turned round to leave, Duncan was in the doorway. His expression was dull, his skin grey and eyes cloudy. He seemed drained of life.

The speech stayed unsaid. Thinking now that too many people were telling Duncan what to do, Cal thanked him instead for letting him look around. He was sorry if he'd upset him earlier.

Duncan neither reacted nor spoke.

'I've left you a note about these . . .' Cal indicated the skull and the encrusted pole. Then he said, 'Look, I know people who might be able to help you – marine scientists, guys I studied with, experts on offshore wind farms and how they disrupt currents and interfere with marine migrations. They could raise objections, delay things until BRC loses patience and walks away.'

Duncan didn't even blink. It felt to Cal as if his offer had also been consigned, unopened, to a dump, just like all those threatening letters. 'Of course, it's up to you,' he added, wishing he'd said nothing.

12

At the bridge over the stream, Violet took a right fork and right again by the stables, following the signs to the estate office. She found she was skirting Brae House, approaching from the side, glimpsing the building through gaps in the trees. Brae, it seemed, was a house of many parts: an elegant central square of three storeys with matching two-storey pavilions at right angles. For all Brae's beauty and drama – Scots-pine woods gave shelter on three sides and a rock crag appeared to overhang it – Violet was more taken with the contrast between the refinement of the property and the bad manners of its owner. If her telephone conversation that morning had been any guide, Matt Hamilton was rude and bad tempered. It was an impression the man himself did nothing to dispel when Violet appeared in the open door of the office and he said, 'You're five minutes late.'

He was a big man, not only tall but also large framed and overweight, with a florid face and a loud voice which he directed without a change of tone or volume at Violet and then at a woman with blonde hair and an impatient expression who was searching through a pile of papers at the desk he was hovering beside.

'How many nights did you say?' he barked at Violet, then at the woman: 'Alexandra, for goodness' sake, I can do that.'

'I'm not sure,' Violet replied. 'It depends . . .'

Matt looked from one woman to the other with a perplexed frown, as though having to deal with two at the same time was an imposition.

'Darling,' he addressed Alexandra, 'why don't you sort out this and let me do that?'

Alexandra gave her husband an exasperated look and surrendered the desk with a parting shot about him never being able to find anything and always surrounded by chaos.

'I'm sorry,' she directed at Violet, who was still just inside the door. 'As you can see, we're in a bit of a muddle.' Violet assumed the 'we' referred to Matt, because Alexandra gave the impression of being anything but disorganized. She wore a white shirt and blue jeans with a thin belt and she approached with a click of heels that indicated purpose. 'Hello, I'm Alexandra Hamilton.' She rolled her eyes at Violet, inviting feminine collusion at the hopelessness of men.

'I wanted to know,' Violet said, 'whether you rent Orasaigh Cottage by the day and, if so, how much it costs?'

Alexandra was about to answer when an eruption of complaint from across the room distracted her. 'Not those, Matt, I've already hunted through those.' He responded with a frustrated growl and Alexandra turned back to Violet. 'Well, we don't really have a day rate; didn't Matt . . . my husband . . . explain that to you when you rang this morning?'

'No, he didn't. He appeared to have other things on his mind once he'd told me how to get here.'

'Yes, he can be rather short on the telephone.' Alexandra looked apologetic, pressing her lips together.

'You were saying you don't have a day rate . . .'

'Normally our lets are for a week or more.'

The implication hovered between them until Violet said, 'Well, your husband could have told me that on the phone, couldn't he?'

An exclamation came from the desk and once again Alexandra's attention drifted. 'Don't say you've found it?'

'No thanks to you.' Matt left the room, flicking over the stapled pages of a document. Quiet restored, Alexandra said, 'Well, there isn't a tenant at the moment so I don't see why we shouldn't let it for a day or two, however long you want, really, since it isn't booked next week either.'

She accompanied the offer with a smile. 'How does fifty pounds a day sound, or,' she paused, 'in view of everything, why don't we say forty?'

Violet clutched the money in her pocket, two hundred pounds, her only savings. 'I think I can do . . .' she hesitated. 'Two, no three days . . . would three be all right?' She separated six twenty-pound notes and said, 'A friend of my mother's used to stay in the cottage. It was a long time ago, you probably wouldn't remember her.'

'Lots of people have stayed there . . .' Alexandra searched a wire basket. 'It's a popular cottage . . . Ah, here it is.' She brandished a notebook and asked Violet for her name, home address and mobile phone number.

Violet gave her details and handed over the rent. 'My mother's friend,' she said, 'was called Megan Bates.'

'Megan?' Alexandra tucked Violet's money into the notebook and returned it to the wire tray. 'Megan Bates.'

She repeated the name. 'No, but as I say, so many people pass through.' She selected a set of keys from a small tin. 'Yellow for Orasaigh,' she said, referring to the coloured tag. 'And you'll need these too . . .' She picked up two sheets of paper. 'The house rules, the dos and don'ts, as well as some useful numbers,' she said, handing over the first sheet with the keys. 'And most important of all . . .' She passed over the second. 'The tide times.'

Violet thanked her and asked if the cottage had recently been done up. 'I had a look through the front windows and it looked smart inside.'

'My mother had the place gutted,' Alexandra replied, 'when my stepfather died six years ago.'

'Was the furniture replaced?'

'Oh, everything was chucked out as far as I can remember.'

Violet held up the keys, thanked her and made for the door. 'I don't suppose,' she turned back, 'you know Duncan Boyd?'

'Yes,' Alexandra looked puzzled. 'Why?'

'Yes, of course you would.' Violet made it sound as though she'd made a silly mistake. 'I suppose you've been neighbours for years.'

'Yes. He was here when I first came to Brae as a child.'

'How long ago was that?'

'Oh, I don't know, about thirty-five years . . .' She still had the puzzled expression.

'You must have been very young.'

'I was six, but why did you ask about Duncan Boyd?'

'Oh, it's just that he remembers her, Megan Bates I mean. By the way he reacted to hearing her name, I think he remembers her quite well.' Violet paused. 'I'm surprised you don't recall her, since you would have been, what, fourteen or fifteen, when she lived at Orasaigh Cottage?'

With that Violet went out. She walked slowly giving Alexandra the opportunity to come after her, to admit her lie. Where the drive led into a copse of yew and holly, Violet looked back over her shoulder. Alexandra was watching her through the estate office window. They regarded each other for a moment before Violet turned away.

Mrs Anderson talked to herself while she cleared up after baking. 'She's going to take Brae from you, *Miss* Alexandra.' The dirty mixing bowls went into the Belfast sink to soak. 'The child will be my heir and will inherit the bulk of my estate.' Mrs Anderson knew that section of Mr William's letter to Megan Bates off by heart. The dirty spoons went into the dishwasher, as she recited from the letter again. '. . . Including my properties in Edinburgh as well as here in Poltown.' She put the leftover chocolate into the cupboard. 'It won't be long now, *Miss* Alexandra.' Then, Mrs Anderson looked out of the window. '*Miss* Alexandra, you're going to lose everything.' How long would it be, she wondered, hardly able to contain her impatience.

Was the girl already out there, searching?

If anyone would know, Jim would tomorrow when he brought her groceries. He'd have noticed any strangers. Mrs Anderson was safe asking him.

Her face darkened.

What if the girl wasn't coming?

―――――

Violet wandered from room to room, imagining the daily routine of Megan Bates's life.

Did her mother rise early? Did she make coffee while running a bath? Did she listen to the radio? Did she read? On which side of the fireplace in the sitting room did she sit? Did she light the fire? Was she tidy? Did she talk to herself? Did she go to bed early or late? Was she in love?

Orasaigh Cottage, Violet discovered, was like a sullen stranger. It gave nothing of its past away. The effect was demoralizing. Within an hour of turning the key in the front door and entering the porch in excitement, she had retreated to the kitchen, her jaw locked in disappointment. The house was empty of personality. Nothing of her mother remained and for a brief mad moment Violet saw the span of the last twenty-six years, starting with her birth, as a continuing and deliberate conspiracy of concealment. It began with a calculated act: her mother walking across a beach and abandoning her daughter for ever. It continued with the sea refusing to give up her body. Another part of the plot had taken place in this cottage where Violet was standing: anything which might hold her mother's memory had been stripped away and still the conspiracy lived on. Duncan Boyd had shut his ears to the sound of her name. Alexandra Hamilton said she hadn't even heard of her.

Later, in a calmer frame of mind, Violet understood

the hurt she felt was that of a child who yearns for a sighting of her mother, even if she has to make do with someone else's dim memory of a meeting long ago. Violet longed for detail, whether her mother had been extrovert or introvert, whether she'd been kind, whether she'd laughed loudly or softly. The answer to any one of these Violet would treasure and she would look for the same trait in herself and then in her daughter Anna.

In the sitting room, she found a telephone directory. She started at the back, going through the Ys, searching for Yellowlees, the name of the detective in charge of the investigation into Megan Bates's death.

On the bus to Poltown she had rung police headquarters in Inverness. Her inquiry caused the switchboard operator some amusement because, 'Mr, rather Chief Superintendent Yellowlees retired nine months ago.' Violet found four Yellowlees in the book: two in Inverness, one in Ullapool and the last in Mallaig. She rang the first Inverness number. There was no reply. The second was answered by a man and Violet asked if he was, by any chance, Mr Robert Yellowlees. He replied that his name was Iain but his brother was Robert. Had she confused the two? Violet told the story she'd prepared. The Robert Yellowlees she was trying to find had been a doctor and lived in Glasgow until his retirement.

'Oh,' Iain Yellowlees replied, 'that couldn't be my brother because he was a policeman, a chief superintendent, and he's never lived in Glasgow, never lived in a big city, not even one the size of Inverness. No, he always liked the great outdoors when he wasn't apprehending villains. He lives in Ullapool now.'

Violet apologized for taking up his time. In the dimming evening light, she circled the Yellowlees Ullapool entry in the phone book. She dialled the number. A man answered and Violet said, 'That's not Tom, is it?' The man, sounding cross, said no and Violet said, 'Sorry, wrong number.' Hanging up, she decided to visit his house as soon as she could in the morning. She ripped out the page and went to the kitchen to find the information leaflet given to her by Alexandra Hamilton. Halfway down the list of useful numbers she found what she was looking for: Turnbull's Taxis. The name registered with Violet. Hadn't Stuart, the bus driver, said something about a family called Turnbull running Poltown?

The woman who answered her call said a return trip to Ullapool with a wait of an hour would be thirty-six pounds.

Violet said, 'That's more expensive than I thought.'

'That's what it costs,' the woman said.

'I'll go one way and catch the bus back.'

'Suit yourself.'

Before confirming the booking, Violet checked the tide tables.

'So that's 8.30 tomorrow morning at the causeway to Orasaigh,' the woman repeated. 'One way. Cash up front, mind . . .'

Violet looked around the cottage's gloomy spaces. She shuddered at the thought of sleeping there. She collected her backpack from the porch and locked the door behind her. Going along the path to her small tent, she watched black clouds gathering to the west. She wondered where her mother's remains were, what little of them must be left. Were her bones buried by sand and seaweed? Were they lying together or dispersed across the sea bed, scattered over the years by storms? The thought of them kept her awake, that and the showers which thrummed on the sides of the tent.

———

Cal watched the rain slant in from the sea. It smeared the pick-up's windscreen, distorting his view of the beach so that he thought he saw a human shape standing by the water's edge. Had the statue returned? He felt a lift of hope followed by a let-down when another squall of rain washed the shape away. Suddenly, the prospect of another night alone seemed dispiriting. He picked up one of the leaflets he'd removed from the pillars to Boyd's Farm. 'Support the wind farm' it urged. 'Say YES to jobs. Say YES to a new school. Say YES to new houses. Say YES to the future of Poltown. Come to the public meeting and make your vote count.' The meeting was tomorrow night. He thought he might attend. Big business taking over the sea; the local population divided – the subject interested him and it gave him another excuse for delaying his return to Edinburgh. Cal glanced into the back of the pick-up. His food had run out. He was also low on diesel. As there was no garage in Poltown, he'd drive to Ullapool in the morning, refuel and go shopping.

13

Intermittent squalls of rain rattled against the bathroom window of Orasaigh Cottage. Violet washed away the overnight chill of the tent with a hot shower and was dressed and running her fingers through her wet hair when a knock sounded at the front door. It made her jump. She was on edge anyway, being back within those walls, on edge as well as in a hurry to meet the taxi which would soon be arriving on the other side of the causeway. She crossed the landing to the front bedroom – its window overlooked the porch and garden – and on the gravel path below was a woman wearing a waterproof hat which concealed her face. She had on a rain-jacket, a skirt which flapped in the wind and wellington boots. Violet backed away into the room, hoping her visitor, whoever she was, would leave, but instead she knocked again, once then twice more. 'What does she want?' Violet said irritably before going to see.

When she opened the door, the woman lifted her head. Under the hat, Violet recognized Alexandra Hamilton from Brae. 'Oh, hello,' Violet said, 'I was just getting ready to go out. A taxi's coming for me . . .'

A squall blew against the cottage. Alexandra turned sideways, the rain striking her back. Reluctantly, Violet retreated to allow her into the shelter of the porch and apologized for having to desert her while she went upstairs for her coat and bag. On her return, Violet found her visitor in the sitting room. She'd taken off her hat and was peering out at the weather, warning Violet worse was to come and they would be better waiting for it to pass. Violet protested weakly about her taxi, aware she had time to spare, a quarter of an hour, and it wouldn't take her more than five minutes to go along the track and cross the causeway. Her objection was more about being trapped with Alexandra.

An uneasy silence followed until Alexandra asked Violet if she was comfortable in the cottage. Violet let her think she'd spent the night there. 'Fine,' she said and added a compliment, the only one which occurred to her, about the shower and the hot water. Alexandra inspected the room, as if in search of a topic of conversation and Violet checked in her bag for her purse. Neither looked at the other. 'I really have to be going,' Violet insisted.

'I should have told you yesterday . . .' Alexandra countered, now examining the fireplace. 'A woman called Megan Bates did live here. I'm sorry. I shouldn't have pretended otherwise, but there was a reason.'

Violet waited, her heart thumping.

'I did meet her a few times. I didn't know her very well,' Alexandra went on, now looking at Violet. 'I didn't acknowledge her name yesterday because it was such a shock to hear it after all this time . . . it's a name from the past and, to be honest, I'd have preferred it to have stayed there.'

'Why?'

The question hung unanswered.

'Do you really want to know?'

Violet nodded.

'Because Megan Bates made my mother's life hell. She was unscrupulous. She was manipulative. She was dishonest. She liked to take what wasn't hers. She didn't have any family of her own – no one knew where she came from – and she tried to take someone else's.' She paused and looked around the room as if some trace of her might have survived. 'And yes, my father . . . my stepfather . . . allowed her to live in this cottage and for the time she was here there was never a second my mother didn't wish her gone. As far as I'm concerned, drowning herself was the only decent thing she ever did.'

For the last sentence she held Violet's stare and Violet said quietly, 'I'd like you to leave.'

The porch door banged shut, but Violet barely heard it. Nor did she move. In all her many imaginings about her mother, she'd never considered the possibility of her being as Alexandra described. Part of her wanted to rush to her mother's defence – to run after Alexandra and protest that it was more lies. Another part was apprehensive: what if other people told Violet the same; what if it was true? She was still paralysed with shock when her phone rang. She dug into her bag.

'Would you be planning to cross this low tide or the next?' It was a man's voice, her taxi driver, sounding impatient at having to wait.

'This,' she said, resenting his intrusion.

The taxi turned out to be a silver people carrier. 'Turnbull's Taxis' was emblazoned on both sides. The driver was a fifty-something man wearing trainers, white socks, olive green shorts and a Celtic shirt stretched across a prodigious belly. He said his name was Graham and as he opened the rear sliding door for Violet he explained that such a big vehicle was useful for picking up parties of hill walkers. 'The state some of them are in after being on the hill eaten by midges,' Graham exclaimed, wiping a fat hand across his face, 'Oh my goodness me.' His belly carried on wobbling jelly-like after his mirth had died away.

Graham, it seemed, was the talkative kind so Violet asked whether he would mind if she sat at the back because she had a phone call to make. A private phone call was the implication. Graham looked as though he thought it was her loss, missing out on his banter. 'You sit wherever you like, love; the taxi's all yours.'

Violet answered with a fleeting smile. No sooner had she fastened her seatbelt than he asked if she was ever travel sick because the road was nothing but twists and turns. 'There's more swing at the back.' Graham, she gathered, would prefer to have her company in the front.

'No, I've never been car sick, air sick or sea sick,' she assured him, immediately concentrating on her phone, keying in Hilary's number. Graham, she hoped, would take the hint; a wish that was accompanied by a flare of indignation. Why did every ugly middle-aged man imagine he was irresistible and interesting to any young woman travelling alone?

When Hilary picked up her call, Violet made her promise to stay on the phone 'for ever' or else, she whispered, 'an old fat bloke will try to have his way with me'.

Hilary laughed. 'How are you?'

Before Violet could answer, Hilary had told Anna 'It's

Mummy' and handed over the phone. 'I've painted Granny's house but it's got a crooked door,' Anna announced.

'That doesn't matter, darling,' Violet replied. 'Will you paint another picture for me?'

'Not a house.'

'No, not a house, what about painting Granny?'

Anna considered the new commission. 'Was she very pretty?'

'Yes, I think she was ... don't you remember the photograph of her in the newspaper that nice Mr Anwar brought?'

'Kind of,' Anna said, before asking, 'What clothes should she have?'

'Let me see,' Violet said. 'What about a summer dress, a white one, and she should have a raffia hat, which is sort of like a straw hat? And the hat must have a big brim, wide enough to shade her face from the sun and with a big red ribbon around it.'

After Anna had gone to tell Izzy, Hilary asked, 'Well, how are you really?'

Violet sighed. 'Frightened that the more I discover about my mother the more I might dislike her.'

'Wow, where did that come from?'

Violet told Hilary about Duncan Boyd's reaction to Megan's name and about Alexandra's description – 'unscrupulous and dishonest'. Hilary tried to cheer her up, saying, 'God, I wish my mum had a reputation.'

Violet asked Hilary if she could put the phone where Anna and Izzy were, so she could listen in for a while. Violet heard Anna telling Izzy what a 'pretty woman' looked like. She had long brown hair which shone like the sun, big eyes which were as big as the moon and lips as red as a tomato.

～～

'You'd better come in.'

Robert Yellowlees was tall and stooped. He had steel-grey hair, brushed neatly and parted on the left, a large fleshy face and the put-upon expression of a man who had something better to do. 'Before the wind takes this door off,' he added.

Violet apologized for dropping by unannounced but she was only in Ullapool for an hour or two and it seemed like an opportunity. He raised an eyebrow (*an opportunity for whom?*) and led her along a broad corridor with beige carpets and bare white walls. 'Well, you've certainly brought the bad weather with you.'

They passed a sitting room in which there was a large television. The sound was off but the picture showed a golfer on a fairway somewhere lush and sunny. Violet said she hoped she hadn't disturbed his viewing.

'I don't imagine a short break will do me any harm.' He put the emphasis on 'short'. By the time they reached the kitchen at the end of the corridor, Violet had grown to dislike retired Chief Superintendent Robert Yellowlees.

She sat at a chair he pulled out from the table and refused his offer of coffee, tea or biscuits. She didn't want to put him to any trouble.

'Any more trouble,' he corrected her and stood across the table, his back to the cooker. He had only caught half of her story at the door. The remainder was lost in the wind. 'So, what is it you want?'

'As I was saying, my mother's childhood friend was a woman called Megan Bates. I grew up hearing stories about her and became fascinated by her life and, more particularly, her death. Wasn't that such an extraordinary thing to do – walk out into the sea?'

Violet waited for the former policeman to respond. When he didn't, she said, 'Well, I've been staying in the area and I thought I'd dig out the local newspaper cuttings about the case. They referred to an Inspector Robert Yellowlees being in charge of the investigation. Then I found your name and address in the phone book and was hoping you might be him.'

'I am,' he replied with a resigned look, as if he knew from experience where this was going and how it would end.

'I was wondering,' she carried on, 'if you remembered the case and whether there was any clue why a woman who had gone through nine months of pregnancy would kill herself and her unborn baby. Didn't you think it odd at the time, Mr Yellowlees?'

He let out a single snort of laughter. 'I don't remember thinking it odd, Miss Wells. Policemen spend their entire careers seeing and dealing with things that don't make any sense.' His expression communicated that he had nothing else to say. In case she hadn't understood, he added, 'You'd be better advised speaking to force head-quarters about this. I am retired, after all.'

But he didn't do what she'd been expecting, ask her to leave. He kept watching her, trying to work out why she was really there, his policeman's instinct for possible trouble still strong. What else could it mean when an old case turned up unexpectedly on your doorstep? So he waited for Violet to say something.

'Do you remember the investigation?' she asked while she had his attention.

His eyes narrowed but he didn't answer.

'I've seen the newspaper reports,' she went on, 'but there's nothing in them to explain why the police decided there were no suspicious circumstances.'

'From memory,' he spoke slowly, still watching her, 'Megan Bates wrote a suicide letter.'

'She left it in the cottage where she was living?'

'No,' Mr Yellowlees replied. 'She posted it and, if I remember correctly, it arrived a day or two after she was reported missing.'

'Who was it addressed to?'

Mr Yellowlees let out another snort. 'Oh, come on, Miss Wells, you don't honestly expect me to remember the name, do you?'

'Can you remember what it said?'

'As far as I can recall it was addressed to her married lover, who was the father of her unborn child. She was upset at what she regarded as his betrayal. Apparently he couldn't make up his mind whether to abandon his wife. Megan Bates threatened to make it impossible for him to see her or the child if he didn't.' He paused. 'In the end he decided to stick with his marriage. I suppose that explains why she took her own life, don't you?'

Violet said, 'I don't know. Is there anything else?'

'What more would you like, Miss Wells?'

'Proof, I suppose. A body.'

'Well, we'd all have liked a body, but there was an eye-witness who saw her going into the sea and some of her possessions were washed ashore later.'

'A hat and a bag, yes.' Violet reached into her pocket for Mr Anwar's newspaper cuttings. She found the one she wanted and read it out. 'Inspector Yellowlees said all the evidence pointed to a terrible tragedy, an unhappy young woman who felt she had nothing left to live for.' She looked at the former policeman. 'Do you still think that?'

'I haven't thought about it for many years, but since you ask, yes, of course I do.'

'You considered every possibility?'

'Yes.'

'Did you at any time consider whether Megan Bates might have given birth to her child and *then* killed herself?'

He shook his head as she spoke but she carried on. 'Let's say she abandoned the child at a hospital some-where and then returned to Poltown, where she drowned herself. If your memory of the letter is correct, isn't that conceivable? That way she would have deprived the father of the child – wasn't that what she said? – as well as mak-ing it impossible for him to see her again.'

Mr Yellowlees said, 'There were no records of Megan Bates having given birth to a baby. We checked.'

'What if she delivered the baby on her own, or some-one helped her? What if the baby was born before she killed herself, if that's what she did?'

'What if, what if . . . where's your evidence? There's not

a scrap. No, Miss Wells, she was still pregnant with the baby when she was seen going into the sea. We had her letter. We had her hat and bag from the beach.'

'What if –?' Violet began and Mr Yellowlees threw back his head in exasperation.

'Enough, enough, Miss Wells. This is fantasyland.' He went to the kitchen door. 'Now if you don't mind, I'd like to get back to my golf.'

She held his glare. 'Why won't you even consider another possibility?'

Instead of answering, he pushed back against the door, opening it wide. She stayed where she was. 'I won't go until you've answered me.'

'I'll put you out myself if you don't leave now.'

Something snapped in Violet. From her handbag she took the letter that Mr Anwar had brought and slapped it on the kitchen table. 'Why don't you read that?' Her voice trembled.

'What does it say?' he asked.

'It was given to me by a social worker. It had been sent to his office in Inverness. It says Megan Bates gave birth to a daughter.'

Mr Yellowlees walked back to the table. He picked up the letter and read quickly. 'I see it's anonymous.' He shook his head. 'Not worth the paper it's written on. Do you know how many letters like this the police get? I'll show you what we used to do with them.'

He tore the page in half and let the two pieces drift to the carpet. 'Now, Miss Wells, I'd like you to leave.'

Violet snatched up the torn letter and ran to the front door. Then she turned back. 'That's the date I was abandoned at Raigmore Hospital in Inverness. I am Megan Bates's daughter.'

～

As he turned left out of Shore Street in Ullapool, Cal saw a familiar figure. Her shoulders were hunched against the rain. But this time she wasn't a trick of his windscreen. She was walking away from him, on the pavement under a sign pointing to the Macphail Centre & Theatre. He pulled up and lowered the passenger window. 'Remember me? You asked me about the tides a couple of days ago, at South Bay. Would you like a lift?'

He saw her hesitation. 'I'm going to Poltown but I can drop you anywhere on the way.'

She glanced at the black clouds. 'Just before Poltown would be good.' She opened the door and got in. 'Thank you.'

Cal drove on while she wiped her face and ran her fingers through her hair. 'You're soaked,' he said. 'There'll be a towel somewhere on the back seat if you hunt through all that junk.'

'I'm fine.'

'Do you live round here? I'm Cal, by the way.'

'No, I'm just visiting.'

He noticed she didn't say her name and that she shifted her body so that she was inclined away and looking out of the side window. 'I was just shopping,' he said, 'not much else to do when the weather's like this.'

She looked at him briefly and turned back to the window.

'Did you find out who owned Orasaigh Island?'

She appeared startled at the question and Cal said, 'You mentioned it when we met before. Don't you remember?'

'Oh, yes, yes I did.' She turned her shoulder again.

Her awkwardness spread to Cal. He wasn't sure whether to keep trying with her or not but the silence felt uncomfortable. So, every five minutes, he would comment on the weather, the scenery or anything else that came into his head. She didn't reply, didn't even acknowledge she'd heard him, and Cal decided to stop making an effort. He turned on the radio and tried to pretend she wasn't there. Eighteen miles later – it seemed more to Cal – she found her voice again.

'That rain's stopped.'

'So it has,' Cal replied.

'How much further to Poltown?'

'Four or five miles,' Cal said.

'Would you let me out here? I just need to walk.' It was an apology of sorts.

Cal pulled in. 'Are you sure?'

She didn't speak until she was outside and about to close the door. 'Yes, and thanks for the lift.'

As Cal drove away, he watched her in his rear mirror and wondered if he would ever know her name.

Violet waited until the pick-up had gone round a bend before checking the time. It was 11.15. It would be nightfall before the tide would be low enough to cross to Orasaigh Island. She had time to kill. It was one of the reasons she wanted to walk. The other was a disconcerting feeling of being out of control. Violet recalled Mr Anwar's warning to 'move slowly and to gather as many of the facts as possible before revealing anything about yourself'.

She wished she had his instinct for appropriate speed.

Too much was happening too quickly.

Why had she told Mr Yellowlees she was Megan Bates's daughter?

Whatever she'd done could not be undone. From now on she must be more careful.

14

Where the road fell down the hill on its way to Poltown, Violet stopped. The first time she'd seen this view, Stuart, the bus driver, had described it as 'a veritable panorama'. If anything it was more dramatic now. The wind was strong and picking up speed. Clouds jostled against each other over the sea, a disorderly and looming procession. More rain approaching. Here and there the landscape was lit by diagonal shafts of sunlight creating intense pools of colour: the rust-red of dying bracken behind Brae, sparkles of silver from a stream flowing to Violet's right; and emerald green surrounding the church to her left. Violet looked from one to another until a movement on the pale sand of South Bay caught her attention. A small black figure was gathering up debris, going backwards and forwards across the beach. 'Duncan Boyd,' she said after watching him. 'You're not going to run away this time.' It took ten minutes to descend to the beach road and another three to find him sitting against a dune, his hair blowing in the wind like stalks of dried grass. She went close to him, as close as she dared, before sitting cross-legged. She looked out to sea and began to talk as if she'd been speaking to him for ages and this was just the continuation of a conversation, one in which he'd been taking part.

She told him how clever he'd been, how hard working,

how lucky that someone like him was prepared to keep the beach clean, how exciting it must be, never knowing what he would turn up from one day to the next, his own tombola, how tombola had been her favourite thing when she'd been a child. Had it been his too?

She laughed. 'Back then I was happy with a bead bracelet. But if I was like you, beachcombing, I'd want to find a necklace, diamonds. Wouldn't that be something? Have you ever found anything as valuable as that? Or . . .' She sounded as though this was a game that she was enjoying. 'I know . . . or a message in a bottle? Have you ever come across one? I bet you have.' She lifted her head to the sky as if dreaming. 'Oh, wouldn't it be extraordinary to find a love letter written a century ago or a message from someone shipwrecked? Have you found any like those? When I was a child . . .' She let out a little snort at how silly she was then. 'I made a raft and wondered where it drifted. Perhaps it washed ashore on South Bay. Have you ever found a little wooden raft with an upturned yoghurt pot for a wheelhouse and a pencil for a mast? No, I guess you haven't, or if you have, it wouldn't have been mine. Mine would hardly have drifted at all; probably it came back on the next tide.'

She kept her voice the same pitch and speed and she punctuated some of what she said with sighs of self-deprecation. She knew he was listening. She knew he was watching her too, but she didn't look at him. She just kept talking.

'I have a daughter. Her name is Anna. She's lovely, with curly hair the colour of dark chocolate and honey-brown skin. If you ever met her you would find her adorable;

everyone does, even though I'm biased. In case you're wondering, Anna is half African; well, North African. Her father is Moroccan, a visitor to Scotland, an economic migrant. Aren't economic migrants like flotsam? In their case poverty, wars or politics drive them to other shores instead of winds and tides; but sometimes winds and tides help them on their way, don't they?'

Then, letting her hurt show, she said, 'What is it about men?'

She dared to look at Duncan. Deep folds had formed on his face; one traversed the thick stubble of his right cheek; another, the left. His eyes were pink-rimmed and bloodshot. His appearance was dishevelled, even more so than at their first meeting. He wore stained blue tracksuit bottoms, probably scavenged from the beach, and an old denim shirt worn open over an old-fashioned vest which had long since turned grimy. Violet was shocked by the deterioration in his appearance but she didn't show it. As she looked away he glanced at her and she wondered whether this was working, whether she was closer or further away from finding a way to him.

She started talking again.

'Sometimes, I'm glad that Anna's father has gone; sometimes I wish he was still here so I could kill him.'

She waited, learning at last from Mr Anwar. 'What's wrong with men like that? Could you run away from a child? A woman wouldn't; I couldn't.'

She banged her fist into the sand. 'I'd do anything to be with Anna, to keep her safe.' She interlocked her fingers and tried to pull her hands apart. 'The bond's that strong.'

She looked at Duncan for a moment before turning away. 'Men seem to have a choice; women don't. As soon as a woman holds her baby, that's that, for life. It's the strongest tie. I was like that with Anna. The love of a mother is the fiercest thing. I know women who would abandon a husband or a lover quicker than they would throw away a cigarette, but none who would abandon a child. Not one. Like you, I've heard stories to the contrary. But, in my opinion, they're put about by the kind of men who would desert a child . . . selfish, horrible men.'

Another pause. She counted to five. 'There's a story like that about a woman who used to live around here. She was called Megan Bates. But I don't believe that one either. No woman could carry a child in her womb for nine months, feel it wriggling and kicking, and not be overwhelmed by love. Ask any woman. No way could Megan Bates have drowned herself and her baby. No way.'

Then she fell silent.

She gazed over the beach at the rolling waves and she waited.

At least Duncan was still there. 'What do you think, Mr Boyd? Could Megan Bates have done that?' She risked another glance at him.

He started in surprise and said, 'I've been looking after this beach for years.' The boy was back. So was the expression of childish expectancy.

'Isn't that good? I bet you've found some amazing stuff.'

He didn't reply and Violet said, 'You were neighbours, weren't you? You must have known her well.' His expression was one she hadn't expected: of sadness. 'I think she was lucky to have you as her neighbour.' Her voice wavered because she could tell that he was about to tell her something. He had the look of someone who had carried a secret for so long and who had longed for an opportunity to share it.

'Yes,' he said simply. 'She was lucky.'

She gave him another fleeting look. 'Did you like her?' she asked.

'Yes.'

Now they were like two children exchanging secrets.

'She was very pretty, wasn't she?'

'Yes.'

Violet gave an appreciative murmur, impressed that he had managed to make a friend of Megan, maybe more than a friend.

'She said I was sweet.'

'Did she? Why did she say that?'

'Because I said I would look after her and the baby.'

'Did you say that?'

'I did.'

Violet's heart was beating so loudly she was worried Duncan would hear it. 'You're a good man,' she said.

'I am,' he agreed.

'Were you the father?'

'No.'

'Hmm.' She was even more impressed: a man offering that to a woman when the child wasn't his. 'Did she love the father?'

'Yes.'

'Did *he* love her?'

'Not as much as I did.'

'Did you love her?'

'I did.'

'Did you know the father?'

'Mr William Ritchie QC.' He boomed the name, like a master of ceremonies announcing a guest of honour arriving at a party.

'Does he live around here?'

'He did.'

'Oh.'

'He used to live at Brae House.'

Violet tried to hide her astonishment. *That* house. Despite her shock, she managed to ask, 'Where does he live now?'

'For the last six years Mr William Ritchie QC has lived in the graveyard.'

Violet listened to the announcement of her father's death and waited to feel some emotion. There was nothing. 'In the graveyard here . . . ?'

'Yes.'

Still nothing. She changed the subject. 'Did Megan love the baby?'

'She did.'

'Did she say that to you?'

'Yes, the last time I saw her.'

'Did she love the baby more than she loved the father?'

'Yes.'

'Did she say that too?'

'Yes.'

Violet kept on asking questions, worried that her voice would crack if she stopped and tried to start again. 'She must have trusted you.'

'She did. We trusted each other.'

'Good friends, then?'

'I would have looked after her and the baby.'

'I know you would.'

'They could have lived here with me.'

'Did you tell her that?'

'I did.'

'What did she say?'

'She said I was sweet.'

'She killed herself, didn't she?'

'I don't know.'

'Why do you say that?'

'I don't know.'

'You found her hat and bag, didn't you?'

'I did.'

'In North Bay?'

'Yes.'

'That must have been upsetting.'

'It was. I love her.'

'I know. You said.'

'I didn't tell the police.'

'What didn't you tell them?'

He glanced at Violet. 'That she'd gone away . . . she said she would.'

Duncan's expression seemed fearful. Violet decided not to press him. She'd come back to it. 'What did you love about her?'

'She was kind.'

'Was she?'

'She was always kind to me.'

Violet smiled. 'That's nice to hear. And what else?'

'She had nice hair.'

'Did she?'

'Yes. It was brown.' He grinned again. 'She let me brush it once.'

'Did she?'

'I keep the beach clean for her. I always have.' He was pumped up with pride.

'Why?'

He shook his head. 'I can't tell you.'

'Yes, you can.'

He shook his head again. 'No, I can't.'

He stood up and she looked away, fearing what was about to happen, hoping he would stay. When she turned back he was walking slowly towards Boyd's Farm.

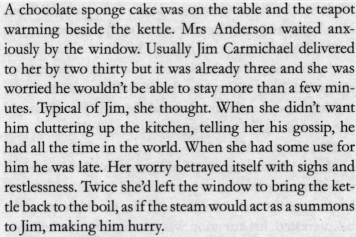

A chocolate sponge cake was on the table and the teapot warming beside the kettle. Mrs Anderson waited anxiously by the window. Usually Jim Carmichael delivered to her by two thirty but it was already three and she was worried he wouldn't be able to stay more than a few minutes. Typical of Jim, she thought. When she didn't want him cluttering up the kitchen, telling her his gossip, he had all the time in the world. When she had some use for him he was late. Her worry betrayed itself with sighs and restlessness. Twice she'd left the window to bring the kettle back to the boil, as if the steam would act as a summons to Jim, making him hurry.

When, finally, his blue van did appear it was three fifteen and Mrs Anderson had a headache. She checked that her bottle of 'medicinal' whisky was in the cupboard – it wasn't fair to Jim otherwise – and called out 'Come on in!' when she heard the latch on the door. She put three teabags into the pot, poured in water, and as she took the tray to the table Jim backed into the kitchen holding Mrs Anderson's grocery order in a cardboard box.

'You're late, Jim.' There was a note of reprimand.

'Afternoon, Mrs A.' It was the name he'd called her ever since he began working part-time at the general store, fitting his deliveries around odd jobs and the demands of his smallholding at the end of the sea loch. He'd been in his twenties then and Mrs Anderson, in her forties, was the housekeeper at Brae House. Calling her 'Mrs A' was still as familiar as Jim thought he dared to be.

Jim swung the door shut with his foot, leaving a muddy mark on the paint (earning a look of disapproval from Mrs Anderson) and placed the box on the worktop by the kettle. 'It's not your usual order, is it?'

Under normal circumstances she would have been sharp with him, telling him that if she'd wanted more she would have ordered more. Instead she said, 'Have I missed out a few things? I must be getting forgetful.'

'Oh, not you, Mrs A.'

Mrs Anderson was alert for any sign that Jim had heard talk about her having to pay rent and her other bills, of her struggling to make ends meet. But he didn't appear to be interested: his attention was on the cake on the table. 'You're not in a hurry, Jim, are you?'

'Not in a hurry at all, Mrs A.'

Mrs Anderson poured his tea and invited him to sit. Usually he stood with his back to the cooker, cup in one hand, biscuit or piece of cake in the other, his chat hardly stopping for a sip or a bite. However, the invitation threw him, as if it required a different standard of behaviour. He inspected his overalls and apologized for the state they were in. He unzipped them and they dropped around his feet. Then he asked if he could use her bathroom to wash his hands but she directed him instead to the sink, putting a clean towel beside the soap tray. Standing back to make way for him, she began to wish she hadn't laid the table after all as he waddled past her duck-like, his overalls threatening to trip him.

'Come and sit down, Jim.' She sat herself. 'Shall I cut you a piece of cake?'

'Please, Mrs A.'

She removed a big wedge for him followed by a slither for her. While he shuffled back round the table, falling into his seat with a thud and a groan, she asked, 'How are you keeping, Jim?'

In her experience, that question was guaranteed to start him talking. Usually he'd say something like 'I'm fine, but have you heard about so and so?' and he'd launch into the details of some other person's misfortune. However, on this occasion he pulled a face, followed by a frown. 'I don't mind telling you, Mrs A, that I've been better.'

The last thing she wanted to say was, 'Why, what's wrong?' but form seemed to demand it so she did, adding, 'It's not like you to be under the weather.' She hoped that might deter a lengthy flow of personal revelation.

'The thing is, Mrs A,' he scratched his head. 'I've made a bit of a mess of things.'

He wrung his hands and shuffled in his seat. She hadn't seen him like this for a long time, since his troubles with the bottle, so she looked interested. 'Go on, Jim, you know you can trust me.'

He nodded, agreeing with her. 'I can, Mrs A, and there's not many you can say that about nowadays.'

Mrs Anderson acknowledged the compliment as well as his meaning. Ever since the military's withdrawal from Poltown and the sale of surplus MoD houses to charities, the village had changed. Few of the older residents stayed on, the exodus accelerated by empty property being allocated to antisocial tenants and the homeless from fifty miles around. 'It's not the place it was,' she agreed.

'I've borrowed from the Turnbulls,' Jim blurted, shaking his head at having done such a stupid thing.

'Oh, Jim.'

His shoulders drooped and he gave a long, deflating sigh.

'Oh, Jim,' she repeated. 'What will you do?' If she sounded hopeless on his behalf it was because of the reputation of the Turnbulls and also because of Jim's experience of borrowing money from the family. He'd been badly beaten up in the past and, according to village rumour, Diana had rescued him, paying off his debt in return for Jim doing odd jobs in the big house and helping out during lambing.

'I don't know what to do.' Jim pushed his plate away.

'You can't pay them?'

Jim had the baleful expression of a condemned man awaiting his fate.

'I wish I could help.'

He shook his head again, this time to let her know he wasn't asking for money.

'Two thousand pounds, that's all it was, to fix the van so it would pass the MOT. Suspension, brakes, new tyres . . .' He threw his hands up in exasperation at this simple shopping list leading to such trouble. 'I'd be sunk without the van.' The irony of his comment brought a fleeting smile: he was sunk with it.

Mrs Anderson sympathized but the sight of Jim's transformation from ebullience, his usual mood, to emasculation reminded her of her own financial predicament: was this the fate that awaited her too? The thought unnerved her. 'There's no good in the Turnbulls,' she snapped, as if warding off encroaching evil.

Realizing her outburst wouldn't help Jim's frame of mind, she said, 'I'm sorry, but those wretched girls . . .'

Jim knew the story. Ten years after Mrs Anderson moved from Poltown to Gardener's Cottage, the military asked her to be a 'wise head' for the young women on the base. She'd agreed as much for the extra money as for having something to do during the week when Mr William and Diana were in Edinburgh. Until then she'd known of Alec Turnbull, the depot's head storeman, only through his son, Ross. She remembered Diana's dismay when he and Alexandra started going out together. Hadn't she told Diana every teenage girl tested her mother with an unsuitable boy?

The father was even worse. Alec, she discovered from

her counselling work, bombarded the base's lonely wives with presents while their husbands were away training. After flattering his way into their beds, he blackmailed them for more sex. Given her head, Mrs Anderson would have reported him to the base authorities, but the victims were terrified of their husbands finding out.

As a result he continued his campaign of conquest and blackmail until a snap audit in the stores uncovered how he funded his seductions. He'd been skimming military rations and clothing and selling them. The scandal was hushed up and Turnbull summarily dismissed. But the village was unable to escape his malign influence since he also ran an illegal moneylending operation (at one time or another at least half of Poltown had been in debt to Turnbull). The profits were laundered through a portfolio of other businesses. There was the taxi company, the static caravans which were rented out to backpackers and the fleet of mobile cafes which patrolled the West Highlands in summer selling burgers and ice creams to holidaymakers and locals alike.

Even a car accident in which Alec Turnbull's spine was crushed hadn't released the village from his grip. Though confined to a wheelchair, he carried on running his operation. The muscle was brought in from elsewhere. And so it continued until a stroke rendered him all but helpless. Rather than let the father's hired hands take over the business, the son had returned to Poltown six months ago to claim his inheritance. Despite the intervening years of working and living abroad, and the impression Ross tried to give of being different from his father, in Mrs Anderson's opinion the apple hadn't fallen far from the tree.

'You've thought about the police, have you, Jim?'

Jim grimaced and Mrs Anderson was thrown back to all those pitiable young women who'd allowed Alec Turnbull to have a hold over them and to Jim's battered and bruised face after he'd missed a repayment on a previous loan.

A look of understanding passed between them. Each had heard similar stories about the Turnbulls, how anyone making a report to the police always suffered retribution and how the family seemed to enjoy protection.

'I'm sorry, Mrs A; shouldn't have bothered you.' Jim stared forlornly at his half-eaten cake. 'Eyes bigger than my stomach, I'm afraid.' He pushed against the table and stood up.

Mrs Anderson said, 'Jim, what's going to happen to you?'

'I'll be running errands in the van, I imagine ... whatever Davie White tells me.'

That name brought another exclamation from Mrs Anderson. Davie White had been Alec Turnbull's enforcer for two or three years. There had been talk of friction when Ross returned, of Davie running freelance operations while Ross negotiated for concessions from BRC, the wind farm consortium. These included the ferry which would shuttle personnel between the land base and offshore. Ross had been involved in something similar in Nigeria, though in the opinion of many people, Mrs Anderson included, it would be a front behind which the Turnbulls could further expand their criminal activities.

'Not drugs. You won't be carrying drugs, will you?' Mrs Anderson asked.

'I don't know.' She could tell he was thinking the same. They'd heard the same stories about Davie White.

'Oh, Jim . . .'

'Ach well,' he sighed. As he pulled up his overalls and fastened them, Mrs Anderson looked aghast that he was going. She asked hungrily if there was any other news, any gossip.

'Funny you should ask that,' Jim said. 'Duncan was a bit upset yesterday morning, up at North Bay.'

'Poor Duncan.' It was what she usually said when his name cropped up. 'Is all the wind farm fuss getting to him?'

'I don't know if it was that. A young woman had been speaking to him and he'd just gone off. She thought it was her fault but I told her not to worry. Nice girl, she was, brown hair, short like a boy, and a couple of earrings.' Jim touched his left ear. 'Pretty name too, Violet Wells, I think she said. Staying for a day or two at Orasaigh Cottage.'

'What sort of age?'

'In her twenties, I'd say.'

15

Violet lay flat in the grass, sheltering from the wind. The sky was black and lowering. *William Ritchie QC and Megan Bates*: for the first time she knew both her parents' names. She said them out loud, practising the unfamiliar sequence of shapes her lips and mouth had to make, as if repeating them would compensate for time lost, would bring them to life or summon the missing story of their affair and project it image by image on the underside of the chasing clouds. She experimented with the names – *William Ritchie and Megan Bates, Megan Bates and William Ritchie* – but reverted to *William Ritchie QC and Megan Bates* because it better suited the little she knew of their relationship: that it was unequal. William Ritchie QC had been a man of position, with property and a wife. Yet it was the spirited and pretty Megan Bates who lost everything: her lover, her baby, her life.

Spirited *and* kind, she reminded herself of Duncan's comment. *She was always kind to me.*

She distracted herself with these and other speculations about her parents while putting off the next thing she had to do, which was to find her father's grave. She'd been delaying because she was worried about how she might react. When Duncan Boyd told her about his death she had received the news with indifference. The clocks hadn't stopped, her heart hadn't missed a beat, her breathing hadn't quickened, nor had a tear formed. Her father was dead: the father who abandoned his pregnant lover; the father who deserted his unborn child. Hadn't he always been dead to Violet? But, as she wondered about her mother and father, she found she was curious about him. When she was standing in the graveyard, reading his carved name, what would she feel? Would she experience a daughter's love for the father she never knew? Would that be a betrayal of her mother?

As it turned out, she needn't have concerned herself. She walked up the broad gravel pathway to the front of the church, her face and her heart as stony and as cold as her surroundings. The headstones on either side of her were all tilting and ancient with inscriptions that had been worn away after long exposure to wind and rain. Looking around, she saw more graves arranged in neat rows behind an old yew tree. They appeared to be newer and some were decorated with flowers. She was approaching them when she noticed a grave apart from any other. It was hard by the wall which surrounded the churchyard. The headstone was white marble with black lettering that was legible from a distance.

IN MEMORY OF
WILLIAM RITCHIE QC
BELOVED HUSBAND TO DIANA
AND DARLING STEPFATHER TO ALEXANDRA

The epitaph's brevity kept her rooted to the spot. More should have been noted: another woman and another child acknowledged. She looked away at the wrought-iron gate in the wall beside the headstone. Through its bars Violet spied the sheltering woods around Brae and it occurred to her that William Ritchie QC had chosen his burial plot with care. Wasn't he interred to provide him with an everlasting view of God's as well as his own house? The headstone was another reminder of the inequality between William Ritchie QC and Megan Bates: he was buried, she was not. He had a headstone; she did not. He had recognition; she did not.

For all her worry about having an emotional reaction, Violet was at her most composed since arriving in Poltown. Striding towards the gate, showing the headstone the same cold disregard the epitaph displayed for her mother, a flutter of paper caught her eye. She glanced down and saw a book, its torn pages turning in the wind. She bent to pick it up and at that moment the grave was an arm's stretch away. She turned her head, stood and walked from the churchyard. Only when she was outside the wall did she examine what was in her hands.

It was a Scottish Prayer Book, the maroon cover soggy from the earlier rain. An idea took hold of her. She flicked through the pages – 'Morning Prayer', 'Evening Prayer', 'A Catechism', 'The Order of Confirmation' – not quite sure what she was looking for. Prayers and religion had not been part of her life. She was hurrying now, turning the pages fast, past 'The Visitation of the Sick' and 'The Communion of the Sick' until she came across 'At the Burial of the Dead'.

She read snippets of text, tasting them for suitability, liking the sound of 'We commend into thy hands, most merciful Father, the soul of this our *brother* departed, and we commit *his* body to the ground, earth to earth, ashes to ashes, dust to dust . . .' The italics encouraged her to think she could change brother to sister, and his to her. She looked at the two footnotes below the prayer and the second of them concerned the alterations that should be made for a burial at sea. Violet gave a yelp of triumph.

She stood with her back to the stone wall, her father's grave on the other side and directed her reading of the prayer towards the sea. 'We commend into thy hands, most merciful Father, the soul of this our sister departed, and we commit her body . . .' she checked the note and substituted 'to the deep' for 'to the ground' and went on: '. . . in sure and certain hope of the general resurrection in the last day and the life of the world to come; through our Lord Jesus Christ, who shall fashion anew the body of our low estate that it may be like unto his glorious body, according to the mighty working whereby he is able to subdue all things unto himself.'

She closed the book.

Later, walking the road into Poltown, she told Hilary about her day and her discoveries: according to the dates on the gravestone her father had been seventy-eight when he died, so he must have been fifty-eight when Violet was born. The gap between him and Megan had been twenty-five years. 'He was married,' Hilary said wearily, adding without waiting for Violet to reply, 'of course.'

'Yes, he was, to a woman called Diana.'

'Children?'

'A stepdaughter,' Violet said. Alexandra Hamilton, the woman who had rented her Orasaigh Cottage. '"Darling stepfather to Alexandra" was on the headstone.'

'The bitch who told you that Megan Bates made her mother's life hell?'

Violet ignored the question. She had other more important news. 'She loved me, Hilary. My mother loved me.' She told Hilary about Duncan Boyd, how he'd fallen for Megan, how he'd offered to look after her and the baby. Her mother had said he was sweet. She had told him she loved the baby.

Hilary asked, 'So why would she kill herself?'

'I don't know,' Violet sighed, 'except there was the letter. According to the police, it was a suicide letter.'

'Oh, Violet, I wish I was there with you.'

'It's OK.'

'Well, at least you've recruited God to your side.'

They laughed. Violet had told her about the prayer and how moved she'd been by the words. She'd be fine, she told Hilary, once she had something to eat. She would go to the shop in Poltown to buy some food, bread and milk, anything she could find, really. Then she'd wait at the causeway for low tide or perhaps she'd go to the public meeting that evening in the community hall. At least she'd be warm and dry if she did.

In the event, the decision was taken out of her hands by the first spatter of rain and by an elderly woman with white hair stopping her car. 'Are you going to the meeting? If so, would you like a lift? It's about to pour.'

No sooner had Violet closed the door and put her carrier bag of shopping at her feet than the rain beat against the windscreen and bounced off the road.

'Wow, I'd have been completely soaked.' Violet laughed at the narrow escape she'd had. 'Look at that . . .'

The car moved off slowly and the woman asked, 'Are you staying locally, in Poltown?'

'Just outside,' Violet replied, a smile of gratitude replacing her wonder at the violence of the storm. 'The cottage on Orasaigh . . . do you know it?'

'Ah, yes. Well, at least you'll have a good roof over your head.'

Violet turned back to look at the rain.

'On account of my age,' the woman said after a pause, 'people seem to think my name is Mrs Anderson or Mrs A, anything but Mary. You may choose which you call me.' There was a prompting tone to her voice.

'Oh, I'm sorry. I'm Violet. Violet Wells.'

'Violet,' replied Mrs Anderson, 'I haven't come across that for a while, but what a pretty name.'

16

Mrs Anderson parked close to the community hall and suggested to Violet they stayed put.

'There's no point in us getting soaked unless we have to.'

While they waited for a break in the rain, Violet ate crisps and a bread roll because she was 'so hungry' and Mrs Anderson reminisced about her childhood, about a game she used to play with her mother whenever it rained, 'and it rained a fair bit'. Most languages had different names for the different varieties of rain, she said. English had shower, drizzle, downpour and deluge (Violet suggested 'torrent'), but Mrs Anderson's mother had only ever used sound and volume, not different words. A shower was 'rain' said in an ordinary speaking voice. Drizzle that lasted for hours was 'rain' said like an extended yawn. A sudden brief deluge or thunderstorm was 'rain' spoken abruptly and loudly like a dog barking, but this was 'RAIN'. Mrs Anderson attempted a shout and immediately apologized for her croakiness. 'Whenever it rained like this my mother would scream "RAIN" over and over and I would join in and the house would echo with our voices. We would become hysterical with laughing and my father would come in from the fields complaining about the racket.'

Mrs Anderson smiled at the memory and Violet said, 'I

must tell my daughter that story. She doesn't like rain but she does like shouting.'

'Oh, you have a daughter . . .' The lift in Mrs Anderson's voice turned wistful. 'Not having children is the thing I regret most; that and not having grandchildren.' Then, watching Violet by sliding her eyes sideways, she added, 'Tell your mother she's very fortunate.'

Violet looked uncomfortable and said nothing, but Mrs Anderson seemed not to notice. She peered short-sightedly through the windscreen and remarked on blurry groups of people running to the door of the community hall, coats over their heads. 'I suppose we'd better brave it, or there won't be any seats left near the front and I won't be able to hear. Why don't you leave your bag of shopping, because there's no point in it getting soaked too?'

After retrieving Mrs Anderson's umbrella from the back seat, Violet pulled up the hood of her anorak. 'Wait there a minute,' she said, letting in a blast of wind as she opened her door. She ran round the front of the car and held the umbrella low over Mrs Anderson as she got out. 'Oh my goodness,' Mrs Anderson said as the storm buffeted at her and the umbrella blew inside out. 'Hold on to me, Violet dear, or else I'll be blown away.'

Violet gripped the older woman's arm and guided her across the tarmac to the awning by the entrance to the community hall. Others were hurrying in the same direction from all over the car park. Two teenage girls screamed as they splashed through the puddles. A man overtook Violet and Mrs Anderson, arriving at the door ahead of them. He held it open while he wiped the rain from his face.

'Oh, hi,' he said, 'we keep on meeting in unexpected places.'

Violet looked up, startled, recognizing his voice. 'Oh yes . . . so we do.'

Before Cal could speak again, Violet was being pushed into the foyer by others pressing behind her. 'I'm sorry,' she shouted back at Cal, who was wedged against the door by the newcomers, but he signalled he couldn't hear above the noise of the wind. Inside, Violet found Mrs Anderson and the man who had delivered Duncan Boyd's box of groceries.

Jim Carmichael nodded at Violet: 'Hello again.'

'Yes, of course, you've met,' Mrs Anderson said. 'Jim had a cup of tea with me this afternoon and told me you were worried about poor Duncan. He'd run off or something, hadn't he, Jim?'

Jim appeared ill at ease at her indiscretion. 'Duncan and Mrs Anderson here are first cousins,' he explained anxiously to Violet, the implication being it hadn't been gossip on his part, more a case of keeping it in the family. 'Mrs Anderson grew up at Boyd's Farm.' He reinforced the point.

'Poor Duncan,' Mrs Anderson sighed in a wandering way, still oblivious to Jim's difficulty. Her attention turned to the hall and the speed with which it was filling up. 'There won't be any seats if we don't hurry,' she said to Violet, deliberately excluding Jim by turning her shoulder. Mrs Anderson led Violet away and Jim remained where he was, looking even more uncomfortable. Violet glanced back over her shoulder and gave him a reassuring smile.

The incident reminded her of school, of the competition to befriend a popular girl, and once she had been won the snubs that had to be delivered to keep rivals away. Violet puzzled at why Mrs Anderson should treat her as some kind of playground conquest. All she could think was that old people often became selfish and that a jealous nature was one of the signs. Another possible explanation came soon after when Mrs Anderson asked Violet if she smelled whisky off Jim, because she thought she had. 'I do hope he hasn't started drinking again.'

The hall was bright, busy and noisy with the storm providing conversation for those assembled as well as a background rumble, as if a predator was prowling outside. Mrs Anderson found two seats by the central aisle and while she settled herself Violet said, 'So you were brought up on Mr Boyd's farm, were you?'

Mrs Anderson let out a little sigh. 'A long time ago, when it was a proper farm with livestock, sheep and cows.' Her tight mouth and pinched white cheeks discouraged further inquiry. Instead, Violet mentioned her visit to Brae House, when she booked Orasaigh Cottage, and how impressive it was.

'Did you notice the walled garden to the right of the drive? I live on the far side, in what used to be the gardener's cottage. Indeed, it still has that name.'

Violet said she thought she'd seen chimney pots. 'It must be a nice place to live,' she added politely, and Mrs Anderson said, 'It is – or rather it *was*.'

Again, Mrs Anderson's sharpness put Violet off from prying further so she steered her back to Brae House in the hope of finding out something about her dead father.

'I met the owners when I collected the cottage keys . . . Matt and Alexandra Hamilton.'

Mrs Anderson rolled her eyes. 'Some people deserve good fortune and others certainly do not.' Clearly, Mrs Anderson believed the Hamiltons belonged in the latter category. 'People,' she said after a pause, 'with little instinct for their responsibilities.' She was clipped and disapproving.

'Did Mr Hamilton buy the property?' Violet feigned ignorance of her father's connection to Alexandra.

'He did not,' Mrs Anderson replied abruptly. 'Brae was passed down from Mrs Hamilton's stepfather, who was a lawyer and a gentleman. His name was William Ritchie. I knew him well because I was his housekeeper for many years.'

'He was your employer?'

'He was, and for the most part he was a good one too.' Mrs Anderson shook her head in sadness. 'A child was the only gift missing from Mr William's life . . .' Once again Violet felt she was being watched but when she looked at Mrs Anderson, the old woman's eyes slid away.

'Talk of the devil,' Mrs Anderson said at a stir behind them.

Violet turned as Alexandra appeared in the hall, followed by Matt. She also noticed Cal. He was sitting at the other side of the hall, a little further back than Violet and Mrs Anderson. He acknowledged Violet with a tilt of his head and Mrs Anderson spotted the exchange. 'Are you acquainted with that young man?' she asked.

'I don't know him,' Violet answered. 'I've met him twice – well, three times now – once at South Bay on the day I arrived and he gave me a lift from Ullapool this morning but, after it stopped raining, I decided to walk. Why do you ask?'

'No reason,' Mrs Anderson lifted her chin and looked at the front of the hall.

'His name's Cal something-or-other. Have you met him?'

'Once,' she said tightly, as though once had been enough.

Again Violet felt discouraged from inquiring further. Instead she glanced back at Cal. He was standing to let two women into his row and Violet took time to study him. His short dark-brown hair appeared black because it was still wet. He had deep-set eyes and his mouth was almost smiling, a transient expression she had noticed before. His nose was slightly skewed to the right. An interesting face rather than a handsome one, she thought. Another observation impressed itself on her. Around Cal, everyone seemed to be dressed in cheap anoraks whereas around her it was as though she had wandered into an upmarket country store. There were expensive-looking jackets in greens and browns. There was another striking difference too. On Cal's side of the hall, everyone seemed to have grey skin – a colour with which she was familiar from her street in a poor area of Glasgow – but on Violet's side, the faces appeared fuller and flusher. It was as if two different races were at the same meeting.

By now, the Hamiltons were going past and Violet felt the expensive swish of their clothes while Mrs Anderson sniffed at fortune 'always favouring the unworthy'.

She lowered her voice. 'If the wind farm goes ahead, they'll sell land to BRC for the Poltown development.'

'I saw something about a new school,' Violet said. 'And a supermarket, premises for small businesses and new housing.'

'Those will all be built on Brae property.' Mrs Anderson's mouth stretched, her lips whitening in disapproval.

Matt and Alexandra's progress was also being monitored by a woman in a floral print dress standing by the speakers' table. She left the stage, all bonhomie and bustling efficiency, and greeted the Hamiltons with a broadening smile. 'Gwen Dixon,' Mrs Anderson said. 'At least she's got a good heart . . . which is more than can be said for those two.'

As Violet was discovering, a compliment from Mrs Anderson wasn't always what it seemed. In Gwen Dixon's case, it turned out to be a plea of mitigation to set against her crimes. 'One of those interfering women who sits on committees and thinks she knows what's best for other people,' Mrs Anderson said before drawing Violet's attention to a side door at the front right of the hall.

Entering was a man of about forty-five with cropped hair and wearing black trousers with a white shirt which stretched and strained as he moved, giving an impression of a muscled chest and arms. He pushed a wheelchair in which sat an elderly man, his head hanging, his face haggard and lined, left side drooping. Mrs Anderson and Violet weren't the only ones watching their slow entrance. Others in the hall were beginning to stare too, the volume of chattering voices suddenly reducing. It was as if an open coffin, the corpse decaying, was being brought into the room.

'That's Alec Turnbull,' Mrs Anderson whispered. 'Not many people have seen him since he had his stroke . . .' As an afterthought, she said, 'If ever a man deserved to lose his looks, it's him.'

'I've heard of the Turnbulls,' Violet said. 'Who's that pushing him?'

'His son, Ross,' Mrs Anderson replied. 'He runs Poltown, just as his father did before him, the taxis, ice cream vans and moneylending. One's as bad as the other . . .' She warned Violet of 'the charade' she was about to witness: 'Ross Turnbull pretending he's interested in jobs for Poltown when everybody knows he supports the wind farm and the expansion of the village because of the concessions he hopes he can get from the developers. Inheritance is a way of life around here. The landowners pass on their acres, the Turnbulls their rackets.'

As Ross Turnbull settled his father at the end of the front row of seats, the babble of conversation started again. Mrs Anderson drew Violet's attention to a group of thuggish-looking men standing at the back on Cal's side of the hall. 'Turnbull's bullies, I wouldn't wonder,' she said.

When the speakers began to take their seats, the hall erupted in noise. The two sides jeered and shouted at each other. Someone shouted 'Poltown scum' behind Violet and suddenly the atmosphere was tribal and menacing: the dispossessed against the propertied; those who wanted jobs and a decent house and those who wanted to protect their interest in keeping the area undeveloped and pristine for tourism. As Ross Turnbull took his seat on the platform, Gwen Dixon called the meeting to order with a voice made for filling halls.

'This,' she boomed, 'is the most important decision for the wider community of Poltown, a chance to make our feelings known.' As the hecklers warmed up again, she shouted, 'The first speaker will be Joanna Dilmott for BRC, followed by Ted Russell for the Stop campaign, Ross Turnbull of the Poltown Action Group and finally Johnnie West, representing the environmental charities.'

Cal smiled at a crop-haired woman in sandals turning out to be the corporate player. Ms Dilmott's hand-knitted look wasn't the only surprise. After thanking the chair, she descended from the stage, talking as she went.

'Who likes being spoken down to? I don't, and I don't imagine the people of Poltown like it any more than me. In case you're wondering . . .' Now she was standing in the aisle between the two front rows, 'how my accent ended up east of mid-Atlantic, it's because I was born in Ireland, raised in England and found success in America.'

She scanned the audience. 'Yes, I'm doing OK, but that's not what this is about. It's not about people like me getting rich by ruining your environment, as some of our opponents like to say. It's about you, whether you want jobs, opportunity, prospects for your families, whether you'll let me and the companies in the consortium give that to you, or whether you'll make us go elsewhere.

'Honestly? I'd rather it was here because you people need it the most. Yes, there'll be a cost. You'll lose some scenery, but not much. Don't turn this down, because nothing like it is going to come this way again soon. Correction: ever. Don't let anyone take this from you.' She paused and looked slowly around the hall: 'And you know who I'm talking about.'

Her last remark drew another bout of jeering and insults, the argument between the two sides in the hall becoming voluble again. Cal heard Duncan Boyd's name being shouted out. A woman behind screamed, 'Take over his farm. Throw him out.'

Cal spun round, 'Leave the guy alone.' The woman looked nonplussed. 'Would you like it if someone here started shouting for you to be thrown out of your home? No, I thought not.'

A disturbance around Cal caught Violet's attention. People were getting up, moving away, pointing. Cal was leaning forward, his head down. 'What's going on?' Mrs Anderson said.

'I don't know,' Violet replied. 'He must have said something.'

The volume of noise fell as the speaker started again. 'I imagine you expected me to come here and talk about the project, the timetable and how you'll be saving the world by backing green energy. But you know all of that, and anyway, it's beside the point. What you've got to decide is whether you want a future, whether you're going to save yourselves.'

She placed her hand on her heart. 'D'ye know something, I think you will.' She bowed before going back up the steps, her sandals flapping, pursued by applause from one side and jeers from around Violet. She glanced at Cal. He was sitting stony-faced with his arms folded while everyone else on his side clapped and cheered.

Ted Russell, in red corduroys, was next for the wind farm's opponents. He rose to his feet with a piqued expression as though he expected a respectful quiet to descend on the hall. Instead there were catcalls and chanting for him to sit down. Mr Russell's face became as florid as his trousers as he struggled to make himself heard. At one point he warned about the threat of unrestrained development and the lasting damage it would do to 'our wonderful west coast way of life, not to mention the tourist industry that sustains us all'. The remark brought more jeers from Cal's side of the hall and a deeper shade of red to the speaker's cheeks. The hecklers didn't seem to regard his 'wonderful west coast way of life' to be the same as theirs. Russell's response was to start shouting back. 'Might I remind you,' he said in a patrician manner, 'that we're custodians of this ancient landscape and history won't be kind to us if we sacrifice it for a technology which is both inefficient and unproven.' Despite Gwen Dixon's calls for quiet, he gave up the unequal battle and sat down, his face glowing like embers in a draught.

'The only things that are inefficient and unproven around here,' a man behind Cal shouted, 'are incomers like you.'

The jibe sparked a counter from Russell's supporters of second-home owners and B&B proprietors sitting around Violet. They clapped their man out of loyalty until Ross Turnbull got to his feet. The hall fell silent, apart from

Russell's bad-tempered complaint to Madam Chair about unfair treatment.

'My definition of unfair is different to Mr Russell's.' Ross Turnbull spoke quietly: 'Unfair is growing up in Poltown and having to leave because there's no work and no prospect of any work. It's families being broken up . . . it's what our children will always have to put up with if we don't back this development. I speak for those without a job or a decent home, those of you who have been held back for too long by people with a selfish interest in keeping the landscape as it is. Well? What are you going to do? Grab the opportunity, for God's sake.' The applause was deafening from the other side of the hall. Everyone around Violet was deathly silent as Ross Turnbull left the stage to attend to his lolling father.

The final platform speaker, the suited environmentalist, talked fluently but drily about the impact of wind farms on bird life in particular (the area around Poltown being important for sea eagles and peregrines) and biodiversity in general. 'You are lucky enough to have miles and miles of wild land and seascape but it's disappearing globally. It's important to protect what's left. You are its guardians.'

It was an unfortunate echo of Ted Russell's speech and elicited another chorus of boos.

No sooner had he sat down than Gwen Dixon stood up. 'Quiet, quiet please.' Even her voice failed to silence an argument that had broken out in the wings of the hall. Violet craned her neck to see what was going on, wondering if Cal had had another disagreement. Two wiry young men in T-shirts were arguing with a landowning type – ruddy face, blond hair, Barbour jacket – who appeared to have found a seat on the wrong side of the hall. A punch was thrown. Violet wasn't sure by whom. The Barbour jacket lunged forward. Suddenly men were running from all over. The two tribes shoved at each other, the preliminaries to a skirmish. The rest of the audience sat transfixed until there was the resounding crack of a head-butt connecting with cartilage. The ruddy face now had a bloody nose. A collective gasp of shock went up as more punches were thrown. It was followed by scraping of chairs and people hurrying for the door.

Violet grabbed at Mrs Anderson's arm. 'I think we'd better go, don't you?'

***

Worse violence happened most Saturday nights in Sauchiehall Street, Cal thought. The head-butt and punches gave way to insults and shouting but the audience still rushed for the exit. There was a yell for a missing child. A woman cried out. Cal caught a glimpse of an elderly man falling. A shout of 'Don't push' went up. Gwen Dixon strode down the aisle towards the crush at the doors, shoulders and hips rolling together, her elbows bent; a practical woman prepared for action. The speakers were on their feet, wondering at what had happened, finding themselves the audience to a drama, all apart from Ross Turnbull, who was wheeling his father towards the side exit. Cal noticed him look back at the melee and grimace, a combination of worry at the crush of bodies and disappointment at the turn of events. Not quite the show of overwhelming support he'd called for or that BRC had demanded.

'Stop pushing.' Gwen Dixon was working her way into the throng. She scolded and shouted, calling for common sense, telling everyone to take a step back, to take their time. Heads turned towards her: the pressure on the door relaxed. 'One by one, please, and no pushing. Everyone will get out safely if you take your time.' Cal joined the queue that was forming. He nodded towards Gwen Dixon, acknowledging her efforts. She glowered back.

Outside, rain was still falling and the wind blowing. Groups of distressed and crying people gathered to exchange stories. A woman Cal's age went from huddle to huddle, inquiring about cuts or other injuries. He overheard her say her name was Doctor Bell. Cal spun round. Where was the statue from the beach and her white-haired companion? He'd come to the conclusion they were granddaughter and grandmother. The old woman was crouching by a car, Cal saw. She'd dropped her keys. The wind was almost tipping her over as she bent to pick them up. Cal ran over, steadied her, retrieved her keys and placed them in her hand. 'Are you all right?' he said.

She blinked at him. 'I've lost Violet. Where did she go?'

17

A hand touched Violet's elbow and again at her forearm. It closed over her wrist in the crush at the community hall's exit. At last outside, the rain and the wind fresh on her face, Violet expected to find Mrs Anderson holding on to steady herself among so many jostling bodies. Instead, she discovered her hanger-on was a man, his face hidden by the hood of his black anorak. Violet was about to thank him, assuming he had appointed himself her guardian through the scrum, but his grip suddenly tightened. 'That hurts! What are you doing? Let go,' she said, her voice rising.

He jerked her arm and kept his face hidden by looking down at the ground. He yanked her again, the violence of the tug dragging her off balance.

'Stop that,' Violet shouted, 'Let me go.' Her voice was lost in the noise of the wind.

She was being pulled along. Violet looked at the other people milling about, hoping they would see what was happening, hoping they would come to her rescue. But no one noticed or heard her. They were gathering up scattered friends or families, checking they were all right.

'Let go!' Violet pulled her arm back, trying to escape. But the man squeezed harder until the bone in her arm hurt. Now she was being taken down the side of the hall.

'Let me go,' Violet tried to dig in her feet. The man's right arm swung round. A fist cracked against her ear. He jerked on her arm again with his other hand. Dazed, she stumbled down the side of the building, away from the glow of the car park lights.

～

He must eat. He must drink. He must ring his son Rahim. Why? Muhammad Anwar tried to remember. Slowly it dawned on him. It wasn't so much that he must do these things. It was just they were all he had left to do.

No case files to read.

No shirt to iron.

No sandwiches to make for his lunch break.

No need for wakefulness in the night, fretting over this or that boy or girl and whether the right decision had been made.

No alarm clock to set.

No flask of tea to prepare.

No emails or texts to read before work.

Not tomorrow, not the next day, not next week. For the time being, he had no work. 'Until further notice,' Mr Hunter, his manager, had said. 'You are suspended and I must ask you to leave the premises.'

Eat, drink, ring Rahim: except Mr Anwar was not hungry or thirsty (despite having had no food or water since he left the office at midday) and he couldn't (wouldn't) ring Rahim. So he remained in Shereen's bedroom, watching the light fade to dark and a Bollywood starlet's airbrushed face on the poster behind the door glowing yellow in the street light. Did he have a reason for leaving his daughter's bedroom? Not to eat. Not to drink. Not to ring Rahim.

Rahim, he sighed. Rahim was all he had left. Rahim, in his final year at Edinburgh University, would soon be a doctor. Doctor Rahim Anwar. How could he admit to Rahim that he had a stupid old man for a father?

Instead he talked to Shereen, as he had since she left home. The theme was a frequent one: how a man like him (a dark-skinned man was what he meant, but also an unassuming man) had to accustom himself to disappointments; how he had become wiser as a result and kinder; how kindness was underrated; how some people confused it with weakness.

'Never judge the man until you know the pressures bearing on him,' he told Shereen, in case she mistook his remark as a criticism of Mr Hunter.

'Always step into the other man's shoes,' he advised with a rueful tilt of his head. Even before Shereen's departure the only shoes she was prepared to step into were peep-toed, sparkly and high-heeled, and beyond her father's pocket. He imagined that nothing had changed except that Shereen's extravagant taste was being indulged by her wealthy husband.

He returned to the subject of Mr Hunter. 'As head of department, his shoes are necessarily big ones.' Mr Anwar held his hands wide apart to show how big.

With a workload growing like Topsy, Mr Hunter didn't have his troubles to seek.

'If your father is sounding regretful,' he told Shereen, 'it's because he is. He's sorry for the inconvenience he has caused Mr Hunter, regretful at being disobedient, though not regretful at what he's done.

'You see,' he said with a degree of caution, 'Mr Hunter doesn't have children. He has no personal experience of the heartbreak that results when parents and children lose touch.' Mr Anwar shook his head, an expression of resigned endurance. The silence was a long one, lasting many minutes. Jagged edges of pain stabbed into his heart. It was twenty-two years since his darling Meera died; Meera, his wife; Meera, the mother of his two children; and four years since he had last seen or spoken to Shereen.

He sighed.

'How could your father have carried out Mr Hunter's instructions? Your father, of all people?'

He told Shereen about the letter he had taken to Mr Hunter. 'It was a mistake, Shereen. Your father is stupid.'

Mr Hunter had said, 'Anonymous letters about something that may or may not have happened twenty-six years ago can wait. Can we just focus on all the vulnerable children we have *today*, please, Mr Anwar?'

Mr Anwar breathed in. 'Shereen, if you had been abandoned as a baby and didn't know your mother's name, wouldn't you want to see that letter?'

Another silence: this time because Mr Anwar was unsure of Shereen's receptiveness to the question. Meera had died when Shereen was only a few months old, the pregnancy accelerating the cancer that killed her. All through Shereen's childhood, Mr Anwar kept Meera's name alive by telling stories about her. When she was sixteen, Shereen had asked him to stop. At different times he favoured different explanations. The kindest to Shereen, the one he reverted to at times like this, was that his daughter carried the guilt of Meera's death. To escape, she had to leave home.

Mr Anwar stared again at the poster, at the starlet's flawless face. Suddenly he felt like a foolish old man. What his heart knew, his head would not admit: glamour, not guilt, had carried Shereen away.

He closed his eyes and tried to remember where he was, his place in the story. Had he told Shereen about his inquiries with the police, about his visit to Violet Wells, the abandoned baby, now a mother with her own little daughter? In case he hadn't, he would tell her anyway.

As he'd known she would, Violet Wells went looking for Megan Bates. Mr Anwar didn't have all of the details but it appeared that Miss Wells had tracked down the officer in charge of the original investigation. Anyone in Miss Wells's position would have done the same, he was sure. It wasn't her fault the officer made a complaint, or that Mr Hunter had suspended him as a result. Mr Anwar glanced again at the starlet and her face brought to mind his dead wife, and how he used to talk to her in the dark. He would sit on his side of the bed, as if readying to swing his legs in beside hers, but instead he would turn off the light and tell her all his ambitions, fears and secrets, the atmosphere of the night becoming so charged that when he lay down beside her they would make love.

Violet had almost reached the far end of the building when a hand clamped against her mouth. No one would be looking for her, he growled. 'So shut the fuck up . . .' His head knocked against her ear, which was already throbbing from the impact of his fist. 'Unless you want another smack . . .' He wrenched at her arm and dragged her some more. Then he threw her to the ground, bent over her and told her to listen because she wouldn't get another warning. Violet looked into the black void of his hood, felt the spatter of his saliva against her lips before kicking out at his legs. He raised his arm to strike her again.

Cal settled Mrs Anderson into the front of her car. He crouched down beside her. 'Now, where did you last see Violet?'

'She was going through the door . . . she was in front of me . . . so many people were pushing . . .' She shook her head with the shock and worry of it all.

'So she got out? Did she? Violet got out?'

'She must have . . . she was ahead of me . . . but when I got outside she wasn't there. She wouldn't have gone without her shopping, would she?'

'Don't worry, I'll find her.' He took out his phone and asked Mrs Anderson for her name and phone number. 'I'll get her to ring you. Why don't you go home now? You've had a shock. Is it far?'

Mrs Anderson shook her head.

'You'll be OK to drive?'

She nodded.

After shutting her door, he searched the car park.

People were still gathered in huddles, swapping stories. Doctor Bell was operating a pop-up minor injuries clinic by the boot of her car. Cal asked if anyone had been taken to hospital.

She looked up from attending to a sprained wrist. 'Not as far as I know. No one's been badly injured, just a few scrapes and bruises.'

Cal went back across the car park towards the hall. He stopped twice to call out Violet's name and once more to give her description to a group of four young women. They said they hadn't seen anyone like that but they'd look out for her on their way into Poltown.

Cal wondered whether Violet had been worried about losing contact with Mrs Anderson and had gone back into the hall to look for her. As he was approaching the front door, he thought he heard a scream. It was the briefest of sounds, there for a moment, then gone in a gust of wind. 'Violet,' he shouted. 'Violet.'

He ran towards that split second of sound. Along the side of the building, at the far end, a faint light cast by a small window lit up two struggling figures.

'Hey,' he called out, running. 'Hey. What's going on?'

The light fell across Violet's face and a small, burly man looked up at Cal. His features were hidden by shadow and a hood. Cal shouted again. 'Hey, leave her alone.'

The man held out his right hand, warning Cal to keep his distance. He backed away, before turning and disappearing into the blackness.

Cal knelt beside Violet and helped her to sit up. 'He's gone. Are you all right?'

She held her hands to her face and nodded. 'Yes,' she said uncertainly. 'I think so.'

'God, what was that about?'

She shook her head.

'Do you know who it was?'

'No.'

'I'll call the police.'

'No, please don't.'

18

Later, driving Violet to the causeway, Cal encountered the same wilfulness. He mentioned Mrs Anderson and how worried she would be about Violet. 'It'd be kind if you gave her a ring. Use my phone if you like. Her number's in my contacts.'

After a pause, Violet said, 'No, I'll wait until I'm back on Orasaigh.'

Cal dropped the subject. He had the feeling she didn't want to speak to Mrs Anderson if he was listening.

Violet's behaviour in the cottage confirmed that impression. He left her in the sitting room while he checked the other rooms, making sure the windows were locked. Although he didn't say so, he was also investigating how secure the cottage was, in case the man came looking for Violet again. While he was upstairs he heard her talking on the phone. It was a brief call, so that when he joined her she was in an armchair in the sitting room, in silence. She was in the dark with the curtains open.

Cal said, 'Are you all right?'

Her answer was slow in coming. 'I'm just tired.'

'I'm not surprised. You've had a nasty experience.'

He sat opposite. 'Was that Mrs Anderson you were talking to? What did she say?'

'About what?'

'About what happened to you.'

'I didn't tell her,' Violet said. 'I arranged to meet her tomorrow, to collect my shopping.'

'I guess you didn't want to worry her.' Cal had the distinct impression that wasn't her reason.

After an awkward silence, he said, 'Can we talk about it?'

'About what?'

'Violet, you've just been attacked.'

Silence.

Cal tried again. 'Have you any idea who he was? Did he say anything? Can you think of any reason why he attacked you?'

'Can't you just leave it?' Violet moved in her chair, curling up, turning her shoulder, as she'd done when he'd given her a lift, letting him know she didn't want to talk, that she'd had enough for one day.

'I'm sorry,' he said. 'Maybe I should go, if that's what you'd prefer.'

She didn't reply and he listened to the wind howling outside. He went upstairs to find blankets. When he draped one over her, she seemed to be asleep. Why, he wondered, was she downstairs in an uncomfortable chair when there were bedrooms upstairs? Was she afraid? Did she want Cal's company after all?

As he kept watch through the long hours of the night he debated whether rest would make her any more receptive or forthcoming. Time would tell.

All he knew about her was her name and that, for a reason to be discovered, someone wished her harm.

One moment Mrs Anderson was fast asleep, the next wide awake and startled at being jolted from unconsciousness. Her eyes strained against the pitch dark of her bedroom and her head shifted on the pillow so that she could listen with both ears. She picked out familiar sounds, those that had accompanied her for her long occupation of Gardener's Cottage: the hollow tick of her alarm clock; tumbling mortar in the sealed chimney at the foot of her bed; the movement of a floorboard; the murmuring and rattling of the pipes which told her it must be past six because the boiler had started to heat the water.

What kept her on edge was a sound she couldn't hear. She listened for the noise that woke her, of someone banging at her front door accompanied by a shout; a woman. She waited for it to be repeated before deciding whether she'd had a vivid dream or whether there really was someone outside.

The seconds ticked away. The fug and confusion of waking from a deep sleep began to clear and with it the uncertainty. Mrs Anderson had heard the noise before; the first time when Diana brought the baby and thereafter at odd occasions like this, when she was deep in sleep and the room was dark and still.

'So much blood,' she whispered. It was what she always said.

Diana at the door, holding a newborn baby, drenched in blood; the baby drenched too, a girl.

Mrs Anderson rolled on to her side and turned on her bedside lamp. Her clock showed 06.23. At seven her alarm would ring.

Twenty-six years ago, she'd have done anything for Diana.

~~~~

Violet's head pressed against the sitting-room window. Her slow breathing made a plume of condensation on the cold glass, its expansion and contraction the only movement inside or outside Orasaigh Cottage. Violet was as still as the branches of the trees behind her.

'Did the storm go in the night?' Cal asked, stirring in his chair, pretending he'd only just woken when in fact he'd been watching her for a while.

His voice startled her but she attempted to conceal it.

'Would you like coffee?' she asked. 'I found a jar of instant in the kitchen. The milk I bought is in Mrs Anderson's car – do you mind black?'

She was talking quickly, as though worried about what he might say if she gave him an opportunity. He played along. 'Black's fine.' He stretched and yawned. 'No sugar,' he called after her.

When she returned, holding a single mug, he said, 'Aren't you having one?' She shook her head, being evasive, barely looking at him. 'Not at the moment.' She put the mug on the table beside his chair and made to leave the room.

'Violet, we've got to talk about this.'

She stopped with her back to him.

'I know what I saw last night,' he continued.

She seemed to slump in resignation. She knew what he was going to say, or thought she did.

Cal hoped she would turn round. 'Well, you know what I think.'

She replied in the same clipped and weary tone of the night before. 'There are creeps like him everywhere. There's always some guy . . .'

'It wasn't like that, Violet. You know it wasn't.'

She grunted in exasperation, as if Cal didn't understand, as if any man could. 'That's *exactly* what it was like.' She sounded impatient, but the emphasis was forced. Cal thought she was trying to persuade herself as well as him.

He was suddenly irritated by her behaviour, by the stupidity of it. 'For Christ's sake, Violet, I'm only trying to look after you.' He regretted his outburst, not only what he'd said but also the investment of emotion. Now she would know he cared what happened to her. He swore silently. He expected her to leave the room but she stood quite still, as if caught between opposing forces: wanting to hear what he had to say but not wanting to; wanting and not wanting his company.

Cal sighed. 'Look, I'm sorry. I don't know what's going on or why . . . maybe it's none of my business.' She stood with her head bowed, arms folded. At least she was listening. 'Violet, what you're saying doesn't make any sense – some bloke just trying it on. Stuff like that doesn't happen in a place like this.'

He watched the rise and fall of her shoulders.

'All I'm saying is that you should take it seriously. Just in case. Go to the police. Tell them what you can.'

She shook her head. 'We've already talked about this. I don't have anything to tell the police. I didn't see the man's face.'

'OK, so why don't you leave? Go somewhere else. Go home, wherever home is. Don't stick around when there's some guy out there . . .'

'I've still got things to do,' she said. 'Things I want to see.'

'What happens if he finds you on your own, when you're walking on a beach?'

Without turning, she said, 'I'm going to have a shower, all right?'

Do what the hell you want, he thought.

While she was upstairs, Cal made another cup of coffee and went outside to the front garden. He leaned against the gate, letting the sun warm him. His clothes were still damp from the rain, his bones chilled by the cold and air-less atmosphere inside Orasaigh Cottage. He was tired. He checked the time on his phone: not quite 8 a.m. Low tide was three hours away. Until then he was stuck on an island with someone who would prefer him to shut up. He remembered seeing Violet for the first time and think-ing she might be a companion spirit, someone who was like him, who found refuge by the sea. How wrong he'd turned out to be. The thought accompanied him uneasily as he wandered along the track. 'Fuck,' he groaned. Had he made it obvious he was attracted to her? Perhaps that's why she was being difficult. Was that the reason she kept a distance between them?

On his return to the cottage, he saw her before she saw him. She was coming out of the porch into the garden. Her hair was still wet from the shower. She had on jeans, a white vest and a blue-and-white check shirt which she wore loose.

'What a difference a day makes,' he said, stopping by the gate.

'Hard to imagine it's even the same place,' she replied, smiling and squinting as the sun caught her eyes.

He wondered if it was her way of making amends: a new beginning after the disagreements of the last twelve hours.

'Can I get you coffee now?' he asked.

'No thanks.' She glanced at him and away. 'I'm sorry.'

'Sorry for what?'

'For being cross when I should have been grateful.'

'It's OK.'

'No . . . No, it isn't.' Her mouth twisted. 'This cottage . . .' She looked behind her. 'It's so depressing.'

Cal nodded.

'Are you in a hurry?' she said, a look of anxiety in her eyes.

'No.'

'Could we do something?'

19

Mrs Anderson's morning walk usually took her over the moor path to the churchyard but today she skirted the walled garden to the main driveway. Turning left, away from the big house, she prepared for the possibility of an encounter with Alexandra or Matt Hamilton. Should either drive by she would carry on regardless, neither stepping on to the verge, nor looking up. She fixed her face accordingly – it drained from milky pink to pallid grey to suit the dourness of her expression. Yet in her breast there was a flutter of excitement at what had been set in train, at its potential.

She was walking along the driveway of the people she would destroy, treading across their property just as surely as she was treading on their hopes and ambitions, just as they had trampled on hers. Yet, if they were to drive past, what would they see: the resourceful adversary who had arranged the return of Mr William's only child, the rightful heir to Brae, or the dry husk they had discarded, a woman barely worth pitying, let alone fearing? She assumed the latter and wished one or other of them would happen by and glance up in condescension. Just for the joy of it: Alexandra or Matt Hamilton being taken in by the illusion she was creating, of a woman brought low by her expulsion from the family she had served beyond duty for all these years.

Where the drive met the Poltown road, she turned right, walking slowly, enjoying the sun's unexpected warmth, until she reached the turn-off to South Bay. She forked left and, after 150 metres or so, stopped beside a slatted bench with a decorated iron frame. She put down her bag and glanced at her watch. She had time to while away before low tide and where better to waste it than there, where she could see the long crescent sweep of the bay, where she could watch for Duncan? She made herself comfortable, the only sign of any restlessness the frequency with which she lifted her eyes. Where was Duncan? Where was the idiot?

While she waited for him to put in an appearance, she occupied herself with memories. Nowadays her head was filled with such bitter recollections that she wondered whether she had been happy for anything more than fleeting periods of her life. So engrossed was she that it seemed no time at all before she noticed a figure moving through the dunes. Mrs Anderson opened her bag, removed a tissue from its packet, dabbed at her eyes and blew her nose. She waited a while longer until Duncan was busily clearing the beach of its latest debris before stirring. Just to be sure.

Now she walked quickly, her childhood knowledge of the folds in the land being put to good use. Only when she reached the stone pillars at the gateway to Boyd's Farm did she rest. There, with the dunes between them, she could no longer see Duncan, nor was there the risk of him seeing her as long as he was working the high-tide line.

She reached out to touch the stone pillar at her side, its

cold surface stirring vivid memories. That was where, as a girl, she used to sit and watch her father working his sheep. She examined the pasture either side of the track to the steading: not only was it no longer lush green, the field was colonized by docks and rushes as well as piles of untidy rubbish and rusting farm machinery. The nearest wreck to her was her father's Ferguson tractor. 'This land is NOT for sale. Turn round here' was emblazoned across it. A 'pah' of annoyance erupted from Mrs Anderson. Everywhere her eye settled she saw neglect, chaos or madness. Was it any wonder it tore at her heart?

The emotion of the moment acted as a goad and she set off towards the steading, her eyes welling up. Following her humiliation at Diana's memorial service, she saw the course of her life as a repeating pattern: one in which she had invested unwisely in people who repaid her trust by abandoning her and – this, the deadliest realization of all – of her complicity. Was there any other explanation when someone time and time again laid themselves open to the same injustice?

It happened here first, on these acres where she'd grown up.

Wasn't this the land where she learned about sheep and cattle, about the growing seasons, about the business of farming, in the expectation that one day Boyd's Farm – its name for three generations – would be hers? Wasn't this where she'd suffered the worst of her betrayals, the one that would set the pattern for the others?

Being the only child of Archie and Catherine Boyd, she imagined the farm one day would be hers, where she would live out her life. A shepherd's expression used by her father explained it best. The sheep, he would often remark, were 'hefted': in other words, they belonged to Boyd's Farm, and so, in her view, did she. She was 'hefted' too, knowing the farm's character and moods better than her own, believing there to be an unbreakable bond between her and its acres and animals, her bloodline and theirs. She'd assumed her father knew too, since there was no sibling for there to be rivalry over the legacy. Yet, she had been wrong, as she had been wrong thereafter on the question of bonds, belonging and the giving of unconditional love.

Boyd's Farm was where it began, with her father, a man who was as knowledgeable about the whims of nature as he was ignorant of his daughter. By the time her mother died, Mrs Anderson was forty-five and divorced, but still she remembered the excitement of thinking she would help her elderly father with the farm. The notion had been short lived. When she suggested moving from Gardener's Cottage to take her mother's place, her father appeared troubled, inquiring why she would want to give up her home when he wouldn't be alive for long. Didn't she know the house and the farm would belong to his nephew Duncan? The farm had always gone to a Boyd. Farming was a man's business and anyway, why would she have expectations of the farm when she wasn't a Boyd? She had become an Anderson by marriage. Despite divorcing, didn't she call herself by that name still?

Mrs Anderson had fallen silent with hurt and rage and he'd shuffled off to find his will among the papers on his desk. Returning with the document, he'd shown her the paragraphs detailing how he intended her to have fifteen per cent of the farm, a share that Duncan would purchase from her once he'd turned a few years of profit. Her father looked at her with bewilderment. He had provided for her better than any Boyd had provided for a daughter. Her charge of unfairness had been unjust. Didn't she owe him an apology?

Beginning with her father, she had always loved jealously. It was true of her husband, who left her pregnant after eight years of marriage and two miscarriages – and the biggest hurt of all, Mrs Anderson's daughter being delivered stillborn following his betrayal. It had also been the case when Mr William brought Diana to Brae. How Mrs Anderson relished the time the two women spent together over morning coffee in the kitchen or tea by the east wall of the garden or at South Bay, where Diana liked to swim (Mrs Anderson following later with the picnic basket and rug). No matter how much time Mrs Anderson had Diana to herself, it was never enough. Mrs Anderson would have contemplated anything to bind Diana to her, done anything.

Mr William's affair with Megan Bates had provided that opportunity.

At the open gateway to the steading, Mrs Anderson looked at the Wall of Lost Soles, hardly believing how much it had expanded since her last visit six months ago. She carried on into the steading courtyard. Despite knowing what to expect, she was astonished at the state of the buildings, astonished and upset. 'And all for what?' she muttered angrily. 'The ruination of my farm.' Under Duncan's stewardship, there had never been a profit and her share remained at fifteen per cent.

She turned left towards the back door of the house. When she'd lived there with her parents, they had used that entrance too, like Duncan, possibly the only tradition that remained unchanged. Two black-and-white cats stirred from the porch roof at her approach. They stretched, arched their spines and raised their hackles. One after the other they jumped down on to an old kitchen chair beside the back step and went careering, back legs askew, as if blown by a gale, across the yard. Mrs Anderson took a deep breath, preparing herself for what she would find inside. It was always a shock. Every time she came.

The door was unlocked. It always was. For years the joke of the village was how Boyd's Farm was an open invitation to thieves; how none had ever accepted because the house contained nothing worth stealing. Instead the boys of the village regarded it as a rite of passage to dash in and scrawl their names on the wall of the farthest attic room, then run out again before Duncan could catch them.

Mrs Anderson closed the door behind her.

She went from dusty corridor to dirty hallway, from chaotic room to still more chaotic room, satisfying the urge that every so often drove her to wander the house. As usual, she chewed at her cheeks at the evidence of her father's wickedness in preferring Duncan over his only child. With each succeeding visit, the case against Archie Boyd grew along with the increasing decay she witnessed.

Ten minutes after going indoors she was back in the yard, her face white, her mood sour, the tendency of a daughter to blame herself and to exonerate her father laid to rest for another while. Usually she would hurry back to the Poltown road to avoid an encounter with Duncan returning from the beach. On this occasion, however, she took the old kitchen chair from the back door and placed it in the shade against the wall by the steading entrance. There she waited for Duncan, for the cousin she hadn't addressed since he'd taken up residence at Boyd's Farm. She sat erect and with her hands folded on her lap, her demeanour composed even when she saw him approaching across the field.

'Hello, Duncan,' she said. Her voice startled him. He lifted his face, the first time she had looked on it in three decades. She could hardly find anything remaining of the good-looking young man she recollected.

The creature before her now resembled a scarecrow. His clothes were rags and his face scored with deep fissures as well as being blotched with different lengths of stubble. His eyes were red rimmed and sunken, his nose bigger than it should be and oddly bulbous at the end, his face somehow smaller. While he gathered himself, she examined him as a pathologist would a corpse, looking for cause and effect. How, she wondered, could a man's skin be so lined? What limit was there to the degradation of a living human body?

Duncan peered at her. 'Is that you, Mary?'

No one had called her by her first name for years; she was surprised to find she was still known by it at Boyd's Farm.

'Yes, it is,' she replied. 'How are you, Duncan?' She looked at him with disapproval and Duncan seemed at a loss to know what to say next. He coughed and fidgeted and looked at the sky.

'I hear you've had a visitor,' she said.

'I have?' His eyebrows arched as though confused by which of his many visitors she might mean.

'Yes.'

'About the wind farm?' he asked. 'I told them not to come back.' He pointed towards her father's old tractor. 'This land is NOT for sale.' He smirked at his cleverness.

She'd heard this about him: that he was a boy at heart, a show-off. 'No, not about the wind farm,' she said. 'A young woman, a pretty young woman.'

A frown formed across his forehead. Mrs Anderson found it surprising there was room, given the competition from all the other lines and wrinkles.

'Her name is Violet Wells. Jim told me you'd met her.'

Duncan held his head to one side, listening.

'Did she ask you about Megan Bates? You remember Megan, don't you, Duncan? Didn't you take quite a fancy to her?'

Instead of answering the question, he fidgeted, one moment picking at his fingers, the next becoming sidetracked by the cats, which had reappeared to welcome him. They rubbed against his legs, tails raised, and meowed.

'You're not very forthcoming, are you?' she scolded. 'Well, Duncan, has Violet Wells been asking you about Megan Bates, or has she not?'

Duncan picked at his teeth, rubbed at his lips and blinked. She could tell he wanted to run away – *so* like a child.

'I wonder why, after all this time. How long would it be, Duncan? Twenty-six years? A long time, anyway.'

Duncan had folded his arms. He hugged them to his chest. 'I didn't kill her. I didn't kill her.' He was shouting at her, his eyes angry, his neck bulging. Afterwards, he seemed anxious as if he hadn't meant to say anything, certainly not that.

Mrs Anderson raised her eyebrows. 'My goodness, Duncan. Where did that come from?'

There was silence for a moment.

'Poor Duncan, you didn't really know what you were getting into, did you?' she said eventually. 'I do hope Violet Wells doesn't start it up all over again, all that nastiness with the police. Oh, I do hope not, Duncan, for your sake.'

She scowled at him, then stood up and brushed down her coat. 'Well, I must leave you, Duncan. A lovely day like this deserves a good walk.'

Examining the field in front of her, she said, 'What a mess you've made of the farm.' Then, looking back over her shoulder: 'I always knew you would.' She took a few steps. 'If you want my advice, you should sell up while you have the chance, before the police come searching through Megan's things again, before they come looking for you, Duncan.'

His head was still shaking.

'Duncan,' she snapped. 'Are you listening?'

'Yes, Mary,' he replied, a chastened boy.

'I hope you are, because this land will never be worth anything again if BRC takes its money elsewhere.'

Without further ado she started back across the field. When she passed the pillars, her hand reached out to touch the smooth curve of the stone. She read the sign: BOYD'S FARM, her farm. She'd had to bear its loss. Why shouldn't Duncan suffer in the same way? Returning along the Brae driveway, she appeared revived, her head high and defiant. She had found another purpose for Violet Wells apart from taking revenge on Matt and Alexandra. She could also use the young woman to torment Duncan and, just possibly, engineer Mrs Anderson's salvation. Talk in the village was that BRC had raised its 'final' offer for Boyd's Farm to half a million pounds. Mrs Anderson's fifteen per cent share would be seventy-five thousand, sufficient to sustain her in Gardener's Cottage for her lifetime. If only she could make Duncan sell.

20

The north-west tip of Orasaigh Island overlooked the narrow entrance to the sea loch. Cal leaned against a boulder standing sentry at the shore. From habit he watched the lethargic progress of seaweed floating on the ebb. Not even two knots, he estimated, maybe only one. Violet was nearby on a gravel beach, gazing towards distant mountains. His assessment of her had changed in the time they had taken to cross the island. He'd started out imagining she might be having some sort of personal crisis, that she'd run away to the west coast (why else would she rent an isolated cottage on a tidal island?), only to find trouble following her. He didn't know precisely what form trouble took: he imagined an ex-lover or an ex-husband, maybe a stalker, something of that kind. Whatever it was, he'd assumed she was the one being pursued.

Now he wasn't so sure.

When they set off along the track, Cal said, 'Don't worry. I'm not going to say another word about last night.'

She sounded relieved. 'A rest would be good,' she replied. 'It'd be nice just to enjoy the day.'

'So what should we talk about?' he asked.

'Anything,' she said. 'Anything apart from me.'

The track narrowed and he hung back to let her go first. When he caught up again, she said, 'Tell me. What sort of person always knows the times of the tides?'

'I'm an oceanographer,' he replied. 'I've been interested in the sea ever since I was a boy.' He'd studied marine science at university and recently completed a PhD. His enthusiasm had never left him, though sometimes it got the better of him. That was why he'd argued with a woman at the public meeting. She was stirring up things against Duncan Boyd. But Cal didn't believe in big corporations being handed large areas of ocean. 'Nor do I like what happens to small guys like Duncan Boyd who stand in their way.'

'So that's why people were getting up and moving away from you.' She nodded, seeming to agree with his view. She squinted at him. 'An oceanographer – is that how you make your living?'

'Mostly I do ocean tracking – using current, tide and wind data to calculate where all kinds of flotsam originated, where it will go and when it will get there.'

'Who employs you – the government?'

'No, I'm self-employed. I work with environmental organizations tracking down ocean polluters or for people looking to recover a body lost at sea. At the moment, I'm involved more with hunting bodies.' He grimaced – he wasn't sure the balance was right but fewer marine charities had money to spare for investigations. 'It's also like that because of some high-profile cases which have attracted media attention. People have got to know what I do and my company, Flotsam and Jetsam Investigations. I'm thinking of changing the name to The Sea Detective Agency.' Cal bit at the side of his lip. 'But I'm not sure. Maybe that would attract cranks and hoaxers.'

'Good name,' Violet said. 'It's easy to remember. Do you prefer environmental work?'

'Yeah,' Cal said. 'I suppose I do, or did. Tracking down a cargo ship that hasn't put out an alert after losing containers overboard is satisfying. Exposing the guilty . . .'

As they walked on, Cal said that missing bodies cases were 'well, a bit different'.

'How?'

'Oh, just about in every way. The clients, for a start . . .'

It was his rule, he said, to emphasize that nothing was certain. All he could provide were possible search areas. A few metres of sea could make all the difference to where a body would beach, *whether* it would beach.

'More often than not, all that's keeping people going is the hope of finding a body.' He sighed, a long exhalation. 'I don't know what's worse any more, finding a half-decomposed body or not finding one at all.

'I didn't realize that at first. Now I do, I dread the effect, one way or the other. I suppose that's why I'm here, avoiding the issue, running away.' He glanced at her, checking her reaction. 'I had a case recently involving an eight-year-old girl. I found her body. She was in a bad way. She'd been in the sea for three months. Her parents couldn't recognize her. I imagine they're still having nightmares. Now other parents want me to find their missing children. I don't think they know what they're asking.'

He hoped his mention of running away would give Violet an opening to talk about herself.

Instead she went quiet and they walked on. He thought he'd lost her until she asked, 'How does it work? Tracking things, I mean.'

'Normally I won't take on a job,' he explained, 'unless I

have three pieces of information: what, where and when. I need a description of the target object. For example, if it's a body, was it wearing a life jacket? Knowing exactly where the target . . .' He apologized for using the word, '. . . went into the sea or where it was last seen is also crucial: that's the LKP or last known position. And I need to know the time it went into the sea. If I know the position and time I can work out the prevailing tides and winds.'

'What happens if you know "what" but you only have an estimate of where and when?' she said.

'There's a greater margin for error. Where things go and at what speed depends on the strength and direction of the currents and the wind, on the size and shape of the object you're tracking, and on how much is above the water, how much below.'

He looked at her to check she was still interested. She was.

'Go on,' she said.

'Well, very few things go straight down the wind. A lilo does because it has no traction in the water. But something with traction will go off at an angle to the wind. The divergence can be five degrees to ninety degrees. Once an object starts to diverge it will continue on that course until the wind changes speed or direction.'

He gave her the example of an oil tanker with a wall of steel above and below the water surface going off at anything up to eighty degrees and described how, at the opposite end of the size scale, small differences in shape or buoyancy had significant consequences for an object's destination.

'What about a person?' she asked.

'You mean a body?'

'Yes.'

'It's a small target for the wind, even a body that's wearing a life jacket and bobbing up and down. At first, it'll tend to go with the current, though that doesn't mean one with a life jacket will end up in the same place as one without. Take shoes, for example. A left shoe will often wash ashore in a different place from a right because of the different curve of the soles and the way the sea works on it.'

By now they had arrived at the tip of the island and Violet peeled off to the pebble beach. Cal stood by the boulder, watching her. He felt he'd been taking a test and was in the unsatisfactory position of not knowing how well he'd done; whether he'd passed or failed.

Whether trouble was pursuing Violet or whether Violet was pursuing it.

After a while, she came to join him, following a sheep's trail through low bracken, apparently deep in thought. He registered the easy way she moved, the white curve of her neck, the billow of her shirt. When she was close he said, 'The tide's about out now, if you want to cross the causeway.'

She looked up and smiled. The tension seemed to have dropped from her. Perhaps it was just getting away from the gloomy atmosphere of the cottage.

'We've got some time before it gets deep again, haven't we?'

'Yes.'

She held up her right hand to show Cal a smooth white stone. 'My daughter paints them,' she said. 'She gives them to me as presents. She's called Anna. She's a sweetie.

Her father ran off when I was pregnant.' She looked across the loch. 'I've never seen him again.'

Cal said nothing.

'Anna's being looked after by my friend Hilary. Her bedsit is below mine. Hilary's daughter is called Izzy. She's Anna's best friend. What else should you know? I live in Glasgow. I went to the art school and stayed on. I was brought up in Inverness. I don't have any brothers or sisters. My mother is dead . . .' She paused. 'And my father. Oh, and I have a night job in a pizza restaurant so my education paid off.' She smiled. 'That's some of the important stuff. All of it really . . .'

Her smile faded. 'Actually, there's more. But you're better off not knowing the rest.'

Cal watched the reflection of the hills in the loch and wondered at the significance of the last few minutes, of Violet telling him the details of her life. Had he passed the test? What did it mean when a woman volunteered her life story when not so long before she had been monosyllabic and resentful.

'Call that a hard-luck story?' He smiled to keep things light, or as light as possible, considering what he was about to say. 'My mother's dead too. When I was seventeen, from cancer. I thought I was grown up until then. But I wasn't. I remember kissing her cold forehead.'

'I'm sorry,' Violet said.

'It's all right. As for my father, well, I thought I knew him, but it turned out I didn't. He suffered a mental collapse after my mother died. When he recovered he went abroad to teach in charity schools. He's never been back. As far as I know he lives in Mozambique with a

Swazi woman who's twelve years his junior and has three young daughters. He's found himself a new family.' Cal heard hurt creep into his voice. 'Oh, and he emailed a couple of weeks ago to announce that he's sold our family home in Edinburgh to the sitting tenants.' Cal shook his head as if shaking off his father. 'It doesn't matter. I'm twenty-nine. I can look after myself but for the first time in my life there's nowhere I can stick a pin in a map and say, "This is where I belong." Do you know what I mean?'

Violet nodded. 'Yes, yes I do.' She looked at the sea. So did Cal. For a while neither spoke. Then Cal said, 'Last night . . . Was that Anna's father?'

'No. Absolutely not.' She answered easily and without offence. 'He's never even seen Anna. She's four. He's gone. I don't know where he is and he doesn't know where I am. Last night . . . I don't know who that was.'

'Do you know what it was about?'

She shook her head. 'No. No, I don't think so.'

'Not some guy trying it on . . .'

'I don't know. It might have been.'

'What else is there?'

'Something to do with why I'm here . . .'

'Which is?'

She glanced quickly at him again, as if weighing up whether she should tell him or not. She shook her head. 'I can't. As I just said, you're better off not knowing.'

Cal decided not to argue. 'OK, so what now?'

Violet had something to ask him. 'What you were saying . . . about things floating on the sea . . . I hadn't thought about it before . . . How likely is it that a hat and a handbag would come ashore together . . . a raffia sun hat with a broad brim and a shoulder bag, quite compact, leather, with a zip-up pocket?'

'They went into the water together?'

'Yes.'

'Did they come ashore at the same time?'

'Yes, I think so.'

'Was there a wind?'

'I don't know.'

'Were they near each other or just in the same general area?'

'They were close.'

'Where?'

'In North Bay.'

'Do you know the time and date?'

'I know the date.' She studied him. 'They were found on 11 September. Late morning . . . I don't have an exact time.'

'Last week, you mean?'

'No.' She hesitated. 'You'll think I'm weird. It was 1983.'

'Not weird. Unusual,' he replied. The temptation was to say more. Interesting. Attractive.

'It just never occurred to me,' she said. 'Not until our walk over here and listening to you talk about objects with different shapes following different courses.'

'I don't suppose you have the hat and bag.'

'No.'

'Do you know where and when they went into the water?'

She appeared relieved at the question, at him taking her seriously. 'Not precisely. Somewhere in South Bay. When?

The day before they were found, around 8 a.m. on 10 September . . .'

'And you're sure about 1983?'

'Yes.'

'So you want to know how likely it is these two objects would turn up together?'

She nodded.

'You're not going to tell me why?'

'No.'

'But you will if there's any more trouble, if you're in danger?'

'I don't know.'

He wanted to hold her, to kiss her.

'OK,' he said. 'I'm going to need my laptop and some oranges.'

At Violet's request, he stopped the pick-up at the entrance to Brae. She said she would walk the rest of the way. The driveway was pretty and anyway she was early – her appointment to pick up her shopping wasn't for another twenty minutes. She might only have met Mrs Anderson the day before but she was certain she knew this much about her: she preferred visitors to be punctual. 'And she disapproves of everyone given the opportunity.'

'You'll be all right?' Cal asked.

'With Mrs Anderson?' She misunderstood him deliberately.

'You know what I mean.'

She did, she said. 'I'll be fine . . . really.'

He considered offering to stay with her but instead said, 'I'm going to the general store in Poltown. After, I'll have a look at North Bay, get a feel for the way the sea works. If you like I'll buy some things for lunch. We can have a picnic on the beach, light a fire.'

'I'd like that,' she answered, climbing out and shutting the door.

'Give me a call,' he shouted through the open window.

A smile lit up her face, a look of happiness, the first he'd seen. He was still working out what it meant when she disappeared along Brae's driveway into the shadows of an avenue of ash trees.

Driving into Poltown, he reminded himself of Rachel, his ex-wife, how similar in looks if not character she was to Violet. He banged his open hand against the steering wheel. Why didn't he learn from his mistakes? There had been enough of them, the names a parade of failure. Apart from Rachel, there were Lydia, Maria and Kate. He remembered Rachel writing bitterly to him before their divorce, saying he was just another geek with a hobby, that girls knew what to expect when they got involved with a trainspotter or some dimwit who boosted his testosterone by watching repeats of *Top Gear*, but Cal's oceanography and all his 'crap about the sea' was a masquerade. It made him out to be some kind of romantic hero when he wasn't. As soon as he was in a relationship he tried to escape. It wasn't deliberate on his part, she had conceded, but still, breaking up with him had left her with a nasty aftertaste of deceit. 'Whoever wrote "no man is an island" clearly hadn't met you.'

At that stage, she hadn't even known about his affair.

Cal turned left, into Poltown's first cul-de-sac, and pulled up outside the shop which used to be twin garages – another architectural misdemeanour inflicted on the residents. For the most part they had little use for garages since few were prosperous enough to own cars. 'Run by the community for the community' was the legend underneath the sign which proclaimed 'Poltown General Stores'. The opening hours were painted in green on the door, along with an indecipherable scrawl of luminous pink and yellow graffiti which extended across the plate glass window. All that was missing was a metal grille, Cal reckoned, and it could have been dropped into any big city sink estate without seeming out of place.

Cal noticed a group of teenagers sitting on a front step opposite. They were watching him in silence. He took the precaution of locking the pick-up.

Inside, the shop was a cross between a small warehouse and a car boot sale. The floor was concrete and the walls lined with a type of shelving Cal associated with DIY stores. The centre of the shop (the car boot sale) was filled by end-to-end trestle tables on which were trays of bread, rolls, fruit and vegetables, boxes of crisps, bags of dried dog food, stacks of cat food tins and, incongruously, a collection of red and gold 'Santa Claus Crackers' (whether relics of Christmas past or stocked early for Christmas coming, Cal wasn't sure). The bread was white only, he noticed in passing, and the fresh fruit and vegetables shared display space with Pot Noodles and packet soups.

Cal's other observation concerned a group of people gathered at the back of the shop. There were half a dozen of them, four men and two women. One of the women sat behind a till around which newspapers were arranged. The others stood leaning against the counter or shelves, talking.

'Hi,' he offered in their general direction. He took a wire basket from the stack at the door and began to search for the ingredients of a picnic. He put rolls into a paper bag, three overripe tomatoes into another and rejected two droopy lettuces before selecting a third. Snatches of conversation drifted over to him. It was about the meeting the night before, who had hit whom, who had been hurt, who had thrown the first punch and who had seen what.

'Excuse me.' The discussion stopped. Six faces turned as Cal interrupted. 'Are there any oranges?'

'I took them off this morning,' the woman at the till replied, 'because they'd gone a bit soft.'

'Just like you then, eh, Helen,' a man leaning back against the counter growled. He had a thin, stubbly face and a mocking expression. Cal recognized him from the night before. In all the panic and commotion, he'd been the odd one out. Instead of running for the door, he'd stayed in his seat observing the melee with apparently detached interest. Cal hadn't paid him much attention – his concern then had been Violet.

Cal ignored the remark. 'Have you still got them?'

Helen glanced nervously at Cal and then at the man who had joked at her expense. 'Aye,' she said uncertainly, 'they're on the floor, by me.'

'Can I see?'

'You wouldn't want to eat any of them.' She bent down

to lift up the box and showed Cal, who was approaching the counter. 'Well, I wouldn't, at any rate.'

He saw what the woman meant: they were discoloured and shrunken, like collapsed old faces. 'Those are perfect,' Cal said, ignoring her surprised reaction. 'Can I have them?'

'All of them?'

'Yes.'

The woman peered at the fruit again in case she'd mistaken their condition. 'Are you sure, son?'

'Yeah, they're ideal.' Cal went to the other side of the shop to buy juice and bottles of water. While he was away from the counter he heard Helen wonder what she should charge since the oranges were 'five minutes from the bin'. She asked, 'What should I do, Davie?'

'Why do you want them?' Cal recognized that growl. It had a distinctive and hard edge. Davie was the one who had made the joke about Helen being soft.

'No reason . . .' Cal picked up a packet of biscuits.

'You were at the meeting last night.' It was less an observation, more an accusation.

'I was there, yes.' Cal returned to the counter with his basket, feeling Davie's eyes on him. After Helen began recording his purchases, Davie said, 'I always remember a face.'

Cal extracted a twenty-pound note from his pocket.

'So what brings you to Poltown?' Davie persisted.

'The sea, the scenery, usual things . . .' His answer was offhand. 'Isn't that why everyone comes here?' He put his money on the counter, while Helen worried aloud about the unresolved problem of charging for the oranges.

'Half price? What do you say?' The others mumbled in agreement. 'Half price is fine,' Cal reassured her.

'Full whack,' Davie said. 'He pays full whack.'

'For them?' Helen asked doubtfully, holding one up, glancing at Davie, wondering what was going on, what she had missed. 'I wouldn't feel right charging thirty-five pence for that.'

Cal was aware of a change in the atmosphere, as were the others. They were looking at Cal then at Davie, as if expecting something to happen.

'Don't worry about it,' Cal said. 'Thirty-five pence is fine.' He'd rather pay three pounds fifty for ten oranges than argue.

'I'll put them in a carrier for you,' Helen said helpfully.

'Make him pay for that too,' Davie ordered. 'Fifty pence a bag.'

Helen glanced nervously at Cal. *That's all right*, he nodded back. She shot another anxious look at Davie. Her face showed concern at the escalating turn of events, at her inadvertent role in what was happening, at Davie turning this into a confrontation. Cal had the impression she'd witnessed similar scenes before and knew what might be coming.

Once Helen finished packing Cal's groceries, she counted his change into his open hand. When Cal lifted up the carrier bag, Davie asked, 'Is that your vehicle outside?'

'It could be,' Cal replied without looking up.

'Didn't I see it at South Bay the other day?'

'It's possible.' He might as well have told him to mind his own business since his voice did. Cal walked deliberately and slowly towards the door. He lingered for a few moments beside the community notice board to show he wasn't in any hurry before going out. As he drove away he glanced in his wing mirror and saw Davie standing in the doorway of the shop, legs apart, mobile phone at his ear. Cal opened his window, extended his arm and raised his middle finger in the air. *'Fuck off, Davie.'*

Along the west wall of the garden at Brae House Violet found a place where she could not be seen from the drive or from the track leading to Mrs Anderson's cottage. She could kill time there without the complication of the Hamiltons or anyone else noticing her and prying into what she was doing. Having ten minutes to waste gave her the chance to ring Mr Anwar, a duty call that had been on her conscience. Usually she was slow to trust people. With Cal, her indecision had a number of causes: caution about involving him in something she did not yet understand, reticence about divulging her purpose and wariness about romantic entanglements (she suspected Cal's interest). Already, she worried she had confided too much. With Mr Anwar, by contrast, as soon as she saw him, she'd trusted him. At the time she'd thought his good manners had won her over. On reflection she realized it was his consideration, a trait he displayed again now once she started to explain who she was and why she was ringing. 'Do you remember? I gave you tea without milk and you met my daughter Anna.'

'Miss Wells, my dear, I was thinking about you, wondering how you were getting on. How are you?'

His quiet civility brought an end to her gabbling. She made a little sound in appreciation. 'I'm well, thank you, Mr Anwar. And you?'

'Oh, it doesn't matter about me,' he replied after a hesitation. Violet noticed the uncharacteristic stumble. She found herself saying, 'You matter very much, Mr Anwar. To me, you do, very much indeed.'

Immediately, she fretted that Mr Anwar would be offended by her effusiveness. To her surprise, it affected him in a different way. Instead of the polite deflection she expected, he told her he'd been foolish and he mentioned people he had wronged in some way or other. A Mr Hunter cropped up a few times, a woman called Meera and, the only one she recognized, Shereen. When she heard her name, she interrupted him. 'Shereen's your daughter, isn't she?' He talked through her question, raising his voice, which was so untypical of the unassuming man she knew that she said, 'Where are you, Mr Anwar? Are you at work?' She heard his breathing and then a different sound, a distant muttering, as though he had put the phone down and he was pacing around a room. Then there was a noise like paper being torn.

'Mr Anwar, Mr Anwar,' she called out. 'Mr Anwar? Are you all right?'

'Shereen will be angry with me.' He was back on the phone.

'Why?'

'I've torn her poster.'

'Mr Anwar, are you in Shereen's room?' She heard him take a deep breath.

'Should I be somewhere else?'

'At work?' Violet tried.

'Ah, work,' he replied.

'What's happened, Mr Anwar?'

'I'm sorry, Miss Wells . . .'

'What have you got to be sorry about? You've been kind.' Then she said, 'It's something to do with me, isn't it?' His silence made her think she was right. 'What's happened? Please tell me. I couldn't bear it if it's something to do with me.'

'It's nothing you've done, dear Miss Wells.'

She could hear he was trying to protect her. 'It's better I know, Mr Anwar, really.'

'I suppose so,' he conceded. 'You've been to see a police officer.'

'Yes, a retired one. He was the man who led the inquiry into my mother's disappearance.'

'He reported your visit to the police authorities and they lodged a complaint with my manager.'

'What has happened?'

'I have been suspended.'

'That's awful. Because of me?'

'Because I was stupid, Miss Wells. Because I disobeyed my superior. Not because of you.'

'I'm so sorry, Mr Anwar.'

'You must go now, Miss Wells. You must carry on. But be careful. It pains me to say this but sometimes people prefer to let things lie than to suffer the discomfort of unearthing the truth.'

'Who, Mr Anwar, who? The police? Tell me, Mr Anwar.'

The phone went dead. Mr Anwar had gone. She dialled

again but there was no answer. She left a message, promising to visit him as soon as she had discovered the truth about her mother. She'd bring Anna too. 'We'd love to visit you,' she said. 'Look after yourself . . . please, Mr Anwar, dear Mr Anwar.'

She stared at her phone, impotent in the face of the havoc she'd wreaked on his unassuming life. She had an unsettling feeling that forces were gathering against her, the police, the violent man at the end of the public meeting – and that her clumsiness had been the cause. Standing there, hidden in the shelter of Brae's walled garden, she suddenly felt exposed. In Poltown, she realized, nothing went unnoticed, herself included.

She was two minutes late for Mrs Anderson.

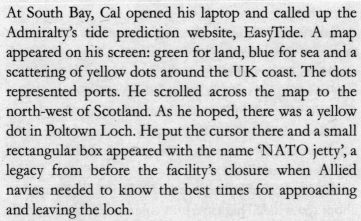

At South Bay, Cal opened his laptop and called up the Admiralty's tide prediction website, EasyTide. A map appeared on his screen: green for land, blue for sea and a scattering of yellow dots around the UK coast. The dots represented ports. He scrolled across the map to the north-west of Scotland. As he hoped, there was a yellow dot in Poltown Loch. He put the cursor there and a small rectangular box appeared with the name 'NATO jetty', a legacy from before the facility's closure when Allied navies needed to know the best times for approaching and leaving the loch.

He clicked on the box and the website asked him whether he wanted historical data or a tide prediction. He opened the calendar icon and selected the year Violet was born and a week either side of 10 September. According to Violet, that was the day the hat and bag were put into the sea. Two seven-day graphs filled his screen, one above the other, separated by grids of numbers. Each graph appeared as a series of blue finger-like spikes. The peak of each spike represented high tide: the base, low tide. On the first graph, the spikes grew longer day by day, the high tides climbing higher, the low tides becoming lower and the cycle advancing towards the highest and lowest tides of all, spring tides. On the second graph they did the opposite as the relative positions of the moon and the sun changed, their gravitational influence on the sea lessening as they moved out of alignment. The tenth was the first day of the second graph. At 8 a.m., the time the hat and the bag went into the water, the flood tide was already flowing, building to a peak one hour and fifty minutes later. According to the graph, it reached a height of 5.2 metres.

Cal started an up-to-date search for the next seven days, this time selecting a tide prediction. When the graph displayed, he could see that the next high tide would be that evening at 17.17. It would reach 4.6 metres, lower than he'd hoped. Still, it would give him an idea. It was past noon now: he'd wait for exactly the same stage, until one hour and fifty minutes before its peak. It'd mean kicking his heels until 15.27.

Next, he called up his ocean database for information about the wind. That gave him columns of figures going back a century: wind speeds and directions for the entire North Atlantic. He searched back twenty-six years to 10 September. There had been a southerly breeze on the coast around Ullapool, ten miles per hour becoming fifteen during the afternoon and moderating to five by nightfall. According to his live weather feed, the breeze today was south-westerly and lighter at five miles per hour. Cal studied a large-scale map of the Poltown area. If anything, he thought, the wind direction today was more likely to push a hat or a bag ashore in North Bay than the one more than a quarter of a century before.

He checked the forward tide data: the new moon was in three days. At 07.14 that morning there would be another high tide of 5.2 metres, the same as the one all those years ago. He brought up the weather prediction. The forecast was unchanged for the rest of the week, an Indian summer they were calling it: highs of seventeen or eighteen degrees in the middle of the day; long sunny periods; clearing skies at night, the temperature falling sharply after sunset; light winds, between five and fifteen miles an hour; shifting from south to south-west. If the forecast was right, there would be three days of more or less similar conditions. If he needed to, he could test the currents again.

His phone rang.

'Cal.' Violet dropped her voice to a whisper. 'Mrs Anderson has just started making me lunch, I'm going to be here for ages. I'm sorry.'

'Don't worry,' he said. 'Violet, I need some information from you.'

'OK.' She sounded wary.

'How did the hat and the bag get into the water?'

'Someone put them there.'

'How far out?'

'I don't know. Whoever it was went deep enough to swim.'

'Is there anything else you can tell me?'

'Only that it was a woman . . .' She hesitated. 'Sorry, Cal, I've got to go.'

Cal wasn't sure if Mrs Anderson had come back into the room or if Violet was protecting secrets.

21

On the map, North Bay's outline resembled a gargoyle. Its northern headland had the appearance of a large, bony nose. The southern jutted like a protruding and sharp chin and the bay itself took the form of a toothless mouth which could no longer open wide. Standing on the hooked nose, Cal estimated the channel between the tip of the northern headland and the protrusion of the chin to be less than sixty metres, a narrow opening for flotsam travelling north-east with the flood tide and returning on the ebb. In this and other respects, North Bay was dissimilar to its southern neighbour. It was sheltered, exposed only to westerlies, with a small beach which sloped into the sea and was protected on the landward side by a collar of boulders. South Bay, by contrast, was open to the elements, vulnerable to any wind between south-west and north-west, with a beach which was wide, flat and long. Instead of boulders, its sweep of sand was bordered by low-lying dunes.

A length of blue rope caught Cal's attention. It was marooned in a stagnant pool among rocks below him. He cast around for more debris, noticing a section of white plastic piping in a tangle of seaweed by the shore. Otherwise the northern headland appeared almost free of flotsam and litter. He walked round the bay, following the high-water mark across the beach, treading on a blue-and-black mosaic of broken mussel shells. Now on the southern shore, he passed a detergent bottle, some bleached wooden planks, sections of rope, the remains of a lobster pot, an orange buoy (which was half-buried under seaweed) as well as two white carrier bags. Considering Duncan Boyd only cleared the neighbouring beach, there was little enough. Still, there was more debris at this part of North Bay than any other: support for Cal's theory about the possibility of a slack water eddy spinning into the open mouth and of the breeze nudging flotsam ashore where the eddy's tail came closest to land, near to where he was standing. He made a mental note to quiz Duncan about whether North Bay had altered much in the last twenty-six years; whether the twin headlands had eroded significantly; whether any other changes had affected the flow of the tides; whether more flotsam washed up on the small beach then than now.

He climbed a chute of loose stones to the top of the south headland, a plateau of grass interspersed with grey slabs of rock. His new vantage point provided a view of South Bay, the dunes and the road end where he had left his pick-up.

Another vehicle was parked there too and three men were walking in his direction. As he watched, they spread out. One stayed on the dune path, the other two on the beach but fifty metres apart. By the way they were walking – their attitude of intent – he knew they were coming for him. It was like watching the closing of a net. Rather than going to meet them or attempting an escape, he stayed where he was. His watchful inactivity seemed to unnerve the two beach-walkers. They came together and parted again; and the man on the path waved at them and shouted. At least Cal knew who gave the orders, who led this little gang. He crouched and picked at the grass, as if he didn't really have a concern about the confrontation to come. Out of the corner of his eye he saw the two from the beach climb the slope of the headland.

By then his only escape was the sea.

Violet refused a second helping by saying how delicious lunch was. 'Shepherd's pie is my favourite.'

The compliment elicited a quick smile from Mrs Anderson. 'I'm so glad you liked it.'

Violet drank some water and, returning the glass to the table, asked if Mrs Anderson might be able to help her with something.

'If I can, dear,' she replied. 'What is it?'

'Well,' Violet seemed embarrassed. 'It's silly really, but one of my mother's childhood friends lived here for a time and I've always been curious about her. She stayed at Orasaigh Cottage – that's why I booked in there – and one bright sunny day she decided to kill herself by walking into the sea.'

Mrs Anderson said, 'You mean Megan Bates.'

'Yes. Did you know her?'

Mrs Anderson nodded a few times as though the name was coming back to her from the dim past. 'I didn't know her well but I knew who she was. Everyone did.'

'I grew up hearing my mother's stories about her and I

could never work out why a woman of thirty-three, who had so much to live for, would kill herself. What made her do that?'

Mrs Anderson sighed, 'It's always been a mystery.' Then, after a shake of her head: 'You've met Duncan Boyd, haven't you?'

'I have,' Violet replied.

'Ask him about Megan Bates. People say he knew her quite well.' Mrs Anderson put on a disapproving frown at finding herself passing on tittle-tattle. 'Ask him if you can see her things.'

'What things?' Violet asked.

'Her clothes, her possessions; furniture and some books, I think.' Mrs Anderson sounded unsure.

Violet looked shocked at the revelation.

'Oh dear, have I said something wrong?'

'No, not at all . . .' Violet said quickly before asking in a puzzled voice, 'Her clothes? Why would he have those?'

'Apparently, Duncan cleared Orasaigh Cottage after Megan's death,' Mrs Anderson continued. 'I don't know whose idea that was. Diana Ritchie's, I suppose.' She pursed her lips in silent criticism.

'Go on,' Violet urged.

Mrs Anderson sighed once more, as though Violet was dragging it out of her. 'Well, you know Duncan was suspected of killing her?'

'No, I didn't!'

'That was before the police announced she'd committed suicide.' Mrs Anderson made a face.

'You don't think she did kill herself.'

'Oh, I don't know if she did or not.' Mrs Anderson stared out of the window, as though looking for the answer. 'There were whispers about suicide being a convenient outcome for the Turnbulls. They didn't want police taking Poltown apart in a murder inquiry, especially not police from outside this area, detectives from Inverness who wouldn't have known the set-up here.'

'Because the police would have found something?'

Mrs Anderson closed and opened her eyes. That's what people were saying, the gesture meant.

'Could Duncan have killed her?' Violet asked.

'I can't imagine he did,' Mrs Anderson replied. 'Though . . .' She'd waited long enough. The time had come to tell Violet.

'What?'

Cal pulled at the grass, throwing pieces into the air as if he was still more interested in the strength of the wind than the three men who were closing in on him. Only when the leader of the trio stopped ten metres away did Cal look up.

'Mr Turnbull wants you out of Poltown.'

Cal glanced at the owner of the voice; then at his side-kicks. They were all of similar age and appearance; Poltown's version of rent-a-thug. Cal had seen similar at the public meeting. The two to his right had muscled necks and sloping shoulders; the one in front, the leader, was taller, leaner and bow-legged. His hair was cropped short, another feature of the breed, and his face was flushed. Not, Cal guessed, from exertion but from an adrenalin rush.

'Mr Turnbull?' Cal said, as if to ask *Who might he be to say whether I can stay or leave?*

The leader stared past Cal, out to sea. Cal wondered if it was a pose he'd been practising in the mirror: studied nonchalance. 'You know who he is and he knows who you are, Mr McGill.'

Cal tore at more grass. How had Turnbull discovered his name? Had someone checked out his vehicle number, someone with friends in the police? He thought of Davie at the shop. Had it been him?

'Mr Turnbull knows the kind of work you do. He doesn't want you here, doesn't want you meddling in something that isn't your business.' He nodded to his sidekicks. 'Tam, you tell him . . .'

The thug closest to Cal swaggered, as though he'd become a favoured son. 'People do what Mr Turnbull tells them.' He tried for menace but his light voice let him down.

The leader shouted again. 'That's it, Tam. Show Mr McGill what'll happen to his pretty face if our paths meet again.' Tam screwed up his right fist and punched it into the palm of his other hand.

'You've been watching too many bad films,' Cal said. Tam took a step towards him.

'That'll do for now, Tam,' the leader shouted. 'Later. You'll get your chance later. Don't say you weren't warned, Mr McGill. You're out of here. You've got till eight o'clock, then Tam's going to come looking for you.'

Mrs Anderson put down her knife and fork. She took a sip of water. 'It's one thing Duncan taking a dead woman's things if he could make use of them . . .' She pressed her lips together, making Violet aware of her distaste at having to discuss such matters. 'But clothes . . . what could he want with them?' She glanced at Violet, watching for her reaction, before carrying on, making sure of her timing. 'Or her hat and bag . . .' She lifted up her eyes in bewilderment.

'What hat and bag?'

'The ones that came ashore, the ones Duncan said he found in North Bay.'

'He's got *those*?'

'Yes, that's what I mean.'

'Who let him have them?'

'The police had no more use for them, once they'd *decided* on suicide.' Mrs Anderson loaded 'decided' with cynicism. 'Megan didn't have any next of kin so they brought the hat and bag to Brae – they knew Mr William was the father of the child Megan had been carrying.' Mrs Anderson slid her eyes in Violet's direction, then away again. 'Diana answered the door when the police called. I don't think she ever told Mr William, but she took the hat and bag and gave them to Duncan with all of Megan's other possessions.'

Violet stared at her. 'He's still got them?'

'I imagine so.' She paused: another look of distaste. 'According to people in the village,' she continued hesitantly, 'he keeps a room upstairs in her memory. Her things are there. Apparently some boys were in the house for a dare and they found the room . . . all neat and tidy.'

Mrs Anderson sniffed. 'The only part of the house that is, people say.'

Violet put down her napkin, excused herself and hurried to the door.

The last time Violet had been in Mrs Anderson's house, she had been a tiny baby, her face screwed up and crying, blood smeared over her and on Diana. 'So much blood,' Mrs Anderson said quietly as Violet ran along the track beside the walled garden.

Cal phoned Violet and left a message to ring him when she left Mrs Anderson's. Afterwards, he wondered whether he should have warned her to keep off the Poltown road in case Turnbull was looking for her too. Perhaps he had already found her – had it been his thug who attacked her after the meeting? Violence, or the threat of violence, seemed to be Turnbull's way.

Cal waited for Tam and co. to drive off before dropping down the flank of the headland to South Bay. Apart from worrying about Violet, he was also concerned about the pick-up, whether his departing visitors had taken the opportunity to show him something of their destructive capabilities. But, when he arrived at the road end, the vehicle appeared to be untouched. Looking through the windows, his laptop, cameras, binoculars and other equipment were as he'd left them on the back seat. He checked the tyres but none had been slashed or damaged. By now it was after 3 p.m. In less than half an hour the tide would be perfect.

Among the disorderly jumble in the pick-up he found a waterproof bag with a strap hanging from one corner. He packed it with eight of the oranges he'd bought, leaving two behind. He stripped to his boxers, then crossed the beach to the sea. When he was in the shallows he put his right foot through the bag's strap and pulled it above his knee. After tightening it, he removed two oranges and waded out until the water was lapping around his thighs. In case the woman had discarded her hat and bag straight away, he dropped one orange there and the next a little deeper. The first gave an impression of a nervous child on a swimming lesson. It moved closer to Cal. The other orange drifted away, parallel to the shore.

How far did she wade before swimming? How far did she swim? How strong was she? What distance could she have gone? The last two were questions he never asked his clients, not any more. They caused too much distress. His clients imagined their son, daughter, husband or wife fighting for life, swimming until their strength was spent, dying from exhaustion and in despair. Now he tried to find out the answers other ways, limiting his questions to whether the missing person could swim and whether a life jacket had been worn. Other factors affecting the distance someone might travel before death he researched for himself: water temperature, weather and the strength of tidal currents. Also, he avoided discussing what might happen after death. In his experience, his clients imagined the body floating, the water lapping: peace at last. When often it sank and sometimes remained sunk. Mostly, it returned to the surface some days or weeks later, the gases of decomposition bringing buoyancy. On this detail, Cal generally said nothing.

He swam breast stroke, then a slow crawl. He counted to fifty before stopping. Treading water, he reached for the bag and removed two more oranges. He released them one after the other, letting them bob to the surface. He repeated the process twice more before returning to the beach and trying to recall when he'd last used oranges for research. Before studying oceanography at the Scottish Marine Institute near Oban, he remembered reading an American school text about ocean currents and a formula for measuring their speed by using oranges. They were easily available, cheap, biodegradable as well as visible, all of which appealed to him then. And they worked.

Back ashore, he removed the empty bag from his leg and walked across the sand. He was dry by the time he opened the pick-up's back door. Finding his binoculars, he spotted two of the oranges: one close in and in danger of beaching, another a hundred metres offshore. He put on jeans, a cotton shirt and trainers before starting back towards North Bay. On the way he worked out how long the oranges should take to reach the gargoyle's mouth.

The distance was about a kilometre. He estimated the tidal current at two to four knots. In theory one of the oranges could be off North Bay in eight minutes or so. But there'd be eddies on the way and other invisible obstacles. Sitting against a rock, he spotted two oranges, both a few hundred metres away, still off South Bay. He marked them against the end of the point to track their progress. Another sweep with the binoculars located one more, nearer shore. It looked on course to pass close by the headland. Cal checked the time. It was 16.47. He hoped one orange would be off the point at 17.17, just as the tide reached its peak and the maximum volume of water was piling up against the headland. It was then an eddy might form and curl into the bay, carrying any flotsam with it. His phone beeped, his screen lit up. Violet had sent a text. She was on her way. Apologies, she added. She'd left Mrs Anderson and was calling on Duncan Boyd. She was crossing the field to his farm. Cal wondered why, but he was thankful she hadn't run into Tam and the gang.

He messaged back:

> I'm at North Bay. Text when
> you're leaving Boyd's Farm.
> I'll look out for you.

The lunch was still on the table; the spoon in the shepherd's pie, the gravy congealed on Violet's dirty plate as well as Mrs Anderson's; the glasses of water where they'd left them, one half-empty, the other hardly touched. The napkins too: Violet's folded and placed beside her clean knife; Mrs Anderson's sitting like a collapsed tent where she'd dropped it as Violet abruptly excused herself. Mrs Anderson watched her go and hadn't moved since, apart from the tremor of a pulse in her neck, an occasional flicker of her eyelids and her left hand kneading its companion on her lap. Like good food, some things were best savoured slowly; the thought of Violet Wells claiming back her mother's belongings, of her taking them from

Duncan, being tastier than the untouched lemon and bramble pudding.

So Mrs Anderson remained in her seat while her mind fluttered restlessly, reviewing her encounter with Violet, teasing at it for errors. Could she have phrased things better? Had her tone been right? Had she sounded sufficiently surprised at Violet's interest in Megan Bates; sufficiently credulous at Violet's 'mother' being a 'childhood friend' of Megan's; appropriately reticent but yet matter-of-fact about Mr William's affair and Megan's pregnancy? Should she have broached the subject of Megan's clothes and her other possessions in the way she had?

Mrs Anderson looked at the kitchen clock.

Tick-tock. Soon the bomb would go off.

22

The clap and clatter of pigeon wings resonated around the courtyard. The birds burst from a broken skylight and were flying in frantic loops and circles above Violet's head. 'Mr Boyd. It's Violet.' She spun around, directing her shouts at one side of the steading, then at another. 'Duncan . . . Mr Boyd. Where are you?'

On first meeting he'd seemed so guileless, a 'poor soul', as her friend Hilary might say. Harmless, Violet had thought, even sweet in his way. Mrs Anderson's distaste and the shock of hearing that Duncan had her mother's possessions had changed Violet's mind. Like a chill, the atmosphere of the steading was also seeping into her bones. The place was sinister, she shuddered, and so was the man who had brought it to such a state of ruination. Like Poltown, she thought, where nothing was what it seemed.

'Where are you?' she said again, as though playing hide-and-seek with a malevolent child. She backed across the yard towards the farmhouse door. It was ajar. 'Duncan?' she inquired into the gap between door and jamb and stepped away, as if expecting him to jump out.

She jumped instead, in anticipation.

'Where are you?' she asked again softly.

'Hello.' Her knuckles rapped on the wood of the door. She pushed it open. 'Duncan. It's Violet. Are you there?'

She went inside.

The smell was what assailed her first – cats – then the mess. She cupped a hand over her nose to stop herself gagging and picked her way across the porch. The floor was strewn with old and muddy boots and lined with scuffed newspapers on which were three chipped enamel plates covered with stale and smelly scraps of food. A black-and-white cat was lying on an old kitchen chair. It watched her, blinked and started to purr as Violet disappeared into the gloom of a passageway. She took a deep breath. Stale air: it tasted of decay, dustiness and something worse. She imagined powdered white bones. 'I love you, Anna,' she whispered, wishing she was back in Glasgow with her daughter, wishing she was anywhere but here.

She emerged into a rectangular hallway, slowly, a step at a time, until she was sure she was alone. She looked at the chipped flagstones, at the broken lumps of plaster scattered across the floor, at the peeling and cratered walls, the cracked ceiling, at the stairs to her right.

Mrs Anderson had said the room was upstairs.

She climbed them two at a time. At the top she experienced something approaching exhilaration. Across the landing, against the far wall, under a faded watercolour of a fishing boat on a stormy sea, was a chest of drawers. Violet glanced to its left, at the closed door.

A name was stencilled on it: *Megan*.

She gasped.

Until then, her mother's name had belonged in the past – in the conversations Violet had had, in the yellowing newspaper cuttings given to her by Mr Anwar. Seeing it on the door was the first time she'd encountered it in the present. How hope waited for just such a thing, how quick it was to flare.

She had to remind herself, *she's dead, she's dead, she's dead*, as she crossed the landing to the unpainted wooden door. Cracks ran up and down the grain and one was wide enough for Violet to feel the faintest puff of fresh air on her cheek. She turned the knob, the door opening on to a tidy and well-furnished room. What would be unremarkable in any other house was a shock among the chaos of Boyd's Farm. Violet stood in the doorway transfixed, her eyes skipping from one item of furniture to the next. Pretty floral curtains flapped in the draught from an open window. Below, there was a mahogany dressing table, bleached by the sun, on which were laid out a hairbrush, hand mirror, scent and nail-varnish bottles as well as a box of tissues. To the left of the dressing table was a wardrobe and on the opposite wall an iron bedstead, the bed made up and with a patterned cover, folded back. A teddy bear reclined against a white pillow. A book was on the bedside table. A fabric bookmark extended from its pages. Was it hers?

'She's dead,' Violet repeated. Everything in the room suggested otherwise, that her mother had gone out but would soon be coming back.

After stepping inside, she shut the door quietly but grabbed at the handle as soon as she'd let go because she had to support herself on something. Behind the door was a cot, the mattress sealed in the manufacturer's wrapping. A large brown-paper-wrapped parcel tied with string rested against the headboard. Someone had written 'for baby'. Violet reached for the side of the cot. Her fingers slid over the tailboard to the side rail. Then she touched the parcel. Instead of wasting time undoing the knot, she slipped off the string and exposed the dark brown of the paper underneath. The remainder was bleached, indicating how long ago the parcel had been wrapped, how long it had been there. After peeling away three layers of paper, Violet examined the contents: six old-fashioned cotton nappies, two sleep suits, two white cot sheets. Everything in white, she imagined, because her mother hadn't known whether her baby would be a boy or a girl.

Looking under the cot, Violet found an upturned baby bath and a nappy bucket.

She stared about her, her face set in an expression of puzzlement, her fingers kneading the soft fabric of the sleep suits. She was looking for an explanation for this room and why it was clean and aired, the bed made, everything neat, tidy and welcoming, as though Megan Bates, her mother, lived there. Why, Violet asked again, when the rest of the house was falling down?

She approached the wardrobe and turned the key. The dark-wood doors opened together. On the left were a series of drawers with half-moon handholds; on the right, a rail from which hung a modest collection of dresses and jackets. Violet was surprised by how few there were and by their muted colours, a mixture of creams, greens and browns. Not only had she expected her mother's wardrobe, if that was what it was, to be full to bursting, but also for her to have a collection of brightly coloured clothes to match her reputation. Violet's impression of her mother had been formed by snatches of information – the white dress and the sun hat she had worn the day she disappeared and the eyewitness Mrs Armitage's comment to the police about her being sure it was Megan Bates because 'no one else wears summer dresses in Poltown'. Neither of these suggested to Violet that her mother had been anything other than showy.

The wardrobe lent a different impression and left Violet confused as well as ashamed of her previous rush to judgement.

She touched a dress, then another and another until she had stroked them all, her fingers sampling the fabrics, this one silk, that cotton, another wool. She registered which was which, though her thoughts were on another attribute of these clothes, how once they would have touched her mother's skin, how Violet's fingers were a slither of fabric away, how this was as close as she would ever come to her flesh and blood.

She lifted out a cream silk dress. The style, like the colour, was restrained: a full skirt and a high-buttoned neck. Violet held it against her, looking in the mirror on the back of the wardrobe door to see whether it suited her too, whether it fitted. She checked the label before returning the dress to the wardrobe – size ten – and the discovery led Violet to examine the labels of the other skirts and dresses. Apart from two maternity dresses which she uncovered in the search, her mother's clothes were Violet's size.

Having entered the room imagining mother and daughter to be different from each other, she found with every discovery her opinion shifting until she arrived at the conclusion that, perhaps, they weren't dissimilar at all. A voice warned her of the emotional danger of veering from one impression to another on such flimsy evidence.

But despite its cautionary effect, Violet experienced a deep-seated and, in the circumstances, odd sensation; one that was close to happiness. In every child there was a desire to belong: in Violet's case it had stayed into adulthood.

She let her hand run along the clothes, feeling again the different textures, the hangers knocking against each other on the rail, before turning to the wardrobe's internal drawers. She removed shirts and cardigans, finding folded-away jeans and underwear, none of it immodest or lacy, and she experienced another shift in her emotions, to anger. She was hurt for her mother, whose mistake had been to fall for a married man and to have become pregnant by him and to have lived on the fringes of a small and narrow-minded community which had an appetite for gossip.

She wandered over to the bed, touched the teddy bear, and noticed the slight wear around its ears and nose. She speculated on its age, whether it would have been her mother's companion from childhood, whether it would have been in worse condition if it had been. She glanced at the bedside table, at the book there. As with everything else she'd seen, her preference was to observe and only afterwards to touch, to acclimatize herself to her mother's possessions a sense at a time. The book's title, written in ornate gold lettering, was *The Far Pavilions* by M. M. Kaye. The illustration gave the impression of the novel being an eastern romance – accurately so, as Violet discovered when she read the cover blurb: 'The famous story of love and war in nineteenth-century India – now a sumptuous screen production.' She opened it at the bookmark, which had been left on page 564, the start of chapter 39. She scanned the text before turning back a page and reading the final three paragraphs of the previous chapter and wondering if they had been the last her mother had ever read. Another impression of her mother formed, of a woman with a romantic streak, who chose to live in isolation. Why?

Violet crossed to the dressing table and sat at the stool. She picked up the hand mirror and watched her reflection, imagining her mother doing the same. She examined the bristles of her mother's hairbrush, looking for stray hairs, disappointed to discover there weren't any. Next, she investigated one of the dressing table's two drawers, observed the tidy array of jars, tubes and bottles, before opening the other. It contained a hairdryer and tortoiseshell hairclips. For a time she was distracted, looking around the room. Then she stood on the stool and felt along the top of the wardrobe. It wasn't level as she'd thought but recessed. Her fingers touched what felt like a cardboard box. She put it on the bed before getting back on the stool. Reaching up, she found another box, bigger and squarer than the first. Placing that on the bed beside its companion, she noticed how little dust there was on them. Either Duncan must have put them on the wardrobe recently or else he must take them down regularly to clean them.

She took a deep breath, as if preparing for a shock.

The lid of the bigger box slid off easily. Inside was a raffia sun hat. It had a red ribbon tied around its broad brim. In places, where the ribbon was stained with water marks, the red had turned to pink streaked with brown.

Violet removed the other lid. Lying in that box was a leather shoulder bag, the strap still attached, the leather blackened and cracked.

All she could think about now was her mother dying and these *objects* surviving. She lashed out at the lids, the boxes and their contents, sending them hurtling from the bed and crashing on the floor.

Afterwards, shocked at what she had done, she stared at the boxes, at the bedcover and at the new creases in it. She straightened them, smoothing the material with her hands, and checked to make sure the door was still closed. Next she removed her mobile phone from her pocket and took photographs of the hat and the bag. Then she went around the room, tidying, wrapping up the nappies and sleep suits, packing up the boxes, returning them to their hiding place, carrying the stool back to the dressing table, and pulling at the wardrobe door to make sure it was locked. She crossed the room and checked everything again. The stool looked to be too far from the dressing table and at the wrong angle. So she adjusted it. At the door she turned the handle and paused, listening. Then she slipped from the room on to the landing.

She crossed to the stairs, descending slowly, checking the ground floor below as it came into view. When she was sure she was alone, she ran across the hall to the back corridor. She stopped by the rear porch. The cat had gone from the chair. Did that mean that Duncan was back? Did it mean anything? She ran again, across the steading courtyard and out into the field. She imagined Duncan pursuing her, shambling and lumbering like a creature in a horror movie. At the stone pillars, safe at last, she stopped and looked back.

'Oh my God,' she gasped in shock. 'You were there all the time.'

Duncan stood still, like a pillar himself, at the entrance to the steading two hundred metres away, watching her.

'What kind of creep are you?' Violet whispered.

23

At Violet's request, Cal pulled off the road below the crest of the ridge, where Stuart the bus driver had introduced her to Orasaigh Island, South Bay and North Bay, the landmarks of her mother's life and death. She'd be five or ten minutes, she said, opening her door. Her meaning was clear. She'd rather be alone.

'Take as long as you want,' Cal answered. He watched her in his door mirror. She stopped at the edge of the passing place: a slight figure against a huge vista of land, sea and sky. An appropriate backdrop, he thought, since Violet had the demeanour of someone taking on the world.

When she had appeared at South Bay, after her visit to Boyd's Farm, she'd seemed withdrawn, even frightened. He'd asked if she was all right. Had something happened? Yes, she replied, but she couldn't talk about it, something shocking. Could they go somewhere else, away from Poltown? She needed time to think. Cal wondered whether she'd met Turnbull's thugs or had a further encounter with the man who'd attacked her, if there was a difference. In the circumstances, getting her away from Poltown sounded like a good idea.

He checked his mirror again. She hadn't moved. Cal opened his door and walked towards her. She glanced back at him and shook her head, as if to stop him as well as his questions.

He carried on anyway. 'While you were with Mrs Anderson, I went to North Bay to look around and I had a visit.'

'Who from?'

'Three men. They told me to leave Poltown.' He waited before adding, 'I was just wondering if they're acquaintances of your friend from last night. The guy who was just trying it on . . .'

She closed her eyes. 'I didn't want this to happen, for you to be involved.'

'Well, it's a bit late for that.' He sounded impatient, his way of letting her know he wasn't prepared to put up with her secrets for ever. 'So what did that guy want? Do you know?'

She slumped with resignation. 'He told me to stop asking questions about things that didn't concern me or I'd get hurt. Then you chased him away.' She wiped her hand across her mouth, remembering the spray of saliva. 'He called me a nosy bitch and then he spat in my face. Ugh.'

Cal looked at the view. 'So, what questions have you been asking?'

'You know.'

He pulled a face. 'About a woman who put a hat and a bag into the sea that turned up the next day in North Bay in 1983 . . .' He glanced at Violet. 'Is that it?'

'The woman was my mother,' she said. 'She was never seen again. She died.'

'I'm sorry.' Cal watched Violet. 'How did she die? Did she drown? Did she take her own life?'

'I don't know. I just don't know.'

'Tell me what you do know.'

She pointed out the faint continuous line of the coastal path from Orasaigh, her finger following it across the grass behind Boyd's steading to South Bay. She indicated the headland, where the path seemed to end. The path went into a gully there, she said, between two sheets of rock, before descending to the beach.

'Around 8 a.m. on Saturday, 10 September 1983,' Violet continued, 'my mother went along that path. She was wearing a white dress and a sun hat – it had red ribbon around the brim – and she had a leather bag over her shoulder. It was a route she took every morning, whenever she could, whenever the tide allowed her to leave the island.'

'She lived on Orasaigh?'

'Yes. In the cottage . . .' She looked away, before he could catch her eye. Cal nodded, as though things were beginning to make some kind of sense.

Violet went on: 'She was seen on the path by a woman who was walking her dog on the Poltown road. The same woman saw her again a short time later. By then my mother was on the beach, at the edge of the water. The woman told police she didn't think it unusual. She'd seen her there often. It was normal for her to paddle or swim but that morning she kept on walking until she disappeared. The woman raised the alarm but my mother wasn't seen again. Her hat and bag turned up the next day. Duncan Boyd found them. A day or two later a letter she'd written came to light. It had been posted just before she died. According to the police, it was a suicide note. The officer in charge of the investigation told newspapers she had taken her own life "on the balance of probabilities". All the usual checks were made to see if she'd taken her passport, money, make-up, clothes . . .'

'She hadn't?'

'Her passport and purse were found in her bag.'

Violet studied the panorama in front of her as if it concealed the clue to solving the mystery. 'She'd been pregnant, almost full-term,' she said. 'The letter was to the child's father. His name was William Ritchie, a big-shot lawyer who worked in Edinburgh during the week and spent weekends here. He owned Brae House and Orasaigh Cottage. My mother was his tenant as well as his lover.' She broke off before adding, 'He was married. Of course. He's dead now, buried in the graveyard.' She directed Cal's attention to the church.

'Pregnant,' Cal repeated it, trying to understand the consequences. 'So the baby died too?'

'That's what the police thought.'

'You don't?'

'No. She'd already given birth. The night before my mother's death, her baby was abandoned at Raigmore Hospital in Inverness. The child was left at the main door, just before midnight, in a cardboard box, wrapped only in towels. There was no note, nothing to identify the child apart from an envelope taped to the side of the box. Inside was a small rectangular section of a cardigan or a jersey, knitted from green wool, and a brooch.'

'So the baby was your brother or sister?'

She put her hand into the pocket of her jeans, removed a small flat box and took out an oval brooch. 'The baby was me. The nurses called me Violet because of this – the flowers are violets.'

Then she took a deep breath. 'I'd better tell you the rest.' And she told Cal about Mr Anwar, about the anonymous letter that had been sent to his office and the newspaper photograph of her mother wearing the brooch, and about Violet's shock at discovering she was dead. 'I thought I'd find her; sooner or later, if I kept looking. I never thought she was dead. Not ever. Not once.'

A smile faded on her lips, as though she'd been a fool. 'I got into the habit of taking the brooch with me. I used to put it on if I was going out into a crowd or shopping, or if I saw someone I thought might be her. I'd walk towards her so she'd be able to see the brooch. I thought I'd be able to tell by her reaction whether she'd seen it before.' She paused. 'You see, I was so certain she was alive. Some days I could feel her.' She pressed her right hand against her stomach. 'Here.'

'Did she leave you at the hospital, come back to Poltown and walk into the sea?'

'It's possible.' Her voice broke. 'Perhaps she did. Perhaps she was just waiting for me to be born before drowning herself, so she didn't kill me too . . .'

'Why would she, though?'

'Revenge, a broken heart,' she said. 'William Ritchie had let her know he wouldn't leave Diana, his wife. In her letter my mother talked about making it impossible for him to see her or the baby again.'

Cal said, 'So she abandoned you and killed herself.'

'But it doesn't make sense. Didn't you say that most bodies wash ashore in time? How did she know hers wouldn't?'

'What do you mean?'

'Because if her body had come ashore, the police would have known she wasn't carrying a baby. They would have looked for me and found me. So she wouldn't have kept William Ritchie from seeing the baby.'

For a while, neither spoke. Violet stared at the brooch and Cal watched the sea sparkling blue in South Bay. Eventually, he said, 'On a day like this it's hard to imagine anything bad happening here.'

Violet let out a bitter laugh. 'That's what I thought when I saw it first. I thought it was heaven.'

She told him about her meeting with former Chief Superintendent Robert Yellowlees, who had been an inspector at the time of her mother's disappearance. 'I made a mistake. I thought if I showed him the letter Mr Anwar brought me, he would realize something terrible had gone wrong, that he'd want to put it right.'

'What did he do?'

'He made a complaint about Mr Anwar, about me harassing him. Mr Anwar has been suspended. Mrs Anderson told me some people thought the police closed down the inquiry into my mother's disappearance as quickly as they could because a murder inquiry would have disrupted the Turnbulls' business operations. The way Mr Yellowlees behaved made me think there was something in that.'

'The local police were being paid off?'

'If it had been a murder inquiry, detectives would have come from Inverness. That's what Mrs Anderson said.'

'Did she say anything else?'

'Have you been into Duncan's house?'

'Yes, once, briefly, when he was letting me see his flotsam collection,' Cal replied.

217

'Like the rest of the place, it's falling to pieces, except for one room, an upstairs bedroom. My mother's name is on the door.'

'Megan? Is that your mother?'

'Yes. Megan Bates.'

'I've seen that room.'

'Did you go in?'

'I just looked in the door. I thought Duncan might be there . . . He was upset. I didn't know where he had gone.'

'All of my mother's things from Orasaigh Cottage are there; furniture, her clothes, her make-up, even the cot she bought for me.'

'Why has Duncan got them?' Cal looked surprised.

'According to Mrs Anderson, Diana Ritchie asked him to clear out the cottage after my mother's death.' She took a deep breath. 'Duncan told me he loved my mother. But she couldn't have loved him, could she?'

'I don't know.'

'Cal?'

'What?'

'Mrs Anderson said the police suspected Duncan of killing my mother . . . until her suicide letter turned up.'

'Duncan, a disappointed lover, a crime of passion, is that what they thought?'

'I think so. And there's something else. Duncan has the bag and the hat.'

'The ones that washed up in North Bay?'

She folded her arms and shuddered, as if she was suddenly cold. 'Why has he still got them, Cal? Why has he kept her clothes, everything?'

'It's odd. He's odd. Maybe it's no more than that.'

She'd thought that too but now she'd changed her mind.

'He makes my skin crawl.' She shuddered again. 'He was watching me, just now when I was walking away from the farmhouse. He was standing there. I've never been so scared.' Every time she thought about him now she imagined his childish smirk. Didn't small boys look like that when they were pulling the legs from a frog or piercing a living butterfly with a pin or throwing a kitten into a pond to watch it drown? Was that what he did to her mother? At school, there were boys with grotesque collections of sad little corpses, boys who recorded the deaths of their victims, kept diaries, private inventories of suffering. Was that why Duncan kept her things?

'Don't you see?' she said to Cal. 'That's why he smiles the way he does. He's smiling because he's fooled everyone. Duncan, the idiot, has taken everyone in. He keeps her room like that because he's a cruel little boy cleaning his private trophy cabinet.'

Cal considered what she had told him and whether he should mention his mother's friendship long ago with Diana Ritchie, or explain his sympathy for Duncan, one beachcomber's affinity for another, his instinct for underdogs. Instead he said, 'Well, someone knows what happened. Whoever wrote that letter Mr Anwar gave you . . . and that wasn't Duncan, not if he killed your mother. Why would he want you back here asking awkward questions?'

'But who, then, and why, after twenty-six years?'

'Guilt, bad conscience, somebody sick or old putting

things right before they die. There could be any number of reasons. The anniversary was last week.'

'Maybe it is as simple as that.' She sounded as though she hoped so.

'But you don't think it's any of those.'

'I've been brought to Poltown for a reason. I just don't know what it is or who wanted me to come here.'

Cal said, 'So what do you do now?'

'I have to go back down there.' She nodded towards Orasaigh Island and South Bay.

'I thought you wanted to get away for a bit.'

'I thought I did too.'

'If you go back, you know what's going to happen.'

'Some guy's going to be waiting for me.' She looked back at Cal. 'I have no choice.'

Cal said, 'Haven't you forgotten to ask me something?'

'What?'

'When's the next low tide?'

'Sometime tonight?' she guessed.

'It's at 23.45. So what are we going to do until we can get back on to the island?'

24

A blue van idled at the bottom of the track to Gardener's Cottage. Jim Carmichael was debating whether to call in on Mrs Anderson. He knew, from experience, that unexpected visitors were unwelcome. But wouldn't she want to hear the news about Violet Wells? He tried to banish from his mind his old blackface ewe which he had named Mrs A because of her truculent and haughty nature.

Having convinced himself a visit would be all right, he drove up the track thinking how much things had changed since his visit yesterday. Then, he'd been apprehensive about the Turnbulls and what they would require of him to pay off his debts. So far all he'd had to do was drive around putting up posters supporting the wind farm and removing those of the opposition. Since Jim had become a convert to the wind farm cause, it wasn't an imposition. In fact, he liked being involved, hearing the chat when he collected posters from the back of the shop, the campaign's headquarters. He'd also had his eyes opened to the advantages of keeping in with Ross Turnbull, who had won the concession to run the new supermarket that would be built as part of BRC's expansion of Poltown. Ross said his plan was to support local businesses like Jim's smallholding.

Far from debt being his downfall, as he'd feared the last time he'd approached Mrs A's door, he now thought it might be his salvation, if Ross stayed true to his word. Maybe Jim would at last be able to enlarge his flock, or keep more bees to supply the new shop with honey. After he'd paid off the Turnbulls in kind, maybe he'd be able to put money aside for a polytunnel to grow tomatoes, peppers and lettuce. He'd pitch the idea to Ross.

Despite this unexpected turn of events, Jim was distracted. As ever, a new worry arrived in on the heels of the one departing. It was this which brought him to Mrs Anderson, not that he would let her know. So when he pulled up at her door, he was experiencing an undertow of anxiety as well as expecting a cool reception. He knocked, and when there was no reply he peered through the side window of the porch. Although the external door was locked, the inside one was open and Mrs Anderson's walking shoes were beside the boot scrape. Still there was no reply and he wondered what to do, his conviction about the wisdom of this visit draining away.

Perhaps she'd seen him coming. Perhaps she didn't want company.

Just as his nerve was about to fail, it occurred to him she might have fallen. He went to the window on the right of the porch. It was Mrs A's lounge, a room into which he had never been invited, although he'd managed enough glimpses through the open door while carrying her box of groceries into the kitchen to have become familiar with it. Looking through the quartered pane, he was surprised to see the mantelpiece and tables empty of her photographs of William Ritchie and his family. They'd been a feature of the room, if rather a peculiar one since Mrs A had no photographs of her own relatives. Hamish Boyd, who farmed on the other side of the ridge, and his brother Duncan were her first cousins. From the bits and pieces Jim had picked up from Hamish or Duncan over the years, it seemed Mrs A had no time for either of them. In Duncan's case, Jim could understand the antipathy. Not only was he peculiar, but Mrs A had had to suffer as he wrecked Boyd's Farm. If Jim had grown up there, as Mrs A had, he would also have cut himself off from the perpetrator of such destruction. In Jim's opinion, and the opinion of the villagers, the only thing the land was good for was the shed BRC wanted to build there.

Mrs Anderson's frostiness with Hamish was less understandable. Once or twice he had asked Jim about her: whether she was well; if she needed anything; whether he could help. On each occasion Hamish wondered why Mrs Anderson was so unfriendly. How could she live so close by and yet never have met his two children, Margaret and Graeme? Jim had thought it might be rubbing salt into Hamish's wound to mention the proprietorial way Mrs Anderson spoke about 'Mr William', her 'good friend' Diana and 'Miss Alexandra', or how many of their photographs she displayed in her home, as though they were her family.

Jim put his hands to the sides of his face, to shield the window from sunlight so he might see inside more clearly. He noticed the wing chair by the fireplace, the newspaper folded over the arm and the tapestry stool in front: more evidence of Mrs A's presence. Puzzled as well as concerned, he went to the other side of the front porch to look in the kitchen window. To his surprise he saw dirty dishes on the table, and when he pressed closer to the pane he saw Mrs A sitting at the table, quite still, looking straight ahead. He wondered why she hadn't responded to either his knocking or his appearance at the window, which surely she must have noticed. He became more convinced that something awful had happened, so he knocked gently on the glass, called out her name, saying, 'It's only Jim,' in case the noise frightened her.

At first she didn't react. Then she turned her head slowly, her expression altering as it travelled. By the time she was looking at Jim, she was glowering with irritation. Jim was taken aback, but also worried, so he waved and asked if she could let him in. Another scowl crossed her face as she rose from her chair and Jim awaited her arrival with trepidation. It had been a while since he'd felt the edge of her tongue.

From the other side of the door he heard a series of terse exclamations, none of which he could decipher, though he imagined he was the target of them. In anticipation of the tirade to come, he took a step back as Mrs A opened the door. She asked crossly what on earth he wanted and why he was bothering her at this time in the evening. Her mood was so at odds with his last visit that he became apologetic and hopped from foot to foot.

'Stand still, Jim, tell me why you're here.' She swiped at a loose filament of cobweb the setting sun had illuminated.

'I was just passing – I'd taken a delivery to the big house,' he attempted to explain. 'I thought I'd just check how you were.' Jim knew that was another mistake. Nothing was more likely to put her in a bad mood than someone taking an interest, uninvited. 'And I've got some news,' he added uncertainly, hoping for salvation, 'that you'll want to know.'

Her face suggested such a possibility was most unlikely.

'That young woman you were with at the meeting last night . . .' Jim blurted.

Mrs Anderson chewed at her lip. 'Violet Wells, what of her?'

'Well,' Jim said, 'you know I'm doing some work for Turnbull . . . Well, there was talk today about Violet Wells being the daughter of Megan Bates.' Jim looked at Mrs Anderson, hoping the revelation would soften her mood, might even tempt her to share whatever she had heard about the young woman, what she was doing in Poltown. 'She told some retired policeman. He passed it on. The boys at the shop were saying Megan Bates mustn't have killed herself after all, that she must have faked her death and gone off somewhere to bring up the baby.'

Mrs Anderson rubbed at a mark on the windowsill, as though it was more deserving of her attention than Jim. 'I can't imagine you're right, Jim,' she said, still rubbing. 'Violet was here this afternoon and didn't say anything to me. As far as I know, she's here on holiday, just passing through. Now if you don't mind, I've things to be doing.'

After Mrs Anderson closed the door with a firm bang, Jim returned to the van and made a mental note never to drop by unexpectedly again. He felt the gap in his stomach where anxiety was still gnawing at him, a gap that, on any other occasion, Mrs A's cake would have filled. As he drove away he thought of Duncan and wondered whether Violet Wells had told him why she'd come to Poltown, whether, as he suspected, she'd talked to him about Megan Bates. Wasn't that why he'd run from her to North Bay?

~~~

Mrs Anderson cleared the table with practised efficiency. The dirty plates and the used glasses went into the dishwasher, the leftovers scraped into an ovenproof dish for reheating for lunch tomorrow. Anything clean, the cutlery and the side plates, she placed on a tray over which she draped a fresh dishtowel. Her habit was to eat only one proper meal a day, usually lunch, unless she had been awake for most of the night and had slept in. Then she'd have breakfast late and, in the evening, scrambled eggs and baked tomatoes followed by toast and jam. This evening, she'd probably make do with biscuits – fig rolls were her favourite – and a cup of leaf tea, Indian for preference. She found it more soporific than China. She put the teapot beside the kettle, followed by a cup and saucer, then the milk jug and the biscuit tin. The sugar bowl was added as an afterthought and she covered the ensemble with another clean dishtowel to keep the flies away. Then she went to the window, as she did when a storm was approaching, to wait for a drama to unfold.

25

Cal told Violet about the oranges, how some of them would have come ashore by now. 'Where they beach will give me a clue to the currents and eddies, to the forces in play the day your mother went into the sea.'

He climbed into the back of the pick-up, looking for his laptop. 'Ah, found it.' Then he asked Violet to hold on to his spare mobile phone, 'just in case'.

'Just in case what?' she said.

'The battery lasts two or three days,' he said, as though he hadn't heard her. 'Keep it with you.'

'I've already got a phone.'

'I know.'

He turned on his laptop and complained about how slow it was before telling her that smartphones could be adapted for all sorts of unexpected purposes. 'I use that one . . .' He nodded towards the phone in Violet's hand, '. . . for tracking currents. I put it in a waterproof box, attach a drogue so that it has traction in the water and then launch it.' He extended his arm as though pushing the box out to sea. 'Although I have access to data collected by drifters and gliders, the ocean monitoring equipment used by marine institutes, more often than not I need precise information about particular stretches of coastal water which haven't been surveyed. A friend of mine has devised an app for that purpose.'

'How does it work?' she asked.

'It lets me know where it is. It transmits its position.' He passed his laptop to her. 'Do you see the map? See the dot flashing?'

'Yes.'

'That's my phone. When it moves so will the dot. It means I can follow where the currents take it. I can calculate speed, direction and so on.' He put the laptop in his backpack and rummaged around on the back seat, addressing Violet as well as the objects of his search as though coaxing them into being discovered. 'Where are you, water bottles?' Having found them, he started another search for a carton of milk and a carrier bag in which he had bread, cheese and biscuits. One by one he put them into his backpack and concluded that it shouldn't be too heavy. 'Are you ready?' he asked.

'Yes,' she replied. She nodded too, letting Cal know she understood why he had been talking. She realized he was trying to divert her from what he had just said about the phone, the implication; of him being able to track her every move, should she go missing.

'Not,' he said, making light of it, 'that I'm planning to let you out of my sight.'

He returned to rummaging, finding his camera and binoculars, putting one into a pocket of an anorak, the other around his neck.

'I don't have a choice, do I?'

'Not really,' he said.

'But you do?'

'Well, I've chosen.' He backed out of the pick-up. 'Are you coming?'

They walked in single file and in silence, South Bay giving way to North Bay, the forestry on the hill looming at them, until Violet asked where they were going.

'There's something I want to show you,' he said. 'Further up the coast. If we hurry we should be back here by dusk.'

They came to cliffs and Cal stopped to scan the shore below. He moved on, repeating the process every hundred metres. 'There,' he said eventually. 'See that sandbar.' He handed Violet the binoculars. 'There's an orange on it.' As she searched, he explained how he'd put it into the sea in South Bay along with seven others. He'd expected some to come ashore where they were looking. If they carried on for a bit he was certain there would be more, because of the curve of the land, because of its exposure to the wind, light though it was, because of the flow of the current which swept up close to that stretch of coast.

After spotting two more oranges, they returned to North Bay. Scrambling over its rock-strewn collar, he asked if she knew precisely where the hat and the bag came ashore.

'On the beach, I think. That's what I've been told.'

Cal showed her how small the area of sand was, how far back from the bay's mouth, how clean of debris, even seaweed, explaining why. He pointed out the narrow sea entrance, the way the high headlands provided shelter from every wind apart from a westerly, and how even that had a small target to hit; how the tidal current went by the bay at between two and four knots, fast enough to carry debris past the entrance before any wind-assisted divergence could occur.

'What are you saying?' she asked.

'Just that it's unlikely a raffia hat and a leather bag would drift ashore on this beach, and even more unlikely they'd end up together. Come and see.'

They picked their way through the boulders going to the bay's protruding chin. After a while Cal began to point out pieces of flotsam, rope, some netting and a buoy. 'Stuff like this comes ashore here because a slack water eddy spins into the bay after high tide. Flotsam gets carried in.' While Violet watched, he clambered among the rocks, lifting loose seaweed, searching the sea pools. Suddenly he tossed an orange into the air, shouting 'catch' to Violet.

'That's what I mean,' he said as she held the falling object. 'The eddy brought it to this side of the bay, but on the day your mother disappeared, the wind had more south in it. Most likely the hat wouldn't have come in here at all. The wind would have taken it further up the coast.'

'What about the bag?'

'The bag, different weight and lying lower in the water . . . it would have gone more with the tidal current. If it passed close by the mouth of the bay around high tide it might have got caught in the eddy. If it did, this is the place it would most likely have beached, where we're standing now.'

'So they wouldn't have come ashore together?'

'The probability is they wouldn't have come into the bay at all. The bag might have, but both together – that's most unlikely.'

'So how did they get there?'

'Someone could have left them to make it look as

though they had floated ashore.' He didn't know the answer. 'It's also odd her body was never found.'

'Why do you say that?'

'As I've mentioned before, in these waters, at these depths, you'd expect a body to be recovered, if not straight away then after a couple of weeks, once decomposition has brought it to the surface. Out in the deep ocean you might not see it again, but in here, you'd anticipate a body turning up along the coast somewhere.' He looked at Violet. 'That might take a few days, or even a few weeks. A body can travel a fair distance, but sooner or later it would catch an eddy. When your mother went missing, the weather was settled like this. Afterwards, there were gales on and off, south-westerlies as well as westerlies and north-westerlies. She'd have come ashore, more likely than not she would.'

The right-hand side of Violet's face glowed golden in the setting sun. Her mouth pulled at the corners. At length she said, 'What you're saying doesn't necessarily prove anything, does it?'

'No. I'm always working with best guesses. Tracking at sea is an imprecise science.'

Violet lobbed the orange into the water. It splashed before bobbing to the surface.

'Although . . .' Cal began.

'Go on,' Violet said.

'Well, if Duncan had been involved in her disappearance he wouldn't have tried to cover it up by leaving her hat and the bag on the beach over there.'

'Why do you say that?'

'He knows where things come ashore. Even back then,

he was collecting flotsam. He'd have known how little came into North Bay.'

Violet wandered off, picking up stones for Anna, turning over shells, reflecting on what Cal had said. On the beach, she crouched and dug into the sand with her fingers, as if trying to disinter its secrets.

When Cal joined her, she said, 'Who, then?'

A few weeks earlier, Jim had watched a television documentary about the flowering of a desert. The location was in Africa or America, he couldn't remember which. Duncan's face reminded him of it now: his cracked and dry skin like the baked earth before the rains; his patchy white stubble like shrivelled stalks of vegetation; his tears like insistent rivulets which pushed out across the arid desert landscape following a thunderstorm in the hills, the trail of wetness colouring Duncan's deadened flesh a pinky-grey. Jim noticed how the tears from Duncan's right eye criss-crossed the wrinkled contours of his cheek, going off in one direction then back in another, whereas those from the left eye dropped vertically into a crevasse beside his nose before splitting into a mini-delta of channels at his mouth. Jim became mesmerized by the slow-motion progress of Duncan's silent misery. He couldn't look away because he felt responsible. Nor could he hold Duncan's hands, as he might a distressed woman's, or put his arms around him. Nor could he leave, not while Duncan was like this.

As he observed the rivulets of tears it occurred to him

that this was the first time he had been confronted by a sobbing man; indeed, the first time he had made a man cry. Both these novelties had left Jim feeling uncomfortable and hoping that Duncan would pull himself together soon. To Jim's dismay, the opposite seemed to be happening. Duncan reached out and grabbed Jim's forearms and held them tight, in the manner of a supplicant or beggar.

'It's all right, Duncan,' Jim found himself saying, 'I'm not going anywhere.'

He hoped the reassurance would simultaneously calm Duncan and encourage him to loosen his grip. Once again, the contrary happened. Duncan stiffened his hold, his tears flowed more freely and he began a mumbling commentary, only some of which was intelligible. When Jim managed to make sense of a few words, he attempted to engage Duncan in conversation – which, after all, had been his purpose for visiting. At one moment, for example, Duncan rebuked Megan Bates for misleading him and Jim asked, 'How did she mislead you, Duncan?' but there was no answer.

At another, Duncan mentioned a 'signal' and Jim inquired, without success, 'What signal?'

At another still, Duncan appeared despairing and repeated, 'Not coming back, not coming, not coming back,' and Jim said, 'Who's not coming back?'

Duncan looked perplexed, as if he could not understand why Jim asked such a question.

'Megan,' he answered, as if it was obvious. 'Megan isn't coming back.'

Duncan's puzzlement reminded Jim of the conversations he used to have with his father, James Senior, in the weeks leading up to his death. Much of their hospital visiting time would be spent sorting out whether Isobel, Jim's mother, would be joining them or not. Jim would start by changing the subject or saying he didn't know when his mother would be coming, but he would always end up telling the truth when his father became enraged by his evasiveness. 'Mum's dead,' he would say. Then he would watch his father's anger subside to be replaced by inconsolable grief. Now the same was happening with Duncan.

'Megan died twenty-six years ago, Duncan,' Jim said.

'I didn't know,' Duncan replied, and his face fractured again with misery.

'You must have forgotten.' Jim lapsed again into the rhythm of conversation he used to have with his father.

'I didn't know. I thought she would come back.'

'No, she can't come back, Duncan. That's why Violet Wells is here. She's Megan's daughter and she's trying to find out what happened to her mother. Don't you remember talking to her?' Jim tried to probe further. 'What did she ask you, Duncan? When she spoke to you. What does she know?' But Duncan's grip on Jim tightened again.

'Megan's not coming back.'

'I'm afraid not, Duncan.'

'She promised.'

'What did she promise?'

'She said she would go away and . . .' Duncan stared into Jim's face with disconcerting intensity.

'And what, Duncan?'

'She said she would go away,' he repeated, 'where Mr William Ritchie QC couldn't find her, and then some day she'd come back, to me.' Duncan pumped Jim's arms. 'She promised.'

'She did go, Duncan. She went for a swim in the sea, don't you remember? Don't you remember finding her hat and bag in North Bay?'

Duncan regarded Jim as though he was the idiot now. 'She left them there. She knew I would know.'

'Know what, Duncan?'

'I would know she had put them there. I would know she was alive.'

Jim asked, 'Was that the signal you mentioned?'

'Yes, yes, the signal,' he said with animation. 'The signal that she'd gone away . . . only I would know.'

The turn of the discussion made Jim wonder whether Duncan had understood anything he'd said. 'You've met Violet, haven't you?'

Duncan's face registered confusion. 'She was here?'

'Yes, she asked you questions about Megan. She upset you. She told me you ran off to North Bay, where the hat and the bag came ashore, where you go when you're upset about Megan.'

Duncan nodded. He remembered.

Jim continued, 'She's asking questions because she wants to know how her mother died all those years ago, how her mother is dead when she is alive; why everyone thought her mother had drowned and the baby with her.'

'Megan loved her baby,' Duncan said. 'She wouldn't have killed her baby.' Then, sounding betrayed, 'She promised.'

'What did she promise, Duncan?'

'One day she'd come back with her baby.'

'But her baby's come back without her, Duncan. Her baby hasn't seen her since the day she was born.'

At last Duncan let go of Jim. 'Megan's not coming back.'

'No.'

'Not coming.'

'No.'

Jim patted Duncan on the knee, withdrawing his arm before it became Duncan's prisoner again. 'You've had a shock,' Jim said. 'It's confusing for you.'

'I loved her,' Duncan said.

Jim stood. 'Well, I'd better be getting back to my rounds and I've my sheep to feed.'

He put his hand on Duncan's shoulder. Later he would remember how bony it felt, how lifeless, as though Duncan's body was already preparing for what would happen, as though Duncan was dying from the feet upwards and all that remained alive were his neck and head.

Mrs Anderson stood at the corner of her kitchen table, her skin suddenly translucent in the evening light, her breathing quickening. Since hearing of Violet's arrival in Poltown she'd been having these turns – one moment she was ecstatic at the prospect of Alexandra's ruin, then this. The two other occasions had been at night when she was in bed. Like now, she was assailed with memories so vivid and distressing her chest constricted until she could barely breathe. Yesterday, for example, a single image of Diana filled her head: blood on her hands, face and blouse, her eyes flashing with hatred. This evening, it was of the baby, lying naked on the kitchen table, the stump of the umbilical cord milky-grey against the pale white of the child's washed skin, the cardigan in which she had been wrapped beside her, where Mrs Anderson had let it fall.

As Mrs Anderson fought for breath, the image disappeared to be replaced by another: Mrs Anderson dripping glucose and water into the child's mouth; dribbles forming into a sticky pool on the table; Diana's face contorted and screaming how detestable the child was, how she wished it dead like its mother. Then, another image: Mrs Anderson swaddling the baby in a white towel and placing her in a cardboard box. She stroked the child's cheek with the backs of her fingers and said, 'There you are. You're safe now.' Then, for the first time, a long scrolling scene: Mrs Anderson was taking Diana to the bathroom to remove her bloodstained clothes and shoes. While Diana washed, Mrs Anderson went to look for the hand-me-downs Diana had given to her over the years. On her return, Diana was standing naked in front of the mirror. Mrs Anderson dressed her in black trousers and a pale yellow shirt and Diana protested about those colours not suiting her. Mrs Anderson dropped Diana's bloodied jersey and skirt into a plastic bag, intending to put in Megan's cardigan too.

But she peered in the baby's box and Mrs Anderson remembered thinking it was already a miracle the child had survived. How many more hardships were to come? She recalled her own childhood, how much comfort her little blue blanket had been. In moments of worry or trouble how she had always sought it out. She spread out

Megan's cardigan and used the kitchen scissors to cut a rectangle from its back, where it wasn't bloodstained. That was when she found the brooch. She unfastened it, took it to the sink and washed off a smear of blood. Thinking it pretty, she pinned it to the piece of cardigan and found an envelope which she taped to the side of the box. She couldn't send a child out into the world with nothing. Mrs Anderson said a prayer then went upstairs to tell Diana she was taking the baby away. She stroked Diana's forearm, leading her to the spare bedroom. She told Diana to sleep if she could, to rest if she couldn't, to relax now because her torment was over.

Another fast-moving series of images: Mrs Anderson in her car, driving to Inverness, the baby box on the seat beside her; Diana gone when she returned but a note on her bed: *I won't ever forget. D*; Mrs Anderson cleaning the floor and wiping the bloody table, before putting the mop, the cleaning cloths and the clothes bag on her garden fire; Mrs Anderson hiding Diana's note in case she ever had need of it.

That was the last scene. By now Mrs Anderson was feeling quite faint. She fell into a chair and remembered how she and Diana had spoken later, Mrs Anderson explaining that she, as always, had acted out of duty to Diana and Mr William. She sought and received Diana's 'absolute assurance' of secrecy and in return, Diana asked Mrs Anderson never to raise the subject again or to inquire how Megan Bates died or where her body was. They never spoke of it thereafter, except with their eyes, one providing the other with reassurance or understanding. It was a silent bond between them, one which acted as a spur to the sharing of confidences in other matters, Diana relying on Mrs Anderson, or so she said, more and more. Now she thought Diana had been acting the part, as a weak pleaser would, because Mrs Anderson knew her awful secret.

26

Cal sat against a slab of rock, Violet nearby on a shingle bank, night closing in, making possible an exchange of intimacies. Violet was explaining why she hadn't been in a relationship since Anna's birth, how she'd been formed by 'the hours, days, months, years' she'd spent yearning for her mother, then by the desertion of Anna's father.

'I don't want any of that: being in a relationship, breaking up, starting again, Anna wondering who'll be next, whether I'll still love her as much when Mr Right comes along; *if* Mr Right comes along.' She screwed up her face, finding even the notion objectionable. 'I don't want her to grow up with that insecurity, with that influence. I don't want her to see me . . .' She glanced at Cal. His face was in shadows. She stared into the gloom, trying to make out his expression. 'I don't want her to see me searching for something she can't give me. That's it, I guess.' She picked at the stones around her, feeling their shapes, selecting one, letting it drop, choosing another until finding one small and round enough to fit her hand. She threw it, the movement making the shingle under her shift and rattle, like a drum roll heralding the splash of the stone in the sea.

Violet glanced again at Cal. 'Having Anna has changed everything.'

'I shouldn't have asked. I'm sorry.' He spoke quickly and quietly. 'It's not my business.'

'It's fine, really it is. I'm glad you did.' She smiled. 'Anyway,' she said, 'it was me. I started it.'

The conversation had begun ten minutes earlier, while they had been waiting for dark, watching its shadows creep across the bay, keeping out of the way of Tam and co. As the colours of the day drained away, she asked Cal about his childhood fascination for the sea. What had inspired it?

'I suppose you could blame my grandfather,' he replied. 'Uilleam. He was from a small island off the north coast and died at sea in World War Two, lost overboard, his body never recovered, or so I'd thought. As a boy I spent hours, days, trying to work out where he'd gone. That was my first case involving a dead body.'

'Did you solve it?'

'Yes, I did eventually, but it took me years.'

She made a sound which let him know she was impressed.

'My grandfather's to blame for everything, for me becoming an oceanographer, for me doing what I do.' He'd never even considered another field, though recently, as she knew, he'd been questioning the direction of his work. He'd always had an academic interest in where and how bodies floated, but dealing face-to-face with relatives, especially 'all those poor, distressed parents' whose pleas currently sat in his inbox, had become both draining and distressing. The last few days' break had given him time and space to make a decision. It would be hard to say no to people whose last hope he was, 'But that's what I've got to do.'

He apologized for being so serious. Then, his voice lifting with enthusiasm, he said, 'The rest of it . . . all the

241

other stuff . . . yeah, I still get a kick from knowing that in three days there'll be a new moon, that the sun, the moon and the earth will be aligned, that it's called syzygy. That the combined gravitational pull of the sun and the moon will make the high tide higher than normal and the low tide lower.'

He laughed. 'Rachel . . . she's my ex-wife . . . used to say I was just another trainspotter, stamp collector, or the guy who played computer games – a loner looking for an escape from the real world. With me it was the sea.' He stopped to consider the accusation. 'Yeah, she might be right.'

'You were married?'

'I was, yes.'

'Children?'

'No.'

'Sorry, I didn't mean to pry,' she said quickly.

'You're not. It doesn't matter,' he answered. 'And you? Were you married to Anna's father?'

'No, nothing like that,' she said.

Usually she'd have left it there but in the circumstances she took the opportunity to say more. She'd seen the way he looked at her. She didn't want him to have a false impression. 'I wouldn't marry now. There's no chance of that. I don't even do relationships.'

'Why not?'

Feeling awkward, she attempted an explanation. 'Well, because Anna will always be the most important person in my life. Being a good mother matters to me more than anything else. That means never letting Anna think she isn't sufficient for me, never letting her worry I might love someone else more than her, so I've decided never to love anyone else at all, never to take that risk. Does that make sense?'

'Can you decide something like that?'

She hesitated. 'Yes, I think you can, if it's for your child.'

She heard him breathe out.

After a while and with night settling in, he said, 'Shall we go now?' She detected a difference in his voice, or thought she did, and wondered if he was bruised by what she'd said, if the difference was disappointment.

They walked back among the dunes, Cal in front, Violet following; going from dip to gully. The sand of South Bay lay to their right. 'Did you see the buoys and the driftwood?' Cal said when they reached the scrub of bushes where the pick-up was parked for concealment.

'No,' she said.

He pointed across the sand. 'See?'

She screwed up her eyes. 'I think so.'

'It's an oil drum. Duncan hasn't been out today. He hasn't been collecting. That's not like him. I wonder what's happened.'

A beech tree reared up from the slope by the back door to Brae. Its lower limbs drooped and hung so that anyone standing close to its trunk was rendered invisible by the murk of evening. Yet, from inside the tree's shroud of branches, it was possible to see out and in particular to observe Brae's large kitchen, as Mrs Anderson had been doing for more than twenty minutes.

She was watching Alexandra Hamilton moving between the Aga and the table with occasional forays to the pantry – so far she'd brought back a bowl of cooking apples, flour and a joint of meat: venison or leg of lamb. Mrs Anderson observed Alexandra's comings and goings with something approaching glee. To think she had produced the ingredient which could wreck this scene of rural domesticity. As tantalizing to Mrs Anderson was the increasing frequency with which Alexandra scowled at the windows from which pools of light spilled across the back courtyard. It was as if she knew she was being watched, as if she had a sixth sense for impending disaster. A minute ago, Alexandra had been peeling an apple at the table when suddenly her head jerked up. She searched the three windows in turn before Matt came into the kitchen, disturbing her. He took a tray of glasses from the sideboard – for the drinks cupboard in the sitting room, Mrs Anderson guessed – and departed by the swing door. As soon as Alexandra was alone again, her eyes flashed back to the windows. It brought a smirk to Mrs Anderson's face.

'All in good time, *Miss* Alexandra,' she said. 'All in my good time . . .'

Mrs Anderson wondered what would happen next. Would Alexandra go to one of the windows to stare out into the darkness? Would she go to the back door, open it and stand in the yard? Mrs Anderson decided to wait and see. After all, she was in no hurry to move things on. She was warm in the tree's shelter. It was dry underfoot and, quite apart from considerations of comfort, she was enjoying the capriciousness of power, her ability to decide when to exercise it. In fact she expected this part of the evening to be just as enjoyable as the next.

There. It happened again. Alexandra interrupted rolling pastry to stare at the middle window. Her face was flushed and fuller than it used to be, Mrs Anderson saw. On its own this was a source of some satisfaction, the thought that Alexandra's departing looks were going to be followed by her property fortune. As Mrs Anderson watched, Alexandra's expression changed from watchfulness to worry. She walked hurriedly to the back door. Mrs Anderson heard the old lock turn, a noise which brought back her days as housekeeper, when she had been custodian of the same key. The outside light came on and Alexandra appeared outside. She glowered in the direction of Mrs Anderson without seeing her before going back indoors. At the kitchen table again, she draped the pastry over a pie dish and trimmed the edges with a knife. When she had finished, she glanced at the window once more. A smile fluttered across Mrs Anderson's thin lips. 'It's time for my visit,' she said.

She moved away from the shelter of the tree and crossed the grass to where steps led down to the drive. She proceeded with care, feeling for each mossy tread with one foot before taking her weight off the other. When she reached the bottom she looked up. Her face shone in the beam of the back-door light and the movement caught Alexandra's eye. By her expression – turning from shock to annoyance when Alexandra saw who was there – Mrs Anderson realized she was unlikely to be asked inside, even into the kitchen. She had imagined Alexandra sitting her down in the hall or the drawing room and

Mrs Anderson having the pleasure of telling her about Violet Wells surrounded by the most precious artefacts of her inheritance from Mr William. But it was clear from Alexandra's opening salvo that would not happen.

'What are you doing, creeping about out here?' she demanded imperiously, pulling the back door open to intercept Mrs Anderson. 'What do you want?' Alexandra stood with hands on hips. 'Well?'

Mrs Anderson did her best to look as though some terrible and unjustified wrong was being done to her by such an ungracious welcome. 'If I'd known this was how I was going to be treated I would have had second thoughts about coming out at night.'

Alexandra laughed; short and bitter. 'Oh please, Mrs Anderson, do me a favour.'

Mrs Anderson thrust out her chin in turn and addressed the black sky above Alexandra's head. 'I refuse to repay your ingratitude with disloyalty. It is not my way.' Her head gave a little tremble of repressed pride, as well as excitement.

Alexandra snorted again. 'I'm tired of this, of you, Mrs Anderson, always trying to interfere. Say what it is you want or I'm going back inside.'

Mrs Anderson glowered. How she wished Alexandra was still small enough to be put across her knee.

'Jim told me this evening about the young woman who is renting Orasaigh Cottage . . .'

'You mean Violet Wells?'

'I am only passing on what Jim said because of the implications . . . for you, the family, for Brae. I thought you'd want to know.'

'Oh, the loyal and faithful servant,' Alexandra sneered. 'What implications?'

'Violet Wells's mother was your stepfather's mistress, Megan Bates. She's Mr William's daughter . . . his flesh and blood.' For dramatic effect, Mrs Anderson waited before carrying on. 'His only child. His *heir*.'

Anyone else wouldn't have noticed the flicker in Alexandra's eyes, a slight widening. But Mrs Anderson was watching and knew what it meant. 'Oh, go away, Mrs Anderson. Go away.' Alexandra collected herself and strode back inside. 'Go away. Go away. Go away.'

The door slammed shut. The outside light snapped off, leaving the yard lit only by the light from the kitchen windows. Alexandra extinguished that too by closing the kitchen shutters, leaving Mrs Anderson in the dark.

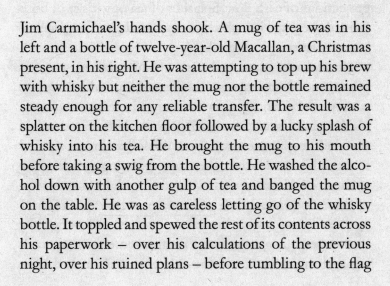

Jim Carmichael's hands shook. A mug of tea was in his left and a bottle of twelve-year-old Macallan, a Christmas present, in his right. He was attempting to top up his brew with whisky but neither the mug nor the bottle remained steady enough for any reliable transfer. The result was a splatter on the kitchen floor followed by a lucky splash of whisky into his tea. He brought the mug to his mouth before taking a swig from the bottle. He washed the alcohol down with another gulp of tea and banged the mug on the table. He was as careless letting go of the whisky bottle. It toppled and spewed the rest of its contents across his paperwork – over his calculations of the previous night, over his ruined plans – before tumbling to the flag floor with a crash. Jim leaned back in his chair and listened to Tommy, his collie, howling. The sound expressed a little of what Jim was feeling: fear and a sense that something irrevocable had happened even though it was only 7.30 in the morning. Tommy, who was shut up in the tractor cab, only knew about the missing blackface sheep. He didn't know the half of it; he didn't know the worst of it.

Jim put his head in his hands and rubbed his unshaven face, groaning and cursing. He berated himself either for his stupidity or for his naivety and followed it up with: 'What did you think would happen, Jim? Well?' The question went unanswered because Jim's elbow knocked against his mug of tea, tipping it over. The remaining liquid spilled across the table and Jim stared at the mingling pools of whisky and tea and then at the damp papers on which he had been estimating the costs of acquiring a polytunnel to supply the new village store as well as his projections of cash flow. Splashes of tea or whisky or both stained the page on which he had made a clean copy of his calculations the night before.

He had retired to bed with an intoxicating sense of optimism, of opportunity finally seeking out his remote corner of the world and rewarding his years of uncomplaining hard work. Unusually for him, he'd even thanked God before going to sleep. Now the sodden pages seemed to mock him and he tore them up, scattering the pieces on to the floor. His mug went flying too, as did a pottery vase of dried flowers, a bottle of ketchup and another of mustard. After so many discordant crashes and bangs the kitchen fell quiet, apart from Tommy's intermittent howling and the clock above the stove. So often it had been

Jim's reassuring companion. Now it was a sound filled with menace. In an hour and a half, Davie would be returning. Then Jim would be told what job he must do to pay off his debt.

He'd woken before sunrise to a ruckus in the front field: sheep calling out in distress and Tommy going mental, yapping and growling. Jim had jumped from his bed and gone to the window. In the grey light of early morning he could see a collie rounding up his blackface sheep. It wasn't Tommy, who was where he always spent the night, on the tractor seat. Jim pulled down the window and shouted, 'Hey. Hey.' The dog stopped its herding and looked at Jim. 'Away with you. *Devil*,' he muttered under his breath and banged on the window frame to frighten the animal. He imagined the dog a stray from Poltown, or perhaps it belonged to a camper but had run off. Those notions were dispelled when he heard a man's confident voice instructing the dog to carry on. Jim rushed downstairs, threats issuing from him. He put on his boots and pulled up his overalls, only managing to hang one strap over his shoulder while struggling to open the door. As soon as he was outside he shouted again. 'Hey, hey. What do you think you're doing?' By now the gate was open and the collie was going back and forth behind the sheep, driving them towards it. A man holding the gate didn't even bother to look up.

Jim shouted again. 'Hey! Hey!'

He had started down the path when a voice seemed to come from behind him.

'Morning, Jim.'

Jim stopped and looked round. Davie White was

leaning against the corner of the house. 'What's going on?' Jim shouted.

Davie waved his arm airily. He had a cigarette in his hand. 'Don't you find it's always so rewarding to get out of bed early?' he said, looking across the glassy water of the sea loch towards Poltown. 'Best part of the day, don't you think, Jim?'

'What are you doing with my sheep?'

'Your sheep, Jim?' He sucked on his cigarette and blew the smoke out of the side of his mouth. 'I don't think so, Jim, not any more.'

By now the sheep were on the track, running. Davie held up his hand and the other man instructed his dog to get ahead of them and to hold them where they were.

Tommy was going demented in the tractor cab. His claws were scrabbling against the plastic sheeting which covered the broken window. 'Tell your dog to stop that,' Davie ordered.

Jim looked at Davie and then at the tractor, which was parked beside the hayshed. 'Settle down now, Tommy lad,' Jim shouted. 'Settle down.' The dog whimpered and fell silent.

'That's better. We can talk.' He wandered over to Jim and threw his cigarette stub at his feet, as if throwing down a challenge. 'You know why we're here?'

Jim said nothing.

Davie shrugged. 'Interest soon builds up on two thousand pounds, doesn't it, Jim?' Davie glanced at the house and the sheds. His expression suggested he didn't see much of value. 'Four hundred and twenty-eight pounds interest after five weeks,' he'd said, shaking his head. 'I thought it might assist you if I took goods to the same value before things got out of control.'

Jim's world was falling around him. He felt winded. Words struggled to leave his mouth. 'I've been driving around doing the posters for Ross.'

'So you have, Jim, and Mr Turnbull is very grateful. Thing is, the money you borrowed is mine.' Davie put his arm round Jim. 'Lovely here, isn't it?' He looked at the view. 'I wouldn't mind a place like this myself one of these days.'

He went towards the garden gate and waved to his colleague. The sheep started bleating again as the collie resumed its herding. Tommy barked and scratched at the tractor windows. Davie looked back at Jim. 'Next time it'll have to be the van or the tractor. The dog too.' He tried to look concerned. 'You don't have much of value, do you, Jim? I can't see you having anything left at all in six months.'

Davie started along the track, hesitated and stopped. 'Tell you what,' he called back. 'There's a job that needs doing.'

'What?' Jim said.

'Why don't you make coffee later and we'll have a chat? Then, we'll see about bringing back your sheep. Let's say nine o'clock. That's when I like to have breakfast.'

27

'Couldn't sleep,' Cal wrote in pencil. 'Gone for a walk. Back soon.' He looked in the pick-up's window. Violet was curled across the back seat, the top of her head poking from the sleeping bag. Cal prised the page from his notebook and secured it to the windscreen with the wiper blade before taking the coastal path to Boyd's Farm. The steading had the same odd atmosphere as the beach at South Bay the night before, of Duncan missing, of something untoward having happened. Cal shouted Duncan's name and waited for a reply, for any sign of life. He peered into the barn into which he had previously been ushered like a courtier. Nothing had changed apart from Duncan's absence. The Neptune Scroll was still nailed to a beam. The Cuvier's whale skull and the barnacled driftwood were exactly where Cal had left them. He shouted Duncan's name again. The barn deadened his voice. 'Duncan, it's Cal, Cal McGill.'

He crossed the steading yard to the back door of the house. To his surprise it was shut, unlike the previous times he'd been there. The handle was stiff but the door sprung free and his nostrils filled with the stench of cats and an unpleasant mustiness. The inside door was also closed. Knocking, he called out, 'Hello, it's Cal,' if only to reassure Duncan that he wasn't a stranger or one of BRC's money-men. Cal remembered Violet telling him how the open door and the emptiness of the house seemed to draw her in, as if leading her to the secrets of Megan's room, and he felt a similar impulse to go further, to look for Duncan.

Walking along the dark passageway towards the front of the house, he continued to call his name, adding by way of explanation, 'I thought you might like some help clearing the beach.' He stopped, as Violet had, where the passageway met the hall, another scene of dilapidation. Like Violet, he couldn't believe a human being lived there, even one as idiosyncratic as Duncan. The house had an aura of terminal decay and a temperature to match. Crossing the hall to the bottom of the stairs, Cal gave up shouting for Duncan because of its futility. Nothing living was within earshot, with the exception perhaps of a cat, a rat or a mouse. Nothing human; of that Cal was certain. The same feeling of absence and death assailed him when he looked inside Megan's room. Cal put himself in Violet's position, to imagine what he would be feeling if these were his mother's possessions, if he had been separated from her at birth and this, to all intents and purposes, was the closest he would ever come to her. Even for him it was a peculiar and unsettling feeling: this pristine room in a house that was falling down; everything present and correct apart from the woman herself.

He crossed to the bed and picked up the teddy bear. Holding it, he examined the room's artefacts, wondering if all they signified was Duncan's enduring attraction to Megan Bates and, of course, his eccentricity. He went to the wardrobe, opening the door and letting his eye track along the clothes rail. Like Violet, he stood on the dressing-table stool to find the two boxes. Unlike her, he opened them where they were, lifting one lid then the other, checking their contents, confirming his view that two such different objects were most unlikely to have gone into the sea at the same time and later to have been washed ashore together. Cal replaced the lids, returned the stool and went to inspect the cot. Once again he considered Violet's reaction, what a powerful symbol this would have been of her lost childhood, indeed of everything she had lost. He touched the wooden frame and went back to the door.

Opening it slowly, he emerged on to the landing. The main staircase lay ahead of him, descending, but another smaller, ascending, flight lay to his left. It was at the far end of the landing and spilling down its few wooden steps was a length of nylon rope. The colour, a faded blue, was the same as one of Duncan's rope piles outside the steading. Approaching the stairs, Cal saw they led to a short corridor, at the far end of which appeared to be an attic room. The door was partially open and through the gap Cal could see the slope of the ceiling and a skylight. As far as he could tell, the room was empty. At least there was no movement or sound. He bent to pick up the rope, a coil about three metres long. It felt damp and Cal concluded it had been carried indoors sometime during the night or early morning. He glanced again at the attic. Although much of the room was still hidden by the door, he had a clearer view of the back wall. What he thought from further away to be stained or grimy wallpaper, he saw now was graffiti and he realized what this room was. Violet had mentioned Mrs Anderson talking about a rite of passage for teenagers from Poltown to run through Duncan's house, how those who signed the back wall of the attic, the room furthest away, were regarded as having shown the most daring. It was the means by which the village had come to know of Duncan's continuing obsession with Megan Bates.

A stair creaked under Cal's weight, making him start. How many of Poltown's teenagers had taken fright at the same place and had gone no further? In two more strides Cal was in the passageway. The rope made him hurry. Despite appearances, the house could not be quite as abandoned as it felt. Duncan or someone else had been there not many hours before. Cal nudged at the door with his left toe, revealing the back wall to be a jumble of signatures, hearts with arrows through them; a romantic and social history of Poltown over three decades. He stepped into the room and gasped, 'Oh, no.' Duncan, his face leathery and vacant, was hanging from a hook in the ceiling. The rope around his neck was blue, like the piece Cal had found on the steps. A chair lay on its side, after being kicked away. Duncan's boots lay below him, presumably dislodged in his death throes by the involuntary thrashing of his legs. His eyes stared sightlessly. His mouth was locked open as though in the act of speaking. Cal was overcome by shock and sadness for this creature, half child, half man, who had chosen to die in this room, of all places.

Had he killed himself there to let his tormentors know they had won?

255

The first thing Jim did on returning indoors was to open the store cupboard, grab the coffee jar and throw it across the kitchen. The glass smashed against a wall; the granules spilled on to the floor. Looking at the disarray – soaked and shredded paper, shards of glass, fragments of pottery and coffee – Jim shook his head, his anger turning to resignation, the impotent gesture of a man finding reasons to choose appeasement over defiance. Jim had sometimes wondered if his aversion to confrontation, his inability to go 'toe to toe' like some men did, would disappear if his life or someone or something dear to him was under threat; whether he too would stand his ground. After his exchange with Davie White, he knew the answer. He wouldn't; he couldn't. He let his head drop and closed his eyes. The dog's howling provided a distraction from his thoughts about cowardice.

'I'm coming, Tommy lad,' he said, going to the open door. 'You hold on there.'

Tommy cocked his head, lifted his ears in expectation as Jim took the side path from the house. When he opened the tractor door, the dog leapt out and ran backwards and forwards in excitement and curled his body around Jim's legs, lifting his nose towards Jim's searching hands.

'There you are, Tommy boy. Did you think I wasn't coming?'

Jim patted the squirming dog's neck and ears. 'I wouldn't leave you, Tommy boy. Course I wouldn't.' He knelt and buried his face in the dog's hair. 'I won't let them take you from me, Tommy boy.' Jim let the dog slobber over him, then stood to slam the tractor door.

In the half second his master's back was turned, Tommy

sprinted along the stony track. The dog jumped the wall into the field and began searching for the sheep, going through his morning routine, running into the corners in case one of the ewes had slunk off on her own. In his bewilderment at the empty field, Tommy added a few tricks. The dog lay still in the grass as if a defiant ewe was standing her ground, foot-stamping, Mrs A more than likely. Then he squirmed forward, legs bent, belly flat to the grass, ears pricked. Jim contemplated Tommy's performance, wishing he had a fraction of the collie's courage. He called out to the dog. Tommy obeyed quickly, running across the field and jumping on to the stone wall. The dog looked back at the empty field, as if the missing flock might suddenly have reappeared. Jim did the same, wondering whether he'd ever see his sheep again.

'Come on, Tommy boy,' he called sadly. In a few bounds the panting dog was lying at his feet. Jim knelt on one knee and Tommy rose to meet him, licking his hands and face.

'What are we going to do, Tommy, eh?' Tommy's breath was hot on Jim's face. 'What are we going to do?'

When Jim went back inside the house, Tommy slunk away to the hen coop, his neck and head flat in the grass, his eyes following every movement of the clucking mother hen and her chickens behind the wire mesh. Meanwhile his master set about tidying the kitchen for Davie White's return visit.

Luckily for Jim, only some of the shattered coffee jar's contents had scattered across the floor. The rest had settled into a heap, like a miniature mole hill, at the base of the wall. Jim scooped some into a mug and searched the cupboards for a jar of honey, from his own bees, and his last packet of digestive biscuits. Putting the honey and the biscuits on the sideboard, he lifted the bread-bin lid and checked the loaf for mould. Then he sniffed the butter, which was all right, if sweating a little. He picked up the broom and started sweeping, its stiff bristles causing broken bits of glass and pottery to skitter across the slab floor. While he gathered everything into a tidy pile, something that Davie said came back to him. 'Business, after all, is business.'

Jim crouched beside the rubbish and picked out the torn sheets of paper. He studied each one before saving half a dozen that he laid out on the table. Bending over them, he tried to decipher his writing, some of which had smudged. Three fragments of paper more or less fitted together. Apart from a jagged tear at the bottom, Jim managed to reassemble the page with his polytunnel calculations. He copied them on to a clean sheet of paper while telling himself off for being spineless.

By the time the table for breakfast was laid, he'd rehearsed 'a proposition' which he would put to Davie. At first, it did little to lift his spirits, but he persuaded himself of its good common sense and he managed, too, to resuscitate a notion that had shrivelled and died round about the time Jim last saw his flock of sheep. Briefly stated, it was that the events of earlier that morning had been a misunderstanding, a failure of communication. The proof, Jim told himself, lay in Ross Turnbull's idea for Jim to grow salads and vegetables for the new village store. Ross had even suggested a supplier of polytunnels in Inverness and had told Jim to mention the Turnbull name to be certain of being quoted the company's 'best price'. As Davie White worked for Ross Turnbull, an accommodation must surely be possible.

Jim put the sheet of figures by the placing he'd laid for Davie. With ten minutes to go, he rehearsed his pitch. He would ask Davie to provide seed capital for his new polytunnel business, Jim would hand over all the projected profits for the first two years (he slid the paper closer towards the seat where Davie would be sitting) – a figure of £10,000, sufficient to pay off his enlarged debt if they could agree a lower interest rate.

In subsequent years they would share the profits fifty–fifty.

Jim was still undecided whether to conclude by holding out the prospect of expansion – say three polytunnels by year five – when Tommy started to bark. Jim looked at the clock. Davie was seven minutes early. He flicked the switch of the kettle, checked that he'd put coffee granules into the mugs and went to the door. As soon as he saw Davie – he had changed into jeans and a short-sleeved T-shirt revealing tattoos on his arms – Jim's confidence began to drain away. It disappeared altogether when Davie barked at Jim to get his dog to 'shut the fuck up'. He shoved Jim from his own front doorstep out into the garden. 'Well, what the fuck are you waiting for?'

The sight of his master being manhandled startled the dog. Instead of yapping and howling, Tommy emitted a rumble of growls and rose to greet Jim, but with none of his usual exuberance. The dog knew something was badly wrong. Jim grabbed him by his scruff and led him to the tool shed, whispering in Tommy's ear that he must be good and quiet. Retracing his steps, Jim felt a stab of fear at the pit of his stomach. His breathing quickened so that by the time he returned to his kitchen and saw Davie lolling back in a chair, legs splayed, he was panting. He swallowed, thumped at his chest as though he had something in his throat and coughed. What made everything worse was the way he started jabbering. A jumble of words emerged from his mouth and proposition wasn't one of them, nor partnership, nor profit, nor even polytunnel. Jim heard himself begging for another chance, promising to do whatever Davie wanted of him, if only . . .

'If only, what?' Davie sneered.

'If only I can have my sheep back. They're my livelihood. I'll do anything.'

Davie smirked. 'You don't get it, do you, Jim?'

'No,' he agreed, hoping even now that conciliation might help.

Humiliation followed fear. His bladder let him down next. He felt warm urine spread out from his groin and run down his right leg.

An expression of disgust crossed Davie's face. 'See all this,' he said. Jim lifted his head and looked around the kitchen with Davie. 'This house, this place . . . you're going to lose it, Jim.'

Then, from nowhere Jim found his voice, the one he'd rehearsed. 'I've been working on a proposition, a business plan,' he said, surprising himself.

Davie thumped his fist on the table, making the plates and Jim jump. 'I've got a fucking proposition for you, Jim.' He paused, waiting for Jim to pay proper attention. 'Either you do what I'm going to tell you or you lose all this, and if you tell anyone, you're fucking dead and buried, Jim.'

His fist banged down again.

'You're a fucking corpse.'

Driving to Poltown for her weekly surgery, Doctor Fiona Bell noticed a police car turning down the single-track road to Boyd's Farm and South Bay. She slowed as she passed the turn-off and wondered if it had anything to do with the public meeting two nights before, whether there had been any spill-over of unpleasantness against Duncan Boyd. Fiona had attended the gathering and even before punches started to fly she'd become concerned. Some of the people sitting by her, patients of hers among them, had been making threatening comments about Duncan whenever Boyd's Farm was mentioned. As she'd been near the back of the community hall, she'd escaped the fracas but had spent the next half an hour patching cuts and bruises, using her emergency bag from the boot of her car.

Afterwards, driving to Ullapool, she'd wondered whether someone should warn Duncan about the passions being stirred up, about the personal risk for him. Back at home, she told Nick, her partner, about the violence and her concerns for Duncan whom she'd met at South Bay walking Pepe, her terrier, after surgery. In her short acquaintance, Duncan didn't seem to be as weird as his reputation. Indeed, she found his shyness endearing, especially on those occasions when she was close enough to say hello and he responded by showing her a piece of flotsam, rather like Pepe bringing back a crab and dropping it at her feet, expecting a pat and some praise for being so clever.

Maybe someone should have a quiet word with Duncan, she suggested to Nick. So he could take some precautions. It was one of those conversations to which Nick hardly paid attention. She persevered because it helped her work out her feelings. At the meeting, she told him, she'd seen a community close to boiling point. Until then, she hadn't imagined there was any threat to Duncan, not really. Now she had changed her view.

'He's such an odd man that he's probably not aware how intense the hostility has become,' she said.

Nick cautioned her against interfering: 'Which is really what you're asking, isn't it?'

She agreed it was. She didn't like to stand by when she might be able to prevent something horrible happening, but she knew there were other considerations, such as her patients thinking she was taking sides, which was why she was asking Nick's opinion. He had grown up in Ullapool and had a better understanding of the area than a newcomer like her, who'd only been in residence eight months and still needed a map to find her way about the roads, let alone the twists and turns of the communities she visited on her weekly surgeries. Nick said, 'In that case, stay out of it. Nothing stays secret in Ullapool for more than two days. Somewhere like Poltown, you're talking two hours. At the most . . .'

At the time, she'd known he was right, but seeing the police car she felt a twinge of conscience. 'God, Pepe,' she said to the dog lying asleep on the passenger seat, 'I hope nothing's happened.'

She made a silent promise to listen to her instincts more and to Nick's cautions less. As she drove on into Poltown, she took her left hand off the steering wheel and ruffled Pepe's wiry coat. The dog stirred and opened his eyes. 'Well, would Pepe like a walk on the beach at lunchtime?' Pepe gave her that longing look he always managed whenever he heard the word 'walk'. 'You would, wouldn't you?' She ruffled his coat again. 'See what Duncan's found for us.'

She parked in front of the surgery – a converted ground-floor flat in Sir Harry Lauder Gardens. Her space had been marked 'Reserved for Doctor', unnecessarily, as she had learned, since most of her patients were too poor to afford a car.

Already she was feeling better. If Duncan was on the beach at lunchtime she'd say something about the atmosphere in the meeting, about the hostility and anger, just in case no one had told him. She wouldn't mention it to Nick.

Her first two appointments were in the waiting room. 'Give me a couple of minutes,' she said, bidding good morning to Mrs Simons and Mr Mackie, 'and I'll be with you.' She carried on along the passage to the kitchenette where Janice McGhee, the caretaker-cleaner, was boiling the kettle and dropping teabags into a pot.

'Morning, Janice.'

'How are you, Doctor Bell?'

In Fiona's opinion, Janice was a frustrated nurse. Every time she greeted someone she asked how they were, or whether they were keeping well. 'Good, thanks, Janice,' Fiona answered. 'Janice, is there something going on at South Bay?'

'Not that I've heard.' A look of puzzlement accompanied the answer.

'I saw a police car there, that's all.' Fiona hoped she'd started a hare running. If anyone could find out what was going on, Janice could. As it happened, Fiona discovered the first piece of information. While prodding circumspectly at a weeping sore on Mr Mackie's big toe, her mobile phone rang. She apologized for the interruption but the call was from 'head office'. She would have to answer. Fiona was still mouthing 'I'm sorry' when Mrs Findlay, the group practice receptionist, began speaking. As usual, she was rather disapproving (whether of new or female doctors or just from habit, Fiona had yet to work out).

'Doctor Turner,' Mrs Findlay said, 'has asked if you could take his appointments this afternoon.'

Doctor Alexander Turner was the senior doctor in the practice. By her tone Mrs Findlay made clear her opinion that Fiona was ill-equipped for the task of stand-in.

'Why, what's happened?' Fiona was deliberately breezy.

'Well, if you must know, he's been asked by the police to attend a death.'

'Where?'

'Near Poltown,' Mrs Findlay said, relishing the opportunity to deliver a slight. 'Of course, if there had been a sufficiently experienced doctor available nearby, Doctor Turner wouldn't have had to go.'

'Where near Poltown?'

Mrs Findlay sounded taken aback by Doctor Bell's abruptness. 'A place called Boyd's Farm.'

Fiona's face turned ashen as she ended the call. Even Mr Mackie noticed the change and, unusually for him, spoke without being spoken to. 'All right, Doctor?'

'Yes.' She nodded. 'A bit of a shock but I'm fine now. Right, where was I?'

After the appointment, Janice put her head round the door. 'You'll never guess, Doctor Bell, the police are at Boyd's Farm. There's been a death. Apparently it's Duncan Boyd. He hanged himself.' She pursed her lips as though a tragedy like that had been inevitable sooner or later. Janice, as Fiona knew, was a supporter of the wind farm for the jobs it would bring to Poltown. 'It doesn't do to speak ill of the dead, Doctor Bell,' Janice said, 'but that one wasn't right, never was.'

'I wouldn't know,' Fiona said diplomatically, but feeling sick. Back in her room she rang Nick to tell him what had happened. 'I feel so guilty.'

'Well, don't,' he replied. 'What could you have said or done that would've stopped him?'

'But I should have done *something*,' she said feebly.

For the remainder of the surgery, each patient entered Doctor Bell's room with a bulletin of the latest news and in between appointments Janice provided updates. After the last patient, Janice stood in Fiona's doorway, shaking her head at such a morning. 'The whole story's coming out now,' she announced. 'Duncan was there when Megan had her baby. He begged her to stay with him, at the farmhouse, but she turned him down and he killed her in a jealous rage. If he couldn't have her, nobody else was going to. Her mistake was letting Duncan see a letter to the baby's father in which she threatened to disappear with the child and Duncan realized it gave him a cover for murder. After killing her, he posted the letter and that's what saved him. If it hadn't been for that, the police would have arrested him.' She paused. Her eyes widened. 'And you'll never believe this bit.' Janice launched into another rush of words. 'After hiding Megan's body and abandoning the baby in Inverness, he dressed up in Megan's clothes, put on her sun hat and went swimming so that old Mrs Armitage would think he was Megan.'

Janice checked to see if Fiona was still following. 'Mrs Armitage is dead now but she used to walk her dog every morning. She'd go to the road end at South Bay before returning home. She'd often see Megan there. Well, anyway, that morning, she thought she saw Megan walking into the sea . . . right deep . . . and she raised the alarm. But really it was Duncan, who'd swum underwater back to his headland.' Janice took a breath. 'The police got suspicious when he said he'd found Megan's hat and bag on the beach at North Bay. He was about to be charged when Megan's letter arrived in the post.' Janice's eyes widened. 'You'd never have thought it of him, would you, being cunning like that?'

The sound of Janice's phone ringing brought a grin of excitement at the prospect of more news to come. 'Do you mind if I take it?'

Janice retreated into the corridor and Fiona went to the window and gazed sadly towards South Bay. She looked at her watch and saw it was nearly lunchtime. She'd take

Pepe for a walk along the shore and remember Duncan. That poor man.

On the beach, Pepe found a dead gull. The bird's body had been buried by sand. Only its black beak protruded. It was at an angle of forty-five degrees and slightly open. In death as in life the gull appeared ready for a fight. The dog was circling suspiciously, growling and barking by turns, sometimes darting towards the beak, hackles raised, before retreating to safety.

'Oh, come on, Pepe, we have to go.'

Pepe dashed in one last time, retreated, barked and trotted nonchalantly towards Fiona, who was by her car at the road end. 'Come on, Pepe. Patients are waiting . . . Doctor Turner's patients.' She mimicked Mrs Findlay's ability to make Doctor Turner's patients sound the most important in medical history. While she waited for the dog, she surveyed the beach, wishing she had the time to remove every piece of flotsam, as Duncan would if he were still alive. Still, she had gathered up all the big pieces – buoys, rope, plastic containers, driftwood – and put them into a pile, then drawn in the wet sand: *In memory of Duncan Boyd who was kind to me.* Looking at it from a distance she liked the idea of the next tide washing away the words and possibly the memorial too, of it being impermanent, even fleeting, like her own acquaintance with Duncan.

28

Police Constable Sandy Buchanan was walking Cal through the house again, double-checking his route to the attic. 'And you're sure you didn't go in there, sir?' The constable indicated the open door to the room in which Duncan kept the doll's house among a jumble of other furniture.

'I've told you already . . .' Cal broke off because Violet appeared in the hall, a policewoman leading her, another following. She looked dazed, as though she wasn't sure whether she was still asleep, whether this was a nightmare.

PC Buchanan nudged Cal. 'Hey, you're paying attention to me.'

'No, I didn't go into that room this time, but I did when I visited before,' Cal replied, still watching Violet as she was led upstairs to the inspector Cal had just left, wondering if she would be treated with the same hostility. Cal had answered question after question: how he'd come to be in Poltown; how he'd met Duncan and Violet; what he knew of her. It had taken him a while to realize why the inspector and now PC Buchanan were so antagonistic. The body hanging in the attic room would lead to more than one post-mortem: Duncan's and into the police investigation twenty-six years ago. Why had the police let a murderer go; why had they allowed a letter to distract them; why had they closed a case without a body? A reporter and photographer from the local newspaper had already been to the farmhouse. Others were on the way. The police seemed to blame Cal and Violet for the media interest, for causing trouble by disturbing the past.

After all, didn't Cal have form as a troublemaker? The inspector had alluded to him 'making a habit of this'. Someone must have Googled his name and discovered other cases he'd worked on where he had fallen out with the police, usually because he'd found evidence they had overlooked. Cal had snapped back at the inspector. 'That's not the point, really.' It was as though Cal had committed a crime for raising the alarm about Duncan's death. 'Is it?'

The inspector had ignored Cal and suggested to Constable Buchanan that Mr McGill – he'd said his name with distaste, like a dog baring its teeth before biting a rat – might like to go through his story again, how he'd come to be at Boyd's Farm when a man was hanging dead upstairs, why he'd entered a private dwelling without permission and where he'd gone, step by step.

Constable Buchanan seemed to be a man who obeyed orders to the letter. He'd escorted Cal from room to room upstairs, making him detail his movements, before going downstairs and doing the same. After the question about the sitting room, he made Cal retrace his steps along the back corridor to the porch and stand exactly where in the steading yard he'd made his phone call to the police and afterwards to Violet. 'Why,' he asked, 'did you go outside before ringing?'

'I just wanted to get out of that horrible house.'

His answer provoked a sceptical look from the constable, who said Cal was being allowed to go, for now. However, he would have to make himself available for further questioning as the inquiry progressed.

Cal waited for Violet by the big barn until he was moved on for 'operational reasons'. As he crossed the field, it became clear what those were. Two trucks and a digger passed him on the track to the farm, followed by a police van carrying a dozen officers. Another hour passed before Violet appeared. By then the officers had cleared one pile of flotsam – the collection of orange buoys – and had filled one of the trucks. The digger had started to excavate the ground underneath.

'They're looking for her, aren't they?' Violet said.

Cal nodded. 'Looks like it.' He touched her arm. 'I'm sorry.' It seemed the only thing to say. She flashed him a smile but he could see how wounded she was, how upset.

'The inspector implied Duncan taking his life was my fault for asking too many questions.'

'He's wrong. You were looking for your mother, doing the job the police should have done years ago.'

'That's not how he put it. He seemed to be saying that even the guilty shouldn't be hounded – that's why countries have systems of justice, police, juries, judges and courts.'

'Did he actually say that?'

She didn't seem to hear him. Her focus was on the field. A digger dumped another load of topsoil into a truck. Police moved in to examine the newly opened ground. 'I just can't bear to think of her suffering,' she said. 'What he might have done to her . . .' She crouched, watching another truck reverse to be loaded up. 'Do you think he hid her there?'

He made no attempt to reply but she didn't seem to mind or notice.

'I don't want her to be buried here.' She shivered. 'Cal.' Her eyes were wide with shock. 'I thought he was sweet too.' Until she'd gone into the house, until she'd seen that room, until she'd seen him watching her. She'd been fooled just like her mother. 'Duncan said my mother loved me . . . How could he have killed her knowing that? How could he have separated us?'

'Jealousy, seeing her loving another man, another man's child . . . it's possible, at least that's what the police think.'

There was hesitancy in Cal's answer. Violet looked at him. 'But you don't?' She sounded puzzled, as if there was no longer anything to doubt.

He shook his head. 'I don't know.'

'Don't know what . . . about Duncan being jealous?'

'Don't know about any of it, about Duncan being a murderer.'

'He admitted killing her last night to Jim Carmichael.' Violet studied his face. 'Jim's given a full statement to the police.' She was trying to work him out. Why was he still taking sides with the creep?

Cal sighed. 'Last time the police took the obvious line. Mother-to-be kills herself and her baby after being let down by her married lover. They wanted a solution that wouldn't involve detectives from headquarters descending on Poltown, turning the place upside down. Now, they're doing the same. It's all neat and tidy again. I'm

271

sorry.' He gave her a regretful glance. 'I don't mean to be difficult, but I've learned to be suspicious of obvious explanations, especially when there are questions without answers.'

'Like what?' she asked.

'Why were you brought here? Who wrote that letter about you being Megan Bates's daughter? Why now?' He paused. 'I keep coming back to that. Whoever wrote that letter knows what happened. And I'm pretty sure it wasn't Duncan.'

He swore, wishing he could make himself clear. 'I'm sorry, Violet, but everything you've told me about Duncan, and what I've seen for myself . . .' He paused. 'I know this is going to sound strange, but I don't think he knew your mother was dead, not until you turned up looking for her.'

＊

For once Mrs Anderson didn't have to tolerate snide remarks. Usually when she visited the shop, a group of villagers would be hanging around the counter. Idle bletherers, she had taken to calling them, grumbling at them under her breath as well as to their faces when the occasion warranted. There were more of them today, a dozen at least, but instead of passing the time making comments about Mrs Anderson (how stuck-up she was; how demeaning it must be for her to do her own shopping) they paid her no attention at all, so engrossed were they by Duncan Boyd's death. Mrs Anderson took advantage of her invisibility by going from display to display, picking up items, returning them, selecting one or two for her basket – a packet of rice, a tin of tomatoes, milk – and taking her time. If anyone had paid her attention, they would have seen how she dithered by the shelves closest to the 'bletherers', how she seemed to concentrate as much on what was being said as on the packets and tins she was examining and how, after being in the shop a while, she left hurriedly and abandoned her basket by the door, the rice, the tin of tomatoes and the milk still in it.

If anyone in the shop had gone to the window they would also have seen Mrs Anderson sitting in her car. They would have noticed her talking to herself and, if they'd watched for long enough, they'd have seen how flustered she was. They might have called the others over to enjoy the spectacle: the dour and disapproving Mrs Anderson discomfited for a change.

The possibility of being observed was one factor in Mrs Anderson's unease. Another was the way she had already drawn attention to herself by leaving her shopping behind. But mostly her disquiet stemmed from the conversation she had just overheard: how Jim Carmichael had visited Boyd's Farm the previous evening; how he'd found Duncan to be tearful and distressed and wanting to unburden himself 'about a darkness in his life which had become too difficult to bear'; how between sobs and howls Duncan had confessed to Megan Bates's murder; how he'd kept on repeating, 'She knows, she knows,' and when Jim had asked who *she* was, he'd replied, 'Violet Wells.' Jim had thought Duncan 'was just being Duncan' and having one of his emotional turns. He'd stayed on at Boyd's Farm until Duncan had calmed down and then he'd returned to his smallholding. As soon as he heard about the hanging, he called the police. Two officers visited him to take a statement in which he blamed himself for Duncan's death. Duncan would still be alive and facing trial for murder if only Jim had realized his confession was the truth.

Mrs Anderson's head was left spinning at the turn of events.

So thrown was she by her eavesdropping that instead of returning to Gardener's Cottage (as she knew she should) she decided to take a chance on visiting Jim to find out what was going on. As she had never been to his smallholding, she fretted about drawing attention to herself again. She started the car in a tizzy of indecision and let it roll towards the road. Left for Jim; right for Gardener's Cottage. She chose left and berated herself for making the wrong decision. She called herself 'idiot' and 'fool' in the vague hope she'd come to her senses, turn the car round and go home. Still, she drove on. A compulsion had overtaken her. She had to find out why Jim had been inventing things, whether he was just being Jim – making himself the centre of attention – or if something else was afoot, something that could spoil her plan.

On the southern shore of Poltown Loch the road narrowed at a cattle grid. Mrs Anderson stopped the car to compose herself (it would never do to let Jim think she was in a flap) and to rehearse her explanation for dropping by – to apologize for her mood the previous afternoon when he'd visited her. After checking her face in the mirror and adjusting her hair, she released the handbrake and let out the clutch. The car progressed slowly along a winding road sheltered by birch and alder trees. Emerging on to more open ground, Mrs Anderson spied Jim's smallholding. It amounted to a patchwork of walled fields around a house and outbuildings set back from the shore of the sea loch. She stopped the car to take it all in and noticed sheep spilling from a trailer into a pasture beside the house. A man was banging on the trailer sides as the animals careered down the ramp. Jim, she thought. At least he looked like Jim: small, round and wearing blue overalls. Mrs Anderson released the brake and drove on only to regret her impetuosity. What concerned her was the Land Rover attached to the trailer. She knew that wasn't Jim's. Someone else had to be there: the thought hadn't occurred to her earlier, so distracted had she been.

She scolded herself again – *idiot, fool!* If only she had gone home and rung Jim. Why hadn't she thought of that earlier? There was nothing she could say to his face that she couldn't have mentioned on the phone. But it was too late to turn back now. Jim, or the figure she thought was Jim, had noticed her car. He was looking in her direction. Although she was still a distance away, too far for her face to be identifiable, the chances were he recognized her car. Even so, Mrs Anderson considered turning round and going home. She could always ring later and spin him a story about not wanting to bother him when he was busy. She looked at the road ahead but couldn't see anywhere to turn; nor, she realized after glancing in the mirror, was there anywhere behind, so thick was the bracken growing at the edge of the tarmac. In desperation she considered reversing all the way to the cattle grid. But her neck was far too stiff to carry off a manoeuvre like that with any degree of safety. She made a muffled exclamation of frustration and resigned herself to the inevitable.

Once she'd parked beside the wall in front of the house, Jim came hurrying towards her. He seemed agitated. She wondered if her unannounced (and unprecedented) visit was the cause or if he was aghast at the thought of someone like Mrs Anderson seeing inside his house. As soon as she got out of the car she attempted to reassure him, complimenting him on his home. A little paradise, she called it, and remarked with feigned exasperation at her unadventurous nature that had prevented her from paying a visit until today.

'I'm so glad I made the effort,' she said, gawping at the buildings and the scenery with exaggerated appreciation. 'It's perfect here, Jim. You've been keeping this a secret.'

Jim, meanwhile, gave a good impression of being appalled at Mrs Anderson's arrival. He stood in front of her with a pleading expression and as he did so the door of the Land Rover opened and a thuggish-looking man with tattooed arms got out. Jim started talking to Mrs Anderson rather too loudly and in a most peculiar way. 'Hello, Mary . . .'

He'd never called her that before.

'Ach, I'm sorry. I forgot this was your day for eggs. I should have put you off coming this week. The ducks aren't laying but I'll give you a call when they're back on. I've got any amount of hens' eggs if they're any use.'

What was Jim talking about!

Mrs Anderson saw his pleading look had become even

more pronounced. It was clear that something was amiss and that she had to play along. As luck would have it, she remembered she had two empty egg boxes on the back seat of her car. 'Don't worry, Jim. I'll leave you the egg boxes and could you drop them off at Gardener's Cottage on your way past when the ducks are laying again?'

While she was at the car she kept an eye on the driver of the Land Rover who had sauntered over to join Jim. Mrs Anderson recognized the face and the name that went with it: Davie White. He was one of Turnbull's thugs and he looked the part too: muscled, with dark stubble over his head and sharp face, as well as an unpleasant swagger. It was also obvious that Jim was uncomfortable in the man's company. Remembering Jim's debt to Turnbull, his odd behaviour started to make a little more sense. Perhaps he'd been alarmed at the possibility of Mrs Anderson being her usual outspoken self, of her taking Davie White to task for preying on unfortunates like Jim. She had been so wrapped up in her own concerns that she had forgotten Jim's.

Returning from the car with an egg box in each hand, she said good morning to Davie, who didn't respond.

Then she turned to Jim. 'Tell you what . . . I might as well have those hens' eggs, a dozen brown ones if you've got them. They do taste so much better.' She smiled as though this was a continuing but good-humoured dispute between them.

She was relieved to see Jim relax. He blinked once and again, which she interpreted as encouragement to continue in the same vein, before going off to fill her egg boxes. Mrs Anderson addressed herself to Davie, 'If I had a place like this I'd have hens too, and geese. I've always had a soft spot for geese.'

'Is that right?' His tone was mocking and was accompanied by a smirk. Then he walked away, waving and shouting after Jim, 'Be good now. Make sure you're only giving her eggs.' The Land Rover's engine clattered into life and the vehicle, pulling its trailer, drove slowly past. Davie nodded at Jim, who was coming back with the full egg boxes, but ignored Mrs Anderson.

'Not a nice man,' Mrs Anderson said.

Jim looked embarrassed. 'I'm sorry, Mrs A.' He pressed her to take the eggs as a thank you.

'For what, Jim? Are you in trouble with Davie White?'

Jim started to gabble on about Davie having done him a good turn. 'He found my sheep wandering on the road. Someone must have left the gate open during the night. I know it wasn't me because I've trained Tommy to run round last thing in the evening and if he finds a gate open he'll bark until I come to close it. Bright as a button is Tommy. So bright I wouldn't be surprised if Tommy could be taught to close gates on his own.' He smiled at Mrs Anderson.

'Talking of Tommy,' Jim said, 'where is the lad?' He whistled and a few seconds later the dog appeared in the open gateway to the pasture where the sheep had been unloaded. And sure enough he stopped and barked.

'See, there he goes,' Jim remarked, before excusing himself to shut the gate.

When Jim returned, Tommy at his heel, Mrs Anderson steered him away from another discussion about the dog by saying, 'I've just been admiring your garden, Jim, and your house.' She needn't have bothered because the Jim who addressed her now was a different character from the one who had gone to shut the gate. What *is* going on, she wondered.

Instead of Jim's expression being evasive – until then he hadn't once looked Mrs Anderson in the eye – it had become one of settled grimness.

'You'll have heard about Duncan,' he said.

'I have.' She was watching for Jim's reaction. 'That's why I'm here. I've also heard what you've been saying.'

Jim rubbed his hands around each other, a display of regret. 'You should have been there, Mrs A – the guilt was eating away at him. I've never seen a man so unhappy. He told me he'd killed her.' He sighed. 'Who'd have thought Duncan capable of murder? If only I'd rung the police last night . . .'

'Yes, indeed, if only you had . . .' Mrs Anderson's features matched Jim's for severity. 'I imagine the reason you didn't is that Duncan didn't confess to anything since we both know he didn't kill Megan Bates.'

Jim stared blankly at the loch.

'Tell me, Jim,' Mrs Anderson continued, 'how many times has Duncan told you about keeping the beach clean for Megan, about keeping her room neat and tidy? About being ready for her when she came back?'

Jim said, 'He must have been lying.'

'He thought Megan was still alive, so why would he confess to her murder?'

Jim said nothing.

Mrs Anderson's eyes formed little hoods. 'Jim,' she snapped. 'Well?' She studied the returning tic in Jim's cheek and slowly her mouth fell open at the thought that had just occurred to her. 'Jim, you haven't . . .'

'Haven't what?' Jim said.

'Made up this cock-and-bull story about Duncan because Turnbull told you to?' Her head shook slowly at the dawning realization, at a Jim she hadn't encountered before. 'Is that why Davie White was here? Is that why he was bringing back your sheep – because you'd done Turnbull's dirty work?'

Then something happened that Mrs Anderson hadn't thought possible. Jim became defiant – with *her*.

'No one put me up to anything. Duncan murdered Megan Bates. He said so last night. He fooled everyone, you too. Now if you don't mind I've got my sheep to attend to.'

29

The egg boxes lay where she'd thrown them. One was the right way up; the other splayed open after falling on its side. Jim's eggs were cracked and broken. Albumen and yolk oozed from the ruptured shells and membranes. Mrs Anderson watched the liquid slipping and sliding while her hands searched out the edge of the kitchen table, its wooden reliability a reassurance after the tremors of the day. From having been the person in control of events she found they were now spinning beyond her reach. The thought of Turnbull being behind Jim's intervention added another and worrying consideration. Why was Turnbull meddling? What did he know?

The sound of an engine and the bang of a car door made her jump, at first with surprise – she hadn't noticed the vehicle's approach – then fright. What new shock awaited her? She remembered too late she hadn't locked the door, hadn't even closed it properly in her rush to reach sanctuary.

'Mary,' a man's voice called out. It was followed by knocking. 'Mary Anderson, are you there? It's Hamish. Hamish Boyd.'

To stop him finding her in the kitchen and her having to explain the broken eggs, she went to the hall before attempting a reply. Duncan's older brother was looking through the gap in the door when they saw each other. 'It's you, is it?' she said coldly.

Hamish was thickset and weathered; his frame and features shaped by a lifetime of physical work and exposure to the elements. His face was ruddy brown and his cheeks latticed with broken veins. His eyes were small, blue and darting below a ragged dome of home-cut greying hair and overgrown black eyebrows.

'You'd better come in, I suppose.' Her umbrage at being disturbed, at his failure to call her first, was evident and eloquent though left unsaid.

'You'll know why I'm here,' he said, stepping from the porch after going through the motions of brushing his shoes against the coconut doormat. He had the lumbering heaviness of a man burdened by sadness.

'Yes, I imagine I do.' She preceded him into the sitting room, or thought she had, but he held back in the hallway. Seeing him hovering there, she said, 'Well, do you want to come in or don't you?'

He mumbled his appreciation at being invited into her house, but stopped in the doorway. It was a throwback to his previous visits when she'd kept him standing outside, like a salesman or itinerant.

'This is about Duncan, I assume.'

Hamish pulled at the lapel of his tweed jacket and glanced down at his grey flannel trousers. Usually he wore overalls and two or three shirts, the number of layers depending on the temperature. 'I've been to identify the body,' he said. 'Thought I should be decent.'

'I see.' Mrs Anderson's mouth hardly opened, so fixed was it in disapproval.

Hamish paid attention to Mrs Anderson's furniture, the window, his feet, anything but meet her gaze. 'Duncan brought disgrace to a good name,' he said eventually.

'He ruined my father's farm, my farm.' Her tart reply made clear the family name was a lesser consideration for her.

Hamish nodded. 'I won't keep you, Mary.'

'What would keep you?'

'Well then, I'll tell you why I'm here,' he went on uncertainly. 'I've decided that Duncan should be cremated when the police release his body . . .' The sentence trailed away, as if he expected an interjection from Mrs Anderson, her approval or otherwise. 'We'll scatter his ashes away from here . . .' He paused again. A frown line creased his forehead. 'As for the house and farm . . .'

If he had been expecting Mrs Anderson to put aside her grudges and hurts because he had lost his only brother, he realized now his miscalculation. She glowered at him, waiting for what was coming next.

'The house and the farm,' he repeated. 'Duncan left his majority share to me.'

'I see,' she said.

'I would keep the property for my boy Graeme, if I thought he wanted it.'

'Not Margaret? Margaret is older than Graeme.'

'What would she want with a farm when she can go off to the city, work in a nice clean office and get married?'

'What indeed,' Mrs Anderson said tersely.

'No life for a girl.' Hamish realized too late his explanation propelled him further into the family minefield.

'No, no.' He shuffled from foot to foot. 'No. It'll be sold . . . that's for the best.'

'To BRC?' Mrs Anderson inquired.

Hamish nodded. 'No one else will want the house. The police think the woman might have been murdered there.' Hamish shook his head again at the shame. 'And the land has been ruined. Pulling down the buildings and covering the place with concrete – what else is it good for?'

Mrs Anderson reminded him of her fifteen per cent shareholding. 'If you have any decency you'll correct the wrong that was done to me by giving me the largest share, if not it all.' Then she asked him to leave, without saying goodbye, without going to the door to see him off.

The sight and sound of the digger unnerved Violet. She hated the way the boom moved, how it jerked like a bony finger, and she loathed the squeal of the engine as the bucket met the rock-like resistance of undisturbed soil. 'Are they sure she's buried there, Cal?' she asked for the umpteenth time.

'I don't know,' he replied again.

Watching and waiting like this was agony. Though she longed for her mother's body to be found so she could take possession of her, she dreaded the moment of discovery. She couldn't help but recall television programmes, documentaries as well as dramas, where skeletons had been unearthed and the skull or ribs showed where they'd been fractured by an axe or some other weapon. Is that what they would find?

Cal said nothing. There was nothing he could say.

After a while she asked, 'Where did she die, Cal?'

'I don't know.'

'The police didn't tell you?'

'I didn't ask.'

'Nothing,' she said turning to him, 'is worse than not knowing.' She studied him for evasion. 'Nothing . . .' She left it hanging, the implication clear. Her imagination churned with all the bloodiest possibilities so she might as well be told the truth.

'I don't think the police know,' Cal said.

The noise of the digger's engine drew her back to the spectacle which had kept her mesmerized for the past hour and a half.

Cal carried on, 'Constable Buchanan let slip that Duncan didn't say anything about how she died or where he hid her. Not in his confession to Jim Carmichael . . .'

The last of these omissions puzzled Cal. If Duncan was guilty, wouldn't he have left behind an explanatory note to guide the police to the woman's remains? Cal would. Wasn't that the only redemption available to a self-confessed murderer on the edge of hanging himself: to allow a daughter finally to bury her mother? Despite Violet's plea to be told everything, he kept this thought to himself. After all, he was only guessing. Perhaps Duncan judged himself past redemption when he slipped his head into his noose. Or perhaps he wasn't guilty of murder. Perhaps that was why he left no note.

Violet interrupted his thoughts. 'Would you do something for me?'

'Of course.'

'Would you go to Orasaigh? Get my things from the house and bring the tent?' She found the key in the pocket of her jeans. 'I can't go back.' She looked at him, her eyes filling with alarm. 'The atmosphere there . . . ' She shuddered. 'I can't.'

Should he try to reassure her it was like a thousand other properties in the West Highlands without damp-proof courses and windows too small for sunshine to penetrate the morbid chill? He decided against it. Perhaps the cottage had the atmosphere of a crypt because Duncan did kill Megan Bates there, as Violet seemed to fear.

He touched her on the arm. 'You'll be OK?'

'Yes.'

'I'll be as quick as I can.'

He was away the best part of an hour, waiting for the tide. On his return, he found her sitting exactly where he'd left her.

'This had been put through the door.' He held out a postcard, one side of which was a photograph of Brae House. She stared at it and then at him as if she had forgotten he'd been away or that she'd asked him to go.

'I found it at Orasaigh Cottage,' he explained. 'It's for you.'

She looked away, at the digger, at the restless searching for her mother's remains: the trucks, vans and a score of police in white or blue overalls.

'Shall I read it?' Cal asked. Violet nodded, a little movement of her head, her focus remaining on the hunt. 'It's from Alexandra Hamilton,' Cal said. 'She wants to meet with you. She says, would Brae House 4 p.m. tomorrow be convenient?'

'Anna is coming tomorrow.' Violet flashed him a brief smile. While he'd been away she had rung Hilary. There was a 6 a.m. bus from Glasgow with a connection in Ullapool. They – Hilary, Izzy and Anna – should arrive early afternoon. Hilary was bringing another tent. They could all camp at South Bay, couldn't they?

After a moment, Violet asked Cal if his mother had taken him to the beach as a child and he said she had.

'I wish I'd had that,' Violet said with feeling. 'Right now I wish it more than anything else.' She'd never been to the beach with Anna. Never paddled in the sea. Never made sandcastles. Never collected shells. Never picked up seaweed and looked for sandhoppers. Never fished in rock pools for crabs.

Hilary had often told her about a beach on the east coast, near St Andrews. It was a mile or two from Hilary's family home. Hilary played there when she was a child. So had her father and her grandmother. Now Izzy played there as well. Violet wished she had that continuity, the simple pleasures of one generation being handed down to the next. It was too late for her. She saw her life as one loss building on another: first her mother, then Anna's father. But she could break the pattern for Anna. Playing on the beach her grandmother loved: it was a small thing but important. For the first time in her life, Anna would know she was following in her grandmother's footsteps. For the first time, she would have something to remember her by which wasn't about loss, or death. Or now murder.

At dusk, Cal brought Violet a sleeping bag. He expected her to be stiff and unaccommodating, but she was the opposite, allowing him to wrap it around her without protest or resistance while remaining mute. Otherwise, he kept his distance, observing her from across the beach road where he'd parked the pick-up. He alternated between leaning against the bonnet and sitting in the driver's seat with the door open. When the police abandoned their search for the evening he stood behind her, in readiness to intervene should any of the officers try to move her on. The vans trundled past in convoy without stopping. Each policeman had the same expression of sombre respect that funeral mourners reserve for a relative of the deceased who remains beside the grave as the crowd departs.

As night fell, he found the scene more affecting than ever, with darkness creating the illusion of threat, of looming shapes emerging from the land and sea, of Violet defying monsters. Of all the thoughts he had about her, one impressed itself on him more than the others. At times of crisis she preferred solitude to company and silence to conversation. In this, Violet and he shared a characteristic. His inclination was to turn in upon himself and so, it seemed, was hers.

After midnight, he retired to the pick-up and pulled the door shut. He dozed restlessly, his sense of duty preventing him from dropping off, or so he imagined until he was awoken by the sound of the passenger door opening. He pretended still to be asleep as Violet settled beside him.

30

They were leaning against the back of the pick-up, Cal and Violet side by side, watching out for the Ullapool bus. Hilary had phoned to say it was running ten minutes late. While they waited, Violet asked about Cal's childhood, the relationship he had had with his mother.

She smiled. 'For one reason or another, motherhood seems to be on my mind.'

'We got on well,' he replied. 'I can't remember her ever being cross with me. Her name was Eilidh. She was a lawyer in Edinburgh. She was fifty-three when she died. Looking back now, I can see that my family died when she did. That's how important she was to me and my father. I think that's why he's found a new family in Africa . . . he wanted to have that strong bond again and why . . .' Cal smiled to lighten things '. . . the nearest thing I have to a home is an office in an industrial estate or a five-year-old pick-up with 102,000 miles on the clock.'

He avoided making a comparison between himself and Violet, though one occurred to him. The death of a mother was formative for each of them, neither really belonging anywhere as a result. He sensed Violet arriving at the same conclusion because she glanced at him, quickly, as if wanting to let him further into her confidence but finding her habit of reticence hard to overcome.

'Go on,' he encouraged.

She looked again for the bus. 'It's funny,' she said slowly, still deciding how much to reveal. 'Sitting last night watching the diggers and the police . . .' She breathed out, a little rush of self-deprecation to pre-empt any reaction from Cal. 'I can't describe the feeling because I'd never experienced that before . . . not in my adult life . . . of being a daughter, I suppose.'

She glanced at him again, a silent apology for the right words being hard to find. 'Of having a responsibility to a parent . . . Do you know what I mean? . . . Of my mother relying on me.' She let out a laugh. 'If the police hadn't been there with their diggers and trucks I'd have used my bare hands to find her.'

He nodded. He understood, or thought he did. 'If you'd asked me two, maybe three years ago, who I was or what I was, I could have produced a list. The top three would have been husband, son, oceanographer, even if I wouldn't have been sure about the order.' He smiled. 'Perhaps that's why my marriage wasn't exactly successful. Rachel always thought husband ranked below oceanographer.' His expression suggested that perhaps she'd been right. 'Now husband's no longer on the list and though, technically, I'm still a son, I don't feel like one any more because my father has gone, emotionally and physically.'

Violet nodded in understanding. 'Until last night, I hadn't considered myself a daughter, because I always thought my mother had abandoned me. Knowing that she didn't makes all the difference.'

She picked at her nails. He said nothing.

'Thank you,' she said after a moment.

'For what?'

'For listening.'

He made a face. *Who says he did?* She flicked the back of her hand against his thigh just as the bus appeared round the side of the hill. 'Today,' she said, setting off towards it, 'is going to be a happier day. Don't you think?'

Cal stayed where he was, watching the reunion of mother and daughter. When Violet started back towards him, a child in each hand, she called out to him. 'I should have warned you.'

'What?'

'How alike the girls are.'

'Twins,' he said. One was milky pale with straight white-blonde hair and the other brown-skinned with wide brown eyes and dark curls.

'That one,' he pointed at the darker girl, 'is yours.'

'How do you know?'

He looked from the blonde child holding Violet's other hand to the blonde woman who followed behind, one a smaller version of the other. 'Pure guesswork.'

'You must be Hilary,' he said, offering to take her rucksack and the extra tent. As he put them in the pick-up he noticed Hilary giving Violet an inquiring look and Violet deliberately ignoring her. Something similar happened at the turn-off to South Bay. Cal caught it in his mirror: Hilary's silent inquiry and Violet shaking her head and mouthing 'stop it'. He wondered if that was why Violet had asked Anna and Izzy to tell her everything they'd seen on their journey. Was she trying to stall Hilary's curiosity about Cal, about whether anything had happened between Violet and him? Approaching Boyd's Farm, he realized Violet had another, more urgent concern. The girls had listed buzzard, seal, mountain, heather, river, sea, bus, rook, seagull and forests and Anna was looking out of the window for other ideas. 'Now,' Violet said, turning her back to the door and covering the window to block Anna's view, 'why don't you ask Cal what he found in the shop for you?'

'What?' Both girls glanced shyly at the back of Cal's head.

'Nets for fishing in rock pools and,' Violet enthused, 'buckets *and* spades.' She mentioned the different creatures Anna and Izzy might catch: 'Starfish, crab, winkle, shrimp, prawn . . .' The girls listened and stretched their arms wide to show how big their catch would be. Having worked out why Violet was behaving in that way, Cal joined in by announcing he'd caught a whale in a rock pool when he'd been a boy, about the same age as Anna and Izzy.

'Could we *really* catch a whale?' Izzy asked Hilary.

'Maybe a small one,' Hilary suggested.

Anna adopted a know-it-all look. 'There aren't small whales.'

By then the pick-up had passed the stone pillars to Boyd's Farm and was approaching the road end by the beach. 'Here we are.' Violet sounded relieved. Anna and Izzy hadn't noticed a thing, not the police, the trucks or the diggers.

Anna was cleaning her beach apartment, patting the sand smooth with her hands, discarding seaweed and gathering up her collection of shells. 'Really . . . honestly . . . how many times do I have to tell you?' Anna greeted each new example of Violet's untidiness with an exclamation. One by one she picked up the shells and placed them beside a puddle of seawater. She scolded each one in turn.

'*You* need to be washed.'

'You *need* to be washed.'

'You need to be *washed*.'

With every change of emphasis she raised her voice. In between, she checked to see whether Violet was listening, whether she was sorry.

'How often have I told you about tidying up after parties?'

Violet still wasn't paying sufficient attention. So Anna pulled her arm. 'Mummy, I'm cross with you. I won't let you stay here if you don't help.' Violet glanced down at her daughter. Whenever Anna called her 'Mummy' she knew she was upset.

'I'm sorry, sweetheart.'

'Please . . . pleeeaaase . . . Mummy, help.' Pulling on Violet's arm wasn't working. So Anna slumped into a sulk. 'There's so much to do, pleeeaaase.'

Violet pulled the little girl to her, hugged her and kissed her head as Anna gave up her struggles of protest. 'Why won't you help with the dishes?' She twisted and turned until she was looking into Violet's face, which was puffy and wet from crying. Anna was suddenly solici- tous and attentive. She'd do the dishes. She liked doing dishes. Anna reached for her mother's face and wiped it, leaving grains of sand on her cheeks. 'I wasn't really cross.'

Violet said, 'It's not you, silly.'

Anna was now pulling at her mother's lips, making her kiss her fingertips one by one. 'What is it, then?'

'Oh, it's nothing. It's just being with you . . . here, on this beach.'

Anna curled up between her mother's legs. 'How many floors will our proper beach house have?' she asked.

'Two,' Violet replied.

'Bigger than this beach apartment . . . ?'

'Yes.'

'And we'll have a bedroom each and one for Izzy to come and stay?'

'Yes.'

'And a separate kitchen?' A separate kitchen was important to Anna. The flat in Glasgow had one room with a bathroom off.

'Yes.'

'And someone to do the dishes?'

'Yes.'

Anna reviewed her mother's answers, checking everything important had been covered. 'All right,' she said.

They lay together until Violet said, 'Anna, if I help you with the dishes, will you come for a walk?'

'I might,' she replied. 'Where to?'

'Just along the beach, and then we'll join the others. In fact,' Violet suggested, 'why don't you put your feet up and I'll do the dishes.' Violet reached for the shells and made splashing noises in the rock pool. 'There,' she said. 'Finished.'

Anna sat and inspected the shells. She pointed at one, claiming it still to be dirty, and set about washing it. 'Did you know . . . ?' Violet was standing up and lifting Anna over the surrounding rocks and planting her on the sand.

'What?'

'. . . What your grandmother did most days?'

'No.'

Violet held out her hand for Anna. Their fingers interlocked and Violet walked her to the water's edge. 'She used to come here.'

'Did she paddle?' Anna let the water approach the tips of her toes before jumping back.

'She did. She used to do this, just like we're doing.'

A black Audi with tinted windows was parked at the stone pillars to Boyd's Farm. The car was clean, shiny and, in Cal's opinion, out of place. It belonged in a swanky city street, not this back of beyond. He walked in its direction, his attention on the progress of the search. The scene was little changed. Teams of police sifted through the piles of flotsam and the numerous small mounds of earth the diggers had scooped from the four shallow pits that had been excavated so far. Even at a distance Cal could see how little topsoil there was, barely enough to cover a body. He would tell Violet that was why the police were concentrating their search on Duncan's flotsam piles: a body in such a shallow grave would need to have another, covering layer for concealment. Something else was obvious: by the numbers of police and the level of activity – there were half a dozen vans as well as two diggers and three trucks – the body had not been found.

By then Cal was almost at the parked car. As he drew alongside, intending to carry on to the Poltown road before returning to the beach a different way, the driver's window opened with an expensive swish. A man in dark glasses, Mediterranean blue shirt open at the neck and a supercilious smile, asked, 'Don't suppose they've found anything?'

'Who wants to know?' Cal said, bending down and looking in. There was another man in the passenger seat. Cal recognized Ross Turnbull. He nodded acknowledgement and Turnbull returned the gesture. The man in dark glasses flashed another bright white smile and his card: *Don Saxby, Executive Director, Development, BRC* was written across the base of a drawing of a wind turbine. 'Just wondering what delay to factor in.'

Cal snorted and shook his head. 'Don't you people ever give up – a man's dead, for God's sake, and a woman.' The window closed.

When Cal returned to South Bay, Hilary and Izzy were splashing at the water's edge and Violet was sitting higher up the beach beside Anna. The girl was turning the pages of her painting book and telling Violet about each picture.

'That's Granny's house. That's her front door and that's,' Anna pointed again, 'her bedroom window.'

Violet glanced at Cal. He shook his head. *No, nothing, they're still searching.*

'And here's Granny.' Anna turned another page.

'So it is, Anna. You are clever. Just as I asked you. Will you paint some more while you're here?'

'Hilary only let me bring crayons,' Anna said crossly.

'Well, draw something for me in crayons. I'd love that.'

Violet glanced again at Cal.

'Alexandra Hamilton's invitation to Brae this afternoon . . .' he reminded her. 'Will you go?'

~~~~~~

After a late picnic lunch of tomato sandwiches, crisps and cans of Fanta, Violet warned the girls they had work to do. It was a rule of camping, she said; everyone pitching in together, children and adults; each having a task. Izzy and Anna drowned out Violet by shouting and Violet told Cal he wouldn't have any young assistants after all. Anna and Izzy would be accompanying their mothers on a long walk and he'd have to put up the tents and collect driftwood for the fire by himself. She suggested the girls put on their shoes because they'd be climbing uphill and the path would be stony and rough. Izzy and Anna looked at each other before Izzy announced she had a sore foot and should probably remain behind to help Cal. 'So it'll just be you walking, will it, Anna?' Violet inquired while busying herself with her backpack. 'Hilary,' Violet asked, 'have you got any of those plasters for blisters . . .'

Anna pulled at her mother's sleeve.

'Can't I stay here, with Izzy?'

'If you help Cal,' Violet replied as a small, red car appeared at the road end, drawing her attention away. 'Come on,' she said to Hilary, 'I'll introduce you.' They started across the sand and Mrs Anderson appeared at the open driver's door. She was barely taller than the car. 'You must think me very rude,' Violet said, 'running out of your house like that, leaving you with all the clearing up after all the trouble you'd taken.'

Mrs Anderson shielded her eyes from the sun with one hand and held on to the door with the other, as if she needed the support. Violet thought how frail Mrs Anderson looked.

'I don't think you're rude at all. Not a bit,' Mrs Anderson replied. 'I should be apologizing to you.'

'Why?'

'I didn't know Megan Bates was your mother. If I had, I'd have been more careful about what I said . . . to be told that Duncan had her clothes and other things. It must have been an awful shock . . .'

Mrs Anderson looked back over her shoulder in the direction of Boyd's Farm. 'Now this terrible thing has happened and done by my own flesh and blood. I don't know what to say to you. It's terrible, just terrible.'

Violet rubbed the old woman's arm. 'You're not to blame.'

'No,' Mrs Anderson replied in the same troubled manner. 'I suppose not, but still, I can't help but feel responsible.'

Violet introduced Hilary and pointed out the children, telling Mrs Anderson which was which. 'Just in case they come over,' Violet warned, 'Anna knows about her grandmother being dead, but not how she died, nor about the police search.'

'Well, I won't say anything.' Mrs Anderson approved of Violet's restraint. 'Far better she doesn't know the details,' she said with the certainty of age. Although she was tactful enough to say, 'What lovely children,' Violet noticed Mrs Anderson's eye remaining on Anna.

'I just want her to enjoy the feeling of having a grandmother,' Violet said, 'of spending time on the beach where she loved to be.'

'Well,' Mrs Anderson said, 'if there are things you have to do, the police and so on, leave them with me . . . or if the weather changes and they need a hot bath. It's been too long since Gardener's Cottage has heard the sound of children.' As an afterthought, she asked, 'Do small girls still like baking?'

'They do,' Violet replied.

The conversation moved on to Alexandra's invitation to Brae, Violet asking Mrs Anderson's advice on whether she should go. Hilary thought she should but Violet wasn't sure. 'Of course you must go,' Mrs Anderson replied, 'and let me have the children. Then Hilary can accompany you.'

Later, as she was showing Hilary her father's gravestone, Violet said she was pleased the girls would be going to Mrs Anderson because she'd seemed somehow diminished. Duncan's death and the police searching her old home must have hit her hard. Having Anna and Izzy would be good for her.

31

Alexandra Hamilton wore a silk print dress belted at the waist and a style of shoe that Anna liked to call 'properly'. They were black patent with heels that elevated Alexandra above her visitors. 'Oh, there you are,' she said, her manner as overbearing as her height. 'I suppose you'd better follow me.' Leaving Violet to close the back door, she went briskly from the kitchen to the front of the house; one pantry opening on to another followed by a wood-panelled corridor. Violet and Hilary lagged half a dozen steps behind, their different progress marked by the noise of footwear on polished floors; the squeak of trainers from Violet and Hilary, the emphatic tattoo of Alexandra's expensive heels.

'Queen Bitch,' Hilary whispered to Violet before they found themselves in a large hall, also wood-panelled, with twin leather sofas either side of a fireplace. Above it hung the portrait of a young woman, her blonde hair cascading artfully on to one shoulder, her face tilted upwards and glowing with the hungry expectation of a charmed life. 'A present from William Ritchie, my father,' Alexandra said, watching for Violet's reaction. 'He commissioned it for my twenty-first birthday.' Alexandra's fingers played with the string of pearls at her neck. The young woman in the painting wore them too. Alexandra saw Violet make the connection. 'Another present,' she simpered, 'for my eighteenth.'

Hilary mouthed at Violet, '*Whose* father?' as Alexandra set off again, this time through an open door into what turned out to be the dining room. A man with wire-rimmed glasses and a crust of white hair sat at the far end of a long mahogany table around which were a dozen chairs with matching tapestry seats. 'I'm sorry, Gordon, for abandoning you.' Alexandra addressed him as if speaking to a crowd. 'I had to go looking for them – they'd gone to the *back* door.'

He raised a sympathetic eyebrow at such odd behaviour.

'This . . .' Alexandra pulled a chair away from the table for Violet, 'is Miss Wells.' She gave Hilary a dismissive look. 'And friend . . .' She carried on to the head of the table without pulling out another chair for Hilary. 'And this . . .' She stopped beside Gordon and placed her hand lightly on his shoulder, 'is Mr Campbell.'

Mr Campbell inclined his head at Violet and Hilary before sliding a document across the table to Alexandra.

Violet watched the transaction uneasily.

'Sit down, please.' Alexandra turned a page and studied it, like a schoolmistress checking up on the record of a pupil brought before her for a disciplinary misdemeanour.

'I'm fine as I am, thanks. Why don't you tell me why this man is here and why you wanted to see me?'

A bored expression crossed Alexandra's face. 'Mr Campbell is a solicitor and . . .' She gave Violet a contemptuous look, '. . . a very old family friend.' She slapped her open hands on the table, indicating the start of proceedings. 'Now, Miss Wells, this might not be what you want to hear but my father died regretting his affair with Megan Bates.' Alexandra lifted her nose, attempting to rise above a bad smell.

'Excuse me, *whose* father?' blurted Hilary.

The lawyer cleared his throat. 'And you are . . . ?'

'I'm Violet's friend, Hilary Reston.'

'Well, Miss Reston, you may not realize this but Mrs Hamilton's biological father abandoned her when she was four. So William Ritchie was really the only father she had and Mrs Hamilton was the only daughter, the only *child*, he acknowledged.' He allowed his left eyebrow to rise again. 'Indeed,' he glanced at Alexandra, 'with Mr Ritchie's encouragement and support she adopted his surname and she used it until her marriage to Matthew Hamilton.'

'Don't listen to him,' Hilary advised Violet before returning to glower at Mr Campbell. 'Why are you being so horrible?'

Mr Campbell cleared his throat again in lawyerly affectation. 'Because it is important that Miss Wells doesn't harbour any illusions about what were and are the facts of Mr William Ritchie's short-lived affair with Megan Bates.' He drew back his lips to reveal worn-down, sharp little teeth before turning to examine Violet. 'It is quite clear he did not love Megan Bates, nor by the end of the affair did he have any feelings for her or for her unborn child.' His lips stretched again, as if attempting to demonstrate his sympathy for Violet's predicament. 'Indeed, given Megan Bates's reputation, there is no reason why he should have formed an attachment to the child, since it was far from certain he was the father.'

'Well, that's easily resolved,' Hilary snapped.

'Not as easily as you or Miss Wells might think.' Mr Campbell regarded Hilary over his glasses with a

considered and concerned stare. 'I assume you are referring to the possibility of a DNA procedure?'

'Yes, I am.'

'That would require the disinterment of William Ritchie's coffin.' He paused and looked from Hilary to Violet. 'I
imagine you realize that, since no other sources of DNA
would be available.'

'I hadn't thought about it, but yes,' Hilary replied,
glancing at Violet to check whether her friend was in
agreement.

'Well, if that is the course of action Miss Wells plans, it
would have to be resolved in a court of law. My client, of
course, would oppose any interference with her father's
grave.' His eyebrow arched. 'I'm sure you realize that
going to court would be very expensive, especially for the
losing side.' He dropped his chin and stared over his
glasses. 'Even more so if there were appeals and the usual
costly delays . . . costs that my clients can easily afford.' He
directed a pitying frown at Violet. 'And that also applies
should you decide to pursue an action for any of the property Mrs Hamilton inherited from her father.'

Violet frowned in return. 'Is that why you think I'm
here?'

'Frankly,' Mr Campbell said, 'I have no idea why you
are here, but in case it's to try to enrich yourself at Mrs
Hamilton's expense . . .' He stopped and referred to the
document in front of him. 'There are two issues to be
resolved. The first is whether you are indeed Mr Ritchie's
daughter, which my client disputes. The second, and the
issue of greater significance, is whether, had Mr Ritchie
imagined himself to be the father, he would have made

any provision for you in his will if he had known you were alive. Of course, if you *were* his child, under Scots law, you could well have a claim for a share of what we call his moveable property – furniture and so on – but again you would have to establish that claim in court with all the risk and expense that might involve.

'In case of any confusion,' he glanced now at Alexandra, 'Mrs Hamilton thought you should be made aware of her father's, Mr Ritchie's, attitude towards Megan Bates. Before his death, he wrote a letter to his wife, my client's mother, expressing his regret at the affair and the hurt it caused. He is silent on the subject of Megan Bates's child but goes on to make specific reference to his paternal love for my client.' He indicated he was talking about Alexandra Hamilton. 'He refers to her as "our darling daughter".'

He let his words have their effect before continuing. 'The difficulty for you, Miss Wells, is this: if you were to pursue the legal route, my client would give evidence that William Ritchie not only regretted his entanglement with Megan Bates but never accepted the child as his own.' He managed to sound perplexed on Violet's behalf. 'As far as I am aware, there is no witness available to you with more intimate access to William Ritchie or knowledge of his feelings at that time than my client.'

Hilary banged on the table. 'Stop this – what are you saying?' she shouted. 'Violet's mother has been murdered and the police are still looking for her body.'

'None of which is my client's concern.' Mr Campbell coughed. 'However, she is concerned at the disruptive effect of Miss Wells's presence here on her family.'

'Meaning what?' Hilary asked.

'Meaning that she is prepared to offer Miss Wells some small recompense for her . . .' Mr Campbell searched for the appropriate word. 'Shall we say for her . . . trouble?' He smirked in satisfaction at his eventual choice.

'What?' Violet said.

'My client,' he indicated Alexandra again, 'is prepared to offer you the sum of one thousand pounds in full and final settlement of any future claim you may bring on the basis of your unproven relationship to William Ritchie.'

He looked at Violet, as if inviting a question. 'There are two conditions: that you agree to take no steps to establish paternity and that you agree to remove yourself from Poltown forthwith and henceforth.'

'What,' Hilary exclaimed, 'for a thousand pounds?'

'Miss Wells would then return to the life she was leading a few days ago, before she'd heard of Mr William Ritchie, before she knew Poltown existed,' Mr Campbell said. Money for nothing, his eyebrow suggested.

Hilary and Violet exchanged glances.

'I would advise you to consider my client's offer with care.' Mr Campbell removed his glasses and his lips pulled back into something between a smirk and a snarl. 'When you think of the alternative . . .'

The sentence was left hanging, along with the implication of unspecified consequences. 'Of course,' he added, 'we will require a signature from you, Miss Wells, at the places marked.'

With that he slid a document across the table towards Violet. It had yellow tabs at the pages where Violet was expected to sign. 'Your friend can sign too, as the witness.' A pen was lying on the top sheet. 'Mrs Hamilton and I will be waiting outside should you have any questions.'

He snapped his briefcase shut. 'To avoid misunderstanding, there will be no repetition of this offer.' He waited for Alexandra to rise and followed her from the room.

After the door closed they heard Alexandra's heels striking against the wooden floor of the hall. Violet stretched across the table and tore the document in half and again into quarters. The pieces of paper fluttered from her hands. Taking the key to Orasaigh Cottage from her jeans pocket, she placed it among the fragments on the polished mahogany table.

'I was wrong,' Hilary said. 'What an EMPRESS of a bitch.' She hugged Violet. 'Are you OK?'

'I'm fine.'

Hilary surveyed the dining room with its gilt mirrors and a sideboard crowded with a menagerie of animals in silver. 'I know what this is about,' she said. 'She's showing off. That's what she's doing. Don't you see? The house, the painting in the hall, the pearls, all this . . . she's letting you see what she's got, her inheritance, the "moveable property". She's daring you to take her on.'

Violet looked around the room too, wondering how she belonged here, *if* she belonged here, how these *possessions* had anything to do with her.

'What are you going to do?' Hilary asked.

'Nothing.' Violet moved towards the door. 'Nothing at all.'

She waited for Hilary before turning the handle. In the hall, Alexandra looked up and Mr Campbell studied Violet over the top of his glasses. 'I presume,' he said, 'that you have been sensible.' There was an unspoken 'or else'.

'Then I suggest you stop making presumptions about me until you're better at it,' Violet said.

'Come on.' Hilary pulled at her arm. 'Let's go.'

They went along the corridor to the kitchen and the back door. Outside, in the yard, Hilary said, 'Did you see the way they were looking at us?' She glanced behind her, as if expecting to find Alexandra and the lawyer in pursuit. Violet walked on without speaking. As they skirted the walled garden on their way to pick up Anna and Izzy from Mrs Anderson, Hilary forced her to stop. 'You weren't supposed to do that. Were you?'

'No,' Violet said.

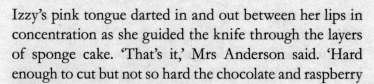

Izzy's pink tongue darted in and out between her lips in concentration as she guided the knife through the layers of sponge cake. 'That's it,' Mrs Anderson said. 'Hard enough to cut but not so hard the chocolate and raspberry filling spills out.'

The knife hit the plate with a clunk.

'Do the same again here.' Mrs Anderson took the knife and scored the icing with the blade. 'Now press down.' Then, Anna and Izzy each delivered a plate of cake to their mothers.

'It looks delicious,' Violet said and kissed Anna, which

elicited an indignant protest: 'Customers shouldn't kiss the waitress.'

'Mm, perfect,' Hilary said, taking a bite.

Anna and Izzy grinned at each other and Mrs Anderson said, 'Now, girls, what about your mothers enjoying their tea in peace?' Handing a plate of cake to each child, she asked Violet and Hilary whether they minded Anna and Izzy watching television next door. She'd promised they could, a reward for helping her to lay the table and clear up the dishes.

'Of course not,' Hilary said. Mrs Anderson herded the girls ahead of her. 'Come on, then.' She pulled the kitchen door to. 'Let's see what's on.'

In the sitting room, Anna and Izzy knelt on the rug, their cake in front of them. Mrs Anderson turned on the television, apologizing for having so few channels. 'That, that,' Anna shouted as Mrs Anderson switched from one to the next.

That was a wildlife programme about a mother monkey and her sick baby. 'It's going to die, isn't it?' Izzy complained to Anna.

'It can't,' Anna insisted. 'I won't let it.'

As soon as they were engrossed, Mrs Anderson remembered she had to shut the window in her bedroom. 'Be sure now to tell me everything when I get back.' The girls looked up before the monkey claimed their attention again and Mrs Anderson went across the hall. She lingered at the foot of the stairs, close enough to the kitchen door to hear Violet and Hilary.

Hilary was saying, 'It's meaningless, don't you see?'

Violet replied, 'I told you, it doesn't matter.' Mrs Anderson heard the hurt in her voice.

'So what if he wrote a letter to his wife just before he died,' Hilary continued. 'What was he supposed to say? That he'd loved another woman? Of course he wouldn't. It doesn't prove anything. Your mother had been dead for years; as far as he was concerned so had you. Of course he'd say he regretted the affair. Of course he wouldn't mention whether he'd had feelings for you, for his child.'

'Really, it doesn't matter,' Violet insisted.

'Well,' Hilary said. 'Don't let it get to you. That bitch is just frightened of you, that's all. Nobody can tell what would have happened if your father had known you were alive; nobody.'

Changing the subject, Violet said she should check whether Anna and Izzy were exhausting Mrs Anderson. 'She's been so good with them.' A chair scraped and Mrs Anderson retreated into the sitting room. Her entrance barely disturbed the children, who were still gripped by the unfolding tragedy of the sick monkey. Its condition had worsened and Anna and Izzy were discussing whether it was still breathing. Mrs Anderson settled into a chair just as Violet looked round the door and saw the girls fixed on an apparently lifeless and almost hairless body.

'Is the poor little thing dead?' she asked and Anna and Izzy explained what had happened, taking it in turns to relate the disasters that had befallen the unfortunate creature. Anna waved her mother closer and Mrs Anderson took the opportunity to excuse herself to put the kettle on.

As she hoped, Hilary was still at the kitchen table. Closing the door, Mrs Anderson wondered whether she would like another cup of tea. 'I don't suppose *Miss* Alexandra offered you very much.'

'Certainly not tea,' Hilary answered with similar disapproval to Mrs Anderson's.

Mrs Anderson replied with a series of tuts. 'In Mr William's time, it was always a very welcoming house. Not like it is now.'

'You worked for William Ritchie, didn't you?'

'I did, for many years, when he was a bachelor and then after his marriage to Alexandra's mother.'

'What sort of man was he?'

Mrs Anderson considered the question and Hilary mistook her hesitation for offence. 'I hope you don't mind me asking?'

'Not at all,' Mrs Anderson reassured her. Her mouth flinched as if in pain. 'Not after the way Alexandra and that husband of hers have treated me.'

'I'm sorry. I didn't know.'

'They wouldn't have dared if Mr William had been alive.' Mrs Anderson managed to look appropriately indignant. 'A gentleman, he was, *and* he had good manners.' In contrast to Alexandra, was the inference. 'Even if he did prefer his own company.'

'You liked him?' Hilary thought it safer territory than a question about Alexandra.

'It wasn't my place to like him.' She corrected Hilary in her precise way. 'I was his housekeeper. I respected him.'

'Did he respect you?'

'I like to think so.' Mrs Anderson saw Hilary's puzzlement at her uncertainty. 'It was the way of things then. Mr William was someone who liked rules and formalities, everything in its proper place.'

'He sounds like a cold man.'

Mrs Anderson considered Hilary's criticism. 'He wasn't an easy man to get to know, that's certainly true. And he could be distant. Emotions frightened him. He wasn't comfortable with them, like a lot of men, I suppose. But you could always rely on him to be fair. You could trust him.' Once again the comparison with Alexandra was left unsaid.

'Stop me if I'm prying, but did you know Megan Bates?'

'I did.'

'You didn't approve?'

'Indeed, I did not.' Mrs Anderson's voice had become clipped.

'Alexandra had a lawyer with her. A man called Campbell. Do you know him?'

'I know of him.' She didn't elaborate. Mr Campbell had signed the warning letters she had received about the rent for Gardener's Cottage.

'Well, he said . . . the lawyer, that is . . .' Hilary dropped her voice and glanced at the door in case Violet was about to return. 'He said that even William Ritchie wasn't convinced that Megan Bates's child was his.'

'Mr Campbell said that?'

'Yes.'

'The nerve of some people,' Mrs Anderson muttered.

'William Ritchie knew he *was* the father?'

'That was my impression at the time.'

'Mr Campbell tried to make out that William Ritchie

had no wish for any other child but Alexandra. He mentioned Alexandra changing her surname to Ritchie as evidence of that.'

'She did change her name, yes.' Mrs Anderson pursed her lips tight together.

'What did her stepfather think?'

'I can't say at the beginning,' Mrs Anderson replied. 'It wasn't long after Megan Bates's death.'

Hilary gasped. 'You mean she tried to replace his dead child?'

Mrs Anderson's eyes flicked to the ceiling, inviting Hilary to draw her own conclusions. 'At that time I don't think Mr William would have noticed whether she called herself Ritchie or any other name.'

'Why not?'

'He locked himself away. I hardly saw him for months.'

'He was upset at Megan's death?'

'That and the baby, and the hurt he'd caused Diana, the shame of being exposed like that, everyone talking about it, the disgrace. It was all of those together.'

'He mourned the baby too?'

'Mr William had his differences with Megan Bates before her death but . . .' She chose her words with care. 'It would be a mistake to think he had no feelings for the child.'

'Go on,' Hilary said.

'He would have been torn in two, between Diana and Megan Bates, between his marriage and the child. Diana was threatening him with a divorce if he continued the affair. Megan Bates was using the child to pressure him to live with her.'

'She threatened to disappear with the baby?'

'Apparently so,' Mrs Anderson replied. 'Mr William wouldn't have known what to do and then it was too late. Megan was dead. Afterwards he blamed himself for everything.'

The sound of Anna and Izzy chattering in the hall penetrated the kitchen door. Hilary turned as the girls entered the room. Violet followed with their dirty plates. 'I think it's time we left you in peace,' she said to Mrs Anderson. 'You've been so kind.'

After saying farewells at the front door, Violet suggested a race to the end of the garden wall. She and Izzy had started running when Anna reached up to Mrs Anderson. 'Thank you,' she said as the old woman bent towards her. Anna planted a sticky kiss on her cheek and ran off, shouting, 'Wait for me,' to Violet and Izzy.

Hilary hung back.

'Don't let Violet know I've told you this,' she said.

Mrs Anderson attempted to conceal the effect Anna's display of affection had had on her. 'What, dear?'

'Alexandra made Violet an offer to settle any claim she has against William Ritchie's estate.'

'Did she?'

'It was laughable really, only a thousand pounds.'

'What did Violet say?'

'She didn't say anything. She tore up the document.' Hilary looked at Mrs Anderson. 'I've told her to fight for what's hers.'

'Of course she must,' Mrs Anderson snapped. Her right hand gripped Hilary's arm. 'She must. Tell her she must.'

'I will.'

Mrs Anderson seemed to struggle for words. 'She can't . . . she can't . . . let that *cuckoo* have it all.'

Hilary remembered the portrait in the hall, the way Alexandra's head tilted upwards, just like a baby cuckoo waiting to be fed after it has evicted all the other fledglings from the nest.

~~~~~

Mrs Anderson felt the warmth and sugary stickiness of Anna's goodbye kiss, such innocent simplicity provoking a storm of emotion and regret. How daft she was for allowing a child's touch to affect her so. What an old fool she had become. She slumped into her chair in the kitchen to mourn what she had lost, what might have been, the memory of her stillborn daughter coming back to haunt her. The forefinger and thumb of her right hand stroked the edge of the table where Violet had lain as a newborn baby, where earlier that day Violet had eaten chocolate and raspberry sponge cake.

One gust subsided and another, of indignation, blew in, at the humiliations Mrs Anderson had had to bear, at Alexandra's ill-deserved good fortune to have children and money, at the injustice being done to Violet and Anna. She imagined Violet and Anna living at Brae. How different it would be. Mrs Anderson would be a cherished and frequent visitor. Anna would drop by to make cakes at Gardener's Cottage. For righting the wrong in which she was complicit, had Mrs Anderson found salvation as well as a new family? 'Violet must fight for what's hers. Of course she must.'

32

The speed of the flames enthralled Anna and Izzy. One moment, delicate tongues of pale yellows and pinks played around the bleached driftwood, the next a roaring brush-fire of livid red devoured a tangle of washed-up fishing nets. The noise reminded Hilary of a breaker crashing on to a beach in a storm.

'Do you think,' she asked the girls, 'that nets and driftwood store the sound of the sea until it's released by fire ... and do you think the sound returns to the waves?' She was kneeling between Anna and Izzy, an arm around each, pulling one then the other back when-ever their fascination with the flames drew them closer. 'Oh look, Mummy's coming back,' she said to Anna. The fire continued to hold the child rapt and she didn't see Violet's troubled expression after her walk along the beach with Cal, or Cal's signal for Hilary to accom-pany him to the pick-up to collect the food for the barbecue.

'What's happened?' she asked Cal as soon as they were out of earshot. 'What's wrong with Violet?'

'The police have suspended the search.'

'Why?' Violet and Hilary had noticed the lack of activ-ity at Boyd's Farm on their way back from Mrs Anderson's. They hadn't discussed it because of the children but they'd assumed the stoppage was temporary, just for the evening, and would start again in the morning. 'Have they found the body?'

Cal shook his head. 'No.' He'd gone to Boyd's Farm after collecting driftwood for the bonfire, to check how things were progressing. He'd arrived as the diggers, trucks and police vehicles were driving away. Constable Buchanan, left behind on guard duty, told him the search had been suspended. The obvious places to bury a body had been excavated, he'd said. So far they'd found 'Nada, zilch, nothing apart from a sheep's jaw bone and some rusting farm tools.' Which left the barns, but they were in imminent danger of collapse and it wasn't worth risking an officer's life for a body that was a quarter of a century old. According to the constable, a plan was being drawn up, involving the wind farm consortium. BRC was in the throes of buying Boyd's Farm. Once the purchase had been completed, it would dismantle the buildings under police supervision and the search would continue hand in hand with demolition. BRC would pay for everything, including the cost of transporting the barns' contents to a police warehouse where they would be sorted, sifted and searched. According to the constable, there would be a delay of two or three weeks before work resumed at the site, though BRC was in a hurry to get things moving.

Hilary blew out her cheeks, imagining her friend's reaction. 'How did Violet take it?'

'How do you think? She's angry.' Cal had mentioned to Violet the 'flash car' he'd encountered on the beach road by the entrance to Boyd's Farm, how the driver had been 'a wheeler-dealer type' working for BRC and the passenger had been Ross Turnbull. Cal said, 'Violet thinks it's happening again – the original inquiry into her mother's disappearance was wrapped up quickly because the Turnbulls didn't want police crawling over Poltown for weeks, disrupting their operations. Now this . . .'

After a barbecue of grilled sausages and tomatoes, Cal suggested an evening foraging trip to Anna and Izzy. He'd identified a place for collecting mussels, another for winkles, and he'd seen some 'good-looking' tidal pools. While Izzy fetched the nets and buckets and Anna her painting book and crayons, Hilary thanked Cal. With the girls occupied, she would have an opportunity to talk to Violet, to persuade her to 'stick with it and fight'.

As they walked along the beach, Cal described some of the creatures Anna and Izzy might encounter: limpets, starfish, blenny, whelks, periwinkles as well as crabs. Arriving at the first rock pool, Cal peered into the still water and pointed out a prawn. Under his instruction, Izzy slid her net behind the wary crustacean and Anna put hers in front. The two girls brought their nets together and lifted them up. Despite Cal warning about its agility, the prawn leapt through Izzy's fingers and splashed back into the water. The next hour or so passed with similar scenes of capture and escape, though increasingly of capture, with Izzy proving to be the more dextrous of the girls.

Eventually, Anna abandoned her 'stupid net' with a flash of temper and took her painting book and crayons to a ledge above the pool.

When Cal asked her what she was doing, she replied sulkily, 'Drawing Mummy.'

'What's she doing in your drawing?' he asked.

'She's doing nothing,' Anna said, her sulkiness turning to mild contempt for Cal's ignorance. 'Because she's a baby and babies can't do anything.'

'They can cry,' Cal said.

'I suppose,' Anna conceded reluctantly. 'But I can't draw crying.'

Cal glanced back at Violet and Hilary, expecting them to be by the fire, but they were at the road end talking to a visitor. Mrs Anderson, Cal guessed, because her car, or a car very like hers, was parked beside his.

Noticing that Cal's attention had drifted to the other end of the beach, Anna asked, 'What are you looking at?'

'Just checking the fire,' he replied before diverting Anna by suggesting they looked for a crab. 'And then we could collect mussels.'

Having become rivals at catching prawns, Izzy and Anna reverted to being allies against the large crab which Cal had seen scuttling away in a deep pool closer to the end of the headland. Despite their prodding and poking, the crab remained hidden. At one point Cal pretended it had the cane of his fishing net in its powerful claws and was dragging him into the pool. The girls helped to pull him back. After they'd stopped laughing, Izzy said, 'What's Mummy doing?'

Cal looked up. Hilary was running towards them.

Izzy had a confused expression, caught between happiness at the thought of showing off her catch of sea creatures to her mother and worry at her urgency.

'Just wait here a moment,' Cal said. 'And watch out that crab doesn't get you.' He loped towards Hilary, hoping his casual manner would reassure the girls. When Hilary was a few metres from him, she stopped, put her hands on her hips and gasped for breath.

'What's going on?' he asked.

She gulped a lungful of air. 'Mrs Anderson,' she gulped again, 'has brought some letters from William Ritchie.' She managed a long, deep breath. 'They were written to Violet's mother. Mrs Anderson found them in his chest of drawers after William Ritchie's death.' Hilary gulped more air. 'She didn't read them because Ritchie was such a private man. He wouldn't have wanted her to look at them, she said, nor was it her place. She waited for the right moment to tell Diana but the right moment never came. Now she's given them to Violet to decide what should happen to them.'

~

There were seven letters, each one handwritten in black ink on a single sheet of blue writing paper. Hilary remarked on the turmoil caused by an affair which warranted so slight a correspondence, a mere seven pieces of paper and about a hundred lines of text.

'I wonder why there's none from Megan,' she said, studying Cal as he read the letters for the first time. She waited impatiently for his reaction, any reaction. 'Perhaps she didn't write any?' she suggested, still watching his face. 'After all, William Ritchie was a married man. In her position would I have risked writing a letter which Diana could have intercepted?'

Cal turned a page and carried on reading.

Hilary looked at Violet, who had taken Anna and Izzy paddling. They were holding hands and jumping over the waves as they rolled in. 'I wonder what she'll decide,' she said wistfully, observing her friend. 'If I was Violet I'd grab as much as I could. I'd wipe the smile off Alexandra's smug little face. I've told her that's what she should do. With these letters, she can't lose.'

Still Cal said nothing.

'Or,' she said, having another thought about the absence of letters written by Megan, 'possibly she *did* write and William Ritchie destroyed them to avoid discovery by Diana.' She sighed at another question without an answer. 'Though why did he keep these ones?' Her face furrowed in frustration. 'I think,' she decided, 'that he kept these letters because the affair had been exposed by the time the police handed them back to him.' Her face brightened, a light going on. 'I know!' She examined Cal, hoping for an equivalent flicker of reaction. 'He couldn't bear to part with them because they were all he had left of his affair with Megan Bates. That would help Violet's case, wouldn't it?'

Cal turned another page, the second last. 'We know she wrote one letter,' he remarked, continuing to read.

'The one the police thought was a suicide note?' Hilary added quickly, pleased to have a response at last, hoping for another. 'The one that Duncan used to cover what he'd done?'

Cal didn't answer.

'I've been thinking about that too,' Hilary carried on. 'Maybe she wrote that letter in desperation, without intending to post it. Maybe that's why she showed it to Duncan, because she was having second thoughts.'

She had lost Cal again. She checked the letter he was reading. 'Dear Megan', it began. The last two opened in that way, indicative of the affair having cooled. The earlier letters started 'My Dear Megan'.

'I can't help liking him for that,' Hilary remarked. 'Dear Megan, even when he was probably thinking she was anything but. Though,' she reflected, 'it can't be easy falling in love with a man who starts letters "My Dear Megan" when he's in the grip of passion, or what passed for it in William Ritchie's case, and "Dear Megan" when he's backing away and telling her he's going to stick with his wife. *Not* very demonstrative . . .'

Cal turned to the last letter in the sequence. It was short. Like the others, it was signed 'Sincerely yours, William'. Hilary read it too, upside down, trying to judge when Cal would be finished. 'Well?'

'Well,' Cal answered. 'He couldn't be clearer. Violet would have been his heir.' Cal referred again to the last letter. 'Megan would have been given a house and an allowance. Diana would have continued to live at Brae and their home in Edinburgh until her death, but the properties would have been put in trust for Violet.'

'Alexandra isn't even mentioned.'

'It doesn't mean he wouldn't have provided for her in some other way.'

'I guess.'

'Having read these . . .' Cal looked through them again. 'I don't think Megan did write to him.'

'Why?'

'Because he never makes any reference to anything she's written. The first four . . .' Cal read the fifth again. 'Yes. The first four are him making up for his reticence when they've been together, or as he puts it in this one . . .' He held up the second letter. 'Yes, here it is . . . where he apologizes for his "lawyer's preference for measured judgement over emotional fireworks". By the fifth letter she must have told him about the pregnancy because he describes the "desperate and difficult decision" he's been forced to make, how "for reasons of duty and morality" he cannot contemplate divorce. Then, in these last two, he's confirming the details of the settlement he's already proposed to her at a meeting. See here.' Cal showed the passage to Hilary. 'He's trying to reassure her that he'll look after her and the baby. He's committing it to paper so that she'll believe him.' He checked the last two letters again. 'That's it, yes. So the letter she composed just before she died, threatening to disappear, the baby too, might have been her only one, because William Ritchie doesn't make any reference to another.'

Hilary drew Cal's attention to Violet and the children. They were walking back up the beach.

'What do you think she'll do?' Hilary asked.

'I don't know.'

'She must fight. She's got to. You tell her.'

～

Cal and Hilary sat by the fire and listened to the rise and fall of Violet's voice, now a dragon, now a pleading child, now a booming giant. They heard the protests of the children as the bedtime story ended and they waited for Violet's decision. Hilary was impatient for an answer. As soon as Violet joined them, she asked, 'Well, are you going to ring her?'

'Do you think I should?'

'God, yes.'

Violet took out her phone and scrolled through her call register to locate the number she had first rung to inquire about renting Orasaigh Cottage.

'A bedtime story for Alexandra.' Hilary looked smug with anticipation. 'Sleep well.'

'I'm still not sure,' Violet said.

'Don't think twice about it,' Hilary said.

Violet pressed the call button and Hilary said, 'Good girl.'

Alexandra's imperious voice answered.

'Hi, it's Violet Wells.'

'So you've changed your mind?'

'There's something I'd like you to hear.' Violet held the letter to the bright glow of the fire.

'What is it now?'

'"Dear Megan,"' Violet started reading, '"I wish another resolution were possible."'

'What is this?' Alexandra demanded.

Hilary shouted, 'It's a letter from *your* father.'

Violet waited for quiet before continuing. '"Dear Megan, I wish another resolution were possible."' She glanced at Hilary, who mouthed 'go on'. '"All that is left to me is to honour the commitments that I have already made verbally. To reiterate: I will treat the child as my own because it is. The child will be my heir and will inherit the bulk of my estate, including my properties in Edinburgh as well as here, in Poltown. I will change my will accordingly."'

'Where did you get this?' Alexandra barked.

Violet shook her head and appeared unable to carry on. Hilary took the letter and phone from her.

'"Should I predecease my wife,"' she continued in a tone more triumphal than Violet's, '"the use of my properties will be rightfully hers for her lifetime. On her death, they will be the child's to dispose of as he or she wishes."' Hilary interjected, 'That's Violet, by the way,' before carrying on to the conclusion. '"I will make provision for you to rent or buy a house within the financial limits I mentioned. You will also receive an index-linked monthly allowance of one thousand pounds. I can only apologize for the distress I have caused. Sincerely yours, William."'

'So what do you think of *your* father now?' Hilary sneered.

'Don't.' Violet snatched back the phone.

'What's wrong?'

Violet cut the call. 'This isn't what I want.'

~

The children were in their sleeping bags, chattering, and Hilary was going to join them since Izzy wouldn't settle without her.

'And anyway, Violet will stay out there all night.' Hilary looked beyond the fading glow of the fire into the darkness. 'If she thinks I'm waiting up to give her a talking to . . .' She was sorry about the flare-up. It was the first they'd had. 'But I don't want her to regret anything. Do you know what I mean?' She made Cal promise to talk to Violet. 'Just what I've said to you. Tell her I'm worried about her making the wrong decision, for her and for Anna. That's all.'

Once Hilary had gone, Cal went to fetch more driftwood. On his return, Violet was standing at the edge of the fire's glow. 'So, not such a happy day,' he said, putting a log into the embers.

'No.'

'Would you like coffee? The fire's still hot enough.'

'What should I do?' She folded her arms.

'You don't have to do anything.'

'I just want her to be found. That's all.' She glanced at Cal, hoping he would understand.

He nodded. 'I know.'

The driftwood began to burn and crackle. They watched the flames until Cal said, 'Hilary thinks you're planning to go back to Glasgow, to your flat, your waitressing job.' He glanced at her. 'She's worried you'll wake up one morning and realize how much more you could have given Anna, if only you'd fought.'

Violet kicked at the sand. 'I know.' It had been playing on her mind too. 'But it's wrong. My mother didn't want William Ritchie's money, she wanted him, and, at the end, she told him she would go away, make it impossible for him to find her. She didn't choose his money even though it would have changed her life. Why should I?'

'He's your father, I guess.'

'He's a name on a gravestone. I don't have a father.' She sounded hurt and angry.

The fire again held their attention, until Violet touched his arm, brushing the back of her fingers against the sleeve of his shirt. 'I'm sorry.'

He nodded. 'Yeah, I know.' Should he say more? He looked at her again. Her skin had turned rosy with the fire. He thought about holding her. Instead, he said, 'Hilary thinks you should go for a long walk in the morning. Climb to the ridge above Brae. Go to Orasaigh. Walk round the loch. Explore. Take your time. Then come back and tell her you and Anna are better off in Glasgow.'

'She doesn't want me to say that.'

'No, but she won't mention it again if you do.'

Violet closed her eyes. She was tired. She would sleep on it. She kissed Cal on the cheek and walked towards her tent. 'Goodnight.'

Cal said, 'And if you do go . . .' She looked round. 'Take your backpack. I've put a bottle of water in it and some chocolate. That phone I gave you too. In case you get lost. Stick it in your pocket.'

33

Hilary struck an early-morning bargain with Anna and Izzy. If they would entertain themselves while she slept for a little while longer, she *might* make sandcastles with them later. The girls said, 'Oh, all right,' in disappointed voices and went to sit by Cal, who was building up the fire and boiling water for coffee. At his suggestion, they sat back against a large log and stretched out their legs, making a table on which to rest Anna's painting book.

'That's Violet, when she was tired,' Izzy said, turning a page.

'That's our flat in Glasgow,' Anna said wistfully, turning another. 'Lovely flat . . .' She patted at the picture with her hand. 'How long is Mummy going to be?' Anna looked perplexed. She was gazing along the beach road.

'I don't really know,' Cal replied, looking too. 'Couple of hours, I imagine, maybe more. She's just gone for a long walk.'

'Why did she go without telling me?'

'You were asleep.'

Izzy raised her hand to Anna's face, forcing her to look at the book again. 'That's me,' Izzy said, 'sitting at Mummy's mirror.'

'And that's Ginger,' Anna said.

Ginger was the cat Izzy had adopted, or Izzy was the child Ginger had adopted. Anna wasn't sure which way round it was.

'That's your granny wearing a hat,' Izzy said.

'And that's the beach house Mummy and me are going to have,' Anna said.

Izzy frowned with jealousy. She turned the page quickly.

'That's Violet when she was a baby.'

Izzy glanced at Cal to check he was paying attention. 'Did you know that Violet had fair hair like me when she was a baby?'

Cal considered Izzy's question with a doubtful expression. 'She has dark hair now.'

'But she *was* fair, wasn't she?' Izzy called for Anna's support.

'Mrs Anderson said so.' Anna was definite.

Cal leaned over and looked at the picture, a pink baby with a big round body, short legs and arms, a small face on top of which was a scribble of yellow crayon. 'When did she say that?'

'Yesterday, when we were doing the dishes,' Izzy said.

'What did Mrs Anderson say?' Cal asked. 'Can you remember? Her exact words?'

Anna and Izzy looked at each other, detecting the difference in Cal's voice.

'I got some soap in my hair,' Anna said uncertainly.

'Bubbles from the washing up,' Izzy explained.

'And *she* said . . .' Anna continued.

'Mrs Anderson, you mean?' Cal asked.

Anna nodded. '*She* said it was funny my hair being so

curly and dark because my mummy's had been blonde and fine, like silk.'

'She said that? Are you sure?'

Anna and Izzy looked at each other. They nodded in unison. 'Like silk,' they echoed.

'Did she say anything else?'

The girls shook their heads.

'Except that we shouldn't tell our mums,' Izzy said.

'Are you sure? Nothing about *when* she'd seen Violet as a baby, *how* she had?'

'No,' Anna said. 'Only that she didn't want to get in trouble for talking about Violet.' Anna's expression was worried. 'But you're not our mums, so it's all right to tell you, isn't it?'

~~❦~~

Mrs Anderson heard banging. Blurry from sleep, she thought she had been in the past again, remembering the baby and Diana at her door. She reached for her clock, expecting the time to be almost seven fifteen. To her surprise it was later, eight thirty. She couldn't decide what had happened, whether she'd forgotten to set her alarm or whether she'd woken as usual and had gone back to sleep. Eight thirty. She never slept that late! She chided herself for being so absent-minded when the banging started again; the pounding of a fist on the door; someone calling her name. Her hands went to her mouth. Not a dream. Not one of those vivid memories from the past. Not Diana. A man's voice. 'Mrs Anderson? Mrs Anderson?' The voice boomed in the stillness of the morning.

'Who is that?' she croaked. 'What do you want?' The sound she made was feeble, hardly loud enough to escape her bedroom, let alone travel downstairs to the front door. Yet, it was as if he had heard her. 'Open the door. It's Cal McGill, Violet's friend.'

She found herself standing by her bed, her feet seeking slippers, her visitor, no, the *drama*, drawing her on. 'I've got to speak to you,' he shouted and struck the door another heavy blow. Mrs Anderson felt the shock travel through the floor as she shuffled from her bedroom. She carried on down the stairs and across the hall, until only the thickness of the front door separated them.

Did he sense her? His sudden quiet made her think so. 'Go away,' she croaked, the silence unnerving her. And again, 'Go away.'

'Not until you open the door,' Cal replied. 'Not until you speak to me.'

She felt the air stir, as if the door was no barrier at all. 'Go away, or I'll ring for the police.'

'Why don't you?'

Mrs Anderson backed away, her slippered feet retreating silently on the hall floor. Cal banged again and swore, as if he knew she was going. 'What colour was Violet's hair when she was a baby?' he shouted. 'Was it fair or dark, Mrs Anderson? Was it blonde or brown? Mrs Anderson.' He banged on the door. 'Mrs Anderson, what colour was it?'

'Blonde,' she whispered. Her fingertips pressed at the place where she still felt the sticky imprint of Anna lips, her cheeks turning alabaster white at the error she had made – at her guard being temporarily dismantled by having two sweet children to herself.

Those girls! She'd made them promise not to tell.

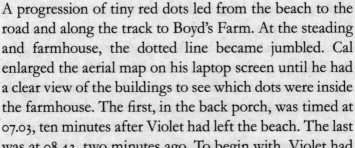

A progression of tiny red dots led from the beach to the road and along the track to Boyd's Farm. At the steading and farmhouse, the dotted line became jumbled. Cal enlarged the aerial map on his laptop screen until he had a clear view of the buildings to see which dots were inside the farmhouse. The first, in the back porch, was timed at 07.03, ten minutes after Violet had left the beach. The last was at 08.42, two minutes ago. To begin with, Violet had been moving around, probably going from the ground floor to the first, Cal guessed. Then she had spent sixteen minutes towards the front of the house, where Megan's room was. But for the last twenty-three minutes, since 08.19, she had been in the same place, towards the back of the house. The signal from the phone Cal put into her backpack showed she hadn't moved.

He stared at the last dot. She ought to be told about Mrs Anderson. Should he ring her? Should he go to the farmhouse? Or should he leave her undisturbed, let her work out what she would do about William Ritchie's letters? A worry nagged at him. The last dot was on the attic room's side of the house. Would Violet go there, to the place where her mother's killer had died? If so, why had she stayed there for so long? He'd heard of one suicide leading to another but no sooner had he reassured himself of the impossibility of Violet doing the same – she would never abandon Anna – than the nag returned. What if she'd been followed by the man who attacked her at the community hall? She'd been warned off once and had been called a nosy bitch. Hadn't the man threatened to hurt her if she carried on asking questions?

He stared at the dot. He called the phone. 'Pick up, Violet, pick up.' He heard his own voice asking him to leave a message.

Accelerating along Brae's back drive away from Mrs Anderson's, he shouted, 'Fuck, fuck, fuck!' His foot was flat to the floor, but the pick-up's response was sluggish. Suddenly every second, every fraction of a second, counted. From the beach road, he went along the track to Boyd's Farm, swerving left and right to avoid the grooves and gouges left by the trucks and police vehicles. He stopped by the steading entrance, at the blue-and-white police tape marked 'Do Not Cross'. Ducking underneath, he ran into the steading yard and pushed open the back door. Going inside, Cal recalled Duncan's hanging body which changed to Violet's in his imagination.

Another fear gripped him. Had the man strung up Violet like Duncan to make her death look like suicide too?

He ran to the hallway, up the staircase and across the landing, stopping at the small flight up to the attic.

'Violet, are you there?'

The door to the room was as open as it had been before. Enough to see in. Not enough to see if a body was hanging from the hook Duncan had used.

'Violet?'

He carried on up the stairs and along the short passageway, opening the door with his foot. He sighed with relief. 'Thank God.' There was no hanging body; there was nobody at all. But propped against the skirting board on the far wall, below the graffiti left by Poltown's teenagers on their night-time dares, was his own phone. He crossed the room and suddenly saw his name on the wall. It was written in sparkly nail varnish beside a message. 'Forgive me. I thought you might try to stop me. Love Violet.' An arrow pointed to the right, to a heart enclosing two names and a date. Ross + Alexandra. 9 September 1983. The day that Violet was born. The day that Duncan was supposed to have killed Megan Bates. But Ross Turnbull and Alexandra Hamilton had been in Duncan's house that night. Two witnesses, but witnesses to what? Cal looked from one name to the other. Which one would Violet have gone to first?

Maybe he should have separated his old ewe, Mrs A, from the rest of the flock. If he had, Jim could have driven slowly along the road, Mrs A bleating in the trailer, the other blackface sheep following on and Tommy, the collie, bringing up the rear. He took a swig from the bottle, and another. The whisky dropped into his stomach and he waited for the hit; the sensation of bobbing around above a sea of worry and depression instead of sinking into it.

'Aah,' he sighed. 'That's grand.'

He wiped his hand across his mouth and propped the bottle against the passenger seat. 'Better get moving,' he mumbled. 'Tommy will be waiting on me.' A grin creased Jim's face as he imagined the dog lying flat, his ears pricked, his flanks quivering in anticipation of Jim's whistle. The sheep would be milling about in front of him, Mrs A stamping her feet in truculence, the others taking their cue from her. Jim grabbed his stick and hauled himself out of the van, leaving the engine running in case of trouble. He checked whether his parking had blocked off the culvert, where Mrs A had led the blackies astray last time he moved them to the loch field. 'Good enough,' he reckoned and wandered the fifty metres back to the bend to watch for Tommy bringing on the flock. He whistled, a long blast. Tommy barked in response. 'Good lad,' Jim said, his habit of talking to the dog so ingrained it made no difference whether Tommy was within earshot or not. 'Good lad. Nice and slow now.'

Jim heard the rattle of hooves on the tarmac, his ears telling him that everything was under control. Rounding the corner and coming into view, the sheep also seemed to be nicely bunched, Tommy showing restraint, working from one side of the road to the other, letting that cussed Mrs A know where he was. As Jim expected, she was at the front but trotting calmly in the middle of the road.

'Good lad,' he shouted and the dog pricked its ears. 'Easy now . . .'

Jim let the sheep come close. Then he walked ahead of them until he was by the van and the culvert. When he stopped to deter another attempted breakout that way, they halted too. 'Bring them on,' Jim shouted to Tommy. The dog chivvied the sheep but Mrs A refused to budge.

Her nostrils flared and her eyes had a wild look which Jim recognized, a look that signalled trouble.

'Damn, damn.'

As soon as Jim had seen the danger, Mrs A took off, her hooves slipping and sliding on the road. She leapt the far ditch and started to climb the bank, the rest of the flock in noisy pursuit. On Jim's command, the dog raced uphill to stop Mrs A from doubling back to the field the sheep had just left, which was what she did the last time. But Mrs A appeared to have a different plan. She wheeled round and started off in the opposite direction.

'Damn,' Jim said. If Mrs A made it to the forestry high up on the hill, he and Tommy would be spending the rest of the day rounding them up. The deer fence had long since fallen down. The place was a jumble of fallen timber. If the sheep got in there, there'd be no easy way of getting them out. Damn. He should have put Mrs A in the trailer after all.

As the last of the sheep disappeared from view, Tommy in pursuit, Jim jumped in the van. Swallowing a mouthful of whisky, he went through the gears, first, second, third to reach the top of the hill track before Mrs A. Changing up to fourth, he gulped another swig of whisky and tucked the bottle between his thighs. The road swung left and entered a tunnel of overhanging trees. Crossing from bright sunlight into shadow, Jim was temporarily blinded. The van hit something, a glancing blow. He gripped at the wheel and braked. Whisky spilled on his trousers. He swore and checked in his mirror, expecting to see a stone which the sheep had sent rolling down the bank or a fallen branch. But the bend was now between him and whatever he'd hit. The noise of the impact rankled too: it reminded him of the time he'd collided with a deer. Flesh and bone against metal made a different thud. Perhaps one of the sheep had toppled on to the road and he'd hit it, not a stone. 'Damn.'

He retrieved the bottle of whisky from the floor by his seat. Most of it had spilled. He gulped what was left and got out unsteadily to check the damage. There was a dent on the van's front offside, a curved impression made by something softer than stone or wood. A sheep after all, Jim thought, or a deer startled by all the commotion. At the speed he was going – less than forty miles per hour – the impact of a glancing blow might not have been fatal. More than likely the animal would have crawled away somewhere.

'Damn.'

Tommy yelped in pursuit of the runaways. He was some distance off, halfway at least to the forestry. As Jim feared, Mrs A was heading for the high hill. He had no chance of cutting her off now. Leaving the empty whisky bottle on the roof of the van, he walked back to the bend. He was alarmed to see the contents of a backpack strewn across the road: alarmed as well as apprehensive.

Not a sheep. Not a deer.

He went from object to object: a pair of sunglasses, a packet of hair-clips, keys, a receipt, roller-ball pen, a bottle of nail varnish, another of water, a packet of tissues.

The backpack was a woman's. Had he hit her?

As he bent to gather up her things, he heard a noise. And again.

It came from the direction of the birch trees below the

road. Fearing the worst, Jim followed a trail of broken and bent bracken. Where the ground flattened, a bare expanse of moss, he came across her body. She was on her side, her right leg at an unnatural angle, and there was blood on her jeans. Her head had also taken a blow. More blood seeped into her hair. For a second, Jim didn't know what to do. The taste of whisky was fresh in his mouth; an empty bottle on the roof of his van. Another that he'd finished a few hours before was in his kitchen.

Just as he was wondering whether there was any way out of this mess, she moaned again. 'Help . . . please.'

'Hold on there,' Jim answered. 'I'm almost with you.'

Resigning himself to losing his licence and worse, he knelt at her side. 'What happened?' he said, and when she didn't answer he decided to tell her a lie, his last hope of avoiding punishment. 'Were you hit by a car? It must have been that one a few minutes ahead of me.' He touched her clenched right hand. 'Can you speak? Can you tell me what hurts?' He looked at her broken leg, at the odd angle of the bone. He wondered if he should try to straighten it, whether a makeshift tourniquet above the break would stop the bleeding, whether he should move her. His knowledge of first aid was limited to sheep. When one of his ewes broke a leg, he cut its throat.

He checked the wound on the back of her head. It seemed to be a graze rather than a deep cut; the blood oozing rather than flowing. He leaned over her body so that she could see him and then he recognized her. The right half of her face was pressing into the moss. 'It's OK, Violet,' he said. 'You'll be all right. I'll get you out of here.'

He squeezed her clenched hand to reassure her. 'Wait till I get the bastard who did this to you.'

She tried to speak, the corner of her mouth opening. Sounds, not words. Jim said, 'It's OK.' Her open left eye watched him. Although bloodshot, it seemed to be able to follow his movement. A good sign, he thought. 'Can you do something for me?' Jim remembered a scene from *Casualty* on the television. 'Can you flex your fingers?' He touched Violet's clenched hand to prompt her. The index finger started to open, the others slowly followed. 'That's good,' he said. 'Can you go all the way?' As the fingers stretched out, a small box fell from her hand. The lid sprang open spilling a brooch, the violet of the flowers framed by the bright green of the moss. Jim grunted as if he'd been winded. His expression altered too; shock, guilt and fright, one reflex after another. He glanced at Violet. Now her bloodshot eye watched him coldly and accusingly.

You've seen it before.

Jim wiped the back of his hand across his face. 'Damn,' he said. 'Why did you have to go and do that? What'll I do with you now?'

～

Not the first entrance. Not the second. At the third, Cal turned left. The sign on the corner house said William Wallace Drive. Someone had spray-painted a line through William Wallace and had scrawled above it Alec Turnbull. At the far end of the cul-de-sac were three bungalows. A woman pushing a pram told Cal which was whose. The one on the left, 'the posh one with a conservatory', was Alec's. The middle one was where Alec's sister-in-law Marjorie lived. The one he wanted was on the right, with the fresh render around the window. Cal parked outside as Ross Turnbull appeared at the side door. He was tucking in a blue shirt. A patterned tie was hanging undone around his collar. He threw a suit jacket on to the roof of his car while he opened the passenger door and put an executive case on to the seat. Then he noticed Cal.

'I'm in a hurry. Sorry.' He watched Cal walking up to the gates. 'Whatever it is, can we make it another time?'

Ross shut the passenger door with his knee and picked up the jacket. Walking round the car, he pulled it on.

'Has Violet Wells been to see you?' Cal demanded. 'Did she ask you about what you were doing on the ninth of September, twenty-six years ago, when you were with Alexandra Hamilton? What you saw that night when you were at Boyd's Farm?'

Ross stopped. 'And that's why I'm in a rush. I've lost too much time already talking to Violet Wells, answering the same question.' Opening the driver's door, he said, 'Come and see me later. Whenever. Happy to chat. But I've got to go.'

'What did you tell her?'

Ross raised his eyebrows and sighed. 'Ask her.' He straightened his jacket and pulled at the cuffs. The sleeves were too short. 'Sorry, I'm running to a meeting, and if I'm late Poltown's going to lose a big opportunity.'

He got into the car, shut the door and opened the window. Reversing down the short driveway, he shouted back, 'By the way, I owe you an apology.'

'What for?'

'Some of my guys trying to frighten you off . . . They thought you were doing work for Boyd, feeding him data on how the wind farm would affect the currents. Someone Googled you, thought you should be warned off. It's the way things used to be done around here. Not now. Not on my watch.'

'Did they also try to frighten off Violet?'

Ross shook his head. 'Nope. Look, I wish I could stay and talk but I can't.'

Cal shouted, 'Where did Violet go?' as the car accelerated away. Walking back to the pick-up, Cal rang Hilary. He related the sequence of events: how Anna and Izzy had told him about Mrs Anderson saying Violet had blonde, silky hair as a baby, what happened when he banged on Mrs Anderson's door and about Violet going to Boyd's Farm, finding Ross and Alexandra's names on the wall, visiting Ross and then her disappearing act. 'Where would she have gone next? To Alexandra?'

Hilary said, 'I can't imagine that. Alexandra's not going to open the door to her now she knows what's in William Ritchie's letter.'

'Listen,' he said, 'has Violet got her own mobile phone with her?'

Hilary said she thought so. In fact she remembered Violet dropping it into the backpack she took on her walk.

'She's not answering,' Cal said. 'I've tried half a dozen times.'

'She might have no signal. It doesn't seem to be that reliable around here.' Then Hilary said, 'I bet she's walking back to tell us what Ross Turnbull said and she's taken the coastal path that her mother used to walk in the morning.'

'OK,' Cal replied, 'I'll look for her there.'

34

Fiona Bell drove slowly down the hill. Thank goodness for four-wheel drive, she thought, as the track became steeper and rougher. In her opinion, visiting the croft of Mrs Macpherson, the practice's oldest patient, was a job for a rally driver, not a doctor. On the way up she'd banged the car's underside three times and going back down was just as bad. The doctor and her dog concentrated on looking through the windscreen; Pepe in his usual pose, back legs on the passenger seat, front paws resting on the dashboard, his body spanning a relative chasm. To Fiona's amusement, dog and driver seemed to be adopting similar strategies. The car's left wheels were balancing on the remnants of the ridge that ran down the centre of the track, the right on the sloping verge, one side or the other threatening to slip into an abyss. The canine and motoring equivalents of a high-wire act, Fiona told Pepe.

As she rubbed the dog's head she noticed he was transfixed by the sight of a black-and-white collie circling a group of sheep a few hundred metres away, close to the forestry. Fiona braked and stopped. 'Isn't that Tommy?' she said to Pepe. The two dogs had met a few times, usually when Jim Carmichael and Fiona passed on the road, each on their rounds. 'No sign of Jim . . .' Fiona searched the hill. 'That's odd. Those two are always together.'

Since the track to Mrs Macpherson's joined the road

close to Jim's smallholding, Fiona thought she would take the precaution of checking up on him. Not only did he have high blood pressure but also a history of alcoholism. The last time they'd met he reeked of whisky. 'That's what we'll do,' she told Pepe. 'We'll park by the cattle grid, then we can walk along the road to Jim's – you'd like that – and come back along the lochside.' Apart from anything else, her visit would appear more casual. If Jim was there and seemed to be all right, she'd say she thought she'd seen Tommy and tell him where.

It took her ten minutes to reach the bottom of the track and another minute or two before she was at the cattle grid. Soon she and Pepe were striding along the road, the dog darting into the bracken, sniffing out the scents of deer and pine marten. Fiona relished being alone in such a wild place. Not for the first time, she doubted she would ever be able to go back to a more domestic landscape. Being among such wildness lifted her spirits. There were so many changing vistas: loch, mountain and a magical September blue sky; so pale it looked ethereal.

Snapping back from her daydream, she wondered where Pepe was. She swivelled round and spotted him behind her at the edge of the road, nosing excitedly at some bracken.

'Pepe, stop that,' she shouted. 'What are you eating?' She hurried back to prevent him from rolling in whatever foul-smelling corpse or excrement he had uncovered. Scattered sheep droppings were on the tarmac, shiny black and fresh. 'Ugh, Pepe, leave it.' She hoped she wasn't too late. 'Pepe!'

The dog responded as though he had been falsely

accused. Patting his head, she slipped the lead around his neck and promised to let him off again as soon as they were at Jim's. Then she parted the bracken with her foot where Pepe had been sniffing and something shiny caught her eye. A phone. Silver. A model similar to hers. She picked it up and pressed the button at the bottom of the screen. It lit up and she saw there had been a missed call. After swiping the phone with the pad of her thumb, she returned the call. A man answered. 'Hi, Violet,' he said, sounding relieved. 'Where on earth are you?'

'Who's speaking?' Fiona inquired hesitantly.

'Violet?'

'No, I'm sorry. My name is Fiona Bell . . . Doctor Bell,' she added without thinking.

'*Doctor* Bell . . . What's happened? Is Violet all right?'

'Who am I talking to?'

'My name's Cal McGill.'

'Let me explain,' she replied hastily. 'I'm walking my dog and I found this phone lying in a ditch beside the road.'

'Where?'

'This might not mean anything to you but it was on the road to Jim Carmichael's smallholding. Beyond Poltown, at the lochside. Do you know where that is?'

'Violet isn't there?'

'No. That's why I'm ringing you. You'd called her.'

Fiona thought there couldn't be many women with such an old-fashioned name as Violet, even in Poltown. 'Would that be Violet Wells?'

Someone was talking, a man's voice. An angry rumble of complaint was followed by a cry of anguish. Now the voice was self-pitying and close by. Inside her head the kaleidoscope of sounds and colours changed again, the pain from her broken leg distorting everything. She became aware of his lips which showered her in spittle as words came from them. She remembered those lips spitting at her before. Then they'd called her a nosy bitch. Now they were telling her she was to blame. He'd saved her life once when she was a baby. Hadn't he warned her off too? After the public meeting. She'd had her chance. Why had she done this to him? What was he supposed to do with her? The lips faded. The sputter of Jim's saliva on her face and the guilty fear in his eyes when he'd caught sight of her brooch accompanied Violet's return to unconsciousness.

Fiona Bell wasn't surprised at there being no sign at the smallholding of either Jim or his blue van. He'd be on the hill somewhere, because Jim and Tommy were never far apart. Maybe Tommy had run ahead to stop the sheep getting to the forestry and Jim had been lower down with a lame straggler. By now it was probable they'd been re-united. Fiona was relieved. At least he wasn't ill. She wrote a brief message anyway, telling him about the phone. 'Just in case you come across the owner looking for it on the road, will you let her know I've made an arrangement to give it to her friend, Cal McGill.' She debated whether to let Jim know the phone belonged to Violet Wells. Would it be a kindness to warn him? Given his walk-on role in the drama of Duncan Boyd's death, she decided to leave it out, erring on the side of caution. She folded the paper and was sliding it under Jim's front door when she heard someone yelling, 'Hey, what do you think you're doing?'

She didn't recognize the voice but, looking up, she saw Jim. Not only was she surprised by his appearance but she was also taken aback by how aggressive he sounded. This was not the mild, obliging, chatty man she passed on the road or saw in the surgery. Jim was still thirty metres away, but even without his angry bellow she could tell something was wrong. It was the hurried way he was walking and the blotchy red of his face under his denim cap. She waved, calling out 'Hi' in case he hadn't recognized her, and waited for him to draw closer. If she thought recognition would soften his mood, he proved her wrong. Stopping by the garden gate, he demanded, 'What the devil are you doing, Doctor Bell?' The red of his cheeks had spread to his throat.

Fiona bristled in return. 'Well, since you've asked so nicely, Jim, I was just leaving a message under your door to let you know I found a phone on the road. I thought you might come across the owner looking for it.' Then she regretted taking umbrage because she smelled the whisky and Jim seemed suddenly lost for words, a poor soul if ever she'd seen one. She wondered if Tommy had taken advantage of Jim's drunkenness to sneak away and find some sheep. Tommy was always herding something, chickens, ducks, even children, given the chance. Perhaps Jim didn't know where the dog had gone. *And* there had been all the upset about Duncan's death. Did Jim blame himself for not preventing it? She'd heard talk to that effect – how Jim should have rung the police as soon as Duncan confessed to killing Megan Bates. In her experience, men became fractious and short tempered with stress. And they drank. Her father had and most of her male patients were the same.

'Jim, have you lost Tommy?' she asked, trying to sound sympathetic.

The question seemed to startle him.

'Why?'

'I saw him on the hill. He was rounding up some sheep.'

His reply was slurred. 'I know where Tommy is.'

'Oh, OK.' Suddenly she noticed Pepe. He was licking a wet stain at the bottom of Jim's overalls. She called the dog to heel but too late. Jim kicked out, catching Pepe in the ribs. The dog let out a yelp.

'Jim, what's got into you?' Fiona knelt to comfort the retreating animal. 'For God's sake, you're like a bear with a sore head.'

'Ach . . .' Jim took off his cap and rubbed it over his face. 'It's been a day.'

'Why, what's happened?' Fiona's tone suggested his explanation would have to be good.

'A walker left a gate open.' He looked around, as if he was still searching for the culprit.

'Is that why your sheep are up on the hill?'

'Aye, it is. Tommy's gone after them. He'll get them all right.' He shook his head, as if there was more to it than that. 'I lost one ewe – broke its leg on some wire. Been skinning her.' He showed her his hands.

347

Fiona noticed how grimy and bloody they were. 'I thought it was blood.'

'What was?'

'That,' she pointed to the bottom of his overalls, at the stain which had attracted Pepe.

He looked too. 'Aye, it'll be blood all right. The wire tore a hole in her, broke a leg as well. I had to put her out of her misery.' Again he rubbed the cap across his face. 'I shouldn't have done that, Doctor Bell.'

'What?'

'Taken it out on your wee dog.'

'It's done now.' An uncomfortable lull followed: Fiona anxious to be going; Jim fidgeting and making grunts of remorse. Eventually the smell of whisky and sweat was too strong a mix for her. 'I'll be off, then,' she said.

By the loch, reflecting on Jim's temper, it occurred to Fiona that she should ring Cal McGill. Might Violet have let the sheep escape? Perhaps they'd taken off down the road and she'd run after them to bring them back. Was that how she had lost her phone? There had been fresh droppings on the road where Fiona found it. She took out Violet's phone again and pressed redial.

Cal listened impatiently to Fiona's voice, trying to interrupt. 'Where are you?' he broke in once Fiona stalled. 'I'm waiting for you, by your car. I've been here for ages.'

Fiona stared at Pepe after Cal ended the call. 'Is it me,' she asked the dog, 'or is everyone bad tempered today? I mean, couldn't he have *mentioned* he'd get here so quickly?'

The more she thought about it, the more hard done by she felt. First Jim shouting at her, now a complete stranger getting stroppy when they'd already arranged to meet in another twenty minutes to hand over Violet's phone. Heading back inland from the sea loch towards the road, she saw an old red pick-up parked beside her car. A man – McGill, she assumed – was pacing backwards and forwards on the road. She realized she'd seen him once before, a brief conversation following the fracas at the public meeting. His restlessness now made her hurry: typical of her, she thought, always the one putting herself out and trying to make things right. However, on meeting him, she found her pique beginning to fade. He was quite good looking with a squint nose (if he was her patient, she'd advise him to get it fixed) and he was apologetic for being short tempered and thanked her when she handed over Violet's mobile. Could she show him where she found it?

'Beyond that bend.' Fiona pointed along the road, which was shaded by the cover of trees. 'On the left-hand side, about fifty metres round the corner.'

Cal looked there too. 'Where does the road go?'

'To Jim Carmichael's place,' she replied. 'He's the owner of the sheep that escaped.'

'So if Violet was walking from this direction,' Cal said, 'that's where she would have been heading.'

Fiona picked up the concern in his voice – he didn't appear to think the phone had been dropped accidentally. 'You're worried about her?'

'Yes,' he said. 'I think I'll have a word with Jim Carmichael; ask him whether he's seen Violet.'

'In that case,' Fiona said, 'I'll lead the way and show you where I found her phone.' She omitted to mention the real reason for accompanying him. She hoped her presence would deter Jim from another display of drunken temper. She thought she'd save Cal from that.

In the event, she needn't have fussed. As the two vehicles pulled up at the house, Jim appeared from a shed beside the big barn and Fiona was relieved at the change in his demeanour. The bull-headed aggression had gone. Trepidation had replaced it, or so it seemed. Perhaps he'd sobered up a bit. She hoped that was it. 'Me again, Jim,' she called over, stopping short of him, keeping her distance in case of another flare-up. Pepe, she was pleased to see, was of the same mind. He sat obediently at her feet. 'This is Cal McGill,' Fiona said. 'He's looking for a friend of his and wondered if you'd seen her.'

'Haven't seen anybody apart from the doctor here,' Jim replied, and Fiona realized she had mistaken his mood. Rather than trepidation, she picked up watchfulness.

Jim shook his head and closed and opened his eyes evasively. 'Not a soul's been here,' he said. 'Apart from the person who let my sheep out between nine and ten.' He gave Cal a hostile look. 'Would your friend have been here then?'

Cal said, 'I suppose she could have been.'

'Oh, do you think it was her?' Fiona blurted, trying to hold Jim's attention, praying he wouldn't notice what Pepe was up to. While she'd been watching Jim, the dog had wandered off and was now crawling under the door of the barn. She hated to think what he'd find to eat in there but she didn't dare call him back in case Jim had another of his tantrums and lashed out again.

One moment Violet welcomed the pain from her leg because it signified life and the possibility of holding Anna again. The next she begged to be spared its torture. Through her agony she heard voices. One was familiar: Cal. Hope at last. She screamed. The sound filled her head yet her mouth hadn't moved. Had she made any sound at all? She listened for Cal again and heard a rustling noise close by. She strained to escape the whisky spit that would soon be spraying across her face. From somewhere she found the strength to strike out and rake at him with her nails, before becoming unconscious again.

Fiona knelt at the bottom of the barn doors where they'd splintered and broken. It was where Pepe had disappeared, where the whimpering seemed to be loudest. 'He's hurt.' Fiona glanced back at Jim then put her face close to the gap. 'Pepe,' she shouted, 'Pepe, love.' When she looked at Jim, he had a peculiar and abject expression. Beads of sweat were running down his face, which had become pale and oily. A tic pulsed at the side of his mouth. Fiona rattled the chain and padlock which held the doors closed. 'Jim, the key, where's the key?'

Jim's head sagged and his clenched right hand opened. A key dropped by his boots, making a tinny sound on a stone. Cal picked it up. 'In case you hadn't guessed,' she whispered as Cal opened the padlock, 'he's been drinking.'

Fiona untied the chain and Cal pulled it free. The wooden doors half opened before sticking on rubble.

A shaft of sunlight penetrated the gloom, falling on a woman's body. She was lying on compacted earth, one of her legs splayed below the knee, her jeans bloody, her face bruised and swollen and her right hand gripping Pepe. The dog squirmed and whined.

'My God, it's Violet,' Cal said.

Fiona knelt and eased Violet's fingers from the dog. She handed him to Cal. 'Put him in my car and get my bag.' She crouched over Violet, feeling at her neck for a pulse, checking on her leg, at the loss of blood. 'Can you hear me, Violet? I'm Doctor Bell.' She shouted back at Cal. 'And call for an ambulance, hurry.'

Outside, Jim hadn't moved, but instead of looking at the ground he was staring across the loch, at the hills which extended into one another like drawn curtains, light and dark catching in the folds.

'What happened? What did you do to her?' Cal studied Jim's face, his mottled skin, his stubborn, stupid muteness. He clenched his fist and swung it. The crack of knuckle on bone made Fiona turn round.

'For God's sake, Cal, *hurry*. She needs an ambulance.'

35

The police arrived within minutes of Cal speaking to the emergency operator. One car with two officers was followed soon after by another. Cal answered their hurried questions about Violet and Jim Carmichael. When Jim was led into his house, a policeman at each arm, Cal inquired how they'd managed to get there so quickly. There'd been another call, a constable told him, a tip-off, about another matter, not something he could discuss except to say the first two cars had been responding to that. More were now on the way. So was a detective inspector from Inverness. He would take charge. 'If you'd just wait here until DI Macrae arrives, sir.'

'Can't I see Violet?' he asked.

'There's nothing you can do, sir,' the constable said, walking towards Cal, holding his arms wide as though practising for a crowd-marshalling exam. 'The doctor's got everything under control.'

After a few minutes, Fiona appeared outside the barn. She waved Cal over, her hands in blue gloves. The constable went with him. Cal asked, 'How is she?'

'Her leg's badly broken. There could be internal injuries too. She's in a lot of pain. Before I sedate her, she wants me to tell you that Jim recognized her brooch. She thinks Jim was at her birth. Violet said you would know what that meant.'

Cal turned to the constable. 'I need to speak to DI Macrae.'

'Sorry, sir. I can pass on a message through headquarters.'

'Does Macrae know about the deaths of Duncan Boyd and Megan Bates?'

'I'm told he's reading the case files as he's travelling. That's why he doesn't want to be disturbed.'

'Tell your headquarters that Jim Carmichael was at or around the birth of Megan Bates's daughter. He must know how she died and, possibly, where her body has been hidden. Also, pass on this message – Mrs Mary Anderson, who lives at Gardener's Cottage, also saw Megan Bates's baby straight after she was born. She should be questioned too. DI Macrae needs to know that there are now two more properties that might contain Megan Bates's body.'

'That'll be for DI Macrae to decide.' The constable moved Cal away from the barn. 'Now wait here.' He walked away, speaking into his radio. When the ambulance arrived, the constable provided a commentary on what was happening. Doctor Bell would be travelling with the patient. Another doctor, a specialist in road injuries, would join the ambulance on its journey. A police vehicle was being despatched to pick up the patient's daughter, Anna, and her friends Hilary and Izzy. They would be taken to the hospital.

Cal asked, 'Which hospital?'

'Raigmore.'

Cal smiled ruefully at the tricks fate played. The constable regarded him with a puzzled expression. 'Did I say something amusing, sir?'

'It's where Violet was abandoned as a baby,' Cal explained as a police van arrived and disgorged ten officers. A uniformed sergeant divided them into three groups. Cal overheard him relaying DI Macrae's orders: three to search the barns, another three to search the house and garden and four to fan out across the fields. What were they looking for, asked one of the field quartet. The sergeant looked sideways at his questioner before shaking his head in wonder at recruits nowadays. *What do you think you're looking for?*

'What you've got in your head, son. Bones.'

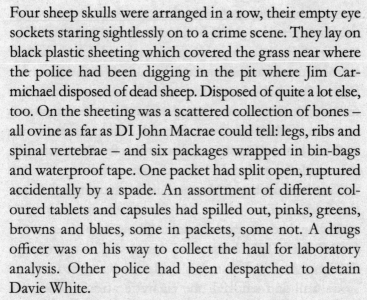

Four sheep skulls were arranged in a row, their empty eye sockets staring sightlessly on to a crime scene. They lay on black plastic sheeting which covered the grass near where the police had been digging in the pit where Jim Carmichael disposed of dead sheep. Disposed of quite a lot else, too. On the sheeting was a scattered collection of bones – all ovine as far as DI John Macrae could tell: legs, ribs and spinal vertebrae – and six packages wrapped in bin-bags and waterproof tape. One packet had split open, ruptured accidentally by a spade. An assortment of different coloured tablets and capsules had spilled out, pinks, greens, browns and blues, some in packets, some not. A drugs officer was on his way to collect the haul for laboratory analysis. Other police had been despatched to detain Davie White.

'And that'll all need to be bagged and taken away too.' Macrae indicated a mound of dug-over earth from which more sheep bones were protruding. Then they'd wait for the forensic team to take away the human skeleton in the pit. Not much had been exposed so far, but that was shocking enough – the head, shoulders, top of the ribcage, an outstretched arm and a hand, the fingers bent as though clawing at the air. Then the pit would have to be properly dug out, the soil and animal remains removed for sieving and sifting. As a precaution, Macrae said, in case of any human material. A scavenger might have burrowed down, might have displaced a bone. Twenty-six years had passed. This time they were going to be thorough. No stone unturned. He winced at his unintended pun.

'So this is where Jim Carmichael used to bury the carcasses of his sheep, is it?' The detective inspector surveyed the packages, the skulls and the dug-up bones until the horror of the skeleton in the pit drew him back. A shadow seemed to pass across his face, his skin blanching in contrast to his slick of red hair: dismay at man's inhumanity to man. He turned away and glared at the loch and mountains, as if they too were culpable, their magnificence nothing but a shimmering distraction for the unwary in their dealings with cold-hearted country folk.

'Get him up here,' Macrae barked, starting off across the field, as if he had to put distance between himself and what had happened there. 'Show him what we've found. See if it'll loosen his tongue.' Then, an afterthought: 'And *make* him look.' Macrae wandered off to a stone wall and smoked one cigarette after another. He examined his shoes. Scenery had never held much charm for him, or fields, or wide-open spaces. Give him a dingy pub, an ugly street and people he knew he couldn't trust. Not this pretence at something natural and finer.

By now Jim was standing at the edge of the pit, staring down.

Staring into his rotten soul, Macrae hoped, glancing at him. The scene reminded him of a film he'd watched recently. An Iraqi had dug a grave for the victim of a car-bombing and his reward had been summary execution with a militia bullet to the back of his head. Macrae held up his hand, shaped it like a gun and pointed it at Jim. An exploding sound came from the back of his throat. His hand jerked up with the recoil. He imagined Jim toppling, just as the Iraqi had done.

'Right . . .' He dropped his smoking cigarette into the grass and walked slowly back to the pit. He gestured to the constables to move away before standing beside Jim. Macrae looked at the set of his jaw, at the bruise from McGill's punch turning purple by his mouth. Jim's eyes were fixed on the skeleton. Macrae waited for a moment. When Jim began to shuffle uneasily, he said, 'The way she's holding her hand, do you see?' Macrae held up his own hand, the fingers and thumb bent inwards, adjusting them so they resembled the hand of the skeleton. 'It makes you wonder. Well, it makes *me* wonder.' His hand clawed at the air again and again. 'Whether Megan Bates was dead when you put her in there . . . you or Mrs Anderson, or whoever else was involved. Whether she wasn't trying to dig her way out with the last breath of her life to find her baby . . .'

The walk had exhausted her, and the upset. By the wall, she hardly had the energy to open the gate, let alone to carry on to the intersection of the paths, to the wooden bench. Yet on she went, propelled by the worry which had pursued her from Gardener's Cottage all the way along the moor path; the thought of being prevented from spending a last moment in the tranquillity of the graveyard. Finally, taking her seat on the right of the bench, her usual place of contemplation, she gazed at the panorama of mountains and water before swallowing the pills. Occasionally she turned her head to glimpse the flat meadow by Boyd's Farm or the canopy of leaves which concealed Brae, but mostly she sat as she always did: her knees together; her hands folded one on top of the other, looking straight ahead, observing the comings and goings on the road, the blue flashing lights, and wishing for death to take her away before the police found her. Once or twice she felt bitterness at how she would be judged. But hadn't she always been misunderstood? A brief half-smile flickered on her lips as she thought of Alexandra. Then she became lost in grief, remembering her stillborn daughter. Her eyes closed. The sun set as evening fell. The chill turned Mrs Anderson's skin as cold as the gravestones and the breath slipped from her.

36

The headlights of Ross Turnbull's car blazed across the beach. Leaving his engine running and his door open, he walked over the sand to the water's edge where Cal was standing. 'The police told me where I could find you.' Cal didn't move, didn't reply. Ross tried again. He'd been upset to hear about Violet's injury.

This time Cal said, 'Yeah.'

'You're not going to make this easy for me, are you?'

'No.'

Ross put up his hands. The shadow of his arms extended over the sea in the headlights. 'OK, I'm sorry. Is that what you want me to say?'

Cal shrugged. *It's something.*

'Yeah,' Ross sighed, 'I should have realized the significance of Violet's visit. I should have worked out where she'd go next. But I'd been living and breathing the BRC deal every minute of every day, making the case for Poltown, arranging with Duncan's brother for the sale of Boyd's Farm rather than worrying about a woman who had died a quarter of a century ago.'

He sighed again, resignation, regret and apology in a single exhalation. 'OK, Violet turning up at my door should have rung more alarm bells.'

So should her questions, when she came to see him.

When had he and Alexandra written their names on Duncan's attic wall, what time of day?

Early evening, he'd told her.

Had he seen Duncan?

Yes, he had. Duncan had been on the beach until late at night.

How late, close to midnight?

Yes, around midnight, and later too. Duncan had been collecting flotsam using a helmet with a torch, like miners used. Ross had seen him.

After Ross had said that, Violet left. He hadn't asked her where she was going.

His head had been so full of worrying about what could go wrong at the meeting he hadn't fully realized what he'd told her. After seeing Cal, and halfway to Ullapool, he got it. *Boom!*

'The night I went with Alexandra to Duncan Boyd's attic was the same night that Violet was born. She was abandoned in Inverness, two hours away, before midnight, so Duncan couldn't have done that, as Jim Carmichael said. Duncan couldn't have abandoned her at Raigmore Hospital.' Ross paused as if he was still working it out. 'Couldn't have had anything to do with Megan Bates's death either, come to think of it, despite Jim saying he confessed to her murder.'

Later that evening Ross had a row with Alexandra. 'Something about nothing,' Ross said. 'She'd had too much to drink and stomped off. I spent the rest of the night on the beach to avoid running into her but also to make a big decision. It was only Alexandra that was keeping me in Poltown. I knew I had no future here apart from following in my father's footsteps. We didn't get on: like night and day, we were. My pa, then, was definitely night. He was a bad man.

'The only way I could escape was just to go without telling anyone. It took me all night to pluck up the courage. I stayed on the beach until daylight then I hitched to Inverness and caught the train to London. But while I was making up my mind I watched Duncan write a message to Megan on the sand a long time after midnight. "Stay with me LOVE you Duncan."'

Ross remembered the capitals in particular. 'He wrote it so that Megan would read it when she went for her walk on the beach the following morning, before the next high tide washed it away.' Ross looked at Cal. 'Why would Duncan be writing messages to Megan Bates if he'd already killed her as he's supposed to have told Jim? Or am I missing something?'

Ross hadn't returned to Poltown for four or five years and then only for a weekend. He couldn't remember when he'd heard about Megan Bates's death but it was some time later.

'And I couldn't have told you what week or month it happened, so there was no reason for me to connect it to that night. Then after Violet asked me all those questions, I got it. As I say. *Boom!* I made the connections. I knew there was something wrong with Jim Carmichael saying Duncan had confessed.'

Ross had pulled off the road on his way to his meeting and called one of his guys, someone he trusted. He asked about Jim, whether there was anything going on he should know about. The answer was one he'd been half expecting.

'Nothing about Duncan Boyd or his confession but a

whisper about Jim borrowing money and being leaned on to hide stuff while the police were about the place looking for Megan Bates's body.'

Stuff meant drugs, Ross told Cal.

'Who's been doing the leaning?' Ross had asked. 'Davie?' His guy hadn't said no, hadn't said anything. That was the way it worked. Silence meant yes.

'Davie White worked for my old pa,' Ross explained, 'and I inherited him.' He shook his head at another oversight. 'When I returned to Poltown I told them all there were new rules.'

He didn't want to know what had gone on before but if he heard of anything illegal he'd call in the police, whatever it was, whoever was doing it.

'Because I've been offshore, Africa, other rough places, they know I can look after myself.' He showed Cal a long ragged scar on the underside of his right forearm. 'I've been in a few scraps. They know I'm not kidding them.'

When his meeting in Ullapool ended, he told the police they might find a stash of drugs at Jim's smallholding. They had too: heroin, marijuana and a 'load of pills'. He also gave them the nod about having a chat with Davie White.

'Stupid,' Ross said, thinking again of Violet, how he could have stopped her going to see Jim if only he'd been quicker off the mark. 'Of course she would have gone to see him after what I told her.'

'Yeah.'

He shot Cal an angry look. 'Give me a break, for Christ's sake. I've said sorry.'

In Ullapool police station, DI Macrae was explaining why he'd asked to see Cal. Violet was refusing to cooperate with the police, for reasons he understood. The force hadn't acquitted itself well. They'd been too slow and sloppy to mount a proper investigation twenty-six years ago and too quick to lodge an official complaint about Mr Anwar. Would Cal be an intermediary? Would he reassure Violet that everything was proceeding to a prosecution of Jim Carmichael?

'Someone has to tell her how her mother died,' Macrae said, 'and under the circumstances that probably shouldn't be a police officer.'

'You want me to do it?'

Macrae deflected the question. 'It's been long enough already.'

Cal nodded and Macrae did too, acknowledgement as well as gratitude. He tapped his keyboard and turned his computer screen towards Cal. 'I want you to see this for yourself so you can tell Violet that nothing's being kept from her. There's no conspiracy, not this time.'

The scene which began to play was one Cal had seen in various guises before, in films, or a thousand television crime dramas.

A guilty man was slumped disconsolately at a table, picking at his stubby fingers, a smart young female lawyer sitting erect beside him. Her demeanour spoke of prospects and achievements; his of disappointment and failure. Jim Carmichael looked a broken man. Then he started mumbling. 'I've seen some terrible things in my life, my father dying of cancer, ravens pecking out the eyes of a horse that was stuck in a bog . . .' He rubbed his face and shook his head. 'The worst was the evening I drove to Orasaigh Island with Megan Bates's weekly grocery order.'

Jim glanced up, full of self-pity.

'Go on,' a voice off camera said. Macrae's.

'The delivery was my last of the day. I'd put her order into the tin box on the mainland shore as I usually did, but when I looked across the causeway I saw Megan over by the island, lying on the sand. I ran over to help her . . .'

Jim looked up.

'What did you see?' Macrae asked.

'There was blood coming out of her. The baby was beside her. A girl. She was still attached by the cord.'

Jim glanced up again, the bewilderment of that evening on his face. What could he have done? He'd never even held a baby before.

'Was anyone else there?' Macrae again.

'No.'

'What did you think had happened?'

'She'd gone into labour waiting for the tide and in the end she couldn't wait.' Jim shook his head. 'Half dead, she was, she'd lost that much blood. All she'd been able to do before losing consciousness was throw her cardigan over the child.

'I hadn't known what to do . . .' That look of bewilderment once more. 'I didn't know whether to move her and risk making the bleeding worse, or leave her and the baby and go for help.' He sighed heavily.

'What did you do?'

'I wrapped Megan's cardigan tight around the baby and secured it with her brooch – flowering violets. I remembered them because everything else that night had been so horrible. Then I drove to Brae, which was the nearest house with a phone in those days. I hoped for Mr William, but Mrs Ritchie came to the door. I was uncomfortable telling her because everyone in the village had heard the rumours about Mr William's affair. But she was calm and practical, going back into the house to ring for an ambulance and returning with towels, a flask of water and scissors.'

'What happened next?'

They'd driven to the causeway.

Jim paused, as if he needed to summon up strength for what was to follow.

'I parked the van and she ran ahead. I followed with the towels and water. When I caught up with her, she was already kneeling beside Megan. I thought she must be comforting her. But she wasn't. She was saying Megan was a slut and a bitch and she deserved to die.'

Jim still looked shocked.

'What did you do?'

'I asked her to stop but she went on and on saying such terrible things.'

Jim sighed. 'The baby was crying and I wrapped her in a towel. Afterwards, Mrs Ritchie turned away from Megan and started telling me about how much she had done for me. She said she'd paid off my debts to Alec Turnbull as well as giving me work at Brae. She'd stuck by me and now I had to stick by her.'

Jim lifted his eyes to the camera, his lids seeming heavy with the burden of guilt.

'Mrs Ritchie said Megan would be dead soon and I had

to dispose of her body, as if she was ordering me to do some job for her at the house. She said the best place for burying bones was with other bones. I knew she meant my sheep pit. I'd disposed of diseased livestock carcasses from Brae before, so Mrs Ritchie was aware of it.'

He tried to resist her, to make her see sense.

Jim glanced again at Macrae and the camera, pleading. *Believe me.*

'So what did you say to her, Jim?'

'I told her she wasn't thinking straight and anyway the ambulance would be arriving soon. But she smiled again. "Poor Jim, there you go again, never quite understanding how things work." There wouldn't be an ambulance, she said. She hadn't called one. She told me to look after the baby . . . "while the slut dies".' Jim stopped talking as his head drooped.

'Go on, Jim.'

'Mrs Ritchie said if I did as I was told she'd help me out again, as often as I needed. She'd stop me falling into Turnbull's clutches again, keep me from getting another beating or worse.'

'Did she help you after that?'

Jim nodded. 'Aye, a few times, what with the drink and everything else. I was never that good with money.'

'How much, Jim?'

He mumbled.

'I can't hear you, Jim.'

'A few thousand, six or seven.'

'What happened next?'

'I tried to comfort the baby. I cut the cord and cleaned her up a bit. Mrs Ritchie kept talking about Megan, things

I'll never forget. How the baby would have no father because he would never know she had been born. How Alexandra was the only child William Ritchie would ever have and ever wanted. Then she looked over at me and said, "She's dead, the slut's dead." Then, a few moments later: "You let it happen too, Jim. Never forget that." And again: "You owe me."'

'And you did as you were told. You got rid of the body?'

Jim nodded. 'I carried Megan to my van and buried her that night.'

'Was she dead?'

'I was sure she was. I looked after her, mind, wrapped her up in a blanket I kept in the back of the van. She wasn't moving. She never moved.'

'What happened to the baby?'

Jim rubbed the back of his hand across his mouth, again and again, as if trying to wipe away a bloody stain. 'Mrs Ritchie took her. I didn't know where.'

'Did she go to Mrs Anderson?'

She might have. He didn't know.

'Mrs Anderson never said anything to you?'

'No.'

'Nor Mrs Ritchie?'

Jim shook his head. 'She instructed me never to talk about it. She never spoke of it again. Not to me. Not a word.'

'When you heard that someone dressed in Megan Bates's clothes had walked into the sea the next morning, didn't you wonder who it was?'

Jim looked sullen. 'Who else could it have been but Mrs Ritchie? She must have collected Megan's things from Orasaigh Cottage during the night. The door was usually left unlocked but even if it hadn't been, Mrs Ritchie had a key.'

'Mrs Ritchie could swim?'

Jim nodded. 'Before Megan arrived at Poltown, Mrs Ritchie used to swim at South Bay in the summer. Mrs Anderson used to join her on the beach with a picnic. I remember Mrs Anderson saying she was a strong swimmer.'

'Strong enough to swim from South Bay to North Bay?'

From what Mrs Anderson had told him, yes.

'Wasn't there a danger of her running into Duncan or someone else?'

Jim shrugged as if he didn't think so. 'Duncan's habit then was to collect flotsam after high tide so that, by the time Megan was able to cross the Orasaigh causeway, the beach at South Bay would be clean. No one else went there at that time in the morning, apart from Mrs Armitage, who kept to the beach road walking her dog.'

'Mrs Ritchie would have known that?'

'What?'

'That Mrs Armitage would be a witness and could report what she had seen to the police?'

Jim nodded. 'Mrs Armitage walked past the Brae driveway every morning before eight.'

Macrae waited before asking another question. Jim's head sagged and he picked at his fingers. After the sound of pages turning, Macrae said, 'Did Duncan Boyd confess to killing Megan Bates?'

'No.'

'Why did you say he had?'

'Violet was asking questions. I was worried where they would lead. When Duncan hanged himself I had the idea of passing on the blame. It was what the police thought anyway, Duncan being the killer.'

Macrae said nothing and Jim began to mumble, working himself up into a last attempt at self-justification. Suddenly he looked up, his eyes shining with indignation. Jim Carmichael had given his loyalty, he said, as though reading a citation from a roll of honour. 'Mrs Ritchie took advantage of me so that spoilt daughter of hers, Alexandra, would get the inheritance.'

'*Given* your loyalty?' Macrae snorted. 'Sold it, more like, to save your own sorry skin.'

The screen went blank and Macrae said, 'Some things we're never going to know.' Which was regrettable, since Violet would believe there was more the police could do. Macrae had a few theories about what had happened, but with Diana Ritchie and now Mrs Anderson both dead there was no longer any possibility of proof. He was as good as certain that Diana Ritchie had taken Violet to Gardener's Cottage after Jim had removed Megan's body, as that was the only way Mrs Anderson could have known the baby's hair colour. His hunch was that Mrs Anderson drove Violet to Raigmore Hospital since she had written the anonymous letter, perhaps out of guilt. The pen she'd used had been found in her kitchen, and similar writing paper. Everything else was informed guesswork, including the identity of the woman who walked into the sea.

That must have been Mrs Ritchie, although he was sure she must have had help from Mrs Anderson.

'There's an estate road through the forestry which runs close to North Bay. Mrs Anderson could have gone there in her car with a change of clothes.' The lack of footprints on the beach, apart from Duncan's, was easy to explain. Diana Ritchie swam in and left the hat and bag at the high-water mark. She returned the same way so that the incoming tide covered her tracks. Then she came ashore again among the rocks at the north headland to make her way to the car. As for Megan's letter, the so-called suicide note, it had probably been intercepted by Diana Ritchie earlier. Megan would have hand-delivered it to the post-box at the end of the Brae drive. It was effectively her goodbye. Since William Ritchie wouldn't leave Diana, Megan intended to go away with the baby. Diana saw how she could use the letter when Jim Carmichael found Megan lying bleeding and close to death by the causeway. Once the body and the baby had been disposed of, all she had to do was seal the letter, put on a stamp and post it to her husband so that it arrived after Megan was seen walking into the sea. More likely than not, Mrs Anderson took it to the Poltown postbox for her. A simple case of suicide.

37

Violet was talking about Mr Anwar, how he had visited her in hospital, how pleased she had been to see him, how worried she was about him still. In his self-effacing way he had deflected all her questions, so she didn't know whether he was all right or not. Anna made him a card inviting him to visit Glasgow. Violet hoped he would.

'If he doesn't, Anna and I will just have to go and see him in Inverness.'

She was sitting in the back of Cal's pick-up, her leg stretched out across the seat, as her consultant had instructed. She had become quiet when Cal pulled in at the side of the road high up on the ridge above Poltown. He asked what she felt, being back there again. Violet stared through the window at the spectacle of an October storm hurtling ashore, a tumult of blacks and greys. 'Nothing,' she said. 'I don't feel anything.'

The landmarks of her mother's life and death lay below her: Brae, Orasaigh Island, the coastal path, Boyd's Farm, South Bay, North Bay, all blurry in the squalls of rain.

'No, that's not right,' she corrected herself, everywhere her eye fell stirring an emotion. 'I do feel something. I hate it, the way it can be like this, you know, wonderful and extraordinary when you're up here. But when you're down there, it's different. It's why I wanted to see it again, just to be sure.'

She looked away to the left, towards the church, the green of the mound on which it sat appearing dull and drab in the rain in contrast to the vivid rush of feelings the graveyard now evoked – her father's last resting place and now Mrs Anderson's. On the drive to the coast, Cal told how she had been found dead from an overdose of sleeping pills, slumped on a graveyard bench. Violet heard the news in silence. After staring at the distant church, she said, 'It must have been her, mustn't it? Mrs Anderson must have written the letter, the one Mr Anwar gave to me.'

'Yes,' Cal replied. 'DI Macrae says she did. He also thinks that Mrs Anderson abandoned you at Raigmore Hospital.'

'Why would she write after so many years?'

'Guilt maybe? Perhaps she felt she couldn't while Diana Ritchie was alive, but after she was dead, well . . . Perhaps your birthday was the reminder.'

'I guess.' A shaft of sun slanting through a break in the clouds claimed Violet's attention. It lit up the hillside above the sheep pit where her mother had been buried and painted it briefly with vibrant russets and greens. The intensity of the colours affected her. 'Cal . . .' Her voice caught with emotion. 'How could Jim Carmichael put her in a place like that? How could anyone?'

'I don't know,' Cal replied. Only a partial skeleton had been found: the remainder probably scavenged over the years by foxes or badgers. Cal hadn't told Violet. Nor had he mentioned DI Macrae's comment that Megan Bates might still have been alive when she was buried. It was speculation and likely to remain that way, though the remains were still being analysed. He glanced in his rear-view mirror, hoping Violet hadn't detected concealment in the brevity of his response. He found she was looking at him.

'It does matter,' she said, their eyes meeting.

'What does?'

'Having a body, even just the bones of one.' She held his gaze. 'Now that my mother's been found I don't feel . . .' She hesitated, uncertain of the word. 'That responsibility any more. Not closure. Something else.' She was anxious he understood what she was trying to tell him.

'Your work – finding bodies for the families – does matter.'

'Yeah,' was all he said, looking away, keeping to himself the email received two days before. It was from the parents of the five-year-old boy who had been swept off the pier by a freak wave. Could Cal McGill help them find 'our missing boy'? Cal's reply? He was busy, regrettably, and would be for a while, the drawback of a one-man operation. He'd email again when his workload allowed him to commit to another investigation.

Violet allowed the view to preoccupy her for a while. 'That's what I dislike about Poltown,' she said eventually. 'Everyone and everything is like Jim Carmichael, seemingly benign but really the opposite.'

Cal nodded in agreement. 'I didn't think you'd want to know this before. But ages ago, my parents knew Diana Ritchie. She was a neighbour in Edinburgh. My mother thought she was a nice woman.'

Neither spoke for a while until Violet found Cal's eyes

again in the mirror. 'I've made up my mind. There's nothing for Anna and me here. Nothing.'

'OK,' Cal said. 'That's why you wanted to see it again, before BRC's bulldozers changed it for ever. To be sure that's how you felt.'

'It is,' she replied. 'Can we go to Glasgow now? I'd like to go home.'